THE MERMAID'S MADNESS

Jim C. Hines

DAW BOOKS, INC.

DONALD A. WOLLHEIM, FOUNDER

375 Hudson Street, New York, NY 10014

ELIZABETH R. WOLLHEIM
SHEILA E. GILBERT
PUBLISHERS

http://www.dawbooks.com

First Printing, October 2009
1 2 3 4 5 6 7 8 9

THE SEA JUST AHEAD
OF THE SHIP EXPLODED

in a fountain of white spray. The lead mermaid arched through the air, higher than any of the others had leaped.

"Lirea," Queen Beatrice whispered.

A scream tore from Lirea's throat, a ragged, furious sound that pierced Danielle's ears, nearly driving her to her knees. Danielle lurched forward, grabbing Beatrice's arm and pulling her out of the way as Lirea cleared the railing.

The mermaid twisted to avoid the lines. She staggered as she landed, ramming the butt of her spear into the deck for balance. Her tails were gone, replaced by feet.

Before Danielle could move, Lirea leveled her spear at the queen. She coughed, spitting seawater onto the deck, then said, "You're trespassing in our waters."

Danielle started to move between them, but Lirea swung her spear, cutting Danielle's arm. Blood seeped into her sleeve.

"You're looking well, Lirea," Beatrice said calmly. "Where is your father?"

Lirea moved closer, driving Beatrice back until she stood against the railing.

"Your sister?" Beatrice glanced at the main deck, where Armand and the men had already gathered with crossbows and spears.

"Don't play games with me," Lirea said. "I hear *every-thing*. I heard you conspiring with Lannadae and my father, just as I hear them planning to attack." She jabbed her spear into Beatrice's side, hard enough to make the queen gasp. A small circle of blood darkened Beatrice's shirt beneath her jacket.

Lirea turned to face Armand and the crew. "Take another step and she dies."

Armand raised his hand. "Let my mother go, and I will—"

"I am queen of the Ilowkira tribe," Lirea shouted. "I will speak to your queen and her alone."

DAW Books presents these delightful fantasy novels
by Jim C. Hines

THE STEPSISTER SCHEME
THE MERMAID'S MADNESS
RED HOOD'S REVENGE*

*   *   *

Jig the Goblin Series:
GOBLIN QUEST (Book One)
GOBLIN HERO (Book Two)
GOBLIN WAR (Book Three)

*Coming in 2010 from DAW Books

Acknowledgments

Douglas Adams once said, "I love deadlines. I like the whooshing sound they make as they fly by."

What Adams neglected to mention was the chilling silence that precedes those deadlines. Calm-before-the-storm silence. Cheerleader-in-a-dark-basement-with-the-serial-killer silence. The kind of silence whose only purpose in this world is to give you a few moments to contemplate the horrors preparing to devour you.

At least, that's what it felt like back in July of '08, as I scrambled to finish the fifth rewrite of this book. Mere words cannot express my gratitude toward my wife and children, who put up with me during this time, and enabled me to actually make that deadline. Living with a writer is never easy, and they have been far more patient, understanding, and forgiving than I have any right to expect.

Thanks also to my agent Joshua Bilmes and my editor Sheila Gilbert, both of whom reassured me that the world would not in fact come to an end if I was late turning in my manuscript. That's very good to know, especially as I look ahead to my deadline for *Red Hood's Revenge*.

I should also single out Diana Francis Pharaoh, author of the *Crosspointe Chronicles* series, for her assistance. I knew any book about mermaids would have to take place at sea, but my knowledge of sailing was rather limited. Thank you, Di, for rescuing me from a number of embarrassing mistakes. (At this point, it's traditional for the author to mention that any remaining mistakes are entirely his or her own, but I think I'm going to blame any goofs on the goblins.)

Thank you, Josh, Debra, Marsha, and everyone else at DAW who helped bring this series into the world. Special thanks to Scott Fischer, whose cover art still blows my mind.

Most importantly, my thanks to you, the reader. Thank you for buying the books, for reading the stories, and for sharing them with your friends and family. Thank you for your wonderfully kind letters and e-mails, and thank you for allowing me to continue doing the most awesome job in the world.

LORINDAR
AND SURROUNDING NATIONS

NORTHLANDS

ALLESANDRIA

MOROVA

KAGAN SEA

LYSKAR

NAJARIN

HILAD

CARIFORNE SEA

LORINDAR

ARANTINE OCEAN

ARATHEA

N E S W

CHAPTER I

PRINCESS DANIELLE WHITESHORE OF LOR-indar clung to the rail at the front of the ship, staring out at the waves. If this wind kept up, she might become the first princess in history to welcome the undine back from their winter migration by vomiting into their waters. The weather had been mild for most of the morning, but the skies had changed as the sun passed its peak. It was as if the sea now took a perverse glee in torment-ing her.

"Drink this." Queen Beatrice's voice was sympathetic as she climbed up from the main deck, holding a steam-ing tin mug. She pressed the mug into Danielle's hand. "Tea laced with honey, just the way you like it."

The queen had discarded the royal gowns of court for clothes that bordered on improper. With her dark blue breeches and loose, pale shirt, she could almost have passed for a sailor. A worn blue flat cap covered her hair, save for a few wisps that fluttered by her ear like tiny gray banners. Only her long jacket, decorated with white ribbon and trimmed in gold, marked her as roy-alty. That and the silver necklace she wore, which held a black pearl the size of Danielle's thumbnail.

Anyone could see the queen's delight at being out to sea. If not for the rules of propriety, Danielle had no doubt Beatrice would right now be climbing the rigging with the crew or manning the crow's nest to watch for merfolk.

For *undine*, she corrected herself. That was what they preferred to be called.

Casual as Beatrice's attire was, she looked far more comfortable than Danielle. Danielle's handmaids had packed for her, and they apparently had as little experience at sea as Danielle herself. The heavy cloak and cream-colored gown might have been acceptable for a casual day back at the palace. Here on the ship, she was constantly struggling to avoid tripping over her own skirt. Spray from the waves clung like tiny glass beads to the purple velvet of her cloak. She was tempted to ask permission to raid the queen's wardrobe.

For the moment, she merely sipped her tea and did her best to keep from throwing up. The honey wasn't enough to mask the more pungent taste of ginger and other spices.

"Too strong?" asked Beatrice.

"Not at all." Danielle forced herself to take another drink. She had grown spoiled over the past year. Living with her stepmother and stepsisters, she had been lucky to brew the occasional cup of lukewarm tea using leftover leaves, and honey was a luxury remembered only from her most distant childhood.

Beatrice laughed. "Snow never has learned to make proper tea."

"What did she put in here?"

"I've learned it's best not to ask. She said it would help your stomach."

Though Snow White's culinary skills left much to be desired, Danielle trusted her. Snow *had* saved her life the year before, after all. The least Danielle could do was drink her overly pungent tea.

If nothing else, the tea helped wash the salty taste of the sea from her mouth. She took another sip, then turned to watch the *Lord Lynn Margaret* following in the distance. The *Saint Tocohl* trailed them on the opposite side, the three ships forming an elongated triangle in the sea.

"You'll adjust." Beatrice clapped a hand on Danielle's back in a manner more fitting a deckhand than the queen of Lorindar. "I do feel for you. I've never suffered from seasickness, but when I was pregnant with Armand, I spent three months unable to eat anything more exciting than oatmeal. Even then, it was an even wager whether I would keep the oatmeal down."

"Yet in spite of your sympathy, you still chose to inflict this misery on me?" A year ago, the mere thought of joking with the queen would have driven Danielle to her knees to beg forgiveness. Now she narrowed her eyes in mock anger. "I never imagined such cruelty from you, Your Majesty."

The laugh lines on Beatrice's face deepened. She leaned closer, lowering her voice. "If I wanted you ill, I'd let your husband take the helm."

Danielle grinned and shaded her eyes as she turned to search for the prince. Though Beatrice had formally given command of the ship over to her son, Prince Armand had yet to take the wheel. The last time Danielle saw him, he had been inspecting the cannons on the right side of the main deck.

The *starboard* side. Armand had inherited his mother's love of sailing, and while they both tried to hide it, neither Beatrice nor Armand could conceal their amusement when Danielle stumbled over yet another nautical term.

Beatrice folded her arms on the railing and leaned out, peering into the water. "I spared you this voyage in the fall when Jakob was born, but there are limits. King Theodore can avoid these journeys if he chooses, but as future queen of Lorindar, you must be presented to the undine."

Her words brought Danielle's nausea back in full force. She gulped the rest of her tea and took a deep breath.

"Also, it was past time you set foot on this marvelous galleon." Beatrice's eyes positively twinkled. "It was named in your honor, after all."

"Yes, I know." Danielle remembered her horror the

first time Armand broke the news. "They couldn't come up with anything better than the *Glass Slipper*?"

The queen shrugged. "I'm told the *Midnight Pumpkin* was also discussed."

"Midnight pumpkin? There was no pumpkin! I never—" Danielle caught herself. "You're teasing me again."

"Perhaps."

Danielle frowned. Beneath the queen's exuberance, she sounded distracted. Her smile faded too quickly, and she kept turning away. Normally, Beatrice gave her undivided attention to whomever she was with, whether that was an emperor or a stable hand. "Bea?"

"Does the tea help?" Beatrice asked without looking up.

Danielle nodded. "Why didn't Snow make some when we first left?"

Another absent smile. "Over one hundred young, strong, hardworking sailors crew the *Glass Slipper*. You should be grateful Snow remembered you at all."

From a platform near the top of the front mast—the foremast—came a shout. "Undine ahead!"

All at once men were racing about, hauling ropes and furling the sails. From the quarterdeck, Armand cupped his hands around his mouth and shouted, "Ease away tack and bowline! Stand by to take in fore topsail!" He waited a beat, watching the men work, then yelled, "Haul taut, and up topsail. Stand by on main topsail!"

He might as well have been speaking a foreign language, but Danielle could hear Beatrice whispering the commands along with him.

Danielle leaned back, studying her husband. His sleeves were pushed back, exposing the lean muscles of his arms. Armand had allowed his dark hair to grow longer over the winter, and Danielle still hadn't decided whether or not she liked the new beard. It filled out his narrow features, but tended to tickle at inopportune times.

Yesterday's
BOOKS

3457 McHENRY AVENUE
MODESTO, CA 95350
(209) 521-9623

DATE 05/27/2011 FRI   TIME 09:07

SCI-FI T1	$4.80
TAX1	$0.40
TOTAL	$5.20
GIFT CARD	$5.20

NO CASH REFUNDS

WHITNEY   046402   00002

Smiling at the memories, Danielle edged around the foremast to the very front of the railing, trying to stay out of the way as the crew climbed up to take in the sails. Nobody had ever warned Danielle how crowded a ship could be. The three masts—four if you counted the bowsprit spearing out from the front of the ship—all trailed ropes and rigging, as though a giant spider had spun its web over the entire ship. With eight cannons secured to the main deck, as well as the longboats, there was hardly room for two men to pass each other.

Danielle watched as her friend Talia made her way across the deck. The chaos didn't seem to bother her in the slightest. She glided through the crew as though she had been born at sea, though from what Danielle knew of Talia's past, she hadn't even set foot on a sailing ship until her late teens, when she fled her desert kingdom in the south.

Shortly after Talia's birth, fairies had bestowed upon her a number of gifts, not the least of which was supernatural grace. Danielle might have been jealous if she hadn't also known the price Talia paid for those gifts. Few knew the true story of Sleeping Beauty, how her century of slumber had been broken by an awakening to make nightmares pale.

"Are you ready?" Beatrice asked, drawing Danielle's attention back to her responsibilities as princess.

"Does it matter?" She knew she shouldn't be nervous. All she had to do was stand there ... stand there and represent the entire kingdom of Lorindar. She who had spent most of her life in rags, with only the birds and the rats for company. Her short time as princess of Lorindar couldn't overcome a lifetime as Cinderwench, and there were still times she thought this new life a dream, an illusion to be swept away come midnight.

"Not really, no." Beatrice gave her a reassuring smile.

To the undine, nobility flowed from mother to child, so it was the queen who was most revered. The former queen of the undine had passed away several seasons earlier, leaving the husband to rule, but they still expected to be greeted by the queen of Lorindar. The queen, and now the princess as well.

Danielle should have been presented the year before, but she had been touring the kingdom with Armand when the undine returned to Lorindar's waters. She had planned to see the undine in the fall, when they left for warmer waters to the south. Her stepsisters had ruined that plan, kidnapping Armand and enslaving Danielle, then trying to steal her unborn child. Even after Danielle returned home, she had been in no condition for a voyage at sea.

She touched her stomach, remembering the dark magic her stepsister Stacia had used to rush her pregnancy along. Danielle had been terrified of what that magic would do to her son. She still thanked God every night that Jakob had been born healthy. No healer could find the slightest problem, and even Snow assured her he was free of any taint or curse.

Beatrice took her hand, gently guiding Danielle to the railing at her right. "Lorindar is fortunate to have such a princess." Turning back toward Armand, she raised her voice. "Lorindar would do well to have a less distracted prince, though. Hurry, Armand!"

Armand was already making his way toward the bow. Etiquette didn't actually require his presence. Indeed, he could have stayed behind with King Theodore, who was known to have the same reaction to sailing as Danielle. But Armand was his mother's son, and he rarely passed up the opportunity to sail.

Behind him, two sailors lugged a watertight wooden chest, sealed as firmly as the ship's hull with pitch and beeswax.

By tradition, Lorindar presented the undine a gift each year to welcome them back from their winter migration. For as long as King Posannes had ruled, that gift had been a chest of strawberry preserves. Last year, Posannes had given Beatrice the pearl she now wore, saying he had gotten the better part of the deal.

"Man the yards!" Armand shouted. The crew in the

yards came to attention, arms held back so they could grasp the ropes for balance. It was an impressive salute, over fifty men stretched out on the horizontal beams which held the now-furled sails.

Talia climbed onto the forecastle, then stepped aside to make room for Armand to follow. The prince leaned down to haul the chest after him, aided by the men below.

"There." Beatrice rested one hand on the rail as she pointed toward the distant shapes. "Where is Snow? I wanted her here as well."

If not for Beatrice, Danielle would have mistaken the undine for rocks in the water. Only their heads and shoulders broke the surface. They swam in an inverted V formation, reminding her of geese.

Without warning, they disappeared beneath the water.

"What happened?" asked Danielle.

Armand stepped toward her, sliding one hand around her waist. Such informality would have earned stern words from the chancellor back at the palace, but such rules were less important here at sea. Danielle leaned against him, the warmth of his body a pleasant contrast to the cool winds. He pointed to the waves where the undine had vanished. "Watch."

The lead undine launched into the air, arching over the water and disappearing with hardly a splash. Two more followed, leaping even higher than the first. Faster and faster they flew from the water in pairs, so close Danielle was amazed they didn't collide.

"There are more than I remember," Armand commented. "I wonder if another tribe has joined with Posannes'."

"Perhaps," Beatrice said, frowning.

Armand flashed a boyish grin as he turned around. "Load the cannons!"

On either side of the main deck, men jammed long rods down the cannons, packing the powder into the barrels. They hadn't bothered to haul cannonballs up onto the deck, as this was only a show for the undine.

"Wait." Beatrice was still studying the water, though the undine were too far away to make out any detail.

"Hold!" Armand shouted. To his mother, he asked, "What is it?"

"I'm not sure." Beatrice sounded troubled, but uncertain. She started to say more, then shook her head.

Armand watched Beatrice a moment longer, then turned back to the crew. "Ready salute!"

The men used ropes and pulleys to haul the cannons into position at the edge of the deck, the barrels protruding through wide gaps in the railing.

Armand glanced at the queen again. When she didn't speak, he raised his arm and shouted, "Fire!"

At each cannon, men brought long poles with burning fuses over the cannons. The resulting explosions sent a shudder through the *Glass Slipper*. The cannons bucked from the recoil, straining at the ropes. Dark smoke billowed from the sides of the ship. Danielle wrinkled her nose at the burned-metal smell.

"I'm sorry," Armand said, still smiling. His tone sounded not the slightest bit apologetic. "I forgot to tell them to only use half a charge."

"Yes. I seem to recall you 'forgetting' last year, too." Beatrice shook her head. "Your eyes are younger than mine. Do any of you see King Posannes?"

Talia stepped to the railing on Beatrice's left, peering through the smoke. "Not yet. What's wrong?"

"Nothing, I hope," said Beatrice. "But you should get down to the main deck. All of you."

By now, the breeze had begun to clear the worst of the smoke, and the undine were close enough for Danielle to make out individuals through the haze. Their skin was a deep tan, a few shades lighter than Talia's. Most were bare-chested, the men and women both, though a few wore tight-fitting gray skins that left their arms uncovered. Some wore weapons, mostly knives and slender fishing spears, secured to harnesses around their arms and chests.

A single mermaid surfaced ahead of the rest.

"Who is that?" Armand stepped past his mother, cupping a hand over his eyes. "Where is Posannes?"

"Armand, I said—" Beatrice's lips tightened. "Talia, get him out of here."

Armand moved to the railing. "If there's a threat, I have to—"

He yelped in surprise as Talia kicked the back of his knees. She caught his collar as he dropped, dragging him toward the ladder.

Armand reached around to grab her wrists, trying to pry her hands free. With a shrug, Talia released her grip, dropping him. Armand lurched to his feet, and Talia shoved him backward. His heel hit the chest of preserves, and he fell again, tumbling down onto the main deck below.

"Talia!" Danielle peered down to see her husband sprawled atop two fallen crewmen. "Are you all right, Armand?"

"He should be. I aimed him at a deckhand." Talia hopped over the chest, following him down.

"You too," Beatrice said to Danielle. "Quickly. Get Snow."

Danielle started to obey, then turned back to take the queen's hand. "If there's danger, you should leave too."

Beatrice shook her head. "Please, Danielle."

The sea just ahead of the ship exploded in a fountain of white spray. The lead mermaid arched through the air, higher than any of the others had leaped. Perhaps her twin tails gave her greater strength, or maybe the others had simply held back.

"Lirea," Beatrice whispered.

A scream tore from Lirea's throat, a ragged, furious sound that pierced Danielle's ears, nearly driving her to her knees. Danielle lurched forward, grabbing Beatrice's arm and pulling her out of the way as Lirea cleared the railing.

The mermaid twisted to avoid the lines. She staggered as she landed, ramming the butt of her spear into the deck for balance. Her tails were gone, replaced by feet.

Even as Danielle watched, the fins running down the outside of Lirea's legs flattened against the skin and disappeared. The scales on her feet and ankles sank into her skin, leaving faint trickles of watery blood. The rest of her scales remained, like purple mail protecting her legs and waist.

Lirea was thinner than the other undine. Her skin clearly outlined her ribs and collarbone. Had she been human, Danielle would have guessed her to be in her late teens. A worn harness crossed between small breasts. A dagger hung on one side of the harness, the handle jutting forward. She wore a necklace of polished oyster shells that appeared far too large for her slender form. A small gold hoop shone in one ear.

Before Danielle could move, Lirea leveled her spear at the queen. She coughed, spitting seawater onto the deck, then said, "You're trespassing in our waters."

Her voice was hoarse, as if she were recovering from a nasty cold. Danielle started to move between them, but Lirea swung her spear, cutting Danielle's arm. Blood seeped into her sleeve.

"You're looking well, Lirea," Beatrice said calmly. "Where is your father?"

Lirea moved closer, driving Beatrice back until she stood against the railing. Lirea glanced at the chest. With a look of disgust, she placed a foot against the chest and shoved. It slid from the forecastle and crashed onto the main deck. "We are undine. We have no need for human fruits. If you wish to travel our ocean in peace, you'll bring us gold. Gold and my sister."

"Your sister?" Beatrice glanced at the main deck, where Armand and the men had already gathered with crossbows and spears.

"Don't play games with me," Lirea said. "I hear *everything*. I heard you conspiring with Lannadae and my father, just as I hear them planning to attack." She jabbed her spear into Beatrice's side, hard enough to make the queen gasp. A small circle of blood darkened Beatrice's shirt beneath her jacket.

"It's nothing," Beatrice whispered, waving Danielle back.

Lirea turned to face Armand and the crew. "Take another step and she dies."

Armand raised his hand. "Let my mother go, and I will—"

"I am queen of the Ilowkira tribe," Lirea shouted. "I will speak to your queen and her alone."

"You killed Posannes." Beatrice ignored the weapon pressed against her ribs. "Just as you killed Levanna."

Water dripped down Lirea's face, making it appear that she was crying. "They betrayed me. Every day, the waves whisper of their treachery."

Motion near the rigging caught Danielle's attention. Talia was climbing one of the lines on the port side. She was already high enough to jump to the forecastle, but even Talia wasn't fast enough to stop Lirea before she could kill Beatrice. Not without something to distract the undine.

Danielle knew little of ships, but she had been to the docks often enough to see the rats climbing the ropes and scurrying over barrels and crates, just as she had seen the cats prowling the docks in search of prey. Every vessel was home to far more than the crew.

All of Danielle's life, animals had helped her. Doves and rats assisted with her chores, cleaning the fireplace or picking slugs from the gardens. Years later, those same doves had blinded her stepmother and scarred her stepsisters. When her stepsisters kidnapped her, the rats had helped her escape.

It was then, imprisoned by her stepsisters, that she had learned to speak to the animals without words. She didn't know how or why they understood her. Perhaps it was another gift from her mother, like the glass slippers and the silver gown she had worn to the ball. All Danielle knew was that they came to her aid.

Never taking her eyes from Lirea, she called in silence. *Help me, my friends.*

"Your father told me what happened to you," Beatrice was saying. "He wanted to help you."

"I've had enough 'help.'" Lirea's words were like needles stabbing deep into Danielle's ears. "Give me Lannadae, and we will allow you to return home. Refuse and we will hunt you all, from the smallest fishing boat to your mightiest warship."

Beatrice bowed her head. "Your father loved you, but he was no fool. How did you do it, Lirea? How did you kill him?"

"He forced me to it!" There was no mistaking the tears trailing down her cheeks now. "He thought of me as a twisted freak, a perversion who should have been left to die. I know what he would have done if I hadn't stopped him."

"He only wanted you to be well again. To be happy." Beatrice started to reach for the spear. Lirea tensed, and Beatrice drew back her hand.

"That's what he told me," Lirea said. "But I heard the truth behind his words."

A stifled exclamation from the main deck drew Danielle's attention to the three rats scrambling up the ladder. Armand had grabbed another crewman, stopping him from crying out. Armand met Danielle's eyes and nodded. Armand was unarmed, but a twitch of his finger signaled the others to ready their weapons.

Lirea didn't notice as the rats climbed the starboard ladder onto the forecastle and raced through the puddles left by her arrival.

Hurry.

Lirea spun, thrusting the long horn on the end of her spear at Danielle's stomach. "Surrender Lannadae, or we will kill your crew, starting with this one."

Danielle raised her head, trying to match the queen's calm, though her hands were shaking.

"Killing her won't end your pain." For the first time, anger hardened the queen's words.

Danielle readied herself. *Now!*

The first rat sank his teeth into the back of Lirea's unprotected ankle. At the same time, Danielle swept her arm up, knocking the spear away.

Lirea stumbled toward the railing as a second rat latched onto the side of her foot. She swung her spear, striking the third rat.

"Take her!" Armand yelled, grabbing the ladder.

Talia was faster. She dropped to the forecastle and kicked low to sweep Lirea's legs from beneath her. While Lirea recovered, Talia grabbed Danielle's arm and flung her into Armand. The two of them fell together, to be caught by the crew below.

Armand jumped to his feet and grabbed a crossbow from one of the men. "If you get a clear shot, take it."

"Your Highness, the undine are attacking the ship!"

Armand swore. "You four, stay with me. Everyone else get to the sides. Raise anchor and signal the *Tocohl* and the *Margaret*. Their archers will have a better angle to shoot the undine off our hulls."

On the forecastle, Talia was trying to get to the queen, but Lirea had already recovered. Lirea jabbed twice with her spear, driving Talia back and keeping Beatrice trapped at the front of the forecastle. The third time, Talia twisted sideways, catching the shaft and yanking Lirea closer. Talia stepped forward and drove the edge of her other hand into the mermaid's throat.

Danielle had seen Talia drop men twice her size with that move, but Lirea merely staggered, stumbling into the pinrail that circled the foremast. The undine must have stronger throats, or else their windpipes were better protected.

Talia hadn't released her grip on the spear. A quick kick to Lirea's wrist broke her hold, and Talia yanked the spear free. She spun the weapon overhead and swung.

Lirea jumped around the mast, colliding with Beatrice and knocking the queen into the railing. Beatrice caught herself, then rammed her elbow into Lirea's side. Someone cheered as Beatrice shoved the mermaid back toward Talia.

Lirea pulled her knife from her harness, slashing wildly. Talia rapped the shaft of her spear against Lirea's wrist, then stepped back, using the tip to cut Lirea's arm above the elbow. Lirea barely avoided the follow-up thrust, which gouged wood from the rail.

"Hurry," Danielle urged. She wanted to help, but knew she would only be in the way.

Beatrice was keeping the mast between herself and the two fighters as she tried to get to safety. The queen was a capable fighter, but Talia's skills were inhuman. Armand was already shoving his way to the edge of the forecastle to help her down.

Lirea screamed again, the sound so painful several men dropped their weapons. Even Talia staggered back. Still screaming, Lirea thrust her knife at Talia.

Talia twirled out of the way, then swung the spear in a wide arc to crack against Lirea's back, breaking Lirea's scream and the spear both.

The impact flung Lirea directly into the queen, driving them both into the railing. Lirea stepped back, and Danielle's heart knotted.

"Beatrice," Danielle whispered.

Lirea's knife was stuck deep in the queen's chest.

"Mother!" Armand started toward the ladder, but one of the crew pulled him back.

The broken spear dropped from Talia's hands, surprisingly loud as it clattered to the deck.

Lirea stared at her hand, still wrapped around the hilt of the knife. She screamed again, a wordless cry of anguish that blurred Danielle's vision. Through watery eyes, she saw Lirea yank the blade free and fling Beatrice toward Talia before leaping from the ship.

Talia caught the queen and lowered her gently to the deck.

Armand was first up the ladder, followed closely by Danielle. Talia already had both hands over the wound, trying to stop the flow of blood.

"She's still breathing." Talia's voice quavered.

"Someone fetch Hoffman," Armand shouted.

"No!" said Talia. "Get Snow."

"I'm here." Snow was already climbing up from the main deck, her face even paler than usual.

"I called for my surgeon, dammit!" Armand stared at his mother's crumpled form. Danielle could see him fighting to maintain his self-control.

One of the men fired his crossbow into the water. "Your Highness, the undine are leaving!"

Danielle reached out to touch Armand's arm. "Snow is a skilled healer. She's helped Beatrice before."

"My mother is dying," Armand replied, his voice flat. "Hoffman is—"

"Your mother trusts these women," Danielle said. "So do I. Please let Snow save her."

Snow wasn't waiting for his answer. She knelt beside the queen and spread her hand over Talia's. "Press harder. Everyone else get back and give me light."

"Will she live?" Talia asked.

Snow didn't answer. She touched her choker, a band of oval mirrors connected with gold wire. Light flashed from the mirror in the center, illuminating the wound. "Pull your hand away now."

Talia drew back, and Snow clapped her own hands down over Beatrice's chest. Her hair fell like black curtains to obscure her actions.

"Talia?" Danielle asked.

Talia's hands had begun to shake. She picked up the broken spear and stepped toward the railing.

Danielle followed. "What are you doing?"

Talia jumped lightly onto the rail, one hand holding a line as she searched the water.

"They've already fled. You'll never catch them." Danielle reached out, but Talia slapped her hand away with the spear. "Even if Lirea remains, she'll kill you. You can't fight them in the water."

Talia might as well have been deaf. She paced along the rail, every step deliberate.

"Snow will save the queen," Danielle said. "Don't leave me to explain to her why you threw your life away."

If Danielle hadn't been watching so closely, she would have missed the faint slumping of Talia's shoulders.

"The sea folk have been known to poison their blades," whispered one of the crew.

Snow shook her head. "It's not poison."

Armand stood. The crew fell silent as he turned to face them. "Make sail for home."

When leaving the docks at Lorindar, he had shouted orders for a quarter of an hour. From the way the crew worked together now, unfurling the sails in near silence, those detailed commands had been little more than a formality.

"What about her?" One of the crew gestured at Talia with her crossbow. "It was her who fought the mermaid and got the queen stabbed."

Talia turned on the balls of her feet. Her expression made Danielle pray the man had already prepared his will and made peace with God. Then Talia looked at the queen. She bowed her head and dropped to the deck, her anger disappearing.

No, Danielle corrected. The rage wasn't gone. It was simply turned inward.

"I said take us home." Armand's voice was soft, but the crew scrambled to obey. He crouched beside Snow. "What can I do to help?"

"Give me space," Snow snapped.

Danielle took Talia's hand and pulled her toward the ladder. It was a measure of Talia's shock that she didn't resist as Danielle led her away.

Snow had spent most of the day in the galley, reading a treatise on the development of marine navigation, from simple star charts to celestial globes of enchanted quartz to the first astrolabe.

The oven had been extinguished after breakfast, as the growing winds made the risk of fire too great, but the smell of fresh-roasted sausage lingered in the air. Snow sat on a wooden bench in the corner, knees pulled close to support her book. She was so absorbed in her reading that she barely noticed the gentle clangs of the pots and pans hanging on the wall.

Her choker cast a soft beam of sunlight on the pages.

Each oval mirror was an enchanted twin to the magic mirror she had inherited from her mother.

This was her second choker. The first had been destroyed a year before. Snow had spent several months working to create a new one. To Snow's surprise, Danielle had proved quite helpful. Her father had been a skilled glassmaker, and though he had died long ago, Danielle still remembered much of what she had learned from watching him. She had shown Snow several tricks to help her improve the quality of the mirrors.

These were slightly larger than the mirrors from Snow's first choker. The gold-rimmed edges dug into her chin and throat if she bowed her head too far, but the larger size made it easier to manipulate their power. In the days leading up to this voyage, she had used the mirrors to capture several days' worth of sunlight. This wasn't her first time at sea, and despite what certain people might think, she couldn't spend the *entire* time flirting with the crew. Three more books waited for her in her cabin.

The first scream shattered her spell, plunging the galley into darkness. She pressed one hand to the wall, rising on unsteady legs. There had been a magical element to that scream, but it was a damaged magic, like an injured boar, wild and enraged.

She waited for the sound to fade, then touched her choker, restoring enough light to make her way safely out of the galley. She passed other crewmen rushing to and fro. "What's happening?"

"Out of the way, girl!" Strong hands shoved her aside.

Snow muttered a quick charm beneath her breath. The man yelled as his boots slid out from under him.

"Excuse me." Snow flashed a friendly smile as she stepped over the groaning man and climbed up into the sunlight.

The scream came again. This time, Snow was able to brace herself. This wasn't a deliberate spell. Her own magic drew on various energies, from the sun's light to her own will, weaving them into whatever pattern she chose. These screams were ... *snarled*. Power without form.

At the front of the main deck, Prince Armand was shouting to the crew. Snow climbed onto one of the long-boats for a better view. A canvas tarp covered the boat, and she moved carefully, feeling for the crossbeams until she found a comfortable spot to stand and watch.

On the forecastle, a half-naked woman holding a spear was fighting with Talia. The stranger appeared human, but her nudity marked her as undine, as did that sharkskin harness. Royalty, judging from the oyster necklace. This had to be Posannes' daughter Lirea.

Queen Beatrice stood behind Lirea and Talia, unable to get past. Already the crew had gathered, blocking Snow's way. She turned to the nearest crewman. "I'll wager a dozen crowns on Talia."

Talia soon ripped the spear from her opponent's grasp, delivering one blow after another. Lirea screamed again, then drew her knife.

Snow's breath caught. Unlike the screams, the magic woven into that knife was deliberate and precise. She could feel only a faint shadow of the knife's power, little more than a whisper, but it was a whisper full of pain and despair. Snow leaped from the longboat and tried to shove her way to the forecastle.

The mermaid lunged, and Talia broke the spear over her back. An instant later, the magic in the knife flared up like oil-soaked rags.

"Bea!" There were too many people in her way. Snow jammed her thumb beneath one man's jaw, a dirty trick Talia had taught her years before. A whispered spell caused another to leap back, even as her illusory spiders flickered and vanished. Tossing spells with abandon, Snow cleared a path to the forecastle, heedless of the injuries she left in her wake.

Moments later Snow knelt beside the queen, her hands over the gash in Beatrice's chest. She sent the others away. Even as she frantically drew on her magic to chill the wound and slow the bleeding, panic threatened to unravel her spells.

The knife couldn't have pierced the heart, or Beatrice would already be dead. Snow grabbed the large mirror at the front of her choker and pulled. The wires untwisted, releasing the mirror into her palm.

She placed the mirror on the back of her other hand, directly over the wound. "Mirror, mirror—" Her mind went blank. The rhymes weren't necessary, but they helped focus her spells. She needed that focus right now. "Dammit, what rhymes with blood? Wait, I've got it."

Snow concentrated on the mirror. "Mirror, mirror, hear my need. Show me whence the queen does bleed."

The mirror's surface frosted, then cleared again. Blood filled the glass, but Snow peered deeper.

There. One of the smaller arteries leading from the heart had been cut, but not completely severed. She could see blood pumping from the cut with each beat of the queen's heart.

There was no way for needle and thread to reach such a wound. Snow touched her choker again. A length of gold wire unbraided itself, coiling around the index finger of her left hand. "Hurry, curse you."

She snapped the wire free, then pressed her finger against the wound. The wire grew hot, remembering the heat of the forge until it was soft and pliable as silk. The tip of the wire snaked into the wound, growing longer and thinner as it sought out the cut.

Six times the wire pierced the artery. More finely than any human hand could sew, it stitched the edges together, gradually slowing the flow of blood. A thought severed the wire, melting the ends together so that no sharp points remained. Snow continued to watch through her mirror until she was certain the bleeding had stopped. Only then did she reach up to touch Beatrice's face.

What she sensed was like a physical blow, knocking her back. "She's gone."

"Nobody's dying if I have anything to say about it." Gentle hands slowly pulled her away. The ship's surgeon, an older man named Hoffman, sat down beside her. "She's still breathing. I'll take over from here."

Snow started to argue, but the words wouldn't come. She squeezed her eyes shut, then nodded.

Someone else helped her to her feet. Her mirror slipped from her hand and broke on the deck.

"Sorry about that," said the crewman.

Snow barely heard. Beatrice's face was pale and still. Her blood covered the forecastle. It had gotten onto Snow's hands, soaked into her sleeves and trousers. She could smell it in the air, the sharp tang overpowering even the salt of the sea air.

"Will she live?" asked someone. The prince? Snow wasn't sure.

She pulled away, trying to get to Danielle and Talia. "The surgeon . . . will do what he can." With those whispered words, Snow fled.

Danielle had seen death before. Her stepsister Stacia had died in front of her only last year. Her father died when she was ten, her mother even earlier.

She had wept for them all, in very different ways. Her mother's death was less a memory than a collection of impressions. Broken glass . . . her father had dropped the bottle he was working on when he heard her mother fall. The bottle had been such a vivid shade of blue. Still warm from the fire, the softened glass had absorbed some of the impact before shattering, spreading shards of oddly warped glass across the floor.

Her father's death had been a slow thing. Danielle had known what was to come, even if her stepmother refused to acknowledge it. Danielle had stolen every moment with him that she could. When death finally came, it was almost a relief, releasing him from his pain.

For her stepsister Stacia, Danielle had wept at the pointlessness of it all.

Sitting on the edge of the cot in the cabin she shared with Armand, she refused to cry now. Snow would save Beatrice. She had to.

"Beatrice found me." Talia's accent was thicker than usual, elongating the vowels and slurring the harder consonants. The finely woven carpet muffled the sound of her footfalls as she paced. She still carried the broken spear she had taken from Lirea. "Four years ago, when I first fled to Lorindar. I was so frightened I nearly killed her."

"This isn't your fault." Worrying about Talia's fear helped Danielle to ignore her own. "You can't blame yourself."

Talia stabbed the tip of the spear into the wall. She twisted, prying up a long splinter. "Lirea didn't intend to kill Beatrice. She wouldn't have, if I hadn't—"

"Beatrice isn't dead."

Talia's jaw quivered. "I've killed before, Princess. I saw the wound. With so much blood—"

"Snow will take care of Beatrice," Danielle said. "You were trying to protect us."

"And what a marvelous job I did." She punctuated her words with another blow to the wall. "I should be on deck. The merfolk might come back."

"You've seen the undine before. Did you know they could take human form?"

Talia shook her head. "They can't. Otherwise King Posannes could have picked his own strawberries. This was something else."

At least she had stopped pacing. Danielle spoke quickly, hoping to keep them both distracted. "Lirea had two tails."

"Most have only one," said Talia. "The royal bloodline has two. They believe it makes them superior, closer to being human. They're faster swimmers, too."

"Beatrice said she was one of Posannes' daughters." Had Lirea killed her own father to take command of her tribe? "Lirea was asking about her sister."

"Power passes through the females." Talia twirled the broken spear in one hand. "Posannes only led the tribe after his wife died. Even though he wears the crown, his daughters hold the true power. The eldest would have taken over in another year or two. If Lirea is looking for her sister, she's probably trying to eliminate her competition."

Beatrice had known. She had been searching for Posannes, and she had recognized the danger Lirea posed. "Did Beatrice ever say anything to you about Lannadae?"

"No." Talia snorted. "But it wouldn't surprise me. You know Queen Bea. She had a thing for taking in frightened princesses."

That made Danielle smile, even as her heart tightened at the word *had*.

The door creaked open, and Snow slipped inside. "She's alive."

Through tear-blurred eyes, Danielle saw Talia relax slightly.

"Prince Armand is writing a note for the king," Snow continued, turning to Danielle. "He would like you to talk to the bird and stress the urgency of the message. Tell it to fly as swiftly as possible."

Danielle rose to go, but Snow stopped her.

"What is it?" Talia asked, clutching the spear with both hands.

Snow sat down on the cot. She looked tired. Tired and *old*. For an instant, Danielle feared she had sacrificed a part of her life to save Beatrice's. Twice now, Snow had summoned dark powers to protect her. Each time, the price had been seven years of her life. The first time, those powers had killed Snow's mother, saving Snow's life. The second time had been last year, when they saved Danielle and Talia.

Since that day, Snow's night-black hair had been mixed with strands of white. Faint wrinkles marked the corners of her eyes. Danielle looked closely, but saw no new signs of age. Snow was simply exhausted.

"Tell me about the knife Lirea used," Snow said.

"The blade was abalone," said Talia. "About as long as my hands, two fingers wide. Double-edged and thin. Not a fighting weapon. It would likely snap if you tried to stab an armored enemy, or even if the blade struck bone."

"No, it wouldn't." Snow clasped her hands together. The skin was red, scrubbed raw. Blood stained the cuffs of her shirt.

"Tell us," Danielle said.

"I've done what I can to help her body heal. Hoffman is stitching the wound, and I've medicines that will speed her recovery. But healing is as much a matter of spirit as flesh."

"Beatrice is the strongest woman I've ever met," Danielle said. "She's the only person I know who can outstubborn Talia. Her spirit—"

"Isn't there," Snow interrupted, her voice cracking.

Talia stepped closer. "You said she was still alive."

"Her heart beats. Her body breathes. But Beatrice—" Snow reached up to take Danielle's hand. "Beatrice is gone."

CHAPTER 2

TALIA HAD LEARNED TWO STYLES of fighting in the years after she was "rescued" from her curse. The first was the formal sik h'ara style. This was long-form fighting, focused on whirling kicks and fast, open-hand strikes.

Talia preferred sik h'adan, close form. There was nothing formal about sik h'adan. It was this style she practiced now in the cramped confines of the cabin, driving a knee into the ribs of an imagined foe, then following up with an elbow to the throat. She stomped a heel to crush the arch of the enemy's foot. She whirled, flinging the broken spear at the floor hard enough to bury the tip in the deck.

"If you're going to attack the boat, would you mind waiting until it's delivered us home?" Snow asked. "Or has the floor insulted you somehow?"

The spear still quivered in place. Talia grabbed the broken shaft and kicked the head, snapping the tip.

"That's right, blame the spear."

As much as she cared about Snow, there were times Talia wanted to throw her through a wall. "Shouldn't you be doing something? Working on Beatrice or talking to your mirrors? We don't even know what that knife did to her."

"I've done as much as I can. I need to get to my mirror at the palace." Snow twirled her hair around her finger, pulling it tight until the fingertip turned red. "My mother might have known. She had a lifetime of secrets collected in her library. I saved some of those books, but most . . . her protections were stronger than I expected. I can't imagine how much knowledge burned that day."

With a sigh, Talia knelt and grabbed the broken spear point, wrenching it back and forth until it came free of the wood. She poked a finger through the hole in the carpet. "I'll mend it when we get back," she said before Snow could comment.

"I haven't seen you this tense since we broke into Lord Pensieve's palace in Colwich," Snow said.

Yet again, Talia restrained herself from snapping at Snow. How could she just sit there? Talia couldn't remember the last time she had felt so powerless. Even Colwich hadn't been as bad, though hiding in the swamps until Lord Pensieve's men gave up the search was an experience she could have done without.

"You were itching for days afterward," Snow said.

"Lorindar has far too many bugs."

"Don't forget the snake."

Talia's mouth quirked. "I'm not the one who screamed."

"No, you're the one who let out a war cry and attacked a foot-long snake with a double-headed war ax."

"It's all I had," Talia said with a shrug. "Besides, for all I knew it could have been poisonous."

Footsteps approached the cabin door.

"Prince Armand," Snow said without looking up.

The door opened, and the prince stepped inside. His expression was cold. "The wind is against us, but I'm told we should reach the palace by dawn. The *Saint Tocohl* will escort us home, while the *Lord Lynn Margaret* remains behind to hunt Lirea and her undine. If . . . if my mother still lives, she will be given into the care of my father's most skilled healers."

He kept his emotions under tight rein. He reminded Talia of his father in that way. To Snow, he said, "Thank you for saving her life."

Snow bowed her head slightly.

"What do the two of you know of Lirea?"

Talia blinked. "Your Highness?"

"I know you've served my mother for many years," he said. "When I was taken by Danielle's stepsisters, you and Snow helped to rescue me."

"We had help from Ambassador Trittibar," Snow piped up. "As well as a friend in Fairytown."

Armand lifted a hand, and Snow fell silent. Talia fought a rush of anger at the gesture. Who was he to wave Snow to silence? But he had been raised a prince, brought up to command those around him, and he had no way of knowing who it was he had dismissed so casually. Most people knew the tale of Snow White, but the idea that she could be living here in Lorindar was too great a leap. At most, people assumed Snow's nickname came from her resemblance to that distant princess.

"Not even Danielle has shared the full details of that rescue," Armand said. "How my wife, with the help of two servants, could defeat goblins and trolls, spirits and dark magic."

"Also darklings and a ghost," Snow added.

"Yes, of course." For a moment, his expression softened. "Don't misunderstand me. I'm grateful for your assistance in Fairytown. But it's clear you are both more than mere servants. What do you know of Lirea's feud with my mother?"

"Nothing," Talia said.

His lips pressed together. He turned to Snow. "And you?"

Snow stared at the wall. "You're an intelligent man. If I had known Lirea meant to attack your mother, do you really think I would have left her unguarded?"

"That doesn't answer my question," Armand said.

Talia had been thinking the same thing. The cabin tilted as the ship fought the wind. Talia adjusted her weight to compensate, watching Snow closely.

Armand pressed one hand to the ceiling. When the ship steadied, he snapped, "I've seen my mother struck down and my kingdom dragged into conflict with an enemy we've never fought. If you truly serve this kingdom, you'll—"

Talia shook her head, fighting for calm. "We swore to serve your mother. Not your kingdom, nor you."

"And you don't want to know what Beatrice puts up with to keep that loyalty," Snow added.

Talia scowled, but Snow only flashed that damnably innocent smile of hers.

Armand drew a deep breath, and the anger slowly drained from his posture. "My mother trusts you."

"Yes." Talia's voice was flat. Beatrice had trusted her, and because of that trust, Beatrice had almost died.

"As does Danielle." Armand hesitated only slightly before adding, "I know you love them both. Thank you for trying to protect them."

Talia managed a small nod. Anger she could accept, but compassion cut through her defenses as easily as she had slipped past Lirea's.

She clenched her fists, trying not to think about that fight. There were so many ways she could have prevented this. A blow to the back of Lirea's knees, dropping her to the deck. An overhand strike with the spear, stunning her. A simple kick to the throat. Any one of those moves would have stopped Lirea without pushing her toward the queen.

"My surgeon will watch over her until we reach the palace," Armand went on. "I would ask the two of you to stay close to Danielle. I've stationed men to watch the water, but we've seen how easily Lirea can board this ship. If she follows through on her threats against Lorindar, we won't be safe until we're back on land."

Talia blinked. "You're asking us to protect her?"

The prince managed a smile. "Somehow I suspect you'd do so with or without my request."

"If Lirea does return," Snow said softly, "tell your men to try to get that knife."

Talia's expression was feral. "If she returns, you can take it from her corpse."

*   *   *

The following morning, Danielle stood on the quarter-deck with Talia and Snow. At sunrise, the cliffs of Lorindar had been little more than a smudge of shadow rising from the water. Now she could distinguish the proud shape of Whiteshore Castle sitting atop the white cliffs. Clumps of green clung to the cliff face where grass and shrubs had managed to take root against the wind and rain.

The palace was made of the same white stone. Glass windows sparkled in the towers, and Danielle could just make out the guardsmen patrolling the eastern wall.

The *Glass Slipper* sailed past the wharf near Fisherman's Canal, where the commercial and fishing ships were docked. Fisherman's Canal was almost a town in itself, with its warehouses, roads, and boardwalks spreading along the rocky base of the cliffs and out into the water. The royal navy used the docks further north, past the road that switchbacked up into the city proper.

The crew trimmed the sails as the helmsman guided the *Glass Slipper* past one of the man-made seawalls, long piles of rock that stretched out from the cliffs to absorb the sea's rage in times of storm.

Sailors swarmed over anchored naval ships, hauling supplies and crawling through the rigging as they prepared to set out.

"What will they do?" Danielle asked. "The undine could be anywhere."

"Not anywhere," said Snow. "In the coming weeks, they'll have to settle someplace safe to birth their young. Their children are vulnerable to cold, so they'll go to a place that's shallow and warm."

Talia leaned over the railing and spat. "Shallow and warm? That leaves the entire coastline of Lyskar, Allesandria, and the Hiladi Empire. We should be able to search them all within about three years. Assuming their respective rulers don't object to the Lorindar Royal Navy snooping about their lands."

"We'll find them," Danielle said. Talia scoffed, but didn't bother to argue.

The *Glass Slipper* slowed, momentum carrying her forward even after the last sail was furled. Behind her, she heard Armand formally relinquish command to one of the officers.

"You and I will be first off," he said as he joined her. "We're not waiting for the tides. I want you back on land." He turned back to Talia and Snow. "Would the two of you assist us in escorting my mother's . . . body?"

Talia hesitated. She looked at Danielle, as though she were checking to make sure she had heard correctly. "Of course, Your Highness."

Danielle took Armand's hand and squeezed. She hoped he understood how much such a request would mean. Talia tried to hide her misery, but it was clear she still blamed herself for what had happened. Knowing Talia, she would continue to carry that blame until Beatrice recovered. Danielle didn't think about what would happen if Beatrice never awakened.

Anchor chains vibrated the deck as they clanked into the water, dragging the ship to a halt a short distance from shore. Hoffman had already moved the queen into one of the longboats. She lay on two padded boards set lengthwise in the boat. Danielle winced as she watched Hoffman strap Beatrice down, securing first her legs, then her waist.

Lowering the longboat into the water was a complicated affair. The crew had emptied the boat of any excess weight, including oars. Others had reinforced the yards with extra lines. The yards were rotated inward, and ropes were run from them down to the longboat. Armand circled the boat, double-checking every knot himself before climbing inside. He rested his hands on his mother's shoulders, then nodded to Danielle.

This was the largest of the four boats on the *Glass Slipper*. Danielle climbed in with Talia's assistance and sat on a bench beside the queen. Talia settled on the opposite side. Snow took up a position near the back.

"Hold tight," Armand whispered, before turning to shout, "Hoist away!"

Danielle held her breath as the ropes pulled taut. Wood creaked and pulleys squealed, and the yardarms bowed as the longboat swung into the air. Danielle fought to ignore the lurching in her stomach. She should have asked Snow for more tea at breakfast.

"Couldn't we just bring the *Glass Slipper* into the docks?" she asked.

"Not until the tide comes in," said Snow. The breeze caught her hair, tossing strands of black in front of her face. "They've dredged the docks to allow the larger ships to come in, but you don't want to risk it at low tide. Not without a shallower draft than this ship has." She smiled and added, "I'm afraid your bottom is just too—"

"Don't make me throw you overboard," Talia said.

The yards turned slowly, moving the longboat past the edge of the ship until it hung suspended over the water. Danielle took one of the queen's hands in hers. Beatrice's skin was cold, like that of a child who had been swimming too long in the chilly water. Danielle removed her cloak and spread it over the queen.

The crew set the longboat down so gently there was barely a splash. The presence of queen, prince, and princess no doubt contributed to their care. Four more sailors climbed down a rope ladder to join them in the boat. They removed the ropes, then stood to receive the oars passed down from the ship.

As soon as the men began to row, Armand turned to Danielle. "My father taught me to see the kingdom as a whole. My mother had a different upbringing. She cares for Lorindar, but she sees individuals first, regardless of their nation. She's a good deal like you, actually."

He glanced at Talia and Snow. "She also kept many secrets over the years. I've seen her ruin dukes and settle wars when all the military might of Lorindar wouldn't have accomplished the same thing."

"She's a good queen," said Danielle.

"Yes." Armand looked down, gently brushing his mother's hair from her face. "Taking in one of Posannes' daughters does sound like something she might do, if he asked her. Both as queen of Lorindar and as a friend to Posannes and his family. They've known each other for many years."

"Beatrice never would have taken us to see the undine if she thought something like this could happen," Danielle said.

"No," Armand agreed. "She was good at recognizing danger. Some believed it was a gift from God."

"She might have relied too strongly on that gift," Snow said, speaking for the first time since leaving the ship. "Even the strongest seer is often blind to his or her own fate. That blindness could have given her a false sense of safety."

Armand stared at her, then nodded.

At the dock, King Theodore stood waiting with a small crowd of guards and bystanders. The cliffs made him appear small, almost fragile to Danielle's eye. The mist from the waves had darkened his jacket and pasted his gray-brown hair to his head.

"I doubt he's slept at all since receiving word," Armand said.

"Have you?" Danielle took his hand. Not that she was any better rested. When she finally drifted off last night, dreams of screaming undine had jolted her awake. "I waited for you to come to bed."

Armand didn't answer, but he squeezed her hand more tightly. "Do you think your friends will be able to help my mother?"

Danielle glanced at Snow and Talia, both of whom sat in silence. Snow had already tried to use her magic to locate Lirea and the undine, just as she had tried to counter the magic that had torn the queen's spirit from her body. Both times she had failed. Danielle had no doubt that Snow would disappear the instant they reached the palace, barricading herself away with her magic mirror. "They love her. We all do."

"Promise me you'll be careful," he said. "Lirea has already threatened to kill you. I don't—" He looked away. "Just promise me."

As they longboat neared the docks, the king jumped into the waist-deep water and waded toward them. The sailors stowed their oars. One tossed a rope to the men on the docks.

King Theodore caught the front of the boat, guiding it alongside the dock. His gaze never left the queen.

"I promise," Danielle whispered.

Padded benches lined the inside of the carriage. The queen lay on the longest, opposite the door. She was stretched out as if asleep, her head resting on the king's lap. The king's breath caught with each jolt as the carriage made its way up the road toward home.

There were few words during the trip, and those were spoken in whispers. Theodore had ordered the coastal towns to be on the lookout for the undine. He had sent word to Hilad and Lyskar as well, though he hadn't yet heard back.

Armand took Danielle's hand, and then they traveled a while in silence. They were coming up on the city wall when Armand said, "I tried to stop Lirea. I was . . . I couldn't reach her. I'm sorry, Father."

The pain in his voice knotted Danielle's chest. Like Talia, riding behind in a second carriage, Armand still blamed himself. "The undine are too strong. Lirea could have killed you. Beatrice wanted you safe."

"As do I," said Theodore.

Armand shook his head, but he said nothing further.

When they reached the palace, they found Father Isaac waiting just inside the gate. With him stood the king's healer, a silver-haired old man named Tymalous. Tymalous didn't even wait for the carriage to stop before climbing inside to check Beatrice's bandages. He muttered to himself, then pronounced her safe to move. With the king's help, they carried the queen to a small cart.

"Bring her to the chapel," said Father Isaac.

Danielle started to follow, but an angry wail demanded her attention. "Jakob!"

Nicolette, Jakob's wet nurse, hurried across the courtyard. Danielle's son kicked and squirmed in her arms. Nicolette's eyes were shadowed, and the shoulders of her dress were stained with tears and snot.

As always, the sight of Nicolette was bittersweet. The same magic that sped Jakob's growth in the womb had left Danielle's body unprepared for motherhood, and she had never been able to nurse her own son. Nicolette was a marvelous nurse and a loving mother to her own children as well as the prince, but seeing her with Jakob always made Danielle feel as though she had somehow failed her son.

Danielle pushed such thoughts aside as she lifted Jakob from Nicolette's arms and rocked him, whispering and bouncing him in her arms. She smoothed his sweaty blond hair back with one hand and kissed his forehead. His cheeks were speckled red from the force of his crying. His voice was painfully hoarse, rasping and pitiful. She held her son tight, and for a moment nothing else mattered. "I have you," she whispered. "You're all right. Mama's back."

Armand reached out to wipe tears from Jakob's chubby cheeks. "Has he been this charming the entire time we were gone?"

"He started crying yesterday afternoon," Nicolette said, her voice raspy. "Hasn't calmed since. Hardly slept two winks the whole night."

"Yesterday afternoon?" Danielle repeated. That was when Lirea had attacked the ship.

"He's been fed, changed, rocked, and nothing soothes him." Knowing Nicolette's devotion to little Jakob, she had probably stayed with him all night. "I even sang him that song he likes, the one about the octopus' shoes. Sang until I could hardly croak another note, but he wasn't having it."

Jakob nuzzled his face into Danielle's shoulder, and a hiccup interrupted his cries.

"Is it true what they're saying?" Nicolette had turned to watch the cart carrying Beatrice to the chapel. "Did the merfolk try to assassinate the queen?"

Other voices drew Danielle's attention from her son. While she had fussed with Jakob, others had approached, forming a loose ring around Danielle and Armand. Peter, the apprentice falconer, cleared his throat and said, "I've a brother who sails on the *Virtuous,* Princess. If the merfolk have declared war, will they—"

The gardener, Laurence, slapped Peter with a dirt-crusted hand. "The undine have been friends to Lorindar for a century. Isn't that right, Your Highness?"

"They say this was a rogue mermaid, an assassin hired by Allesandria to avenge some imagined slight," said Rebecca, one of the women who worked in the laundry. "They mean to—"

"A lone mermaid did attack our ship," Danielle said. Rumors would spread regardless of her words. At least this way the rumors would have some basis in truth. She glanced at Armand, uncertain how much more to say. "She escaped, and we don't know why she attacked. The undine . . . they appear to follow her."

"Will the queen live?" asked Peter.

They never would have pressed Armand this way. Even now, they carefully avoided his gaze, trying to close in around Danielle while dodging the prince. An impressive trick, given that Armand stood with his arm around Danielle's shoulders.

But until a year ago, Danielle had been a servant, not a royal. Though she wore her crown when the chamberlain forced her to, she still thought of the palace staff as friends and equals, far more than the nobles at court.

"That's enough," Nicolette snapped, shooing the crowd back. "Jakob's just beginning to settle down. Anyone riles him up again will answer to me."

"Thank you," Danielle smiled as she watched Nicolette chase the crowd back. "We'll be all right. You should go and rest. Stop by the kitchen and tell Simon to give you whatever you'd like, on my orders."

"Thank you, Highness," Nicolette said.

Danielle hummed to her son as she and Armand walked toward the northwest tower, where the royal family resided. After only a few steps, Jakob began to struggle. By the time they were halfway across the courtyard, he was screaming loudly enough to draw stares from atop the walls. His pudgy fingers reached for Armand.

"Looks like it's my turn." Armand's expression was a blend of fondness and exasperation. The prospect of fatherhood had terrified him in the beginning. He still tended to treat Jakob as though he were made of glass, but there was no mistaking the love in his smile. "I'm sure I was never so fussy, but when I tell that to my mother, she merely laughs." He reached out, but Jakob kicked so hard Danielle nearly lost her grip.

"He's pointing past you," she said. "Toward the chapel." Toward Beatrice.

Danielle tightened her hold on her son. Queen Beatrice had been known to sense things. One of her premonitions had alerted them to Armand's kidnapping the year before. Perhaps Jakob had inherited that gift.

Or perhaps he had received something darker. Despite Snow's assurances, Danielle still worried. She had been surrounded by so much magic while carrying Jakob. It was possible Snow had missed something.

"Maybe he spotted his grandfather," Armand offered. "You know how they spoil him. Is it any wonder he wants to follow?"

Danielle tried again to take Jakob to the tower, but he jabbed his tiny fingers at the chapel, kicking with all his might. With a sigh, she turned toward the chapel.

Armand chuckled. "My father may sit on the throne, but little Jakob is well on his way to ruling Whiteshore Castle."

Jakob raised his head, studying his father for a long moment, then turned and blew a snot bubble onto Danielle's shoulder.

A wooden cross inlaid with polished silver topped the steeple of the small church. A single step at the front led through a stone archway. The air inside was cool and still. Past leather-padded benches, Danielle spotted Father Isaac arranging dried palm fronds around the base of the altar. The king sat in the front bench, his head bowed in prayer. Queen Beatrice lay on the altar with her hands folded over her chest.

Danielle's throat tightened at the sight. She knew the queen still lived, but seeing her laid out as if for a funeral . . .

Jakob twisted in her arms, staring first at the altar, then turning his attention to the stained glass windows along the tops of the walls.

Father Isaac strode across the chapel until he reached Armand. Without breaking stride, he wrapped his arms around the prince and kissed his cheek. Isaac was the prince's age and had known Armand since childhood. He had officiated at the wedding between Danielle and Armand, both the public ceremony in the great hall and the smaller, more intimate ceremony here in the chapel. "I'm so sorry, Armand."

He turned to Danielle and embraced her as well, being careful not to block Jakob's view of the window. His faded black robe smelled of incense, and the brown curls of his beard tickled her cheek. "As I told the king, the wounds are serious, but not fatal. Whoever treated her did well. Even your father's healer pronounced her care 'adequate.' "

Danielle forced a smile. Coming from Tymalous, that was high praise indeed.

"I'm told her wounds go deeper than the body," said Armand.

"I know." Isaac backed away, straightening the rose-red collar of his robe. The collar was wrinkled, the edges dark with sweat. A jeweled crucifix hung from a leather thong around his neck, seeming out of place against his oft-patched robe. Small rubies capped each of the tiny nails holding the silver figure to the cross.

"Spirit has been torn from flesh," Isaac said as he led them to the altar. He picked up another palm frond, his hands moving with well-practiced assurance as he folded the frond into a cross. He gently tucked the cross into the queen's hands. "This will protect her until I have time to erect a stronger ward. She should be safe here."

"A ward?" Danielle asked.

"Not all churches frown upon the magical arts." A smile flitted across Isaac's face. "Given the nature of this kingdom, it would be a foolish ruler who didn't bring a magical adviser into his circle."

"You said she would be safe," said Armand. "Safe from what?"

Though the king didn't look up from his prayers, Danielle saw his shoulders tense. He was listening as closely as his son.

"Her body is vulnerable," Isaac said. "There are forces in this world that might seek to use such an unprotected host."

Danielle hugged Jakob tighter. Jakob squirmed in protest. He twisted about to stare at Beatrice, his small mouth pursed in concentration. Slowly, his face stretched into a yawn.

"Magic is a gift from God, like anything else," Isaac said. "The blade that struck your mother is a perversion of that gift. I can care for her mortal body, but even here, protected by God's power, the body can survive for only so long without the soul."

Armand nodded. "How long?"

"A week. Perhaps two. The queen is strong, but she is not a young woman."

For a moment, Danielle felt like a child again. She wanted to flee to her mother's hazel tree and hide within the branches where she would be safe. But her mother's tree was gone, and hiding wouldn't help the queen. She moved closer to Armand, drawing on his strength instead. He did the same, stepping toward her until their shoulders touched.

"What can we do?" asked Armand. "I mean no offense to your knowledge, but there are other mages in Lorindar. We can summon help from Fairytown as well. They will—"

"And what will you offer the rulers of Fairytown for

their aid?" asked King Theodore. Here in the chapel, he didn't bother to conceal his bitterness. "What price will you pay for the life of a queen?"

"Without knowing how her spirit was taken, they could do no more than I," Isaac said. "For now, Armand, you should comfort your father. Take strength in your shared love for her and for one another."

"We've little time," Armand said. "Lorindar may soon be at war with the undine, and love will not find the mermaid who did this."

"No. But it will help you through the days to come." Isaac turned to Danielle. "As for you, perhaps you should take your son to the nursery?"

Danielle looked down at Jakob, who had fallen asleep and was now drooling on her shoulder.

Isaac bent down to kiss Jakob's forehead. "God be with you all."

Lirea floated in the shade beneath the dock, listening to the creak of wood as the humans finished unloading their ship. One hand clutched her knife in its sheath. The sea had washed the human queen's blood from the blade, but it didn't matter. The attack had roused the voices, like blood to sharks.

Quiet, she sang, but the knife wouldn't listen. She crossed her hands over her chest, trying to muffle the knife's cries. It was like an infant, wailing an incoherent song of fear and grief. So loud . . . she had huddled in the cold depths throughout the night, trying to block out the sound and the memories.

A school of minnows swam past, laughing at her. She tensed and waved them to silence, but they ignored her. Fortunately, the humans didn't hear. Minnows had tiny voices, and she knew from experience how weak human ears were.

You'll never find her.

Stupid minnows. She snatched at them, but they darted between her fingers.

You've killed the human queen. They're all against

*you now. If they don't destroy you, then Lannadae will
find you and kill you, just as you killed your father.*

Shut up! She grabbed again, this time catching one
unfortunate minnow in her fist. She stuffed him into her
mouth, then glared at the rest, daring them to speak.

They swam away in silence. The one she had caught
squeaked *Murderer!* from within her jaws. A little vicious chewing took care of him.

Lirea waited until the humans left, then swam out
from beneath the dock. She followed a white sandbar
toward the ships anchored farther upshore.

The water tasted faintly of blood. She could hear scav-
enger birds crying and fighting near the shore, swooping
down as they tried to swipe a meal from the humans' nets.

Lirea swam along the seabed, stirring clouds of sand
as she approached a small, single-masted vessel near the
end of the harbor. The ship was in poor repair, judging
from the peeling paint and the taste of rot in the water.
Lirea swam around to the far side, where the ship would
conceal her from the others.

The water was deeper here. The humans must have
dredged the bay to allow their vessels to load and unload.
The morning sun rippled along the surface. Anyone looking
down should have a hard time seeing past that reflection.

Lirea fought tears as she shifted her body to human
form. Scales cut her legs, piercing skin and muscle as they
were absorbed into her body. Blood trickled from her
legs as the flesh sealed over countless cuts. She swam to
the surface, spitting seawater from her lungs and sinuses.

Slowly, she paddled toward the anchor chain that
trailed from the ship. She stripped off her harness, tying
it to the chain beneath the surface. It was easy to feign
weakness as she called out.

A tousled head peeked down from the ship. Lirea
heard shouts, and then a strange contraption of wood
and cork splashed into the water beside her. She guessed
it to be a buoy of some sort. Cork ringed a wooden disk.
The rope was secured to an iron loop in the center. After studying the device, she grabbed the rope and pulled

her legs onto the disk like a human stool. She used her other hand to keep from bouncing against the hull as they hauled her on board.

Two men stared at her. At first Lirea thought some of her scales might still be showing, but then she remembered the human taboo against nudity.

"What happened to you?" one asked.

Lirea hugged herself, trying to cover her body the way a human might. She hobbled past them, putting the cabin between herself and the other ships. "I don't want to talk about it." A true enough statement.

"Geoffrey, fetch a blanket for the lass," said the one with the tousled hair. He appeared to be the older of the two. He was coiling the rope from the flotation device.

Geoffrey's eyes lingered on Lirea a moment longer, then he turned away. Lirea waited until he ducked into the cabin, then moved toward the other man. "Let me help you."

"No need. You've been through enough."

Lirea took the rope anyway. He started to protest, but Lirea looped the rope around his neck and pulled.

The crack of bone brought Geoffrey from the cabin. He stared at Lirea and the crumpled body of his friend.

Lirea broke the flotation ring over his head. He fell, still clutching a rumpled blanket in his hands.

The ship swayed in the wind. Somewhere beyond the harbor, a small band of undine waited beneath the waves for Lirea's return. Lirea would have sent them with the rest to begin their war against the humans, but Nilliar had insisted they escort their queen.

They couldn't help Lirea now. Traitor Lannadae might be, but she was also of royal blood. No single-tailed undine would dare kill her. It was up to Lirea to find and punish her sister.

She should have attacked the human queen's ship, sinking them all, but the shock of the knife's rage had been too much. By the time Lirea recovered, the humans had already fled.

Perhaps it was for the best. The human queen had

been Lirea's only hope of finding Lannadae, and now she was dead. Let the survivors carry her warning back to their king. When their vessels began to disappear, they would remember Lirea's price for safe passage.

Raindrops sprinkled Lirea's skin as she lowered the flotation ring back into the water and climbed down to retrieve her knife. Once she was back on the ship, she knelt to remove Geoffrey's clothing. Both men were larger than her, but it would do. She slipped the loose shirt over her head, then used a skinning knife from the older man to shorten the sleeves. She performed similar alterations on the trousers, then sat down and massaged her legs, trying to rid her muscles of the worst of the pain.

She searched the rest of the ship, but she found no other occupants. With the cabin blocking her from the other ships, nobody else appeared to have noticed her presence.

She dragged Geoffrey's groaning body below. If anyone had heard rumors of a mermaid living along the shores of Lorindar, it would be a sailor. If not this one, there were plenty of others to talk to.

Lannadae had evaded Lirea once. She wouldn't escape again.

CHAPTER 3

IN THE YEARS SINCE SNOW HAD FLED her country, she had never been able to completely accept Lorindar as home. The endless rain, the fog that rolled in each morning, chilling the air, the cry of the gulls ... and had she known how often she would be forced to eat seafood, she might have stayed in Allesandria, even if it meant facing a death sentence for the murder of her mother the queen.

Though she never spoke of it, there were days when she longed to look out and see not endless ocean but the jagged mountains topped with snow.

The place where she felt most at home was far beneath the palace, in the room she had claimed as both library and laboratory. Books lined the walls on shelves of oiled wood. The walls were bare stone, as her room in Allesandria had been. The blue and gold carpet in the tight-stitched styles of home must have cost a fortune. Beatrice had imported it two years ago for Snow as a birthday gift.

Stains and burns marred the carpet now, the result of two years of magical experimentation.

The most valuable artifact in the room, one of the few items Snow had been able to smuggle out of Allesandria, was the magical mirror that hung from the wall. Flowering vines cast in platinum framed the oval mirror, which was taller than Snow herself. Every once in a great while, Snow would sneak down here and ask the mirror to show her the mountains of home.

Today she was ready to smash a chair through the glass. She sat on a barrel, her bare heels thudding against the wood as she glared at the mirror. The mirror reflected her glare right back.

"Mirror, mirror, of silvered glass. Find Lirea or I'll break your—"

"How exactly would one break a mirror's ass?" asked Talia, stepping through the archway into the room.

"It's metaphorical." Snow rubbed her eyes, then grimaced. Her joints were stiff, and her eyes felt as though Danielle had scoured them on one of her cleaning binges. "How long have I—"

"About an hour." Talia sat on the floor, folding her legs beneath her. "I take it you haven't been able to find Lirea?"

"I caught a glimpse once. She was somewhere in the water."

"Well, that certainly narrows it down."

Snow reached out to touch the platinum frame of the mirror. She had tried one spell after another, searching for both Beatrice and Lirea. Her first efforts to find Beatrice had come up against a magical ward. Recognizing Father Isaac's spells, she had tried again, this time concentrating on Bea's spirit. The mirror had revealed only darkness. "My mother would have been able to find her."

She peered more closely at her reflection, studying the strands of white scattered through her hair. Her mother's hair had been the opposite, white with wisps of black.

"As I recall, you defeated your mother," said Talia. "Twice. Anything she could accomplish—"

"I cheated."

Talia shook her head. "When you're fighting for your life, there's no such thing as cheating."

Snow smiled absently. "She tried to teach me when I was younger. With every spell we cast, I could feel her power creeping into my body. Looking back, I suspect she was hoping to prepare my body so she could claim it for herself when she grew too old. I didn't understand at the time, though. All I knew was that I didn't like the feel of her hands on mine as we practiced or the nightmares I had afterward. So I pretended to fail until she gave up on me."

Finding new and inventive ways to fail had been the best part of those lessons. From a levitation spell that blasted the ashes from the hearth to that sleeping draft that loosened the bowels, it hadn't been long before Snow's mother proclaimed her magically worthless. Though it was what Snow had wanted, a part of her had mourned the end of their lessons. They were the only times her mother had paid her any attention.

"I would sneak in to read her books when she was away, but I was never as skilled as she was. I could never create a mirror this powerful." She touched the gap in the front of her choker. "Without her mirror, I doubt I'd even be able to create these."

"Would you like me to tell Danielle to look for a more powerful witch?"

"*Sorceress.*" Snow glared at Talia, who matched the expression. Snow broke first, smiling despite her weariness. "Keep it up, and I'll show you what powerful really means."

"So what's stopping you from finding Lirea?"

Snow turned back to the mirror. "Each time I get close, something pushes me away. I don't know if it's the magic of the knife, Lirea herself, or something else."

Talia turned away at the sound of footsteps in the armory. Through the doorway, Snow saw Danielle standing in the armory, studying the ceiling.

Snow hopped down from the barrel, grimacing at the cramps in her legs as she joined Danielle. "What are you doing?"

"I've never realized how big the ocean really is," said Danielle.

An intricate tile mosaic formed a map of Lorindar on the armory ceiling. Amethysts marked the borders of Fairy-town near the center. A crystal palace sat on the northeast tip of the island. Slate tiles crept through lapis lazuli seas, each one a different ship from the Lorindar navy.

Weapons of every shape and size hung from wooden pegs on the walls, from the sharpened steel snowflakes Talia had made for Snow to the weighted training sticks Talia used for her workouts.

Danielle's enchanted sword hung point-down by one of the lanterns, the glass blade reflecting the flicker of the lantern flame. The hilt was cast in the shape of a hazel tree, with wood inlaid in the glass for a better grip. Though it appeared fragile, Talia knew from experience that weapon was as deadly as anything in this room. The blade was smooth and perfect, clear as rainwater save for a handspan of glass above the cross guard. There the glass was thicker, frosted white where Snow's magic had repaired it a year before.

Danielle bent down, retrieving a small tile that had fallen to the floor. Snow reached out to take it from her.

"The *Branwyn*." Snow pressed the tile to the ceiling. Magic should have held it in place, showing them the ship's location. Instead, the tile dropped to the ground.

"How?" Danielle asked, staring at the ship. "I thought the *Branwyn* was a warship."

Talia watched the other tiles creep across the ceiling. "Merfolk tear a ship apart from beneath. By the time you realize they're beneath you, your ship is already taking on water. We're fortunate they didn't sink the *Glass Slipper*."

"You think Lirea did this?" Danielle asked.

"Maybe." Snow slipped the tile into her pocket. "Even if she attacked the *Branwyn*, she'd be long gone by the time we reached the wreckage."

"I don't suppose you could craft a tile to find Lirea?" Talia asked.

Snow shook her head. "I spent months enchanting that map and sneaking down to the docks to plant a matching tile on every ship in the fleet."

"Beatrice doesn't have months," said Danielle. "According to Father Isaac, her body won't survive more than a week or two."

"We can't search an entire ocean in two weeks," Talia protested.

"No." Snow stepped to one side, making sure Danielle was between Talia and herself. "If we can't find Lirea, maybe we should look for someone else who might be able to help us."

"Her sister Lannadae." Danielle studied the map again. "If Beatrice really was hiding her, she'd be close by. We could start by searching near the harbor, and then—"

Snow braced herself. "Or I could take you to her."

"You know where Lannadae is?" Talia asked.

"Kind of."

Danielle folded her arms. "What does 'kind of' mean?"

Snow stepped back, trying to guide the conversation back into the library and away from all of the weapons. "It means yes. Beatrice swore me to secrecy."

Talia followed her. She was unarmed, but Snow had once seen Talia kill a troll with nothing more than tableware, so that wasn't as comforting as it might have been. "How long have you known?"

"Since the fall. Beatrice needed me to set up a mirror so that we could check on Lannadae while she hibernated through the winter."

"Why didn't you tell us?" Danielle asked. She sounded angry too, but she was better at keeping that anger under control. Unlike Talia, who tended to wield her anger like a sledge hammer.

"Because I promised." Snow retreated farther into the library, hurrying to one of the trunks against the wall. She opened the lid and pulled out a dark cloak. "According to Posannes, Lirea was sick. She slept for days at a time, refusing to move. When she woke, she spoke to herself, ignoring those around her. I guess she started to believe her sisters were conspiring against her. She attacked and killed her older sister."

Talia followed, throwing words like knives. "And you didn't think to warn us about a murderous mermaid?"

"Lirea wasn't a killer." Snow's shoulders slumped. "I mean, she was, but not like that. She loved her father. She wept over her sister and begged for the king's help. She tried to kill herself."

"If she'd succeeded, Beatrice might not be dying in the chapel," Talia said.

"Posannes sent Lannadae to the queen to keep her safe while he sought help for Lirea." It had been Snow who recommended the healers of Najarin. Najarin was far enough south to be accessible during the tribe's migration, and their healing skills were second to none. Several of Snow's own tomes were hand-copied from Najarin.

Talia snorted. "A daughter who had already killed once."

"Posannes was no fool," said Snow. "He kept Lirea under guard. She was unarmed, escorted by other undine at all times. He should have been safe." She stared at the cloak in her hands. "Posannes sent messengers throughout the winter, telling us Lirea was getting better."

"Better enough to murder her father and take over the tribe." Talia spun away. "So you knew Lannadae was here, and you've been wasting time with your mirror instead of taking us to see her?"

"I thought I could find Lirea myself." Snow kept her head low, hair hiding her face. "Beatrice asked me not to tell."

"Beatrice is dying!"

Each word was like a blow to the stomach. Snow blinked back tears, but before she could respond, Danielle asked, "Talia, would *you* break a vow to Beatrice?"

Talia hesitated.

"Posannes was king of his tribe," Danielle continued. "I don't know how it is among the undine, but I've watched human royalty. What would happen if the other tribes learned one daughter was mad, the other hidden away? Beatrice was protecting them. It's what she does."

"Here." Snow flung the cloak at Talia before she could say anything more, then grabbed another for Danielle. "Do you want to yell at me some more, or do you want to find a mermaid?"

"Why can't I do both?" muttered Talia.

The wool cloak smelled of dust and cedar, but Danielle pulled it over her shoulders. Behind her, Talia gathered knives and other weapons from the armory.

"Do you really need so many weapons?" Danielle asked. "Beatrice was helping Lannadae. She wouldn't—"

"Who says they're for Lannadae?" Talia tucked a small whip into her belt. "I wasn't ready when Lirea attacked the ship. That won't happen again." She glanced at Snow and added, "Though I *might* have been prepared if someone had warned me about Lannadae."

"The last messenger Posannes sent told us Lirea was doing better," Snow said. "He said—"

"It doesn't matter anymore," Talia interrupted. "Where have you been hiding this mermaid?"

Snow ran her fingers over the books on the far wall, selecting a heavy leather-bound tome with *Dwarven Architecture: A History of Rock, Iron, and More Rocks* written on the spine in silver ink. She gave it a tug, and the bookshelves swiveled away from the wall with a painful screech.

"A secret passage behind the shelves?" Danielle asked. "Isn't that a little cliché?"

"Sure, if that passage were the real one." Snow grinned and moved to the other end of the wall. "Beatrice didn't want the trap to be *too* difficult to find."

Talia peered into the darkness. "What trap?"

"The sixth step triggers a counterweight that slams the shelves shut, locking them behind you. If you're lucky, someone hears you screaming and comes to let you out." Snow grabbed a second set of shelves on the other side of the wall and pulled. These slid open without a sound, revealing another staircase. "The architecture book also unlocks the real passageway over here."

Talia grunted with reluctant approval. "How long has this passage been here?"

"You would have found it long ago if you ever bothered to pick up a book." The mirrors on her choker glowed like tiny moons as she stepped into the darkness.

Talia looked at the trapped passage, then back at Snow, as if contemplating how hard it would be to toss Snow down those steps.

"If Beatrice wanted us to know about Lannadae, she would have told us," Danielle whispered. "Don't blame Snow for Beatrice's secrecy."

"She should have trusted us," Talia snapped.

"How many people should she trust with *your* secrets? Or Snow's?"

Talia glowered, then followed Snow down the steps.

Danielle didn't bother to pull the shelves shut behind them. As far as she knew, only Beatrice and the three princesses even knew these rooms were here. She hurried after the others while she could still see the light from Snow's choker.

The rock to her left was slick with algae and mildew. The wall to the right appeared to be made of loosely stacked stone, the kind of thing a child might build with rocks from the garden . . . if the child were playing with rocks the size of wagons. Sunlight peeked through the cracks, adding to Snow's magical illumination.

"These stairs are over a century old," Snow said. "This was the old seagate path. Beatrice hired dwarves from Fairytown to dig this passage after a rockslide buried the path twelve years ago." She kicked the stones and grinned. "I know it looks like a loud sneeze will collapse the rocks, but the mortar the dwarves used to reinforce the rock is stronger than steel."

"It's filthy," Danielle said.

"It was supposed to be an escape route," Snow went on. "But the rockslide also opened up a few caves down at sea level. So when Lannadae asked for sanctuary—"

"Beatrice brought her here," Danielle finished. Despite what she had said to Talia, a part of her was stung that Beatrice hadn't told her. "Lannadae must have been terrified, to turn to humans for help."

"She was frantic," said Snow. "Beatrice tried to get her to talk, but that only upset her more. Undine have actually been known to die of terror. Whatever Lannadae saw, it frightened her near to death."

Danielle stopped to peer through a gap in the rocks. The ocean was closer than she had expected. They were already more than halfway down the cliff.

"Beatrice thought Lannadae would be safe here," said Snow.

"*Lannadae* was safe," Talia snapped.

Normally, Snow would have either responded to Talia's jabs in kind, or else she'd have stuck out her tongue and ended the whole thing. Not this time. Snow bowed her head, ostensibly watching the steps.

Danielle searched for words. A part· of her simply wanted to shove Talia down the steps, hoping the fall would knock some sense into her. This wasn't Snow's fault any more than it was Talia's. But Talia was the kind of person who liked to seize a problem by the throat and throttle it into submission, preferably in such a way that left her other troubles too frightened to bother her. With Lirea out of reach, that left only Snow and Danielle as targets for her anger.

Nobody spoke again until Snow's footsteps began to splash in the water. Snow stopped to remove her boots, setting them against the inner wall on a higher step. "We're close now. The tide is rising, so you'll want to leave your things high enough to avoid the water."

Danielle removed her cloak and bundled her shoes inside. She retreated up the stairs, setting her things where they would be safe from the sea. The damp air raised goose bumps on her arms.

The stairs descended into cool seawater. A bed of algae and seaweed covered the bottom steps. Danielle held the outer wall for balance, frightening a tiny crab who scuttled through the cracks and disappeared.

Snow turned sideways, and the light from her choker dimmed as she squeezed through a narrow gap in the inner wall. Talia followed, and then it was Danielle's turn. The rocks smeared mud and algae over her shirt and skirt. After a few steps, the passage widened into a shallow cavern filled with water.

Snow was already wading toward the center of the pool. "Lannadae?"

At the back of the cavern, a dark shape slipped into the water. Too large to be an animal, it had to be the mermaid. Danielle started to speak, but between one breath and the next, the mermaid exploded from the water.

She hit Snow with one shoulder, knocking her aside before turning to brandish a large rock at Danielle and Talia.

"Stay back!" Talia shouted, her knives appearing in her hands as if by magic. She leaped into the water, twisting sideways to avoid the next attack.

"Lannadae, these are my friends!" Snow shouted.

Even Danielle could see how clumsy Lannadae's attacks were. The mermaid swung wildly, clearly panicked by the arrival of strangers. "Talia, don't hurt her."

The next time Lannadae swung, Talia brought the hilt of her knife down on the back of Lannadae's hand. The mermaid squealed and dropped her rock. She splashed back, barely avoiding Talia's knives.

A powerful tail slammed into Talia's hip, tossing her to the side. Lannadae tried to use her second tail to shove Talia beneath the water, but Talia was faster, pushing sideways, then jabbing a knife at Lannadae's stomach.

"Talia!" Danielle waded deeper into the water. "That's enough."

Talia hesitated. Lannadae shot to the rear of the pool, surfacing with another rock.

"Both of you, stop." Danielle stepped between them,

her heart pounding. She watched Lannadae's hands, waiting for the telltale twitches that would signal another attack. She had trained with Talia long enough to defend herself, but her reflexes would be slower in the water. "Nobody is going to hurt you." She glanced at Talia, who scowled but didn't argue. "We came here for Beatrice."

Lannadae kept her rock raised. Her tails were bent in opposite directions on the bottom of the pool, allowing her to match Danielle's height. "I don't understand. Why would Beatrice tell you about me? Has my father returned yet?"

"I told them." Snow raised her hands, either to show she was unarmed or because she was preparing a spell, Danielle wasn't sure. "These are my friends. Talia and Danielle. Beatrice trusts them."

Lannadae stared at Snow, then pulled herself up to perch on a wide shelf of stone, watching them all.

She was similar in appearance to Lirea, with the same long, split tails. Her scales were redder in color, and the fins on the sides of her legs seemed fuller, though perhaps the spreading of her fins was simply a sign of fear. She appeared roughly the same age as Lirea. Blue and yellow jewels sparkled on tiny braids in her matted hair.

She was plumper than her sister, though still thin compared to the other undine Danielle had glimpsed. The winter had eaten away at the thick layer of fat that would have protected Lannadae from the cold. Her skin was pale, tinged with blue.

Snow's choker brightened as she studied Lannadae more closely. "You haven't been eating enough."

Lannadae slapped her tails against the water. "Bring me something that hasn't been dead for three days, and I'll eat that."

"The undine only acquire that blue-green pallor through poor diet," explained Snow. "We brought as much food as we could last fall to prepare Lannadae for her hibernation, but—"

"Why did you bring *them*?" Lannadae demanded, staring at Danielle and Talia.

"Because we need your help," Danielle said. "Beatrice was attacked yesterday. By Lirea."

Lannadae dropped into the water. Turning to Snow, she asked, "Is that true?"

Snow nodded. "Beatrice is still alive, but she's not well. Lirea stabbed her."

Lannadae dove beneath the water and stayed there.

"It's all right," Snow said. "She does this when she's afraid. She'll come out soon."

Danielle looked around the cavern. Several books sat on a crude shelf chipped into the rock. Gifts from Snow, brought down from the library? She couldn't imagine Snow risking her precious books to the water. Even from here, Danielle could see that the leather covers were heavily stained, the pages swollen from moisture.

"Beatrice gave them to her," Snow said. "I did my best to protect the pages, but . . ." She shook her head, her disapproval obvious. "I've already had to repair the bindings on two of the books."

The air smelled of seaweed and old fish. Bones and cracked shells littered the rock to Danielle's right, along with a tarnished knife. A stone flute lay tucked against the edge of the cavern. A pair of open barrels had been crammed into a nook near the back.

Talia climbed out of the water and picked up the knife. "This came from the palace kitchen."

"Beatrice brought a number of supplies when Lannadae awoke last month," Snow explained.

"How did they bring those barrels in?" Danielle asked. "Beatrice couldn't have hauled those down the seagate stairs by herself."

"There's a tunnel below the water, at the very bottom of the staircase." Snow pointed back toward the narrow cave. "It's only visible at low tide. Beatrice and I—"

"How much longer is she going to hide?" Talia asked.

Snow waded toward Lannadae. "You're safe, Lannadae. Lirea doesn't know where you are, and my friends aren't going to hurt you." She jumped back as Lanna-dae's tails thrashed beneath the water.

"Fine. We can do this the hard way." Snow dragged her fingers along the surface of the water. Fog spread over the ripples, and a crackling sound filled the cavern. Ice spread outward, moving toward Lannadae.

Lannadae thrashed again, then swam to one side, nearly colliding with Danielle as she burst from the water. "I told you I don't like the cold!"

"Beatrice needs your help now," Snow said. "The ice was fastest. Or would you prefer I let the princess here call a sea snake to chase you out of the water?"

Lannadae yelped and turned to stare at Danielle. Her eyes grew inhumanly wide. "Princess? You're *her*, aren't you? Princess Cinderella?" She ducked beneath the pool, swimming so close that her hair tickled Danielle's feet. Lannadae arose moments later, whipping her head back so that water sprayed from her hair. "You're not wearing your glass slippers!"

Danielle fought a smile. "They're not very practical for stairs and caves."

"Beatrice told me your story. I've been practicing until I can tell it almost as well as she does. I could tell it to you, if you wanted." She ducked her head, suddenly shy.

"That would be lovely," Danielle said. "But first, we have to—"

"Cinderella and Snow White both. How exciting!" Lannadae spun around to stare at Talia. "So who are you?"

"Nobody," Talia said before anyone else could answer.

"Oh." Lannadae sounded disappointed. She turned back to Danielle. "Can you explain something to me? You attended the ball in a magic gown and slippers, but that magic ended at midnight. If the gown vanished, why didn't the slippers disappear too?"

"Actually, I've wondered that too," said Snow, cocking her head at Danielle.

"The gown didn't vanish." Danielle closed her eyes, remembering how hard it had been to tear herself away from Armand each night before midnight. "But my step-sisters and stepmother stayed at the ball each night until the stroke of twelve. I had to flee before they left. I returned to my mother's tree each night to hide my things, changing back into a filthy serving girl so nobody would suspect me."

Talia cleared her throat, and Danielle sighed, remembering the days when the worst she had to fear was a beating from her stepmother. She knelt in the water, lowering herself to Lannadae's height. "Your sister attacked Beatrice with a magical knife."

Lannadae drifted back. She sank deeper until her mouth was level with the surface. Snow tapped the ice in warning, but Lannadae didn't try to hide. Water flowed over her lower lip, causing her voice to warble. "An abalone blade, the hilt bound in hair?"

"You know it?" asked Talia.

Lannadae moaned. The sound sent ripples over the water, and Danielle backed away. The mermaid's voice grew louder, a song of despair that resonated through Danielle's bones, stirring feelings she hadn't felt in months.

For weeks after Jakob's birth, nightmares had torn Danielle from her slumber. Dreams of Jakob left unattended on the northern wall of the palace, giggling as he looked down at the ocean far below. Her own screams as she tried to run to him, but her feet wouldn't obey. Every step painfully slow, watching Jakob totter on the edge, too far to reach, and then he was falling.

Danielle rubbed her eyes, trying to blot those visions from her mind. Trying to keep from shaking.

"Stop it," Snow shouted. "Lannadae!"

Lannadae jumped, and her song trailed off.

"The undine's voices are magical," Snow said, wiping her face. "Particularly those of royal blood."

Danielle nodded, remembering Lirea's screams back

on the *Glass Slipper*. "Thank you," she whispered. "Talia, are you all right?"

Talia had turned to face the cavern wall. "Tell her if she does that again, I'm going to—"

"I won't," Lannadae said. "I'm sorry. I didn't mean to hurt you. I forgot how our song affects you." Tears dripped down her cheeks. "My father is dead, isn't he? Lirea killed him."

Danielle rubbed her arms, fighting the urge to run to the palace to check on Jakob. She could still feel Lannadae's grief, as strong as if it were her own. "I'm sorry, Lannadae. I lost my own father when I was young."

"I should have stayed with him," said Lannadae. "He insisted on protecting me. On protecting us both, Lirea and myself. He said the tribe couldn't afford to lose either of us."

"Tell us about Lirea's knife." Talia's voice was colder than usual. Lannadae's song had obviously hit her as hard as it had Danielle.

"The hair wrapped around the handle is mine. Mine and my sister's." Lannadae floated on her back, fingers tugging the beads in her hair. "We were told it would save her."

"Who told you?" asked Snow.

"My grandmother."

"Tell us what happened," Danielle said.

Lannadae swam to the rear of the cave and retrieved a knotted loop of yellow sinew. Beads and bits of shell were tied along its length. She twined the cord between her fingers, weaving a simple pattern of diamonds within a larger square. The motions appeared to calm her.

"I am Lannadae, daughter of Gwerdhen, of the line of Ilowkira." This was the loudest she had spoken. Her words were almost a chant. "This is the story of Lirea and Prince Gustan.

"Lirea was the most daring of Gwerdhen's three children. She would follow the humans and their ships, learning their songs and eavesdropping on their words.

She soon learned more of humans than any undine before her.

"One spring day, powerful waves drove a human ship against the rocks." Lannadae's fingers looped through the cord in her hands. When she pulled the cord taut, it suggested the shape of a ship with a single sail. "Lirea swam with all her strength, but she was able to save only a single human. He was a Hiladi prince, strong and handsome. She brought him to safety and fell in love. She gave herself to him that day on the rocks.

"When our father learned what Lirea had done, his fury shook the oceans. But his rage only made Lirea's yearning stronger."

"Forbidden love is much more exciting," Snow agreed.

Lannadae shuddered, sending tiny wavelets from her body. "The undine have frolicked with your kind upon occasion, but for one of the royal blood to love a human ... she could have been banished from the tribe. Prince Gustan's people would have done the same, thinking the undine little better than animals. For much of that summer Lirea would sneak away to be with her beloved, despite the dangers. Gustan's palace sits in treacherous waters, where wind and waves threaten even an undine. Often she returned bruised and battered from the journey. They both knew there could be no real future between them, but still she went to him.

"As spring passed into summer, Lirea turned to our grandmother Morveren for help. Morveren, who had spent her life gathering the secrets of the sea. Morveren offered Lirea the chance to assume human form, though the transformation was not without cost. But Lirea cared only for her prince."

"I've heard this story." Talia's posture was stiff. Danielle could see how much Lannadae's song of despair had shaken her. "Sailors talk about a mermaid who became human to be with her prince."

"There's a song, too," Snow added. "Six verses, one for each night of the seduction, ending when the prince takes the girl down to—" She flushed and looked at Lannadae. "I'm sorry. I never realized that song was about your sister."

"I don't like to tell this story," Lannadae said, seemingly unoffended. She allowed the cord to fall loose, then twisted a second loop. She adjusted the second loop so a line cut through the first about halfway up. Two of the stones suggested eyes. Lannadae added a third loop, so that blue beads hung beneath the stones. Tears, Danielle realized.

"What was the price?" asked Snow.

"Humanity is only half of our nature," said Lannadae. "With the rest stripped away, Lirea was incomplete. Her human body was imperfect, causing her great pain with each step she took. Morveren wasn't strong enough to truly change Lirea's nature, but she wove a second spell, one that would give Lirea everything she wanted.

"Morveren's magic would last for six days. By the seventh, Lirea had to secure Gustan's hand in marriage, binding his life to her own. Their marriage would complete the spell. Lirea would remain human and would live with her prince for the rest of her days. If she failed ... nobody can survive for long with half of her being torn away."

Danielle flinched, thinking of Beatrice. "What happened?"

Lannadae tugged her hands, eradicating the shape of the face. "He took what he wanted this one last time, then sent her away. Lirea called to us from the shore, her ragged voice full of pain and grief. I found her ready to end her own life. She told us how he rebuffed her.

"I begged her to wait, to let my sister and me help. We sought out Morveren, who prepared the knife you saw. Morveren said that only the life of Lirea's prince could sustain her now. If he would not bind his life to hers, she would have to take it from him." Her index finger hooked the center of the cord, elongating it into the shape of a blade.

"She killed the man she loved?" asked Danielle.

"Loved?" Talia snorted. "She killed the man who used her."

"We brought the knife to Lirea. She wept, vowing not to use it. On the seventh day, as her lungs constricted and her body felt as though it dissolved from within, we persuaded her to return to him to ask again. She did so, telling Gustan she would die without him. He scoffed, saying he had already taken another woman. In her grief, Lirea shoved the blade into his heart."

Outside the cave, the crash of the waves had grown louder. The reinforced wall of the rockslide absorbed most of the water's power, but the pool still pushed Danielle's legs with each ebb and flow.

"His life for hers," said Lannadae. "Lirea survived, though not as Morveren's magic had intended. Her voice was broken, her body neither human nor undine. Some say it was Lirea's unfulfilled yearning that trapped her between worlds, whispering to her beloved in the shadows."

Tears left salty tracks down Lannadae's cheeks. She wiped her face, then gripped her cord with both hands, fighting to compose herself. "Thus ends the story of Lirea, daughter of Gwerdhen, of the line of Ilowkira." She looked up. "Did I tell it well?"

"Very well," said Danielle.

"Afterward, Lirea was changed. For a long time she refused to sing or speak. When at last she began to recover her voice, she blamed Levanna and me for what had happened." Lannadae no longer spoke in the formal rhythm she had used for her story. She sounded much younger now. "She moved so quickly."

Danielle closed her eyes, guessing what was to come next.

"All three of us had warriors who guarded us against the dangers of the sea. Lirea said she smelled a shark nearby. As soon as the guards turned their attention elsewhere . . ." Lannadae began to tremble. "By the time they pulled Lirea away, Levanna was already dead. Lirea stabbed her with that knife, again and again until the blood clouded the water and turned them to shadows."

"With all of her trauma, your father still let her keep the knife?" Talia asked.

"Would you swim unarmed in the deep ocean?" Lannadae asked. "Would you risk one of the future rulers of your tribe? An undine child receives her first knife as soon as her fingers are strong enough to hold the handle."

"I'm so sorry," said Danielle. "You must have been terrified."

"What happened to Morveren?" Talia asked.

"Our father banished her after Levanna's death." Lannadae dipped beneath the water again. While she appeared to breathe water and air equally well, the water seemed to bring her comfort. She rose a few moments later. "He had commanded Morveren to undo her spells, but Lirea wouldn't let her approach. She threatened to kill herself before she would let Morveren touch her. Morveren used magic to lull Lirea to sleep, then took Lirea back to her home to try one last time to save her. Lirea threw off the spell. She attacked Morveren, then fled to our father, begging him to keep her safe."

Lannadae moaned again, but she stopped herself after a glare from Talia.

"He sent Morveren away for her crimes," Lannadae said. In a softer voice, she added, "I should have stayed with him."

"You were afraid," Danielle said gently. "He wanted you safe."

Talia waded closer. "Do you know where Morveren went?"

"It's several days north of Lorindar, where the northern and southern currents come together and the taste of the water becomes bitter from the seaweed."

"Somehow I don't think our charts track the taste of the ocean," Snow said.

"I can show you the way. I tried to go to her once, to ask for her help. The sea grew angry, and the waves battered me against the rocks." Lannadae lowered her voice. "Lirea knows I'm here, doesn't she? That's why she attacked Beatrice. She'll be hunting for me."

Had Lannadae been human, Danielle would have embraced her, but she wasn't certain how the undine offered comfort. Lannadae was barely more than a child. Danielle knew the pain of losing a family, but to lose them like this . . . she could understand why Beatrice had taken pity on Lannadae. "We'll keep you safe. I promise."

"How do you intend to do that?" Talia asked.

"By finding Morveren," Danielle said. "She might be able to help us stop Lirea."

"Assuming Lirea hasn't tracked her down and killed her, too," Talia muttered.

Danielle glared at her. "We'll leave tomorrow. I'll ask Armand to prepare the *Glass Slipper* for—"

"No," said Snow. "Tell him we're taking the *Phillipa*."

Danielle's throat tightened. "Isn't that the queen's ship?"

"It's also the fastest thing in the harbor." Snow smiled. "And I suspect Captain Hephyra will be a little more tolerant of an undine on her ship than most captains."

Talia was already wading toward the stairs. She paused. "Are you two coming, or do you expect me to pack for all of us?"

CHAPTER 4

DANIELLE HAD WORKED HARD over the past year to break the habits of her former life. For months after she moved into the palace, she had cringed at every stain or smear of mud, instinctively bracing herself against her stepmother's wrath. Eventually, Armand had pulled her aside to explain that her anxiety was catching, and the palace staff were working throughout the night attempting to meet what they saw as their new princess' demands for perfection.

Danielle had learned to stifle her reactions after that day. Of course, there were parts of the palace no servant knew about. Danielle still cleaned the secret chambers beneath the palace from time to time. If she waited for Snow or Talia to do it, the job would require a shovel. She also dusted the passage that led from those chambers up to her room.

Up to her privy, to be precise.

Today, she barely noticed the occasional cobweb stretched across the dark shaft. When she reached the top rung, she pressed her ear gently against a wooden panel hidden in the wall. Danielle dreaded the day she scaled these bronze rungs, only to interrupt one of the chambermaids relieving herself.

There were no sounds from the other side save the howl of the wind from outside the palace.

"Sounds like a storm coming," Snow commented from the darkness below.

A quick tug of a metal lever opened the panel. Danielle stepped into the privy and listened again before exiting into her bedchamber.

The window had blown open, and rainwater puddled the black and white tile floor. From the size of the puddles, the window couldn't have been open for long. Danielle started toward the window to close the shutters, but Talia caught her arm from behind.

"You know better." Talia dropped to her knees, checking beneath the bed before moving to the window. She peeked outside, then reached out to pull the shutters closed. She latched the windowpanes back into place, muffling the sound of the wind. "Leaving the windows open is like sending out a royal invitation to any assassin who cares to eliminate the prince or princess of Lorindar."

"The last time someone tried to kill me, she used the door," Danielle said. "Besides, I shut those windows myself. The wind must have blown them open."

The rain sounded like pebbles bouncing off the shutters. She could hear the water rushing through the copper gutters outside.

"That storm isn't natural." Snow moved past Talia and pressed her fingers against the glass.

"What do you mean?" asked Talia. "I can't remember the last time a week passed without a thunderstorm. You need gills to live in this country."

"This is different," said Snow. "It's angry."

Danielle stared at the puddles, fighting the urge to fetch a mop or rags. "Is it some sort of magical attack?"

"I don't think so. Even if I'm wrong, the palace should be protected." Snow wiped her hand on her skirt. "If the storms continue, we could have an interesting time on the *Phillipa*."

Danielle grimaced. "I'll need an extra strong batch of that tea before we leave." She walked toward the wardrobe, hoping to grab some dry clothes. "Where is Armand?"

Snow touched her choker for a moment. "On the north wall."

So much for getting dry. Or dinner, for that matter. She hadn't had much of an appetite earlier in the day, but after hiking back up the seagate path, not to mention the climb from below the palace, her stomach was making its displeasure known to all within earshot.

Danielle tried not to think about how easily Snow had located her husband. Snow had planted small mirrors throughout the palace. Wall-mounted sconces were mirror-backed, giving her eyes in nearly every room and hallway. Other mirrors had been hidden in the mouths of gargoyles along the rooftops or fitted into mosaics in the ceilings.

Snow always assured her she would never violate anyone's privacy without good cause. "Besides," she had added the first time Danielle asked, "I can't see anything interesting through that silly canopy on your bed anyway."

Danielle had requested thicker curtains that same day.

"Armand is with the king and some others," Snow said. "The rain makes it hard to see."

Danielle grabbed a cloak and pulled it tight around her body. Like so much of her wardrobe, the cloak had a few too many frills for her taste. Gold thread and lace only covered half of the material, making it one of the less extravagant outfits.

The lamplighters had just begun to make their way through the hallways, touching flame to the oil lamps mounted in the walls. The flames flickered in the drafty air, and several lamps threatened to die completely.

By the time Danielle and her companions reached the north wall, the sky had begun to fade to black. Both Armand and the king stood in the rain, along with several guards and a man wearing the burgundy vest and gold seabird pin marking him as admiral of Lorindar's navy. Behind them stood a second sailor. His face was swollen and bruised, and he shifted about as though he didn't know what to do with himself.

Ambassador Trittibar of Fairytown was here as well, human-sized as he usually was when in Lorindar. Wisps of white hair plastered his face where they had escaped from the long braid draped over his shoulder. As always, he dressed in such a way as to make Danielle suspect the fairy folk perceived color very differently from humans. A green shirt clashed with his purple jacket, and Danielle couldn't even imagine where he had found trousers in that particular shade of rusty orange.

A white falcon named Karina perched on his shoulder. Splotches of red mottled the bird's chest. Trittibar scratched the falcon's neck, and she responded by raising her crest like a tiny crown.

"Karina confirms it, Your Majesty," Trittibar was saying. "The storms are strongest along the shore but die quickly the farther you travel from the palace."

"Demons fly in those clouds," said the admiral. Hays, Danielle remembered. She had seen him about the palace on occasion. Hays licked his lips, eyes searching the skies. "I've spent forty years of my life on these waters, and I've never seen a storm arise so suddenly. The *Reginald* was barely out of the harbor when the winds hit. Cracked her mainmast before she could take in her sheets."

"We were less than an hour out of Lorindar when we saw the storm building," said the sailor. "We stopped to lash supports to the mainmast. That's when the undine attacked."

"You were on the *Branwyn*," Danielle guessed.

"James Harland. I've been a waister on the *Branwyn* for two years."

Armand raised an eyebrow, but he didn't ask how Danielle had known. He beckoned her closer, putting an arm around her shoulders when she joined him. The gesture seemed to be as much for his comfort as hers.

" 'Waister?' " Danielle whispered.

Armand bent his head close. "He worked the deck at the foremast."

"Were there other survivors?" Danielle asked.

"I don't think so, Your Highness," said James. "I was working to bring in the bowsprit when the wind tossed me overboard. The merfolk dragged me away almost before I hit the surface. They left me on the outer seawall. They promised safe passage if we paid proper tribute to their queen."

"Lirea asked for gold," Armand said. "The undine have never used money before. They barter with other tribes for what they need."

"The undine aren't known for this kind of magic." The king waved a hand toward the clouds. "Could Lirea have allied herself with the fairy folk? The gold could be payment for their aid."

"Anything is possible, Your Majesty," said Trittibar, but he sounded dubious. "But I believe I would recognize the magic of my people. It would be a serious violation of Malindar's Treaty, and few of our kind would risk the wrath of our lord and lady. No, this is something else."

"You believe it's coincidence that this storm assaults the palace the day we bring my mother home?" Armand asked. He spun away, moving so fast the water sprayed from his arms.

A page hurried onto the wall, his jacket held over his head against the rain. The king waved for him to approach.

"We've received a note from Lord Montgomery. He sends his sympathies to you and the prince and asks how you intend to protect Eastpointe from the undine. He requests twelve warships be diverted to escort trade ships to and from his docks." The page bowed and took a step back.

King Theodore simply shook his head. "Word spreads quickly. By this time tomorrow, I imagine half the lords will be demanding similar protection." He dismissed the page, then rested his arms on the crenellations of the outer wall. "Who do you think Montgomery's spies are, to alert him of the undine threat so quickly?"

"Does it matter?" Armand asked. "He's within his rights to ask the crown for help."

"He is," Theodore acknowledged. "Just as I'm within my rights to call on Montgomery's resources in a time of war. If he's not careful, I'll send him and his ships out to sea to hunt Lirea."

"Until this storm eases, what help does he expect us to give?" Hays asked. "The weather would cost us a quarter of our ships before we even left the docks. We've already had one cargo ship run aground."

"Order the hurricane bells rung," Theodore said. "Any incoming ships should be diverted away from Whiteshore. Send them to Griffon's Vale."

Admiral Hays bowed his head. "I'll have hurricane warnings rung on the hour."

Armand shook his head. "We know they've attacked near Whiteshore. Let me take our ships out to search for Lirea. Warships sailing together will be better able to defend themselves, and they should lure the undine away from our civilians. If we could take prisoners, we might be able to find where Lirea is hiding."

Danielle's throat tightened. He meant to draw the undine away by making himself a more obvious target. She looked at James, his eyes still haunted by the undine attack on his ship.

"It's a big ocean, Highness," said Hays.

"Would you prefer we huddle along our shores, waiting for the undine to attack at their leisure? We know where the *Branwyn* was attacked. Once this storm recedes, we can begin our search there."

Danielle cleared her throat. "Exactly how difficult would it be for a ship to sail through this storm?"

"Anything's possible," said Admiral Hays. "I'd not want to try it if I had the choice."

"Why do you ask?" Suspicion sharpened Armand's voice.

"We've learned of someone who might be able to help the queen. I'm told the *Phillipa* is a fast ship. Would she survive these winds?"

The king straightened. "Who have you found? Where is this person?"

"The mermaid who created Lirea's knife." Danielle

hesitated to say more in front of so many people. "If we can find her, she might be able to help us undo—"

"You promised me you would be careful," Armand said, pulling her aside. "Even if the winds don't capsize you, Lirea and her undine are lurking out there. What makes you think they won't come after the *Phillipa*? It's too dangerous for you to—"

"As dangerous as searching half of Fairytown to rescue a captured prince?" Danielle answered.

Armand's eyes widened, and the king coughed to cover what might or might not have been a smile.

"You found Lannadae," Armand said softly.

Danielle didn't answer. "Lirea may come here in search of her sister. We should make sure the docks are well watched."

"For all the good it will do in these storms," Hays said. "A man can barely see his own—" He glanced at Danielle. "His own hand."

Snow stepped forward to stand beside Talia. "The spells on Lirea's knife are strong. If we can find the mermaid who created it, she might also have the skill to find its wielder."

"Why would she help us against her own kind?" Trittibar asked.

Talia's chin rose ever so slightly. "We can be very persuasive."

"Let me go." Armand turned to the king. "I can take the *Phillipa* to find this mermaid."

"Because somehow this is less dangerous if you go instead of me?" Danielle demanded. She folded her arms. "I'll tell you what. I'll stay here where it's safe if *you* promise to do the same."

"It's my duty as prince—" Armand began. His shoulders drooped slightly, and he gave her a rueful smile. "You're about to turn that argument back at me, aren't you? Don't expect me to be happy about this, Princess."

"No more than I am." She gave him a quick kiss, trying to ease the moment. "You think I wouldn't rather be here with you and Jakob? It tears my heart to leave him with

Nicolette again so soon. Sometimes I think he knows her better than his own mother." She swallowed hard, refusing to lose her composure in front of so many people, but Armand saw. He reached for her, and she rested against him. "But if I stay here where it's safe, and Beatrice ... I have to, Armand. We both know a mermaid is more likely to listen to a princess than a prince."

James cleared his throat. "I'd like to come too, with your permission."

"Are you sure?" asked Danielle.

He bit his lip, but he nodded. "I've spent most of my life at sea. I won't let the merfolk take that away from me."

The king had been quiet, listening to their argument. Now he nodded to James. "Your experiences could be helpful if the undine attack again. If you're sure, you may accompany the princess on the *Phillipa*."

James bowed his head, but not fast enough to conceal look of apprehension. "Thank you, Your Majesty."

"A single ship would be too obvious a target," Armand said. "An escort—"

"An escort is precisely what will mark us as a target to Lirea and her warriors," Snow said. "Even with the hurricane bells, you'll still have individual ships seeking to escape the storms. Fishermen need to eat, and the cargo ships lose money every day they delay. Most will obey the warnings, but a few will not. The *Phillipa* will be just another ship sneaking away to try her luck against the storm ... unless you draw attention to her."

Armand whirled. "So you think I should send my wife out unprotected?"

"Unprotected?" Talia repeated, raising an eyebrow.

"I won't be," said Danielle. "An escort is a good idea."

Armand stared. "Perhaps I've fallen prey to some spell, but I could have sworn your friend just finished arguing against sending additional ships."

"Who said anything about ships?"

*   *   *

Danielle had only taken a few steps down the tower stairs when she heard the door open again behind her. "Armand?"

It wasn't her husband, but the king himself. Theodore pulled the door shut behind him. "I won't keep you. But if you could spare a moment?"

Talia took Snow by the elbow. "We'll grab something for you from the kitchen and meet you in your chambers."

Danielle almost called them back. While she had grown close to the queen over the past year, she hadn't spent much time with King Theodore. He might be her father-in-law, but she still saw him first as ruler of Lorindar.

Danielle waited until Snow and Talia vanished down the stairs. "Armand is angry at me, isn't he?"

"No. Not at you, at any rate. Mostly he's scared." The king leaned against the wall, showing the fatigue he had struggled to hide before. "He's already angry that he couldn't protect his mother, and he hates the idea of you putting yourself in danger. I can't really blame him for that."

"I'm not thrilled about the danger either," Danielle said. "But I can't—"

"I know. Armand knows too." He sat down and patted the step for Danielle to join him. "Beatrice and I had been married less than a year when I realized she was sneaking away from the palace. I was furious. I tried to follow her once, believing—" He bowed his head. "Well, what any man might suspect."

Danielle tried not to stare. She had never seen the king blush before.

"At that time, I was working to settle an inheritance dispute between twin brothers, both of whom believed they should rule South Haven. Their father's body was still warm, and already they were at each others' throats." He shook his head. "After holding court for two days with these spoiled brats, I was ready to throw them both from the cliffs. I'm afraid I took my frustrations out on Beatrice that night, shouting at her and accusing her of various infidelities."

He chuckled. "She walked away in the middle of my rant, slamming the door in my face."

"What did you do?" Danielle tried and failed to imagine the king shouting at Beatrice.

"Nobody had ever turned her back on me before. I stood there for quite a while. Long enough to realize I might have made a mistake. I was too proud to follow her, though. Eventually I retired to bed.

"A noise woke me later that night. I sat up, thinking she had finally returned. Instead, a man swathed in black stood over my bed. He held a knife in one hand, and a mask hid all but his eyes. He took a single step, then flopped onto my legs, a single arrow protruding from his back.

"Beatrice stood in the doorway. She lowered her bow and stepped inside to apologize for interrupting my sleep. There had been a second assassin, and stopping him had taken longer than she expected."

"What about your guards?" Danielle asked.

"Stunned," said the king. "Charles, one of the twins, had planned well. He hoped to frame his brother for my death, earning South Haven for his own and moving himself one step closer to the throne. I never suspected—" He turned to look in the direction of the chapel, and his voice softened. "I didn't, but Beatrice did. Things were far easier between us after that night."

Danielle tried to smile. "I did help rescue Armand from my stepsisters. Does that count, or do I need to stop actual assassins?"

That earned another chuckle. "He's prince of Lorindar. He's not used to feeling powerless." He climbed to his feet. "There are things Beatrice has done which I don't know about. Things I *can't* know. I have no doubt she's saved my life more than once. Perhaps the kingdom as well. But it was never without danger."

He looked at the wall, as if he were trying to peer through the stone to the chapel where Beatrice lay. "She chose that risk. I hope you don't feel forced to make that same choice or to accept those same risks."

"Beatrice has been like a mother to me," Danielle said.

The king's face was hard to read. Hope and fear and sadness all battled behind his furrowed brow and shadowed eyes. "The *Phillipa* will be ready to depart at sunrise."

Danielle spent a fitful night, between the rain pounding against the palace and the warning peal of the hurricane bells. The sky was still dark when Talia knocked on the door. It had to be Talia. Anyone else would have hesitated to awaken the prince and princess so early.

Danielle sighed, kissed Armand, and climbed out of bed to get dressed.

Armand rolled over, watching her through the silk curtains. "I talked to my father last night after you went to bed. He's arranged to have a small chest of gold brought to the *Phillipa*. If the undine do attack, you might be able to buy your freedom. Let Captain Hephyra do the talking, and don't let them find out who you are."

"I thought we had decided not to pay." Danielle sat on the edge of the bed to lace her boots.

"We had." He sat up and pushed a curtain aside, then kissed the back of her neck. "However, that decision was made before you insisted on sailing out alone." He kissed her again, moving to the side of the neck, then to her ear. His beard tickled the skin along her cheekbone.

Danielle closed her eyes as her blood pounded harder. She placed a hand on his thigh. "You'll try anything to keep me safe, won't you?"

"Mm . . . is it working?"

She laughed and turned to kiss him. His plan might have worked well indeed, if Talia hadn't chosen that moment to knock again. With a groan, Danielle pulled away and picked up her sword belt. "And what will you be doing today, Prince Armand? Unless your plans have changed, it was my understanding that you meant to lead your warships out to hunt for undine, to deliberately lure them into attacking."

He lay back, still watching her. "I've also ordered extra nets sent to the *Phillipa*. They should be strong enough to use against the undine."

"Thank you." She turned around. "I will be careful, Armand."

"We received word late last night that the undine sank a Lyskaran frigate in their own harbor early yesterday evening." Armand rubbed his face with both hands, as though he thought he could scrub the fatigue away. "Once again, they left only a single survivor to relay their demand for gold."

"I'm sorry," said Danielle.

"I dreamed it was your ship." He watched as she tugged her hair back into a loose braid. "I watched them pull you down . . ."

Danielle kissed him again. "I have to do this. Your mother would do the same thing."

"My mother's actions are the reason she's laid out in the chapel, a breath away from death." He climbed out of bed. "Tell your friends I expect them to bring you back to me."

"Tell your crew the same from me," Danielle said. She hugged him once, running her fingers through his sleep-tousled hair before pulling away. "Tell them it's a royal command from their princess."

She found Talia dressed and ready. She wore only a handful of visible weapons, most notably a curved dagger on her hip and several shorter throwing knives on the opposite side. Danielle had no doubt a small armory was tucked about her person. Talia glanced at Danielle's outfit and grunted. "I was starting to think you'd changed your mind."

They stopped at the nursery so Danielle could kiss Jakob good-bye. Jakob hardly stirred at all as she lifted him from the crib. A small puddle of drool on his pillow showed that at least one member of the royal family had managed a good night's sleep. Danielle dried his cheek as she cradled him to her chest.

"The *Phillipa* is waiting," Talia said. "The tide will be turning soon. If you want to leave today—"

"I know." Holding her son, a part of her wanted to send Talia and Snow along without her. They had served Queen Bea for years before Danielle came along. The words were at her throat, but she forced them down. She kissed Jakob again, then gently laid him back into the crib. "I'll be back soon. I promise."

"Sleep well," Talia added. "I'll do my best to bring your mother back in one piece."

Danielle smiled at that, though she knew there was truth in Talia's words. How many had Lirea already killed? The idea of Jakob growing up without his mother, as Danielle had done . . . She bowed her head and followed Talia from the nursery.

Outside, the storm showed no sign of letting up, and they were both soaked by the time they reached their carriage. The cold water washed away her fatigue but left her even more depressed about leaving Jakob and Armand. "Where's Snow?"

"Waiting with Lannadae. She's been agitated ever since she found out about her sister."

"How are we going to get her onto the *Phillipa* without anyone seeing?" Danielle asked. "She can't exactly scale the ladder with the rest of us."

"Snow will be bringing her in on the ship's dinghy, along with various supplies. Including your special request." Talia wrinkled her nose. "Better her than me."

Danielle dug her fingers into the embroidered cushions as the carriage rocked in the wind. The road was wide, but a strong enough wind might still upend the carriage, even with the extra weight of the trunks packed in the back.

"I should warn you, it's dangerous letting Snow do this on her own," Talia said.

"You think someone might attack her?"

"Worse." Talia leaned back in her seat. "I think we're going to spend the rest of the day listening to her make 'dinghy' jokes."

The *Phillipa* was loaded up and anchored near the mouth of the harbor. Snow and Lannadae waited at the dock to row Danielle and Talia out to the ship. The dinghy was already crowded, with three barrels packed into the back and a tarp strapped over Snow's trunk against the rain. Lannadae hid beneath the tarp as well, curled into a smaller space than Danielle would have thought possible.

By the time Danielle and Talia settled into the boat, it sat so low in the water Danielle feared it might capsize. Danielle tried to adjust her sword to keep the cross guard from jabbing her in the side. She didn't know how Talia carried so many weapons on her person without bruising herself every time she moved.

Talia squeezed onto the bench beside Snow, taking one of the oars. They rowed together, pulling the boat toward the *Phillipa*.

The *Phillipa* was smaller than the *Glass Slipper*. She was a two-masted ship of unusual design, with a narrower beam than most of the ships Danielle had seen. Her hull was unpainted, the wood oiled to a rich brown. Even in the cloudy morning light, the furled sails gleamed as though they were woven from silver threads. A carved swan was mounted at the bow, her long head extending beneath the bowsprit.

"She was a gift from the fairy queen." Snow pointed to the mainmast. "The spars are freestanding, which means she has a broader range of motion. The sheets are much lighter than canvas but just as strong. The rigging was woven from—"

"She's fast and she's strong," Talia snapped. "We get that. Now would you mind paying attention to what you're doing before you completely turn us around?"

"I want to see," said Lannadae.

Danielle pressed gently on her shoulder to keep her down. "You will. We're almost there. Stay down until we reach the far side of the ship."

"We'll secure the lines to the boat before we board," Snow said. "Lannadae, you'll be alone when they raise it from the water. Too much weight makes it harder to hoist their dinghy." She smirked. "Stay out of sight until we get you. Captain Hephyra knows you're coming, but I'm not sure how the rest of the crew will feel."

"I understand." Lannadae's breathing was faster than normal, and her scales were puffed outward. A sign of fear, Danielle guessed. This was the first time Lannadae had been out of her cave since the past fall.

"Captain Hephyra had no objections to taking an undine passenger?" Danielle asked.

Snow grinned. "If anyone will take a mermaid on board, it's Hephyra." With that odd proclamation, Snow stood up in the boat and waved to the crew.

Once Snow and Talia had finished knotting the ropes to the front and back of the dinghy, one of the crew lowered a rope ladder. Danielle followed the others onto Queen Beatrice's personal sailing ship.

The *Phillipa* was a madhouse. Rain splashed against the deck as the crew rushed to secure the last of the supplies. She spotted James helping to haul several barrels up from another boat and waved. James returned the greeting. He appeared nervous, his bruised face grim as he turned back to his duties.

"Captain?" Danielle called, shouting to be heard over the storm.

"Princess Whiteshore?" The speaker was a tall woman perched on the platform near the top of the mainmast. The maintop, if Danielle remembered the terminology correctly.

"You'll be wanting to back up," said a passing crewman.

He hurried on before Danielle could respond, but she did as he suggested. Moments later, the woman leaped from the platform. She landed in front of the three princesses, one hand hitting the deck to help absorb the impact.

Danielle stared. For an instant, the woman's bare feet had sunk *into* the boards of the deck. The woman straightened. "Snow. Talia. Nice to see you both again."

"Captain Hephyra," Danielle guessed, still staring. Not even Talia could have made such a jump without breaking her legs.

Hephyra was easily a head taller than most of the crew, dressed in a fashion that might have come straight from the more risqué section of Snow's wardrobe. The rain had soaked her white shirt, and a dark green bodice did little to preserve her modesty. Auburn hair hung nearly to her waist. Her sleeves were tied back above the elbow, revealing a slender gold tattoo around her wrist in the design of a chain. Her trousers were a style Danielle didn't recognize, dark brown and tied at the knee to reveal well-muscled legs.

Her eyes drew Danielle's attention, being a deeper green than she had ever seen before. They reminded her of new-budded leaves.

Captain Hephyra tugged a bandanna from her belt and tied her hair back from her face. "You're welcome to hide out in your cabin while we prepare. Personally, I prefer the rain." She spread her arms, tilting her face back.

"You're mad," Snow said cheerfully. "You know that, don't you?"

"I'm not the one who decided to sail through this weather," Hephyra answered. "The king's man said it was important."

Before Danielle could answer, one of the crew swore. "Captain, we've got a mermaid here!"

Hephyra strode to the side of the ship, where the dinghy hung just below the railing. "That would be our other passenger, I presume?"

"Her name is Lannadae," Danielle said. Already a handful of men gathered at the railing. Several carried knives and shortswords. "She's a friend of the queen."

"And you're bringing her on my ship why?"

Snow folded her arms. "*Your* ship?"

"Fine." Hephyra rubbed her wrist, scowling at Snow. "The queen's ship."

Danielle looked at Snow, trying to understand the hard edge beneath Hephyra's words.

"The *Phillipa* was a gift to Queen Beatrice," Snow explained.

"From the fairy queen. I remember." Danielle looked back at Hephyra.

"Carved from the tree of a dryad." Hephyra's fingers caressed the rail. "*My* tree."

Danielle looked around. "The whole ship?"

"It was a big tree."

"Hephyra had trespassed on the queen's land," Snow said. "The queen meant to make an example of her by killing her tree. She had it cut down and turned into this ship. She assumed that would be enough to kill Hephyra as well, but—"

"But the ancient trees are tougher than even the queen knows, may termites burrow her a second arsehole." Hephyra turned her head and spat. "Beatrice understood what this gift was. I had hidden within the grain to avoid the royal bitch's wrath, but by the time we arrived in Lorindar my tree had begun to die. Beatrice found me and had her witch here do what she could to save the tree. The fairy queen's oath binds this ship to Beatrice. None can break that bond, which makes me her servant. But as long as I stay, the *Phillipa* and I both survive."

"Sorceress, not witch," Snow muttered.

"So the *Phillipa* is alive?" Danielle asked.

"That's right. And you still haven't explained your pet mermaid."

Lannadae must have realized she was discovered. She sat up and peered up at the crew.

"You've heard what happened?" Danielle asked. At Hephyra's nod, she said, "Beatrice is dying." A knot tightened her throat. "Lannadae can take us to one of her kin, someone who might be able to save the queen."

Hephyra leaned against the rail. "Why would I want to help you save her? Her death means my freedom."

"Beatrice saved your life," Danielle said. "She could have let you die."

"That was her choice," the dryad said with a shrug. "I'm bound to her, Princess. Not you."

"Fine." Danielle turned to Snow, suddenly furious.

"Your spells helped Hephyra and her ship survive. Does that mean you can reverse those spells?"

"No need," said Snow. "The fairy queen said this ship would serve Beatrice. Hephyra doesn't have to obey us, but she does have to serve. Beatrice needs this."

"Stupid oaths." Hephyra spat a second time, then turned to the crew. "Bring the mermaid on board. The rest of you, get back to work."

The crew seemed reluctant to obey. Danielle couldn't hear their words, but their tone was angry. Lannadae shrank down into the bottom of the boat.

Hephyra smiled again, but this time it was a hungry expression. "If any of you feel you've no duties to perform, the ship could use fresh fertilizer."

"Fertilizer?" Danielle asked.

"The bottom of the ship is filled with earth, to feed the ship," Snow explained. "You'll smell it if you go down a few decks. On most ships they dump the chamber pots overboard, but Hephyra has a better use for them." She grinned. "Lugging the pots through the dark lower decks is not one of the more popular duties."

Most of the crew hurried away, though one lingered behind, watching Lannadae. Young as she was, the sight of her wet body clearly held him captivated. "This could make for a worthwhile journey after all," he commented.

Danielle tensed. "Who is that man, Captain?"

Hephyra glanced back. "Martin. Tough sailor. Drinks too much, but he's good in the sheets." She grinned at the double entendre.

"Will he be a danger to Lannadae?" Talia asked.

"No danger," Hephyra said. "He plans to have his way with her as soon as he can get her alone, but he knows better than to kill her or anything like that."

"No danger?" Danielle repeated. "She's a child."

Hephyra stared. "I was four days from the sapling the first time I knew the pleasure of a man. She's what, ten years? Fifteen? Hard to tell with you mortals."

"How can you know what he'll do?" Danielle asked.

Hephyra cocked her head to the side, studying Danielle. "It's been two weeks since you last slept with your husband. Though you wanted to this morning, I think."

Snow's snickering only added to Danielle's embarrassment. "She's a dryad," Snow explained. "A nymph."

Talia's voice shook. "If your man lays a hand on her, I'll break it. And then I'll make sure Snow sinks this ship to the bottom of the sea. How long will you and your tree survive in the sunless depths?"

"Don't get your knickers in a knot." Hephyra shook her head. "Martin, are we going to have any trouble with you keeping your mast under control?"

"No, ma'am!" Martin broke away from Lannadae and turned to go.

With a sigh, Hephyra crossed the deck and seized him by the belt and collar. Martin barely had time to scream before Hephyra tossed him overboard. "Never try to hide your lusts from a dryad, you foolish man." She turned around. "Anyone else so much as thinks about bothering our guests, I'll do worse to you." To Danielle, she said, "Happy now?"

"Thank you," said Danielle.

Hephyra turned to Lannadae. "I'm not entirely sure where we'll put you."

"I can stay in the boat for now," Lannadae said. "I like the rain and the puddles."

"A girl after my own heartwood." Hephyra clapped Danielle's shoulder. With her other hand, she gestured toward the barrels James was bringing on board. "Just tell me one thing, Princess. These three barrels of bait and fish offal you brought along. Don't tell me you mean to divert this ship for a spot of fishing?"

"Oh, those?" Danielle matched her smile. "Just keeping a promise to my husband."

Lirea walked among the humans throughout the night and into the morning, searching for any clue to her sister's whereabouts. On a calmer day, she might have tried to track Lannadae through the water, but today the waves were too violent. Lannadae's taste would have swiftly washed away.

Eventually, her questions led her to one of the taverns, a crowded place that smelled of old beer and dead fish. She looked around until she spotted a bedraggled fisherman with a curly brown beard, crooked nose, and hair so thick it could have been undine. Robson, if the last person she had talked to was to be trusted. Robson was huddled in the corner by the hearth, waiting out the storm with a half-empty mug of beer.

Lirea sat down across the table from him, her back to the fire. She forced a smile and asked, "You hunt lobster?"

Robson studied her for a long time. The heat of the flames raised steam from his damp clothes. "That's right."

"Have you sold any to the queen?" This was the ninth fisherman she had spoken to. She had received five drinks and two propositions, but the closest she had come to answers was one man's suggestion that Robson had been seen making deliveries to the palace.

He frowned. "Not the queen, no. There was a woman who came to me a month or so back, asking for a barrel of live lobster. She didn't say who it was for, but she dressed too well to be a commoner. Gorgeous eyes, lips as red as blood. Saucy lass. If I weren't married, I'd have—"

"What did she want them for?" Lirea asked.

"Can't rightly say. I can't imagine a lady as fine as her eating something so crass. The commoners enjoy them, but you'd never catch me dining on bottom-feeding sea roaches."

"Where did you deliver them?"

"To the lady's boat." He scratched his chin. "I suppose she might have been a shipowner, stocking food for her crew. Though live lobster is a strange choice for a sea voyage, and I can't imagine an owner rowing her own boat about."

Lirea stood. "Thank you."

"Lannadae will kill you, you know," he said casually.

Lirea's hand went to her knife. "What did you say?"

"Easy, girl. I only asked why the interest in lobster."

"I thought you said . . ." Lirea closed her eyes, trying to shut out the voices in her mind. A simple fisherman wouldn't know Lannadae's name.

The conversation in the tavern had grown louder. She heard someone else mention her name, but when she turned around, nobody appeared to be looking her way.

"You should kill them all before they kill you." Robson's voice was a chorus, taunting her. "Take your place as ruler of both land and sea."

"No!" Lirea backed away. His words sounded real, but he couldn't know who she was. This was a trick of her mind.

"Give it up, child." The words no longer matched the shape of Robson's mouth. What was he really saying? Other humans were beginning to stare as well. "You'll never find her."

Lirea held her breath until the pounding of her blood pushed the voices back. Staring at Robson, she said, "Lannadae *is* here."

He shook his head. "Who's that?"

Her sister would have been hungry when she awoke, and she had always been fond of lobster. No undine would eat dead meat the way humans did, not if they had a choice. "Where did the woman take your lobster? Was there an undine with her? A mermaid?"

Robson shook his head. "A friend of mine claims to have spotted the soulless bastards circling the waters outside of the harbor late last night." He downed the rest of his beer, then wiped his chin on his sleeve. "Some say they mean to sink our ships from below, that they've declared war on us all. Ought to scale and gut the whole lot of them."

"Oh, but Princess Cinderwench would never permit that." Another man stumbled toward the table. He was well built and wore the dark vest Lirea had seen on some of the sailors. He caught Lirea's arms and pulled her close, squinting at her face.

Lirea restrained herself from drawing her knife from beneath her shirt and cutting him open. Instead, she grabbed his wrists and pried his arms back. "Cinderwench? You mean Princess Danielle."

"You look a little like her," he said. "Same eyes. Same hair."

"Like the princess?" asked Robson. "I think you've had too much to drink this night, friend."

"No, not the princess. The fish-girl she brought on board. Pretty young thing, naked as a babe, but budding like a fresh—"

"Mind your tongue in front of the lady." Robson started to rise, but the sailor shoved the table. The edge caught Robson in the waist, knocking him down.

Lirea grabbed the sailor's hand and yanked him away. He started to resist, then grinned and slipped a hand around her waist.

"Name's Martin," he said.

Lirea pulled him toward the door, the voices in her head roaring their hunger.

"Careful, lass," said Robson. "Be sure you know what you're doing before you walk out with the likes of him."

Martin snarled, but Lirea held him close. "Don't worry. I know exactly what I'm doing."

CHAPTER 5

NILLIAR WAS THE FIRST TO RESPOND to Lirea's call. She was soon joined by other warriors, fourteen in all. More than enough to sink a single human ship.

You've found Lannadae? Nilliar sang.

Lirea sliced her hand through the water, ordering silence. Her tail twitched, spinning her about as she searched the sea.

They gathered at the true edge of Lorindar. Humans thought their isle ended at the cliffs, but the land stretched well beyond. It was here that Lorindar truly ended, as the seabed dropped away into the cold black abyss. With the clouds blocking the moon and stars above, Lirea's fellow undine were little more than shadows. She could taste their presence, feel the movement of the water as they swam, but she couldn't see their faces.

Which one would be next to turn against her? How many were working for Morveren or for Lannadae?

The voices had grown worse since she killed Martin. The whispers seemed to come from all around her, chastising her while at the same time urging her to return to shore and murder every last human.

Lirea swam to the drop-off. Warty barnacles clung to the rock. Perhaps they were the source of the voices. She grabbed one, trying to break the shell from the stone.

What is it? asked Nilliar.

I spent the day searching, questioning the humans. Lirea tugged at the barnacle as she tried to remember. *I think I might have interrogated a rowboat, too.* Or was the rowboat where she had hidden Martin's body? She wasn't sure anymore. *There was a ship that left early this morning. Her hull unpainted, with two masts and silver sails.*

We saw it, said Nilliar. *She struggled against the wind, but she kept afloat. The humans also launched a fishing ship, and a cargo vessel snuck away late last night. I allowed them to leave so that our presence would remain secret until you returned.*

Lannadae is on the silver-sailed ship. Lirea swam to the surface, rising and falling with the waves. She could see nothing through the rain. Coughing water from her lungs, she sealed the gills along her neck and said, "Show me which way they went."

"Are you certain? Why would Lannadae—"

Lirea drew her knife, and Nilliar fell silent. "Take me to them."

The human's ship had made poor time against the wind. Even so, Lirea grew weary long before one of her warriors sighted the ship in the distance. She needed sleep. Fatigue always made the voices worse.

Lirea took her spear from Nilliar and dove, thrusting the spear forward. Her warriors drew their own weapons and followed.

Exertion warmed her body as she raced through the water. The currents were more favorable here, giving them extra speed. They would reach the ship with ease, and this time there would be no mistakes. She could almost taste the salt-metal tang of blood in the water.

Lirea slowed as imagination and reality blurred. The taste of blood was real, if faint. Or was this another illusion?

Shark! Nilliar's warning was low and calm. The undine responded instantly, swimming into a half-sphere formation around Lirea, protecting her from attack.

Lirea could see the shadow swimming toward them, but she wasn't worried. A lone undine might fall prey to a shark, but an armed group had little to fear.

There's another!

Moments later, Lirea spotted a third. The sharks swam together, their formation almost as tight as that of the undine. Her people could face three sharks, but it would be costly, and the blood would only enrage the sharks further.

Ready spears, sang Nilliar. *Form a ring, and try to herd them toward the center.*

The undine moved with one purpose: to protect their queen. Nilliar swam into the center of the circle, where she twitched her arms to simulate injury and lure the sharks into the trap. But as they waited, the sharks slowed. One turned away, swimming back toward the human ship. A second followed.

Lirea waited, heart pounding, to see if the third shark would still attack. This one came close enough for Nilliar to swim forward and strike its nose with the butt of her spear. The shark turned back, pausing only to snap at something in the water. It returned to the human ship, where a fourth shark now waited.

They're following the humans. Lirea swam after, being careful not to get too close to the sharks. Something floated on the waves nearby. She jabbed it with her spear. A fish head stared at her with empty eyes. *They're tossing fish parts overboard to attract the sharks.*

That wouldn't cause them to attack us, sang one of her warriors. *Or to break away once they decided to attack.*

They say the human princess can speak to the animals, answered Nilliar. *They obey her wishes and protect her from harm.*

Lirea spun around, her song angry. *When I speak with animals, you look at me as though I'm mad.*

The undine looked away. In a low voice, Nilliar said, *You also told us you interrogated a boat earlier today.*

Lirea's anger faded as quickly as it had come. Nilliar had a point. Lirea swam to the surface and watched the ship sail away. "They have only four sharks. We'll summon more warriors. We can—"

"The rest of the tribe will have reached the spawning grounds by now," Nilliar said quietly.

Lirea struck her across the face.

"Your body knows," Nilliar continued, her tone unchanged. Blood dripped from her nose. "Perhaps you can't taste it, but the rest of us can."

Lirea could have screamed. Without the scent of a royal to fill the water, the undine would be sterile. No matter how loyal they might be, some pressures were impossible to fight. If Lirea didn't return home soon, those undine of breeding age—easily half of her tribe—might leave to join other tribes, destroying all she had accomplished these past months. "It's too early."

"Spawning has been known to come quickly in times of danger," Nilliar said. "The pressure to breed is strong. The urge was building even during the migration. You can't fight it anymore, Lirea."

"No . . ." Lirea could hear the knife's anger, a match for her own. "Then we attack now. The sharks—"

."Could slaughter half our number, and the blood would draw more sharks to serve their princess." Nilliar wiped her nose. "Even if Lannadae is with them, the risk is too great."

Lirea was no longer listening to her fellow undine. Another whisper floated on the wind. This new voice was seductive. Familiar. Lirea began to tremble. "Where are we?"

"North of the humans' island kingdom," said Nilliar.

The clouds blocked the stars from view, but there were other ways of navigating. Lirea dove, seeking out the deeper currents to confirm her fears.

A shark taunted her in the distance. *You can't stop us.*

She swam back to the surface. "I know where they're going."

Lannadae has slipped through your grasp again, and

she'll never let you be queen, called another shark. *She's going to kill you.*

"Where?" asked Nilliar.

"We have to stop them. The sharks don't matter. We can't let them reach—"

"Lirea, no." The other undine drew back, leaving Nilliar alone to face Lirea. "Please, my queen. Your people need you."

Lirea would have been within her rights to kill Nilliar for such defiance. If Lirea so wished, she could drive a spear through Nilliar's heart for such insolence, and Nilliar knew it. "Lannadae is taking them to Morveren."

Nilliar sank lower. "I've hunted sharks before, my queen. If you order us to attack, we will obey, and we will die. *You* will die, and Lannadae will have won."

Kill you dead! the sharks taunted. *Dead as a really dead thing!*

Nobody had ever claimed sharks were creative. But their voices were little more than whispers next to the rage of her knife. *You let her escape before because you were too slow and weak. Lannadae is there! She'll free Morveren!*

"Nilliar—" Lirea watched the ship go. She bowed her head. Nilliar was right. "Send a singer to find Captain Varisto. Order him to destroy the human ship."

The knife screamed its fury, filling her eyes with tears of pain.

"Where will we find him?" Nilliar asked.

"Swim north." Lirea lay back, listening to the wind. "Swim until the sea turns red. He will be there."

To Nilliar's credit, she asked no further questions. She knew the place Lirea described, as did the rest of the undine. Nilliar gestured, and one of the warriors stripped off his harness and weapons. He dove beneath the surface, seeking the deeper currents that would speed his journey.

"By the time he reaches Varisto's ship, it might be too late to intercept the humans," Nilliar said.

The sharks cried out again, adding their voices to that of Nilliar and the knife. *Dead!*

"Oh, shut up."

Only Nilliar and the sharks obeyed.

Despite Talia's fears, the day passed without incident. She hadn't decided which was more likely, the undine attacking the *Phillipa* or one of the crew taking out his fears on Lannadae. But either the undine weren't worried about a single small vessel, or else Danielle's sharks had done their jobs. One of the younger crewmen, barely more than a boy, had been charged with dumping the occasional handful of offal into the water. At those times, Talia could see the dark forms of the sharks as they came to the surface to feed.

As for the crew, whatever their feelings toward Lannadae, not one of them disobeyed their captain. Talia saw one or two men stop to stare at the mermaid, only to be dragged away by his fellows, usually with harsh words of warning.

Most of the crew wore lifelines against the storm, long ropes that secured them to the ship. Talia had reluctantly allowed Captain Hephyra to loop one of the lines around her waist. The sheets were furled, all save the foresail and main topsail. Any more sail in such weather would risk cracking the mast. Hephyra herself took the helm, holding the wheel steady against the wind.

She showed no sign of strain, but when she had stepped away earlier in the day, it had taken two men to keep the wheel under control.

Talia increased her scrutiny once night fell, pacing the edge of the ship and searching the water for any trace of motion. As she passed the boats, Lannadae peeked out and beckoned with one hand. The dinghy was nested within the larger cutter, both boats resting on chocks and secured with double-lines.

"What's wrong?" A canvas tarp covered the back of the boats, though the bottom of the dinghy was ankle-deep with water from the rain.

"I can't sleep," said Lannadae.

Talia allowed herself a slight smile. "Neither can I."

"It's too dry, and sound travels so strangely above water. So many voices. And no way to seek deeper waters to escape the wind." Lannadae sank lower in the boat. "You must think me a coward."

"You're young," said Talia.

"Have you been friends with Cinderella and Snow White a long time?"

"Danielle for about a year," Talia said. "Snow... we've known each other longer." She glanced at the cabin, wondering what they were doing. Danielle was probably huddled in her cot with a bucket. There was only so much Snow's teas could do. Snow, on the other hand, had been known to sleep through anything. The lurching of the ship might be enough to ruin even her sleep. Still, Talia wouldn't have put it past Snow to simply tie herself to the bed and dream merrily through the night. Assuming she didn't find someone else to do the tying.

Lannadae rested her chin on the edge of the boat. "Snow told me the women in your city decorate their shoes with glass beads, to make them look like Cinderella's slippers."

"Some do." Talia smiled despite herself, remembering the first time Danielle had learned of that trend. Seeing Danielle's outrage, Snow had naturally hurried out to buy a pair for herself. "A few of the more well-to-do families even tried to capture rats and doves as pets, but that fashion passed more quickly."

"I'm working on a new story of how Cinderella summoned the sharks to protect us." The cord Lannadae had used for her story back at the cave was now looped around her wrist like a bracelet. She started to tug it free. "Would you like to hear?"

"No." It came out more sharply than Talia intended, and Lannadae shrank back. "Perhaps another time."

Lannadae pulled herself up onto the frontmost bench in the boat. "Do you have any sisters, Talia?"

Talia's fists tightened. "I did. One sister and three brothers."

"Where are they today?"

"Dead." She rubbed her neck, trying to work out some of the tension in her muscles. "Look, I know you're frightened. I'm just not very good at comforting people."

"Why are you so mad at Snow White?"

And there was the tension again. "I'm not mad."

"You press your lips together every time I mention her. I thought that was one of the things humans did when they were angry." She smiled. "Yes, like that."

"Go to sleep."

"I can't, remember?" said Lannadae. "The wind is too—"

"The wind is starting to die down."

Lannadae pulled herself higher, looking out at the sheets of rain pounding the ship. "But—"

"Go to sleep."

Talia hadn't lied. The storms were finally slowing. Talia threw off her lifeline the instant Hephyra did, figuring if it was safe enough for the dryad, it was safe enough for her. Soon the wind eased enough for Talia to fully explore the ship. She could see much more from atop the masts.

Morning found her on the footrope that hung below the foremast top yard. One hand held the yard for balance as she moved through a simple combat form, testing the lines. The better she knew the *Phillipa,* the faster she could get where she needed to be if the undine attacked again.

Hephyra had replaced the lines since Talia's last time on the queen's ship. The new ropes were slightly thinner than she was used to. The masts appeared thicker as well, though that was to be expected. Like trees, the masts added a new ring of growth with each year.

She spun on one foot, switching hands as her opposite foot swept the legs from an imagined opponent.

"You move as though you were born to this ship."

Captain Hephyra stood on the topyard, arms folded as she watched Talia finish her form. "You're distracting the crew, though."

"*I'm* distracting them? What kind of captain wears a skirt, anyway?"

Hephyra grinned. Her skirt flapped like the blue and white banner atop the mast. Only the heavy tassels at the hem kept her thighs covered. "My invitation still stands, you know."

"No, thank you." Talia pulled herself up onto the yard. "I told you two years ago—"

"Yes, yes. You serve Beatrice. As do I." Hephyra rubbed the gold tattoo on her wrist. "And if Beatrice doesn't survive? What then, Talia? My crew could use a woman of your skills."

"To do what? You can't go back to Fairytown."

Hephyra ran one hand down the mast, caressing the wood. The gesture was sensual enough to make Talia flush. "I can't return to the grove of my sisters, no. But there are other ways to return. I know the smell of your magic and your curse, Talia. I know you have scores to settle with the fairies, as do I. Tell me, when was the last time one of the silver fleet fell prey to pirates?"

"Not in a hundred years."

Hephyra winked. "Consider your future, Talia."

"My future lies with Beatrice," Talia said firmly.

"For now, perhaps." Hephyra began to climb down the mast. She didn't bother with the ropes. Her bond with her tree allowed her to cling to the wood like an insect, moving with even greater ease than Talia herself. "Snow will never return your feelings, you know."

Talia grabbed the ropes to keep from falling. "What?"

"Never think you can conceal your longing from a dryad, dear Talia." Green eyes caressed Talia's skin. "There could be other benefits to joining my crew. My kind is far less . . . *particular* than you humans. You don't have to remain chained to them."

"They're my friends." Talia's throat was dry. Damn dryad magic, anyway.

"Perhaps. But I'm friendlier." With that, Hephyra laughed and jumped down to the deck, leaving Talia muttering words unbecoming for any lady, let alone a princess.

By the middle of the second day, Danielle had imbibed more tea than she normally drank in a week. The *Phillipa* was fast, but her smaller size made her more vulnerable to the motion of the waves. Last night had been one of the most miserable of her life, and that was saying a great deal. Thankfully, Jakob had helped inure her to sleepless nights.

She had little luck with breakfast but had so far managed to keep down a small lunch of porridge topped with cinnamon. So long as she remained above deck where she could see the horizon, the rolling of the ship wasn't so bad. She rested one hand on the hilt of her sword as she watched the sea. As always, the touch of the wood and glass handle soothed her tension. With her other hand, she tried to comb the tangles from her hair. She had cut it shorter after Jakob's birth, but the wind and rain had snarled the shoulder-length locks.

"We're down to less than half a barrel of fish guts," Snow said brightly, coming up behind her. She had acquired a worn leather tricorn hat, no doubt charmed from one of the crew.

Danielle groaned. "What happened?"

"One of the barrels washed overboard sometime last night." Snow yelped as a bundle of black fur hopped past, something purple and slimy clutched in its teeth. "And it doesn't help that Stub keeps getting into what's left."

The three-legged cat leaped onto one of the deck guns. The sun had warmed the metal, and Danielle could hear him purring as he chewed his prize. She walked over to scratch the scraggly fur behind his ear, which made the stump of his rear leg twitch madly. "How long until we reach Morveren?"

"Lannadae wasn't sure," Snow said. "We lost some time in the storm, but now that we're under full sail, we might make it by the end of the day. Assuming the winds don't change, we could have you back home to your prince before the week is out." Her face brightened. "That reminds me, I have a present for you. I meant to have it ready before we left, but things were so rushed. I finished it after lunch."

She pushed up her sleeve and tugged off a bracelet. Three thick strands of copper were braided together, and in the center they held a small, circular mirror. Snow grabbed Danielle's arm and pushed the bracelet over her wrist.

"Go on," said Snow.

Danielle looked at the mirror. All she saw was the greenish pallor of her face, and the windblown mess that was her hair.

"Give it a kiss."

Danielle shrugged and touched her lips to the glass. A familiar giggle made her smile. The mirror blurred, and then she was staring down at her son. She could hear Nicolette's voice, trying to persuade him to eat a biscuit. Jakob seemed much more interested in putting the gummed biscuit into his hair.

"Jakob?"

He jumped and looked around. "Mama?"

"He shouldn't be able to hear you." Snow yanked Danielle's arm, wrenching her shoulder as she studied the mirror. "I enchanted the glass to work through the mirrors in the palace. This is the sconce to the left of the doorway in the nursery. The magic of those mirrors should go only one way."

She grinned and added, "I left a mirror like this for Armand as well, so the two of you could talk. I told him it was a good-luck necklace. You'll have to kiss the mirror a little differently to make that spell work, though."

Danielle twisted free of Snow's grip and studied her

son. "Oh, no. He's gotten his hands on Armand's shoe again."

Jakob's latest infatuation was with one of Armand's shoes, a fancy thing of polished leather and velvet trim. Always the left shoe, for some reason. Jakob would gnaw it all day if he could. Unfortunately, the dye in the velvet always left Jakob with a purple-stained mouth and chin for several days afterward.

"What is it with your family and shoes?" Talia asked, coming over to join them. "First Armand runs around half the kingdom carrying that slipper, and now your son decides to devour the things."

"I still want to know how he heard you." Snow leaned over Danielle's wrist. "Jakob? It's Snow. Wave if you can hear me."

Jakob was too preoccupied trying to wedge biscuit into his right nostril.

"Thank you for this, Snow." Danielle touched the edge of the glass, and longing filled her chest. That should be her with Jakob, laughing and trying to get him to eat his biscuit. How many times would duty take her from her son? "Can we use it to check on Beatrice too?"

Snow's smile slipped. "Not with Father Isaac's wards protecting her."

Danielle scratched her nose. The skin was already sensitive to the touch. Talia's brown skin gave her some protection against the sun, but Danielle would have to find a hat for herself soon. "Has there been any sign of the undine?"

"Nothing yet." Talia leaned over the railing. "But they could be right behind us, and we'd never know until they decided to show themselves."

"That makes me feel better." Danielle watched as Jakob's image faded from the mirror. "What do we do if they're just waiting for the sharks to leave?"

Snow patted the railing. "Then we find out how tough the *Phillipa* really is."

*   *   *

The weather held for the rest of the day, allowing the *Phillipa* to continue under full sail. Danielle eventually found a moment alone to experiment with Snow's mirror. Snow hadn't been joking about the kind of kiss required to reach Armand. Danielle hoped she wouldn't have to contact Armand while anyone else was around.

He had been in the bow of his ship when Danielle reached him, and the sound of her voice made him jump so hard he bumped into the rail.

"It's good to hear your voice," he said, once he had recovered from his shock.

"And yours," said Danielle, holding the mirror close. "Have you found anything?"

"No sign of Lirea or her undine yet." His voice tightened as he summarized the past day's hunt. The storms had eased enough for him to take four ships out in search of Lirea. Two men had been found murdered on a fishing boat. Another ship had been wrecked from below while still in the harbor.

"You can still see the top of the masts sticking out of the water," Armand said. "They cracked her hull and left her to sink. It probably started taking on water yesterday evening. Most of the crew survived. This was meant as a warning, to make sure every man in the bay knew what could happen to him."

He moved closer. Danielle could see the gold chain stretching out from the mirror, circling Armand's neck. His eyes were shadowed. He was angry, but trying not to let it show.

"How is Beatrice?" Danielle asked.

"Unchanged. Father Isaac and Tymalous have done all they can."

The cabin door opened, and Snow peeked inside. "Lannadae is asking for you."

"You have to go," said Armand. "I wish I knew what it was Lirea really wanted, aside from her sister. Why would they ask for gold? The undine are migratory. Gold is heavy and clumsy to move."

"Maybe Morveren will be able to tell us."

"I hope so." Armand managed a small smile. "Be careful, Danielle. And please thank your friend for the gift."

"I will." Danielle kissed the mirror, and when she drew back, Armand's image was gone. She held it a moment longer, then left the cabin. Snow waited outside with Lannadae, who had finally ventured out from her makeshift cave of wood and canvas.

"We need your help," Lannadae said, hurrying toward the bow of the ship. Danielle walked with them, trying not to stare.

Lannadae used her arms to keep her body upright, pushing herself along with her twin tails. The motion reminded Danielle of thick snakes. Lannadae gripped the rail and pulled herself higher, studying the water.

"I think we're close." Lannadae leaned farther over the railing. "But I can't say for certain. Without tasting the water, feeling the currents ... how do you people keep from getting lost all the time?"

"We use maps," Danielle said. "You'd have to ask Snow for the details."

"The position of the sun and stars give you a general location, so long as you adjust for the seasons," said Snow. "I can show you how to read the charts in the map room if you'd like. I've been plotting out our route as we traveled."

"Maybe later?" Danielle interrupted gently.

Lannadae was searching the water. "Are the sharks still with us?"

"Two of them." The rest had left earlier this morning when they ran out of food. These two would depart soon enough. Danielle called to them often, thanking them for their help and asking them to stay just a little longer, but eventually they would grow hungry and need to hunt.

Lannadae smiled and pulled her body up onto the rail.

"What are you doing?" Danielle grabbed her arm.

"Tell them to protect me. I need to make sure we're

still going in the right direction." Lannadae moved one
tail over the railing.

"They're sharks, and they've got to be hungry by now.
They might—"

"They'll listen to you. You're Cinderella!" With that,
Lannadae pulled free of Danielle's grip and dove into
the water.

"She certainly trusts you," Snow commented.

Danielle leaned out, trying to find where Lannadae
had gone. She dreaded what she would see. *Please don't
eat her.*

The mermaid surfaced a short distance ahead of the
ship, giggling like a child. She dove again, then leaped
from the water. Her leaps were smaller than the ritual
greeting of Lirea and her tribe, but what Lannadae
lacked in strength and form she made up for in sheer
joy.

Both sharks swam over to investigate, but a combi-
nation of shouting and begging convinced them to turn
away. By now, several of the crew had come to watch
Lannadae frolic in the water. Even Captain Hephyra
chuckled as Lannadae skimmed the surface, crossing to
and fro in front of the *Phillipa.*

"We're close," Lannadae shouted. Her gills were red
slashes along the sides of her neck. Even though Danielle knew what they were, the sight still shocked her. "I
know this place. Morveren is that way."

Hephyra turned to shout, "Steady a-starboard!" The
Phillipa turned slightly, following Lannadae's directions.
"Steady!"

"Captain, do we have any meat to spare?" Danielle
asked.

"I'm sure we could find something. Why?"

"To thank the sharks for not eating our mermaid."

Hephyra grinned and ordered one of the men down
to the galley.

"Forget the sharks," Snow said, her forehead wrin-
kling as she studied the sky. "You'll want to throw her
a line."

"What is it?" Danielle asked.

"Another storm." Snow pointed ahead.

"Captain!" The cry came from atop the mainmast. One of the sailors leaned out from the crow's nest, ropes twined around his wrist and hand for balance. "Rough seas ahead."

"Rotted hell. We've barely dried out from the last one." Hephyra cupped her hands to her mouth. "Secure the ship. Reef the sails, and keep her on course. And someone get that mermaid out of the water."

"I wanted to stay," Lannadae was saying as two men hauled her up. She had managed to catch a large silver fish, though she had at least been smart enough not to start eating until she was out of the water and away from the sharks. Her nails had to be sharper and stronger than a human's, the way they pierced the fish's side. She sat down on the deck, water puddling around her, and began to eat. Between bites, she said, "I'll be safer beneath the waves. My tails have been so dry. The scales are already starting to chip."

"Your scales won't matter if those sharks grow nervous enough to take a bite out of you." Danielle started to take her hand, but Lannadae waved her away. She stuck the whole fish in her mouth and crawled along the deck.

"Not the cabin," said Snow. She tugged Danielle toward the map room at the very back of the ship.

The masts bowed as the crew hurried to furl the sails. Danielle glimpsed Captain Hephyra taking over at the wheel, fighting to keep the ship turned into the wind. Talia met them in front of the map room, taking Danielle's hand and helping her inside. When the door opened, the wind created a miniature storm of paper. Lannadae slid in after her, and Snow hauled the door shut.

With three people and one undine, the map room was quite cramped. Snow's choker flared to light, illuminating the room. A single desk occupied half the room. An enormous map of Lorindar and its surrounding countries dominated the far wall. To one side, long drawers of red-stained wood were mounted to the wall, each one latched with a small brass hook.

Stone weights held another map flat on the desk. One of the mirrors from Snow's choker stood in the center of the map, thin gold wires acting as both legs and pins.

Wind howled, and the *Phillipa* rocked to the side. One of the rocks slid onto the floor. Talia grabbed the ornately embroidered chair behind the desk before it could topple over.

Snow squeezed past Talia to claim the chair. The desk itself was secured to the floor to keep it from sliding. She jabbed a finger at the map. "The wind is all wrong for this part of the sea. This is magical, like the storm that chased us from Lorindar."

Danielle held the other side of the desk for balance. The lines and arrows covering the map made no sense to her, but she trusted Snow.

"Could Morveren be the one controlling the storms?" Talia asked. She didn't seem to notice the pitching floor. Her knees bent to shift her weight, easily compensating for the motion.

"She couldn't have sent them all the way to Lorindar."

"What about Lirea?" asked Lannadae. "If she's followed us here—"

"I don't think so," said Snow. "This storm . . . it feels settled, somehow. It's been here a while. Lannadae, you said that when you tried to find Morveren, the sea grew angry and the waves tried to batter you against the rocks."

"That's right." Lannadae pulled herself up to look at the map, her tails spread back in a V for balance. She jabbed her partly eaten fish at the map. "You think the wind was deliberately keeping me away?"

Another rock slid from the desk, and the map curled back over Snow's mirror. "I don't know," said Snow. "But it's really starting to irritate me."

"The *Phillipa* is tough, but if the wind smashes us into

the rocks, we're still going down. If this thing is guarding Morveren, we have to fight through it," said Talia.

Snow cocked her head. "What do you mean 'we'? What are you planning to do, throw a knife at it?"

"Can you fight it?" Danielle spoke quickly, trying to cut off the annoyance she saw in Talia's eyes.

Snow grabbed her mirror from the map and returned it to her choker. "There's no body to attack. It's not a demon hiding in the center of the storm. It's the whole storm." She rose from her chair. "I need to be out there. I need to feel the wind on my skin, to allow its power to touch my own."

Snow stepped to the door and pushed it outward. The wind yanked it from her grasp, slamming it open so hard the topmost hinge cracked loose from the frame.

Danielle and Talia both moved to brace Snow's arms. When Snow cast her spells, she sometimes lost track of the world around her.

Waves crashed against the side of the ship, washing over the main deck below. None were tall enough yet to reach the map room, but that could change at any time. Salty spray chilled Danielle's face.

Sailors shouted as they fought to secure the boat below. The guns were still lashed tight from the previous storm. Lifelines spread from the mainmast like a spiderweb. How could any storm have built so quickly?

Even with the sails furled, the wind still carried the ship along at a good pace. So far, Captain Hephyra had managed to keep the ship aligned with the wind. Danielle tried not to think about what would happen if Hephyra lost control of the wheel, and those winds struck the *Phillipa* broadside.

The door started to blow shut, but Talia snapped her foot out to stop it before it could slam into them. She grunted at the impact. "How long do you need to stand here, Snow?"

"The wind is bound to this place." Snow's eyes were squeezed shut, her face crinkled against the rain. "I've never seen a binding like this. I might be able to break it eventually, but it's like trying to snap steel chain with a cooking knife."

Danielle squeezed Snow's arm to get her attention. "If it's a guardian, can you hide us somehow?"

"Illusion doesn't work too well on things that don't have eyes."

"So what *would* work?"

Snow tilted her head back, like a child tasting the rain. "That depends on what it is. If it's elemental-based, it's 'seeing' us by sensing where we block the wind. A demonic or spiritual creature would taste the blood and life aboard the ship. Given the nature of the *Phillipa*, it would probably see the ship just as easily. Though it could be some sort of controlled projection, in which case its master is probably watching through—"

Danielle tugged her arm again. "Guess!"

"Guess?" Snow opened her eyes and looked at Danielle. Wind whipped her hair into her face, spoiling her offended pose. "I suppose ... I don't sense a scrying, which means it's likely to be an independent creature of some sort."

A scream drew Danielle's attention to the deck. One of the lifelines had snapped, and a man clung to the railing to keep from falling overboard. "Hurry, Snow!"

Snow ripped a mirror from her choker. With her other hand, she pulled a short-bladed dagger from her belt. She nicked the ball of her thumb, then smeared the blood over the mirror's surface. After returning the knife to its sheath, she brought the mirror to her lips and began to whisper.

"Is she doing magic?" Lannadae asked from inside the map room. "I want to see!"

"She'll show you some card tricks later," Talia snapped. "Snow?"

Snow closed her fingers around the mirror. "We have to get this as far away from the ship as we can."

"Give it to me." Danielle grabbed the mirror, then

stepped into the room to swipe the remains of Lanna-dae's snack.

"Hey!" Lannadae tried to take it back, but Danielle was already moving out into the storm.

Danielle paused only long enough to jam the mirror deep into the half-eaten fish. "Talia, I could use some help."

"That's disgusting." Talia shoved Snow into the map room and slammed the door.

"Try changing a diaper." Danielle managed a grin. "Think you can get me to the rail without letting me go overboard?"

Talia pulled a small, spindle-shaped whip from her belt. Danielle recognized the zaraq whip as one of her preferred weapons. Talia pulled out the thin line and used it to lash her arm to Danielle's.

They crouched low, practically crawling as they made their way toward the starboard rail. Bad as the wind had been before, now it was all Danielle could do to maintain her footing.

"Keep your head down," Talia yelled.

By now, most of the crew had hunkered down, clinging to whatever they could find. The sails were furled, the deck secured, and there was little to do but wait for orders and hope the storm passed soon.

The whip bit deep into Danielle's arm. The railing was only a few steps away, but Talia held her back.

"Not yet." The ship tilted again, rearing back as another wave passed beneath them. "Now!"

Danielle stumbled forward and thrust an arm through the rail, clinging with all of her strength. The water was far too close for her liking. The ship settled again, raising her away from the waves. The ocean was too rough for her to see whether any sharks remained. Praying they hadn't fled, she reached through the rail and threw the fish and mirror into the water. "Eat it and swim away as far and fast as you can!"

The *Phillipa* tilted again. Danielle braced her feet

against the rails and tried to turn around, but Talia held her in place.

"Just wait!" Talia shouted. "Don't go until the ship pitches forward."

"What?" Danielle shook her head. "You're crazy."

"Don't you trust me?" Talia grinned. The waves tilted the ship forward like a toy, and Talia shouted, "Come on!"

Danielle lurched to her feet. Water flowed over them both as Talia dragged them onward. There was no way to stop, and she would have fallen if not for the whip tying her to Talia. Danielle held her breath, but the *Phillipa* settled flat, allowing them to recover. The stern began to sink, tossing them both back toward the map room. Danielle's shoulder slammed into the door, cracking the frame further. Talia managed to catch herself with her free hand.

Talia was laughing as she pulled open the door. "After you, Your Highness."

"You're a madwoman," Danielle said, though she could feel her own manic laughter struggling to burst free. Or maybe that was her last meal. She gave silent thanks for Snow's magical tea.

"Fun, wasn't it?" Talia began untying her whip from Danielle's arm.

"Can you tell whether it worked?" Danielle asked.

Snow nodded. "The mirror is racing away at a good pace."

Even as she spoke, the motion of the ship began to ease. The wind quieted, and slowly the *Phillipa* steadied herself in the water.

"I knew it!" Lannadae cheered. "I knew Snow White and Cinderella would save us."

"Snow White and Cinderella saved us?" Talia repeated. Shaking her head, she tucked her whip away.

A short time later, Captain Hephyra opened the door. Sunlight streamed into the map room. Water dripped from Hephyra's clothes. Stub the cat was curled in her arms, meowing pitifully.

"Is he all right?" Danielle asked.

"He's fine." Hephyra scratched the cat's ears. "He decided to hide out in one of the boats. By the time the storm passed, he was up to his neck in water, but he was too petrified to climb out. He's not the brightest animal."

Outside, Danielle could see the crew mopping the worst of the water from the deck. Those who had recovered enough to move, at least. Some were still doubled over the railing. Experienced sailors or not, such weather was enough to twist any man's stomach.

"Are you expecting any more surprises on this voyage?" Hephyra asked.

"Probably," said Danielle.

"I figured as much." Hephyra wiped her face, then ran a hand over the cracked doorframe. "I'd appreciate it if you'd refrain from breaking my ship any more than you need to. It stings."

Danielle nodded. "So noted, Captain."

Hephyra turned to face the crew. "What are you lot waiting for? Bring the ship about and stand by to anchor."

"To anchor?" Snow repeated.

Hephyra pointed to the front of the ship. "We've got rocks ahead. Any longer in that storm, and we'd have ripped the bottom out from beneath us. The *Phillipa* can't sail through those waters. The rest of this journey, you make in the boat."

"It's all right," Lannadae said, crawling past Hephyra to the rail. She pulled herself up and drew a deep breath. "We're here."

CHAPTER 6

LOOKING OUT OVER THE WATER, Danielle understood why Captain Hephyra didn't dare take the *Phillipa* further. Rocks jutted into the air, as though the sea had flooded an ancient mountain range and only the peaks still protruded. Some were barely the size of their boat, while others were large enough to support clusters of tight-packed grasses and even trees.

Lannadae sat at the front of the boat, her tails pressed to either side. For this journey, Hephyra had ordered the cutter lowered. This was a larger boat than the dinghy, with room for them all as well as two oarsmen and, if all went well, a second mermaid passenger. James had volunteered to row them out, along with a heavyset bearded man named Douglas. James clung to the rope ladder to hold the boat in place as Snow climbed down.

The waves filled the air with mist. "You're certain you know where Morveren is?" Danielle asked.

"Morveren told us all before she left," said Lannadae. "She said she went to live with the giants."

Talia stepped from the ladder into the rear of the boat, seating herself in front of Danielle. "If we're hunting giants, I'm going to need to grab a few more weapons."

"There are two rocks that look like the heads of giants," Lannadae said. "Morveren lives there."

James pushed them away from the *Phillipa* as Douglas fitted the oars into the oarlocks. Though James sat facing Lannadae, he deliberately avoided looking at her.

"Are you all right?" Danielle asked.

"I'm fine, Highness," James said. "Thank you."

"If you prefer to stay—"

"I said I'm fine." He flushed, apparently remembering who he was speaking to. "I'm sorry. The last time I was this close to one of them, they were dragging me under. I thought I was about to die." He stared out at the waves. "We had over a hundred men on the *Branwyn*. Why am I the one who survived, Princess?"

Danielle searched for comfort, but what good were words to a man who had watched everyone he knew die?

It was Talia who answered. "Asking that question is a quick path to madness. There's no reason. You lived. Use that life."

James nodded and began to row. "I intend to."

Atop the *Phillipa,* Captain Hephyra leaned over the railing to shout, "I want you back here by nightfall, mermaid or no mermaid. If you spy dark clouds, turn back at once."

James and Douglas soon settled into a rhythm. Mist sprayed the air as the waves broke upon the rocks. Danielle could see the black shells of barnacles packed together on the rocks near the waterline. Higher up, some of the rocks carried patches of dark green moss.

"I've sailed past these parts," said James. "They say the rocks are graves. Every time a ship is lost, another rock rises from the sea."

"Pah," said Douglas. "Everyone knows they're the teeth of the old gods, left here a thousand years ago."

"Really?" asked James.

"No. They're rocks." Douglas splashed him with an oar. "Quiet down and row."

Danielle had donned a long jacket before leaving the ship. She pulled it tight, folding her arms for warmth, but there was no way to avoid the dampness. Only Lannadae seemed unaffected by the wind and the water. The mermaid leaned over the side, trailing her hand through the waves.

Behind them, the *Phillipa* was little more than a shadow in the mist. "Not exactly the most comfortable place to live," said Talia.

"I don't know," answered Snow. "Strange winds, cold fog . . . my mother would have killed to create this kind of atmosphere."

Soon the *Phillipa* had disappeared from sight, and they were alone with the rocks and the waves. Danielle studied each one as they passed, searching for two rocks shaped like giants. Nobody spoke. Even the splashing of the oars grew quieter as the cutter slowed.

"There," whispered Snow, pointing at two shadows up ahead. A flock of birds exploded from a nearby island at the sound of her voice.

"Kraken bugger us all!" The boat rocked as Douglas stood, yanking his oar from the lock and brandishing it like an enormous staff.

"They're only birds," said Danielle, trying not to smile. "Cormorants, like the ones who live in the cliffs back home."

The cormorants skimmed the water, many coming close enough for Danielle to make out the individual black and white feathers on their wings. Several nabbed fish from just beneath the surface before flying back to the closer of the two islands ahead.

James and Douglas rowed the boat, following the birds. Both rocks were twice as high as a man and almost as long as the *Phillipa*. The sides were nearly vertical, miniature cliffs of crumbled black rock. As they approached, Danielle could see a submerged path of stone connecting the two.

"I guess that one sort of looks like a giant," Snow said dubiously.

If so, it was a sickly giant indeed. The nose had fallen into the water, and the cheeks were streaked with bird droppings. Though the moss and barnacles did give the impression of a beard, and the clump of trees up top could be hair.

The second "giant" was easier to discern as they approached, though one "eye" held an enormous nest of woven grasses and leaves.

"Where would she be?" Danielle asked.

Lannadae sank lower in the boat. "I'm not sure."

Danielle leaned over the side. The water was shallow enough to see the plants swaying on the bottom.

The wind moaned as it blew past the rocks. Danielle fought a shudder at the sound. It made her think of her father's breathing during his last days in this world. The long, strained gasps as he fought for air. The groans of pain he fought and failed to suppress, knowing Danielle was listening.

"She's here," Snow said.

Danielle wiped her face. "What's that?"

"It's Morveren." Snow's eyes were glassy. "The song of the undine is magical, remember?"

"She was always a strong singer," said Lannadae. "In her youth, she would sing messages to other tribes."

"Sounds like the cries of the drowned," said James.

Talia hadn't spoken. She was staring at her hands, and her eyes were haunted. Danielle reached back to touch her arm.

Talia slapped Danielle's hand aside, then froze. "Sorry. I was—" She shook her head. "Where is she?"

Snow pointed to the trees which topped the left rock. Talia barely rocked the boat as she stood and drew one of her knives.

"What are you doing?" Lannadae asked.

A moment later, the knife spun between the trees.

The moaning sound Danielle had thought was the wind stopped with a yelp. Talia pulled out a second knife.

"No!" Lannadae grabbed Danielle's leg. "Cinderella, stop her!"

Danielle put her hand over Talia's. "She can't help us if she's dead."

The song began again, angrier this time. Talia's eyes shone. "Shut her up or I will."

Danielle nodded and turned to face the cormorants nesting in the rocks. *Sing, my friends.*

To call the cries of the cormorants a song bent the meaning of the word to the breaking point, but as their squawks grew, the mermaid's spell lost its hold. Barely audible, a furious voice from the trees shouted, "What are you doing to my birds?"

"That's her." Lannadae stared up at the trees. "What is she doing up there?"

"Let's find out!" Snow said brightly. Either the mermaid's song hadn't affected her, or else she had thrown off the effects far easier than anyone else. Before Danielle could stop her, Snow jumped overboard and began swimming toward the rocks.

"Cooperative of her to walk into whatever trap Morveren might have waiting, don't you think?" Talia shook her head and jumped in after Snow.

Danielle cupped her hands to her mouth. "My name is Danielle Whiteshore, princess of Lorindar. I've come with your granddaughter Lannadae to ask for your help."

"Liar! Lannadae's dead. Lirea murdered her sisters, just as she murdered my son!"

Danielle turned to Lannadae. "How would she know that?"

"I don't know." Lannadae raised her voice. "Grandmother, it's me!"

There was no answer. Danielle stripped off her jacket. "Lannadae, please swim around to the other side and make sure Morveren doesn't try to escape."

Lannadae slipped out of the boat. Danielle removed her shoes, but she hesitated to follow. She had never learned to swim as a child. She wouldn't have learned as an adult either, if not for Beatrice's insistence. She still remembered her first lesson. The queen's exact words had been, "Either jump in or I'll get Talia to throw you in."

Holding her breath, Danielle jumped into the water. It was colder than she expected, weighing down her clothes and dragging her under before she bobbed to the surface. Coughing and spitting seawater, she paddled after the others.

Snow was already climbing up the side of the rocks. Talia leaned down to haul Danielle from the water. Danielle grabbed a handful of grass with one hand while her feet searched for cracks and outcroppings in the rock.

The first few handholds were tricky, being slick with moss and water. By the time Danielle reached the top, Talia and Snow were already there, crouched in a small clearing among the ferns and trees.

Discarded fish bones covered the ground next to a sunken hollow filled with mud. The trees were no thicker than her arm, but there were dozens of them, their roots climbing over one another for purchase. Water puddled among the roots and in depressions in the rock.

The treetops bent together overhead, where branches and driftwood had been interwoven to create a thick canopy against the sun. Broken bits of twine littered the earth. Snow picked up one of the pieces. "Seaweed fibers."

Four paces brought Danielle to the opposite side of the rock. The water below wasn't deep enough to dive into, at least not for a human. An undine might be able to make it without breaking her neck. But she could see Lannadae swimming past, and surely Lannadae would have noticed if Morveren tried to flee.

"Nobody said anything about invisible mermaids," Talia said.

Snow was investigating a clay bowl which had been shoved beneath a fern. She made a sour face. "Yummy. Drowned worms."

Danielle stepped into the middle of the clearing. "Morveren, we need your help. Lirea attacked my queen with the knife you made."

"Then your queen is dead." The branches overhead quivered. Morveren peered over the edge of a kind of hammock woven between the trees. Thick as the branches were, Danielle hadn't even noticed her.

"A mermaid in a tree." Talia pulled out her whip. "That's one I haven't heard before."

"Morveren, your granddaughter is alive," said Danielle. "She's here. You can see her swimming through the water below."

Morveren grabbed the edge of the hammock and tumbled out, dangling in midair. She clutched a braided rope in her hands, which she used to lower herself to the ground. She groaned as she moved, and her upper body was hunched as though her bones struggled to support her weight.

"What happened to you?" Danielle whispered.

Like her granddaughters, Morveren had two tails. But where Lannadae's and Lirea's tails ended in wide fins, Morveren's were nothing but stumps. The scales at the end of her tails grew in an irregular pattern, poking through lumps of pale scar tissue.

That would explain why she stayed out of the water. The fins running down the sides of her legs would still help her to get about, but without her tails, she would swim little better than a human.

Morveren was nude save for a worn harness. Twigs and bits of leaves were tangled in her black hair. Her scales were rough and filthy. White cracks marred many of the scales, and some had torn away to reveal pale skin. Her skin had the same unhealthy blue tinge as Lannadae's.

Morveren dragged herself along the ground until she reached the edge of the rock. "Lannadae?"

"Grandmother!" Lannadae bobbed from the water.

"It is you." Morveren turned to Danielle, tears dripping down her face. "She's alive."

"So is our queen," said Danielle. "Lirea's knife ripped her spirit from her body, but her body still lives."

Morveren moaned and crawled back to the mud pit. She lowered herself into the mud with a grunt of pain. "Do me a kindness and hand me that bowl?"

Snow carried the bowl from beneath the ferns, setting it at the edge of the mud. Tiny wormlike creatures swayed in the water, their tails stuck to the bottom of the bowl. White hairs surrounded the other ends like tiny crowns.

"Thank you." Morveren plucked out a worm the size of her smallest finger. Danielle grimaced, wondering if she meant to eat it, but instead she squeezed the worm until greenish goo seeped from the back end. Morveren smeared the goo onto a bloody scratch on her arm, then tossed the worm back into the water. "The secretions of the flowerworm are as good as a second skin. It keeps the blood scent from spreading through the water." She pointed to Danielle. "You scraped yourself climbing up here. Would you like me to tend the cuts?"

"No, thank you," Danielle said.

"This dry air is torture. Weakens the scales and the bones and cracks the skin." Morveren used two more worms to treat various cuts, then crawled out of the pit toward her granddaughter.

"She calls this dry?" Snow asked.

Danielle sat down beside the mud. "How did you know Lirea had tried to kill her sisters?"

Morveren hesitated, then turned away. Her expression was difficult to read, but Danielle thought she looked ashamed. "Through the knife. For a time, I could hear fragments of her thoughts. Back when my magic was stronger." She bowed her head. "My son?"

"I'm so sorry," Danielle said.

New tears spilled from Morveren's eyes.

"Tell us about the knife," said Snow. "How did you construct it? What spells did you cast?"

"Lirea wanted to die." Morveren dug at one of the scales by the edge of her scar, scratching and pulling until it finally came free. "She was so young. You can't blame her for what happened. Blame me, if you must. Lirea begged me for a spell that would allow her to be with her human prince. She said he loved her, and I believed her. Once I learned the truth, it was too late."

"So instead of removing the spell, you gave Lirea a knife that rips the soul from its victims," said Talia. "That makes sense."

Morveren flicked the scale at Talia. "You think removing a spell is as easy as changing those ridiculous clothes you wear? Spells like the one I cast on Lirea can be woven in two ways. One is temporary, lasting less than a day before wearing off. Lirea wanted to be human forever. She insisted on it, pleading and begging until I gave in. She was in love, charmed by a man she thought she knew. I should have insisted she wait, but I've never been able to refuse my granddaughters. Lirea told me her prince wanted to marry her. I thought that bond would be enough to sustain the spell."

"Since he's human, that connection would help to define and maintain her form as well," Snow said, nodding. "When his body died, the spirit still sustained her, but she lost that clarity of form. She's trapped between human and undine."

"You know magic?" Morveren asked, her voice eager. "Then you understand the cost of such a transformation."

Snow shook her head. "I've read about transformation magic, but I've never been able to master it."

"The spells are ... difficult." Morveren slumped lower. "I should have refused."

One of the cormorants swooped down, wings pounding. The bird seemed on the verge of panic. A fish tail protruded from his beak, and his head convulsed as he tried to swallow. Danielle started toward him, but Morveren was faster.

Morveren sang a low, warbling note, and the cormorant hopped toward her. The mermaid grabbed him gently behind the head. She slipped the fingers of her other hand into the beak, slowly working the fish free. The fish still flopped weakly, so she slapped it against a rock.

"What's wrong with the bird?" Danielle asked.

Morveren picked up a sharpened flake of stone and used it to cut a loop of twine from the cormorant's neck. The bird fluffed its feathers, then flew up into the trees. "I trained them to fish for me. The string stops them from swallowing their prey, so they have to come back to me to remove it." She bit into the fish, scales and all, then spat the meat into her hand. The cormorant cried out, and Morveren threw the meat, smiling faintly as the bird flew after it. "They're not terribly smart creatures, but I can't hunt as well as I used to."

"What about your magic?" Danielle watched the cormorant disappear into the mist. "Why do you need birds to hunt for you? Can't your spells take you away from here?"

"My magic . . . isn't what it once was," Morveren said. "I used most of my strength helping Lirea. Trying to help her. Even if there was a way to completely restore her to what she was, I no longer have the power to do it. Nor, I think, would she allow me to do so."

"Lirea has turned the undine against us," Danielle said. "She demands tribute in exchange for safe passage through the sea. Gold and other treasures."

Morveren crawled to the edge of the rock and lay flat, staring down at Lannadae. "There are stories of a time, thousands of years ago, when the undine were one tribe. They say the first undine were more like you, able to walk and live on land as well as the sea. We were one family, enslaved to the humans. We ruled the sea in their name, and all paid tribute to our masters."

"What happened?" asked Snow.

"Some believe we turned against our rulers, wrecking their ships and stealing their treasures until they were too weak to protect themselves. It may be Lirea hopes to do the same. To unite the tribes and regain our former glory. And perhaps to punish your kind for what was done to her."

"Help us to stop her," said Danielle. "And to save our queen."

Morveren sat up to face Danielle. Despite her filth, there was something regal in her bearing, a strength that hadn't been there before. "Your queen's soul is trapped within the knife, along with Gustan's. I will help you retrieve the knife and save your queen." Morveren tugged a leaf from her hair and flicked it away. "In return, you must help me save Lirea."

Before Danielle could answer, Talia stepped around to the mermaid. "Lirea attacked our queen. She threatened Princess Danielle. She killed your son and one granddaughter and still hopes to kill your other granddaughter."

"None of which would have happened if not for me." Morveren turned to Danielle. "The knife wasn't meant to cure her. It was meant to keep Lirea alive until I could complete the spell. I fear the knife has trapped her in the moment of Gustan's death. A part of her is always reliving what she did to save herself. I've condemned her to torment enough to drive anyone to madness and hatred. Please let me try to undo the damage I've caused her."

A thunderclap echoed over the water. Danielle's first thought was that the storms had returned, but the sky was clear.

"That was cannon fire," said Snow.

"Could Lirea have found the *Phillipa*?" Danielle asked.

Talia shook her head. "The *Phillipa's* guns are smaller. That's another ship." She tensed as a second explosion followed, slightly higher in pitch than the first. "*That* was the *Phillipa.*"

Below, Douglas and James were shouting for them to return.

"Please," said Morveren. "Lirea's actions aren't her own. Let me try to make amends for what I've done to my family and to yours."

Danielle nodded. "If you can help us save Beatrice, we'll do what we can for Lirea."

"Assuming we live long enough to reach her," added Talia.

Danielle searched for the *Phillipa* as she climbed down from Morveren's island, but the mist was too thick. She dropped into the shallow water with a splash, biting back a gasp at the cold.

"Princess!" James shouted. He and Douglas brought the cutter alongside and helped Danielle climb on board.

Lannadae was already there, dripping puddles into the front of the boat.

Morveren followed them down, a woven sack looped over one arm. She gripped the tree roots and grasses to control her slide, then dropped into the deeper water at the back of the island. She circled around to the boat, reaching it just after Snow.

Once everyone was on board, James pressed his oar against the rock, pushing them back toward the *Phillipa*.

Morveren and Lannadae sat in the front, holding one another and crying together. Morveren sang softly, though there didn't appear to be any magic in the sound. It reminded Danielle of the crooning, meaningless sounds she sometimes made to comfort Jakob.

Several more cannons fired in quick succession. "Who are they fighting?" Danielle asked, knowing the question was a foolish one. They could no more see the *Phillipa* from here than she could.

She counted six more shots before the mist thinned enough to make out the shape of the *Phillipa* and a larger ship with red sails.

"Hiladi mercenaries," Talia said.

Douglas stopped rowing. "Hold here. We're not bringing the princess into the middle of a fight."

Danielle turned to the undine. "Lannadae, you said Lirea's prince was Hiladi."

It was Morveren who answered. "He was, but why his people would help Lirea, I couldn't say. They see our kind as little better than animals. Given what she did to him, they should be the last to come to her aid."

Snow squinted at the second ship. "I count four masts."

"That's a galleon." Talia swore. "She shouldn't have been fast enough to catch the *Phillipa* with a broadside."

"They're riding Lirea's winds." Morveren had taken the remains of her fish from her sack. She chewed as she spoke. "They speed the Hiladi ship while slowing your own."

Danielle stared. "The storms that tried to sink our ship. Lirea controls those?"

"She inherited them," Morveren corrected. She picked a piece of fin from her teeth and tossed it into the water. "Nine spirits of the air. They were Gustan's guardians. When he died, they remained with Lirea. She doesn't control them, exactly. She may not even understand what they are. But they serve her."

"What do you mean?" asked Snow.

"After Lirea killed Gustan, I tried to help her. I used magic to calm Lirea, but her spirits attacked before I could complete my spells." Morveren jabbed her half-eaten fish back toward the clouds. "I could feel Lirea's fear and rage through the winds."

"So it's an empathic bond rather than true mastery," Snow said. "Less precise, but harder to break. No wonder I had such a hard time fighting them."

"You fought Lirea's spirits?" Morveren sounded impressed. "One of them remained behind to guard my island. I meant to ask how you had gotten through."

Lannadae beamed. "Snow White is a powerful sorceress. She's done many amazing things, Grandmother. I can tell you some of the stories. How she fled to the woods to escape her mother, or how she fought her mother to avenge the death of her lover."

"I'm more interested in how you beat those spirits," Morveren said. "I was never able to destroy them. It was all I could do to stop them from killing me."

"Mirror magic." Snow raised her chin, showing off her choker. "I didn't try to destroy the spirit. Instead I used one of the mirrors to capture the spiritual emanations from the crew. When we sent the mirror away, the winds followed."

"Given the size of those mirrors, how do you maintain the strength of the emanations?"

Snow beamed. "These aren't the true mirrors. Each one is clear glass, bound to a much more powerful mirror at the palace. There's plenty of magic in that one to—"

Danielle touched Snow's arm. "Is now really the best time for magical theory?"

"Oh. Sorry." Snow flushed and turned around.

"The *Phillipa*'s having trouble holding her position," said Talia. "The winds again?"

Douglas spat over the side. "She's outgunned. The *Phillipa*'s a tough old bitch, but she can't take on a Hiladi galleon with the winds against her."

More shots thundered over the water. Screams followed, making Danielle flinch. "Snow, can your magic affect the Hiladi ship?"

"I can't do much from here." Snow stood up in the boat. "If I can reach the ship, I might be able to stop them. The smoke should cover my approach."

"No," said Talia. "The wind is too strong. It sweeps the smoke away between shots. If even one person spots you, you're dead."

"So what?" James snapped. "We wait here in the cutter and watch Captain Hephyra go down with her ship? I'm not watching another ship sink! We've got to do something."

Danielle leaned toward Morveren. "When we came to your island, you sang to us. Can you do the same to the Hiladi? Frighten them off, or at least lull them into stopping their assault?"

Morveren's smile revealed missing teeth and a fish scale stuck in her gumline. "That's one of the few powers left to me. My voice isn't what it once was, and I can't sing to them without affecting your friends on the ship as well, but I'll do what I can. You'll want to seal your ears."

"With what?" Danielle glanced at the boat's contents, finding nothing beyond an extra oar, a small barrel of fresh water, a length of old rope, and a sodden mouse nest.

"Oh, that's right. Humans can't close their ears at will." Morveren reached into her sack and pulled out a small basket. Inside was a flat black stone. A cluster of flowerworms clung to the surface of the stone, their bodies limp. "These might work."

James scooted back. "You're not putting worms in my ears, mermaid."

"No, of course not." Morveren cradled the stone in her lap. "Just their secretions. The paste should muffle my song enough for you to resist. You don't have to use them, but if you refuse, don't hold me responsible. The song of the undine is known to have a powerful effect on men. A few find themselves irresistibly drawn to the singer." She lay back and winked. Beside her, Lannadae muffled a giggle.

Douglas and James spoke as one. "We'll take the worms."

Morveren smiled and plucked one of the worms from the rock. "Don't know what I'll use for my poor skin," she muttered. "Who's first?"

"Me." Danielle held the side of the boat for balance as she crawled closer to Morveren. She sat down and tilted her head to the side, pushing her hair back. "How do we clean this stuff out when we're finished?"

"It will dry and crumble away in a day or two." Morveren's cold fingers pinched the top of Danielle's ear.

The slime was cool, trickling into Danielle's ear like syrup. She swallowed, trying to relieve the sense of pressure inside her head. It felt as though she had jammed a finger deep into her ear.

Morveren gently turned Danielle's head and repeated the process on the other ear. She squeezed the rest of the slime out of the first worm and grabbed a second before pronouncing Danielle done.

Danielle rubbed a finger along the outer edge of her ear. Her fingertip came away smeared with a film of pearly wax.

She moved to the side to make room for Snow. She could still hear the others talking, but their voices were muffled. She could hear the cannons as well, and the screams of the wounded. "Please hurry."

Lannadae plucked two worms from the stone and helped, squeezing the paste into James' ears while Morveren tended to Snow. Even with both undine working together, it seemed to take forever before they were finished with everyone.

Morveren returned the worms to their basket, then wiped her hands on her scales. "Are you ready?"

Her words sounded flat and distant. Danielle nodded, as did the others.

Morveren began to sing. There were no words, only a deep, mournful melody. Even Danielle could feel the longing behind the song, the sorrow and the despair. She touched the mirror on her wrist, thinking of Jakob and Armand. Tears filled her eyes.

If things went badly, she might never make it home to Lorindar. She would never see her son or husband again. She would die here, alone and forgotten. Abandoned, as Morveren had been.

Morveren. This was her song, her sorrow and grief. Danielle was too close. Even with her ears plugged, the song overpowered her. She struggled to climb out of the boat, but her muscles wouldn't obey.

"Morveren, stop." Either Danielle's words were too weak or Morveren couldn't hear over her song. Danielle fell to the side, banging her shoulder on the bench before toppling into the bottom of the boat.

Snow closed her eyes, feeling the magic of Morveren's song as it swept past her. In some respects, it reminded Snow of a trick her mother used to use, forcing power into her voice in order to command obedience. Morveren's power was both broader and more focused. Even with her ears plugged, Snow could feel the song tightening its grip on her.

Snow smiled and set about crafting her own magic. As a child, she had learned to resist her mother's commands. She had concealed that power, obeying at all times so her mother wouldn't learn of her rebellion. But she obeyed by choice, not because she was forced to. It might have been a meaningless distinction, but to a little girl, it was an important one.

She whispered one of her earliest shielding spells, repeating the simple singsong rhymes she had devised as a young child.

> *"Gray stones, gray stones,*
> *hear my call.*
> *Gray stones build a*
> *great big wall.*
> *Build it high as the clouds I see.*
> *Build it strong as strong can be."*

The stones of the spell were from her bedroom; the clouds were her only view through the high, narrow window in her wall. On those nights her mother worked magic, Snow would lie awake, fighting off the nightmare sensations of that power. She hadn't understood what it was she felt, only that it was dark and wrong and hungry and that it would consume her if she dropped her guard.

As when she was a child, she imagined those stones leaping forth in rows, stacking one upon the other until they formed a barrier between herself and Morveren. She opened her eyes to find Lannadae staring at her, so close their noses almost touched.

"I'm all right," Snow said. Lannadae didn't seem to be affected, but the other humans sat stupefied.

"If she stops singing now, the Hiladi will come after us," Lannadae shouted. "They know we're here, but they shouldn't be able to do anything so long as the song continues."

"I understand." Snow considered trying to expand her spell to protect Talia and Danielle, but that would require too much time. With a grin, she grabbed Danielle beneath the arms and hauled her up onto the bench. The cutter rocked dangerously, nearly dumping them both overboard, but she managed to recover.

"Sorry, Princess." With that, Snow tossed Danielle overboard.

Danielle splashed to the surface. "What are you doing?"

Oh, good. She had hoped the water would muffle Morveren's song enough to weaken the spell. To Lannadae, she said, "Help me with Talia?"

Talia had been grouchy ever since learning Snow had hidden Lannadae's existence. So it was with a certain degree of pleasure that Snow dumped her overboard after Danielle.

"Help them swim," Snow said. Danielle wasn't a terribly strong swimmer, and every time she and Talia surfaced, they had to fight Morveren's song.

Lannadae slipped into the water, grabbing Danielle's left hand and Talia's right. Her gills flared open, and her powerful tails propelled them toward the Hiladi ship, leaving Snow struggling to catch up. By the time they passed the *Phillipa,* Danielle and Talia seemed free of Morveren's spell. Snow risked lowering her own shield. She could still feel Morveren's magic, but the wormwax blocked enough of the sound for her to ignore it.

The air spirits were also unaffected. They continued to blow, rotating the *Phillipa* away from the Hiladi ship. The wind made swimming much more difficult, as the waves battered Snow back toward the *Phillipa.* Lannadae helped the others to reach the Hiladi ship, then returned to pull Snow along.

Talia had drawn two of her knives. Where did she keep them all, anyway? Talia slammed one into the side of the ship, pulled herself up, then drove the other home. She shifted her weight and pried the first knife free. Hand over hand, she scaled the side of the ship.

Snow turned around to study the damage to the *Phillipa.* The railing had been shattered in three places, and one of the cannons was gone. Several holes punctured the side of the hull. They had torn some of the rigging as well.

"What about the rope from the cutter?" Danielle shouted, cupping her hands to her mouth. "Could we use that to climb?"

Snow shook her head. "That rope's old and wet. Even if you could hold on, I wouldn't trust its strength."

Lannadae bent double. Her tails kicked air, and then she disappeared into the darkness of the water. Snow searched to see where she had gone.

Moments later, Lannadae shot up from the waves. She didn't clear the side of the ship as Lirea had done, but she flew high enough to catch hold of the railing. She swung from side to side until she hooked a tail over the rail. From there, it was a simple matter to pull herself onto the ship. A rope soon tumbled down into the water.

Snow smiled and began to climb. She stopped beside Talia to say, "Don't take too long. Morveren can't sing forever."

Danielle was next up, and then Talia reached over to take the rope. She yanked her knives from the ship with a scowl, tucking them back into their sheaths before scrambling up the side.

The crew weren't moving. Many sat on the deck their heads bowed, weeping. A smaller group stood at the edge of the ship, peering longingly toward Morveren. They wore typical Hiladi garb in fiery colors. Beaded black cords secured billowing sleeves at the elbows and wrists. Broad, flat hats protected them from the sun. Snow grabbed one and tried it on, then tossed it aside. Too sweaty, and far less stylish than her tricorn back on the *Phillipa*.

Splintered wood covered part of the deck, proof that the *Phillipa* had fought back despite her disadvantages.

Snow turned slowly, fingers brushing her choker as she drew on the mirrors to enhance her vision. There was magic on this ship. Not as strong as the enchantments on the *Phillipa,* but still respectable. There . . . a spell carved into the mainmast to protect it. Another woven into the wheel to enhance the strength of the helmsman.

Talia and Danielle were arguing about what to do first, but Snow was more interested in the ship's spells. She had never studied Hiladi magic before. Most appeared to be runic in nature, like the characters embroidered along the edge of the sheets to give them strength.

To undo the spell would require hours of careful work, but there were alternatives.

"What are you doing?" Lannadae asked.

"Playing." Snow smiled as she traced new symbols in the air. Painting them directly onto the sails would have been better. Casting with only her fingers meant the spell would be easy to remove ... but first they would have to find it. How long would it take for the Hiladi to realize their sails had a flavor, one the rats should find particularly appetizing?

"Come on," Snow said. "Let's see what we can do with their navigation equipment."

Having reached the ship, Danielle wasn't sure how to best disable their attackers. Talia had no such problems. Knife in hand, Talia approached the closest sailor.

"Wait!"

Either the plugs of wormwax in Talia's ears kept her from hearing, or else she simply chose not to. Danielle hurried to catch her arm.

Talia spun, nearly cutting Danielle before she stopped herself. "Sorry," she mouthed.

"They're helpless," Danielle shouted, pointing to the crew. "You can't just kill them."

"They meant to kill us, remember? Your duty is to your people, Princess."

Between the wormwax and Morveren's song, Danielle had to watch the shape of Talia's mouth to make out what she was saying. "Not like this. We can cut the ropes and disable the cannons."

"We don't have time to be civilized."

Snow had already wandered off. She appeared to be casting some sort of spell on the mainsail. So far, the crew hadn't even acknowledged their presence. A few glanced up, but not one managed so much as a frown before Morveren's voice lured them back under the mermaid's spell. Some were barely more than children, the soft fuzz on their chins the closest they could come to the beards worn by the older men.

"No," said Danielle. "Cripple the ship, but leave the crew alone."

Talia shook her head, but put her knife away. "If Morveren's song fails, they'll kill us all."

"And if you start killing them, that might be enough to break Morveren's hold." Danielle drew her sword. The enchanted glass blade cut easily through the ropes behind her. A few more swings sent lines snapping back across the ship. She crossed the deck and raised her sword.

Talia caught her arm and pulled hard enough to throw Danielle to the deck.

"Do you even know what you're destroying?" Talia pointed upward to a yard that now hung at a dangerous angle. "Cut those ties, and you'll likely kill us both when the topsail yard comes crashing down."

Danielle stood, her heart pounding. She brushed black sand from her palms and clothes. The sand covered most of the deck. "Thank you."

Talia was already storming toward the ladder to the gundeck. A man stood enthralled beside the ladder. Talia knocked him out of the way, bloodying his nose before dropping him to the deck, unconscious.

Talia had never been a cheerful woman, but Danielle had never seen her like this. She was hurting, that much anyone could see. She was still punishing herself for what had happened to Beatrice. But any time Danielle had tried to talk to her, Talia brushed her aside. Beatrice was the only one who could get through to Talia when she was this upset.

What would happen to them if Beatrice didn't recover? Officially, both Snow and Talia were personal servants of the queen. Danielle could have them reassigned to herself, but she could never take Bea's place.

Pushing such thoughts aside, Danielle hurried to the back of the ship and cut the ropes that connected the wheel to the rudder. She hacked through the wheel itself for good measure, then followed Talia below.

The Hiladi kept their cannons in a lower deck. Dust

shimmered in the sunbeams coming through the open gunports. Small pyramids of cannonballs sat in triangular brass frames beside each one. Danielle had to hunch to keep from banging her head on low-hanging beams.

Talia was already assaulting one of the cannons on the port side with a large hammer, driving an iron nail into the touchhole. Two men stood beside her, leaning out the gunport to better hear Morveren's song.

Danielle moved to the starboard side. If the ship came about, she didn't want them to be able to fire another broadside. Low partitions separated each cannon from the next. She grabbed one of the ramrods and tossed it out through the gunport. If they couldn't load their guns, they could hardly continue their attack. She threw out the linstocks as well. The iron rods with their slow-burning matches left thin lines of smoke as they arched down into the water.

At the last gun, as she tugged the ramrod from the man's hands, he blinked and pulled back. One hand grabbed her wrist. His eyes slowly focused on hers.

Danielle stomped on his foot. He shouted and swung the ramrod into her arm, knocking her down. He appeared disoriented, still fighting to shake off the effects of Morveren's spell, but it was clear that the spell was weakening.

Danielle pulled out her sword and swung two-handed, knocking the ramrod from his hands. On the other side of the ship, two men stumbled toward Talia as she finished spiking another cannon. One raised a club overhead.

Talia jammed a nail into his gut, grabbed his shirt, and shoved him headfirst into the cannon. The second man wrapped his arms around her from behind, but Talia snapped her head back into his face. He let go, blood dripping from his lip.

"Time to go," Talia shouted. She swung her hammer at the nearest stack of cannonballs, sending them rolling across the deck.

Danielle's sword was too long a weapon for the

cramped gundeck, but most of the crew were still too confused to put up much of a fight. She knocked several men aside with the flat of her blade. Talia cleared two more with well-placed kicks.

Topside, Snow stood with Lannadae, knife in hand as she tried to fight her way toward the edge of the deck. Talia jumped into the sunlight and threw her hammer. It spun past Snow's shoulder and dropped one of her attackers. Snow cut a second while he was recovering from the surprise of Talia's attack.

Danielle wasn't sure exactly when Morveren had stopped singing, but the air was strangely quiet. The plugs in her ears muffled the shouts of the crew as they tried to rally against both the intruders and the *Phillipa*.

Light flashed from Snow's chokers, driving the rest back long enough for her and Lannadae to break away. Lannadae leaped overboard, but Snow waited at the rail for Talia and Danielle.

An explosion cut through the silence, and the ship shuddered beneath Danielle's feet. The *Phillipa* had resumed her attack.

A man in a red sash moved to intercept Danielle. Where some of the crew had decorated the cords on their sleeves with beads and other trinkets, this one wore gold coins with square holes in the center. A sparse beard shadowed his jawline.

He drew a short, curved saber, which he pointed at Danielle. Though his blade was shorter, his size made his reach a match for her own. His broad shoulders suggested greater strength as well.

"Surrender the mermaid and you may live." Between his heavy, rolling accent and Danielle's blocked ears, he repeated himself twice before she understood.

Danielle answered by raising her own sword. She had worked with Talia over the past year, but she was no match for a trained swordsman. She tried to circle past him, but there was no clear path. The rest of the crew were shaking off the effects of Morveren's song. Some hurried to their posts, trying to respond to the *Phillipa*. Others spread out to fight Danielle and her friends.

"Talia?" Danielle called, keeping her back to the mainmast. Talia still stood at the ladder from the gundeck, keeping the men below from following while fighting anyone who approached too closely. She almost appeared to be dancing with the Hiladi crew, but each time she spun, another man fell back.

Danielle's opponent swung, trying to beat her sword aside. The steel blade rang against the glass, jarring her wrist and forearm. Danielle sidestepped and blocked a second swing. He was trying to disarm her, not kill her. Some Hiladi men had strong beliefs against striking women. Hopefully this was a fervent believer.

Danielle pursed her lips, concentrating on his sword and his stance. She allowed her guard to fall slightly, as though she were growing tired.

He took the bait, slashing at her blade. Danielle released her grip a moment before he struck. Her sword spun away, stabbing the deck. Expecting resistance, he stumbled forward, off-balance. Danielle grabbed his sword arm and slammed her knee into his stomach. He doubled over, and she pushed him headfirst into the mast.

She wrenched her sword free and ran.

Snow pulled a sharpened steel snowflake from a hidden pocket on her shirt, flinging it at the next man who tried to intercept Danielle. He went down howling and clutching his leg. A wide swing of Danielle's blade tore a bloody gash in another man's shirt, driving him back. Talia dispatched a third, and then they were leaping overboard.

The impact of the water stunned her, and her sword slipped from her grasp. Danielle ducked beneath the surface, salt water stinging her eyes as she searched. *There!* She spotted the glass blade sinking through the water. She kicked as hard as she could, but the sword was already beneath her, falling faster than she could swim. Her chest ached, but she continued downward, even as the sword shrank away.

Lannadae shot past her. The mermaid snatched the sword and doubled back. Her other hand caught Danielle's wrist, pulling her up and away from the Hiladi ship.

They reached the surface a short distance ahead of Talia and Snow. Behind them, the crew of the Hiladi ship appeared to be more worried about escape than pursuit. As Danielle watched, the *Phillipa* put another hole through the hull near the bow.

"Thank you." Danielle's hands shook as she took back her sword. "This is . . . it's all I have left of my mother."

"It's beautiful," said Lannadae. "I saw you fight. Would you—" She dipped beneath the water, then tried again, apparently overcoming her shyness. "Would you mind if I composed a story about it?"

Danielle smiled. "Just don't let Armand learn how close I came to being killed by some Hiladi sailor."

"Hiladi captain, actually," said Snow, swimming alongside. "The red sash is a symbol of rank. He's young for the rank, but those gold coins also mark him as a noble."

Talia splashed them both as she swam past. "Could we chat later? You're still within range of their crossbows."

Danielle sheathed her sword and took Lannadae's hand, allowing the mermaid to tow her toward the boat. "Is everyone all right?"

The water swallowed Talia's response, but she appeared unharmed. As for Snow, she merely grinned and said, "That was fun!"

CHAPTER 7

EVEN THROUGH THE WORMWAX plugs, the sound of the cannons made Danielle wince as she climbed over the railing onto the *Phillipa*. The Hiladi ship was moving away, aided by a strong wind. Captain Hephyra stood by the cannons, shouting at the men to quicken their pace.

Hephyra shoved one of the gunners aside, grabbing a cannonball one-handed and ramming it home. If she could have, Danielle had no doubt Hephyra would have simply thrown the cannonballs at the other ship.

"I think she's annoyed," Snow commented.

The *Phillipa* was in far worse condition than the Hiladi ship had been. Sand and splinters littered the deck. One of the cannons had been destroyed, the wooden frame cracked and broken beneath the barrel. The dinghy where Lannadae had slept was in pieces. Several men lay groaning on the deck, and pools of blood darkened the sand.

Danielle dug a finger in her ear, trying to scrape out the worst of the worm goop. "Where did the sand come from? The Hiladi ship was covered in it as well."

"The crew spreads it across the deck," Talia said. "To keep the men from losing their footing in the blood."

Danielle swallowed and moved toward the closest of the wounded crew, a man whose legs had been crushed when the cannon tore free. "Snow?"

"I've got him," said Snow, stepping past.

"They're moving out of range," shouted one of the gunners.

Hephyra snatched the linstock from his hand and fired another cannon. The shot fell short, splashing in the water behind the retreating ship. "Get back here, you miserable cowards! I'm not finished with you yet!" Hephyra's breathing was hoarse, and she limped as she walked toward Danielle. "Seedless bastards came upon us without warning. I hope you found what you were looking for."

"Morveren is with Lannadae down in the boat," Danielle said. "Are you all right?"

"They hurt my ship." Hephyra dropped to her knees, pressing her hands to the deck. The contact appeared to bring her strength. "Iron shot tears right through the wood, but we'll be all right." She looked up and shouted, "Bring the cutter on board, and get this ship ready to sail! Anyone with nothing better to do can haul themselves down to the bilge pumps."

Danielle returned to the rail, trying to stay out of the way as the men prepared to bring the boat on board.

"Where will you be putting the mermaids?" Hephyra asked, coming up beside her.

Morveren lay sprawled in the bottom of the cutter, her head in Lannadae's lap. She was still panting for breath, and her skin was flushed. James and Douglas remained in the boat, securing the ropes in preparation for hauling the cutter back on board.

"Morveren needs rest," Danielle said. After living alone for so long, the mermaid would probably need time to acclimate to so many people. "Somewhere quiet and wet."

Hephyra shook her head. "Unless she means to sleep in the bilgewater, I've got nothing for her."

Below, Morveren stirred and pulled herself upright. "Don't worry about me, Princess. I'm used to sleeping on rock and mud, remember? Tell your crew to sail southwest until you clear the rocks and the mist. Then northwest."

"Why northwest?" Hephyra asked. "What do you hope to find there?"

"My home. If you want to find my granddaughter, there are things I'll need." Morveren lay back. "Food would be nice, too."

The royal cabin in the *Phillipa* was smaller than Danielle's chambers back at the palace, but even the closet was more luxurious than anything she had known in her childhood. The room was at the aft of the ship, and it even boasted a glass window looking out at the sea. Stub the cat lay sprawled on a leather-padded bench in front of the window, basking in the sun. Large cots took up both walls, and a trunk sat to one side of the door.

Morveren studied one of the cots. Her body was longer than a human's, but the amputation of her fins meant she should be able to curl onto the mattress without too much discomfort. She grabbed the side and pulled herself up, bending her tails and tucking the stumps beneath the rumpled covers. *For warmth or from shame at her deformity?* Danielle wondered.

Morveren's nose wrinkled. "This smells like birds."

"The mattress is stuffed with down," Danielle said.

Morveren settled back with a long, satisfied groan. "I'll make a new deal with you. I'll give you anything you want, and in exchange you'll provide me with one of these beds for my own."

Lannadae sat beside the head of the cot, her tails tucked beneath the mattress. "Will those Hiladi come after us again?"

"Probably," said Snow. She waited for Talia to enter, then pulled the door shut behind her. "The captain of that ship was no mercenary."

"A Hiladi ship with red sails?" Talia asked. "One that attacks without warning, firing upon a ship flying Lorindar's colors? What else could they be?"

"Their captain was a Hiladi nobleman," Snow said.

Danielle stared. "You said that before. How do you know?"

"I was born in Allesandria," said Snow, digging her little finger into her ear and scraping out a chunk of wormwax. "Our kingdom borders Hilad. In my great-grandfather's time, we were a part of the Hiladi Empire. I saw the man you fought. The honor of wearing gold is reserved for Hiladi royals. No mercenary would violate that rule."

"Why not?" asked Danielle.

"Fear and honor. But mostly fear." Snow sat down on the bench and scratched Stub's neck. "The punishment for impersonating a member of the Hiladi imperial family takes a full month, as various parts of the offender are removed and fed to different sea creatures."

"Is that where Lirea got the idea to do *that*?" Lannadae asked, staring at Morveren's tails. "From her Hiladi prince?"

"Who can say?" Morveren pulled the covers higher. "Lirea is sick. I doubt she even knew what she was doing when she crippled me."

"That doesn't change what she did," said Talia.

"If my magic hurt her in this way, then is it any less than I deserve?" asked Morveren.

Talia turned away. "Maybe not. But Beatrice didn't deserve it."

Stub stretched and stood. His ears flattened when he spotted Morveren and Lannadae. He trotted over and hopped onto the cot, sniffing Morveren's tails.

"When I was a child, a minor prince of Hilad attacked one of our border towns," said Snow. "My mother seared the flesh from his body, then used gold wire to lash his bones into a birdcage. She hung the cage in her throne room when the Hiladi ambassador arrived a week later. She even captured a little songbird and cast a geis to make sure he would spend the whole time whistling, just to draw the ambassador's attention to the cage."

She sighed. "Afterward, she gave the bird and cage to me. He used to sing every morning to wake me up."

Silence filled the room. Eventually, Morveren said, "You had an unusual upbringing, child."

Talia snorted. "You have no idea."

"This makes no sense," said Danielle. "Lirea killed a Hiladi prince. Why would another royal help her?"

"His name is Varisto," Lannadae said, her voice quiet. "I met him once. He was Prince Gustan's younger brother. It was springtime, and I had gone with Lirea to meet her prince. Varisto was arguing with Gustan. He left when he saw us."

Danielle silently scolded Stub, stopping him from trying to take a bite out of Morveren's left tail. She sent him back to his sunbeam on the bench, then asked, "Why would he attack the *Phillipa*?"

"You wouldn't ask that if you had been raised noble." Talia paced along the carpet. "Gustan's death put him in line to inherit the empire. He might feel indebted to Lirea for helping him toward that goal. Hiladi are fanatical when it comes to repaying debts."

"But Gustan was his brother." Danielle knew her protests were naive. She had seen enough squabbling at court to know how far people would go for power, but knowing and understanding were very different things.

"He wants to kill me too, doesn't he?" asked Lannadae. She had grown quiet, curled at the head of Morveren's cot. "Lirea killed his brother, so he'll repay her by killing her sister."

Morveren reached over to comb her fingers through Lannadae's hair. "I'll never let that happen, little one."

"I hated her for what she did to me." Lannadae bowed her head. "I hated being trapped in that cave. Having to stay hidden, feeling afraid every time a ship passed by and wondering if each day would be the day Lirea found me. When I went to sleep in the winter, a part of me hoped I wouldn't wake up. I just didn't want to be afraid anymore."

Morveren's eyes had filled with tears. She wiped them away with one hand. "I'll find a way to save you both." She looked at Snow. "But I'll need help."

"I'll do whatever you need if it helps Beatrice," said Snow.

"Good." Morveren studied Snow. "How skilled a witch are you?"

"Sorceress, not witch." Snow grinned. "I was skilled enough to chase off Lirea's air spirit, wasn't I?"

For the first time since returning to the ship, Morveren smiled. "You'll have to show me what you can do, once I've rested. For now I hope you'll excuse me. That song took a great deal out of me."

"Let me know if you need anything," said Danielle, rising to leave. The others followed, even Lannadae, who appeared troubled. "What is it?" Danielle asked.

Lannadae waited until the door was closed behind them. "She wants to save Lirea. I know I should too, but I don't. She killed Levanna. She killed our father. How am I supposed to feel safe while Lirea still lives?"

Only hours before, Lannadae had been leaping and splashing in the water like a child. Now she appeared lost, haunted by fears and memories no child should have to face. Danielle searched for words of comfort, but found none.

"Did you ever fear your stepsisters would kill you?" Lannadae asked.

"Once, yes."

Lannadae looked up at her. "What did you do?"

"I fought them," Danielle said. "And I found friends to help protect me." She managed a smile for Lannadae's sake. "The same friends who are protecting you. We'll keep you safe, Lannadae. I promise."

Snow sat in the cutter, flirting with James as she finished off a second peach-filled pastry from dinner. One hand rested on the ropes securing the front of the boat to the deck. She smiled at James, then licked the crumbs from her fingers. He was supposed to be swabbing the rest of the sand and water from the ship, but for some reason he appeared to be having trouble concentrating.

Snow sucked a bit of fruit from her index finger. If poor James clutched that mop any more tightly, he would snap the handle. She stretched, then lay back to rest against the canvas folded over half of the boat. When that didn't work, she crossed her legs on the edge.

James dropped his mop.

Victory! Snow fought to keep from smiling. Never underestimate the power of bare feet and a little ankle.

"So this is how a sorceress spends her time?" Morveren climbed the chocks and grabbed the edge of the cutter, grunting in pain as she pulled herself inside. She straddled the bench, resting her tails in the puddles on the bottom of the boat.

"Are you all right?" Snow asked.

"Too much time out of water," Morveren said. "Our bones aren't as strong as yours. We're built for the lightness of the sea. Up here, I feel as though my bones have turned to rock."

"I could mix up a willow tea that might help," Snow offered.

"It's no less than I deserve." Morveren sank down, resting on the bench. "My magic isn't what it once was, and I spent most of that strength protecting you and your friends. When we reach my home, I'll need you to help me unravel the defenses I left behind."

Snow glanced at James, but Morveren's arrival had clearly reversed the effects of Snow's charms. He was hard at work, though his face remained slightly flushed. "What kind of defenses?"

"Nothing as powerful as Lirea's air spirits," Morveren said. "What type of magic do you practice?"

Snow shrugged. "I use mirrors a lot, but I've studied a little of everything."

"A dabbler, you mean." Morveren snorted.

Snow reached down to touch the water puddled in the bottom of the boat. She whispered a quick spell, and frost spread across the surface. Morveren yelped and yanked up her tails. Bits of ice rimmed her scales.

"Not bad," Morveren said, rubbing the ice off. She turned around, searching the ship. "That cat. Can you command him to come to us?"

Stub was trotting along the starboard rail, a bit of fish

clutched in his teeth. "Command him?" Snow repeated. "You haven't known many cats, have you?"

"Magic is about strength of will. If yours is no stronger than that of a ship's cat, how can you hope to overpower my old spells, let alone subdue my granddaughter?"

"Talia usually does most of the subduing." Snow brushed her fingertips over her choker. "Mirror, mirror, shining bright. Bring that cat into the light."

Glimmers of sunlight danced along the railing, guided by her mirrors. Stub's tail lashed as he watched the lights jump down to the deck. He shifted his weight, then pounced. The lights raced away, Stub in pursuit. Moments later, Stub stood on the side of the cutter. He sat and lifted one paw, then the other, searching for the lights, which had mysteriously vanished.

"I told you to command him, not trick him with your mirrors," Morveren said.

"He's here, isn't he?" Snow said, more sharply than she intended.

"True enough. You did well, considering your youth."

Snow stopped herself from touching her hair. Her appearance made her look older than most of the people on this ship. "My youth?"

"I've been practicing magic for over two centuries," Morveren replied. "You've spent perhaps twenty years? Thirty?"

"Perhaps."

"You lack subtlety. If your spells were songs, you would be shouting at the top of your voice. I noticed it before, when you wove your shield against my voice. And your mirrors make powerful tools, but you use them as a crutch. Whoever taught you should never have allowed you to become so dependent on—"

"Nobody taught me."

Morveren leaned back, studying Snow as if for the first time. When she spoke, the scorn was gone from her voice. "You learned on your own? And you didn't kill yourself in the process?"

"Not yet," Snow said.

"You might have potential after all." She was smiling as she spoke. "Close your eyes."

"Why?"

Morveren splashed her. "Do you want to learn or not?"

Grudgingly, Snow closed her eyes. "Now what?"

"Now you listen to my song."

Snow waited. She could hear the waves breaking against the hull. A pair of deckhands walked by, whispering about the Hiladi ship. Pulleys squeaked as the crew trimmed the sails. "You're not singing."

"You're not listening," Morveren countered. "You're trying too hard. You're so tense, like a child who believes she can shit pearls if she pushes hard enough."

Snow opened one eye. "Undine can do that?"

"No. But my older brothers told cruel stories when I was young. Now shut up and listen."

"Easy for you to say." Snow tugged her earlobes, trying to clear the congested feeling. "You're not the one with worm goop corking your ears."

"So stop using them."

Resting her hands on her thighs, Snow tried again. She had learned at a young age to see things that weren't there. It was the only way to detect the spies her mother sent to watch her. Imps and minor demons, little more than flickering afterimages. They weren't invisible, not in the traditional sense. Rather, they hid among the real, blending into their surroundings. The trick was to push the real world out of focus in order to see what lay beyond.

She tried to do the same with the noises around her. Voices faded to a buzz. The waves melted into a steady crash of sound. She could hear the drumbeat of her own heart. Even that sound faded, the thrum of her blood becoming little more than a distant rhythm.

For a moment, she thought she heard it. Humming, faint and fragile as a whispered breath through a flute. Snow stretched out with her senses, but the sound slipped away.

"Subtle as an amorous squid, you are," Morveren said. "You waste more magic searching for my song than I've used for the actual spell. You overwhelm it with your clumsiness."

Snow stuck out her tongue, keeping her eyes closed. Stillness had never come easily to her, but she did her best. Slowly, the humming returned. A simple scale in a minor key, rising and falling again and again.

"Good. Open your eyes."

Snow found Stub sitting on the edge of the boat, head tilted to one side, the tip of his tongue protruding from his mouth. "How did you do that? Your song wasn't even strong enough to command a butterfly."

"Lannadae told me what happened when you brought Talia and Danielle down to meet her. Lannadae was afraid, and she attacked them. Lannadae is undine. She's stronger than any human, but Talia beat her. How?"

"To start with, Talia carries enough weapons to arm a battalion." Snow raised her hand before Morveren could speak. "Fine, so strength isn't everything."

Morveren reached out to tickle Stub's ear. "It only takes a single thought to direct the mind. Your job is to provide the right thought. Sing with me."

"What?"

Morveren hummed out loud this time. "Sing with me." She spoke without interrupting her song.

Snow nodded, humming along with the mermaid. A single scale, reminding her of music lessons when she was young. That tutor's breath had smelled like old fish too.

Morveren sang lower. Snow matched her. Morveren changed keys in midscale, jumping to a higher pitch. Snow grinned and chased her song. Their voices grew quieter.

"Sing to the cat," Morveren said. "Don't let me hear."

Snow did her best. She lowered her voice even more and concentrated on Stub. His ear twitched.

"Good. Now weave a vision into the music and scare him off."

She imagined a troll sneaking up to yank Stub's tail. Between one note and the next, she shoved that vision at the cat.

Stub's claws dug into the wood, and he scrambled away, hissing.

"You sang louder at the moment of sending," Morveren said. "I could see that hairy beast as clearly as the cat did." She pointed to the aft of the ship. "They say a true master will weave a song loud enough to deafen your helmsman there, and she would sing it so precisely that the man next to him would never hear a single note."

Snow flexed her legs, trying to work the stiffness from her muscles. She glanced at the stumps of Morveren's tails. "If you're so skilled, why couldn't you stop Lirea from doing that to you?"

Morveren bowed her head, staring at the lumps of scars and misshapen scales. "I never claimed to be a master. Her wind spirits took me by surprise, and her madness gave her strength. I was able to stop her from killing me, but that was all. Even if I had the strength to overpower her, I would have destroyed her mind in the process. That's the other risk of sheer, brute force. You may crush that which you hope to control."

"Sounds like Talia again," Snow commented.

Morveren lay back and smiled. "Now see if you can persuade that poor beast to bring me some of that fish."

By the following morning, Stub refused to come out on the deck if Snow was anywhere to be found.

Morveren had assigned one task after another. She would splash water onto the side of the cutter, telling Snow to freeze a single drop without affecting the rest. When Snow finally managed that, Morveren sent her off to cast an illusion only one person would see. That took most of the evening, but eventually Snow returned, ex-

hausted and exhilarated, leaving behind one very confused chef.

Morveren divided her time between rest, Lannadae,
and Snow. Currently she and Lannadae were shut away
in Danielle's cabin, enjoying a morning nap. How much
sleep did mermaids need, anyway?

Snow turned her attention back to the carpenter who
was working to repair a section of the starboard railing.
Morveren hadn't given her any more lessons, so Snow
had been making up her own. She hummed to herself,
gathering her magic for another attempt.

"There you are." Danielle smiled as she approached.
Talia followed close behind. Danielle carried Stub in her
arms, but the cat hissed and fled when he spotted Snow.

"Can this wait?" Snow asked, still concentrating on
the carpenter. "I'm *this* close to making him pick his
nose."

Danielle held up a biscuit. "I'm glad to hear you
missed breakfast for something important."

Snow tried one last time, but the pick turned into a
scratch at the last moment, and she gave up. She scowled
at the carpenter, then grabbed the biscuit. Her mouth
watered at the taste of raisins and cinnamon. "Thank
you," she mumbled between bites. "I've been practicing,
that's all."

"So we've noticed," said Danielle. "You wouldn't
know why Bradley refused to cook this morning, would
you? He was saying something about last night's peas
screaming in pain and trying to climb out of the pot
when he boiled them."

Snow tried not to laugh and nearly choked on her
biscuit.

"The poor man's still praying for forgiveness for every
legume he's ever tortured," Danielle added, lips curled
as if she couldn't decide whether to smile or scold.

"Captain Hephyra says the water ahead grows thick
with seaweed." Talia twisted her hair into a braid as
she spoke. "It's slowing our progress, and it could be
dangerous."

"It is dangerous," Morveren said, her voice as clear as if she stood beside them. Morveren crawled across the deck, followed closely by her granddaughter. "We're here."

"Where is here?" Talia leaned out to study the water ahead. "This is practically a swamp."

Snow joined Morveren at the rail. Up ahead, clumps of dark red plants carpeted the waves. From here, it looked thick enough to stand on.

"It's gotten a little overgrown," Morveren commented.

"A little?" repeated Talia. "That morass could sink an unwary ship."

"That's the idea." The muscles in Morveren's arms were like ropes as she pulled herself higher. "I like my privacy."

The crew was already trimming the sails, bringing the *Phillipa* around so she skimmed the edge of the seaweed.

"I'll need help getting through this mess," Morveren said. "I enchanted the plants to stop anyone who tries to get too close."

"Why would you do that?" asked Talia.

Morveren looked at Snow. "I'm sure you've collected other trinkets over the years, in addition to that mirror you spoke of. Would you let strangers snoop through your things? Unfortunately, the plants have spread in my absence. And there may be ... other dangers. I never expected to be away so long."

Snow hoped her eagerness didn't show. Enchanted plants? She knew the fairy folk used similar magic, but they guarded those secrets closely. "What other dangers?"

"That depends on how much those plants have grown," said Morveren. "You'll need to escort me to the bottom. Have you ever tried shapeshifting?"

Her stomach tightened. "I've tried, yes." The books she had inherited from her mother included spells for changing the body. That was how her mother had fooled Snow into taking a poisoned apple. Snow would have seen through mere illusion. Her mother had physically transformed herself to lull Snow's suspicions. But Snow had never been able to master that trick. She had tried a great many times over the past year, usually with insects. The most she had managed to do was change a living beetle into a dead beetle.

"I should go," Lannadae said. "There's no need for more magic. I can help you through the plants."

Morveren smiled and kissed Lannadae's hair. "Thank you, Granddaughter. But you lack the skill to help me. Don't worry about your friend. She will be—"

"Don't worry?" Talia asked, moving to stand between them, facing Morveren. "Look at what happened to the last person you changed with your magic. If you think you're going to lay that kind of curse on Snow—"

Morveren scowled at Snow. "How do you tolerate such ignorance?" To Talia, she said, "The spell I cast on Lirea was meant to last forever. Such a change carries a much greater cost. Snow will be undine for less than a day. She can cast that spell herself once she learns how, and with far less exertion than she used against your Hiladi friends."

Talia looked ready to toss Morveren overboard, but Snow spoke up first. "I want to learn this, Talia."

"She destroyed Lirea's mind," Talia said. "You can't risk—"

"She didn't mean to," Snow countered. "Morveren tried to help her. It's not her fault Gustan betrayed her."

"My parents tried to use magic to 'help' me, too. Remember?" Talia's voice was cold. "There's always a cost."

"Then I'll pay it," Snow said. "Wouldn't you do the same to help Beatrice?"

"There will be pain," Morveren said.

"I've eaten Talia's blackened nadif chicken. I can handle pain." Snow grinned at Talia. "Don't worry. I'll be careful."

"That would be a first," Talia muttered.

Snow stuck out her tongue.

"I'll tell Hephyra what's happening," Danielle said.

"She knows." Snow patted the railing. "This ship is her tree, remember? You think she hasn't heard every word we've spoken?" With that, she handed her hat to Talia, tugged off her shoes, and jumped overboard.

Even here on the edge of the seaweed the plants tangled her legs, slowing her plunge. She could feel Morveren's enchantment within the ropelike stalks, trying to pull her down, but the magic was weakest here. She kicked to the surface and tugged her feet free just as Morveren dove into the water beside her.

"Hurry back, Grandmother," Lannadae called.

From the rear of the ship, Captain Hephyra waved at them both. "I'll bring her about and anchor in clearer water, where the chain won't tangle in the weeds. Try not to get yourselves eaten."

"That's the least of our worries," Morveren called out. She swam to Snow. "Tell me what you know of shapeshifting."

Snow's heart pounded. "I know the theory. Runes traced on the skin to shape the desired form, and then—"

"Undine don't spend a lot of time drawing," Morveren said dryly. "Runes are only one way of shaping the magic." She reached down with one hand, flinching as she twisted a chipped scale from her hip. "Unless you want those trousers bonded to your flesh, you should probably be rid of them."

Snow held her breath and bobbed beneath the waves, kicking her trousers and undergarments free. There was something delightfully wicked about floating half-naked in the sea. She adjusted her belt, tightening it higher over her shirt. The sunlight reflecting off the surface should preserve her modesty from anyone on the ship.

Snow bundled her things into a ball and pressed them against the side of the ship. A quick spell spread a patch of ice from her clothes, freezing them to the hull to await her return.

"If you humans weren't so skinny, maybe you wouldn't need all those clothes," Morveren muttered. "It's a wonder you don't freeze to death come winter."

The seaweed tickled Snow's skin behind the knees, making her giggle.

"Stop that." Morveren pressed the scale into Snow's hand. "Cut a line down the inside of each leg, deep enough to draw blood. Don't worry, sharks won't come anywhere near this place."

Snow touched the scale's edge to the inside of her thigh. Gritting her teeth, she pressed until the scale broke the skin, then sliced downward. Blood was a common ingredient for many kinds of magic, but usually she found a less sensitive place from which to acquire it. Breath hissed as she finished the cut. She paddled in place, letting the initial pain pass before starting on the other leg. She studied the scale. The edge was chipped ragged. No wonder it hurt. "My knife would be less painful."

"The scale gives your body a taste of the form it's to assume," Morveren said, swimming around behind Snow. She grabbed the back of Snow's shirt, supporting her while she recovered. Even with her tails gone, Morveren was a strong swimmer, and the fins along the side of her stumps kept them both afloat. Supported by the water, she moved more easily than she had on board the ship.

Snow's blood drifted through the water like smoke. "I think I like the runes better."

Morveren laughed. "If magic were easy, everyone would do it."

The second cut was harder. Now that she knew how much it would sting, she had to force herself to press hard enough to cut the skin. Morveren held her until she finished.

"Press your legs together and try to cast the spell. The pain will help you focus. Concentrate on the shape you wish to assume."

Snow nodded and began to chant the words she had learned from her mother's spellbooks.

"Don't speak," Morveren said. "Sing. All the spoken words in the world can't match the power of a single song. Sing for your ears alone, as you sang to the cat. Force your flesh to obey."

Snow obeyed, improvising a simple melody to match the words. She could feel the skin of her legs tugging together, but it wasn't enough. Then Morveren joined her voice to Snow's.

"It's working!" She could feel her legs clinging together, as though a single scab bound both cuts.

"Brace yourself, child."

Pain erupted down Snow's legs. Her body pulled taut, breaking free of Morveren's grip. Scales pierced her skin in a thousand places. She tried to scream, and seawater flooded her mouth. Her joints popped and her bones smashed together. Muscles tore and re-formed. She bent double, the sea closing over her head.

Morveren hauled her to the surface, and Snow gasped for breath.

"You *can* breathe water, you know," said Morveren.

Tears streamed down her face, blurring her vision. Already the pain was fading. "Why can't I stop crying?"

"Larger tear ducts," Morveren said. "It's one of the ways we rid our bodies of excess salt."

Snow swallowed and tried to stop herself from shaking.

"You did well, child."

Snow lay back and raised her tail out of the water. Her scales were deep red, like Morveren's own. She laughed, though the sound that emerged was closer to a hiccup. "I did. But why only one tail? Why not two, like you?"

"Because this is the form you imagined," Morveren said. "I confess, I pushed you toward this shape myself. Swimming with two tails is more complicated, and I don't have time to teach you to use them."

Snow spun in the water and threw her arms around Morveren. "Thank you!"

Morveren laughed and pushed her away. "Enough of this. Are you going to help me tame this garden or not?"

Snow ran her hands over her body. Her shirt felt uncomfortably tight against her torso. "I'm plump!"

"You're healthy," Morveren said. "Follow me. If we're lucky, you'll only need to deal with the plants. Use your magic to calm them. I'll do what I can to help."

"What if we're unlucky?"

"Don't fight unless you have to. The magic around this place has been mostly dormant. Whatever you face, simply lull it back to sleep. And don't forget to breathe."

Snow gave her new tail an experimental kick. Long fins rippled along the sides, but she wasn't sure how to control them. She dove beneath the surface. Her body felt buoyant, dragging her toward the surface. She kicked harder, paddling with her arms to steer herself after Morveren.

Her chest was already starting to ache. She opened her mouth and took a cautious swallow of seawater.

Instantly she began to gag. She doubled over, coughing and fighting to breathe.

Water filled her lungs, and the coughing slowed. Cautiously, she tried to exhale. The skin on either side of her neck parted, and cool water flowed from her gills. She tried again, fighting the instinct to drink rather than breathe. Eventually she managed to take another breath of water.

Her chest felt stiff and heavy. She had an easier time swimming now that she had expelled most of the air from her body. She could still feel a small bubble trapped in her chest. She belched it out and drew a full breath.

The water tasted like spoiled vegetables. Something to do with the seaweed?

She pressed her fingers to her gills. Three long gashes stretched along each side of her neck, following the curve of her jawline. She plucked off one of her mirrors and held it out, trying to see the red gills beneath the flaps of skin.

A soft, two-toned call drew her attention to Morveren, who had grabbed one of the stalks. Thin red fronds clung to her skin. Morveren sang to the plant, a gentle song with a thread of magic woven through the notes. Slowly, the fronds released their grip.

A tendril of seaweed brushed across Snow's stomach. She tried to push it aside, but the plant was stiffer than it appeared. A second reached toward her arm.

Snow replaced her mirror and did her best to mimic Morveren's song. By the time she mastered the trick of singing underwater, the seaweed had begun to pull her down. But the leaves relaxed as soon as she switched to a lullaby she had heard Danielle sing to Jakob.

Commanding the plants was actually easier than controlling animals or humans. She grinned like a child as the seaweed fell away.

She passed Morveren, clearing a path. As they swam deeper, she activated the magic of her choker, surrounding herself in soft, blue-tinged light. She floated in an endless forest of undulating plants, which concealed both sky and seabed. Small yellow fish flitted through the leaves.

A clump of seaweed looped around her tail. Snow turned her song on the weeds, but nothing happened. Twisting about, Snow saw another tangle of red reaching past her toward Morveren. The leaves and vines twined together, their form almost human.

Snow grabbed her knife from her belt and slashed at the vines. The figure held its shape, squeezing Snow's tail while it stretched to grab Morveren. This would be one of the other dangers Morveren had mentioned, then.

Snow stabbed her blade into the center of the form and flicked a tiny catch on the cross guard. A metal plate in the center of the guard swiveled aside, revealing a small mirror. Snow sang again, using the mirror to carry her song into the heart of her attacker.

The seaweed shuddered, then relaxed. Leaves began

to drift away. The vines Snow had cut before fell through the water.

Morveren swam down and plunged her hands into the figure from behind. Snow caught a hint of something cold and hungry, and then the seaweed unraveled completely, becoming simple plants again.

Morveren clasped Snow's arm, then swam lower.

Snow continued to sing a path through the seaweed. Twice more they were attacked by the strange figures. Her scales protected her tail, but her arms burned where the leaves cut her skin. Each time she used her knife to enhance her song, stilling the attackers long enough for Morveren to destroy them.

Eventually the plants began to thin. Snow's light broke through the forest to illuminate a wrecked ship on the rocks below. Debris covered the seabed: old barrels, a length of chain, even the bones of the former crew. Mollusks covered the ship's hull. Both masts were broken near the base, and a large gash tore through the port side, near the back.

The shape and size of the hull marked it as a Lyskaran cargo ship. From the position and rakish angle of the foremast, this ship had to be close to a hundred years old. Nothing grew around the wrecked ship, and as Snow swam closer, she could see where Morveren had set white stones in a ring, a magical fence to keep her plants from devouring her home.

The water was colder here, and it tasted of silt. Snow followed Morveren through the broken hull into what would have been the main hold.

Morveren was already racing about like an oversized minnow, shooing away an eel, wiping silt and sand from crude shelves, and inspecting every bit of her former home.

The lay of the ship meant the starboard side of the hull served as the floor. Shelves made from broken planks lined the walls, nailed into place wherever the structure of the ship was still strong enough to support them. Jars and bowls lined the shelves. Dark algae covered most of the wood, making the water taste thick and sour. A white patch on the walls and floor near the far corner turned out to be an overgrown bed of those flowering worms Morveren liked. Several of the jars had apparently fallen, their remains broken and half buried.

Morveren turned to Snow, her hands and fingers dancing. She hummed a quick-paced tune with no consistent melody.

Was this how the undine communicated underwater? Snow spread her hands and shrugged.

Morveren swam to a nearby shelf and grabbed a small, sealed jar. She scraped away a layer of algae with her thumbnail, then held the jar to Snow's light. Apparently satisfied, she turned and smashed the jar against the wall.

Bubbles of air exploded from the jar. Morveren poked a finger into the largest. Slowly, the bubble expanded until it filled the upper part of the hold.

Morveren spat great lungfuls of water, then gasped for breath. "I apologize. I forgot you wouldn't know how to speak."

Snow was too busy coughing to answer. Water exploded from her mouth and nose. She felt as if she were vomiting up half the sea.

Morveren chuckled and swam toward the back of the hold, where strands of blue ropes formed a crude curtain. Snow felt the tickle of magic as Morveren passed through the ropes.

Snow floated on her back and waited for her stomach to stop spasming. Eventually, she felt well enough to look around. She could still feel water in her chest, but so long as she didn't think about it too hard, it didn't seem to bother her in this body. She just couldn't inhale as deeply as she was used to doing.

She pushed toward the shelves and brushed her fingers over a slender green jar. The magic worked into the glass made her jump. She could feel—no, *hear*—the presence of life within the jar, though it appeared empty. She picked it up and inspected the lid, which was sealed in place with some sort of wax.

"Don't open that," Morveren said as she returned. Her voice was stronger than before, and her face was flushed. She appeared almost euphoric. She set a small sack on the floor and swam over to join Snow.

"What is it?" Snow asked, cradling the jar in both hands.

"Some of the ship's crew refused to abandon their ship after passing on. Nasty, vindictive men who did everything they could to interfere with my work and drive me away. I hate to think what they were like in life." She took the jar from Snow's hand and returned it to the shelf. "That's what tried to kill us out there. A few of them must have escaped since the last time I was here."

"I've never felt magic like this." Snow had fought spirits before. The last time had cost her seven years of her life. Yet Morveren had dozens of such jars, not counting any that might be hidden in other parts of the ship. A vessel this size could have carried a crew of a hundred.

"The soul jars keep them from mischief until they're ready to move on," Morveren said. "These spells are the basis for the knife I made for Lirea."

"Do all of these jars hold trapped souls?"

Morveren laughed. "Not all. Some are ingredients for various spells. Others are more mundane." She grabbed a clay pot and offered it to Snow. "Dried snails. They're delicious."

"No, thank you." Snow was still studying the soul jar. She could see bits of hair or string pressed into the wax. "How do you know when the souls are ready to move on?"

"So many questions." Morveren dragged a metal chest from just beyond the curtain. "I promise I'll teach you what I can. But not here. Your friends are waiting, and you don't want to be trapped this far from the surface when your spell wears off."

"What's in there?" Snow asked, pointing to the chest. When Morveren turned away, Snow grabbed another soul jar and tucked it into the front of her shirt. The jar pressed uncomfortably against her chest, but the added fat of her mermaid form provided some cushioning.

"Memories." Morveren ran a finger over the pitted metal, then opened the lid. She pulled out a tiny necklace of yellow and green stones. "This was Lannadae's. I made it for her when she was born, but she kept trying to swallow it."

She looped the necklace around her wrist. Next she retrieved a tiny doll. The upper torso appeared to be made of woven seaweed. The lower portion was covered in tiny purple scales, ending in a thin shell carved into the shape of the tail fin. "These were the first scales Lirea shed. Her mother collected them, and I sewed them into this doll. Baby scales are softer and much easier to work with."

"It looks like it's missing a head," Snow said.

"My sewing was no match for Lirea's teething phase. I never got around to fixing this." Morveren smiled as she shut the chest. "She was such a sweet child. So loving, with such potential. Her voice held incredible power. I'm afraid she took advantage of that gift. Her parents spoiled her shamelessly. Even I had a hard time resisting her."

"Did you ever teach her magic?" Snow asked.

"I tried." Morveren brought the doll to her mouth, using her teeth to tighten a loose thread. "Lirea had talent, even more than her sisters, but she lacked the desire. Magic requires more than mere skill. It requires love. I hoped she would change her mind as she grew older. There was so much I wanted to pass along."

"I wish my mother had felt the same way. She would have killed me if she knew I was sneaking in to read her spellbooks." There were times Snow wondered if that discovery was what had first led to her mother's attempts on Snow's life. The stories claimed she was jealous of Snow's beauty, and that was certainly true. But had jealousy of her daughter's power played an even greater role?

"She didn't want you to learn?" Morveren sounded surprised.

"My mother didn't like to share." Pushing those memories aside, Snow reached out to touch the doll. "If these are Lirea's scales, we should be able to use them to find her."

"That's right." Morveren released the doll. The carved fin sent it spiraling through the water to the floor. "But the scales are old, and the connection is weak."

"Blood creates false life," Snow said. "That should strengthen the bond long enough for us to cast our spell."

"Very good." Morveren gestured for her to proceed.

Snow hesitated. "Normally I would use my mirrors to—"

"No mirrors." Morveren yanked Snow's hand away from her choker. "You're too strong for such shortcuts."

Snow's face grew warm. "Thank you."

Morveren squeezed her hand. "Thank *you*, child."

CHAPTER 8

D ANIELLE HAD REMOVED HER BRACELET
and now cradled the small mirror in both hands.
She sat with her back to the oil lamp, her body blocking the flames from the mirror. "Does Nicolette know
you're still awake?"

Jakob's response was clear, confident, and completely
unhelpful. "Mama!"

"That's right." Danielle smiled. Snow's magic allowed
her to see Jakob clearly, even in the darkness.

"Tala?" Jakob asked, leaning forward until his face
pressed against his crib. He had started looking for Talia as soon as he realized Danielle was there. Snow still
hadn't figured out how he was able to see through the
mirror. Danielle longed to let her study the bracelet
again, to determine whether this was a trick of the mirror or something to do with Jakob himself. But Snow
continued to spend all of her time with Morveren.

After following the small mermaid doll for the past
day, Snow and Morveren now believed Lirea was hiding
on the northern coast of Hilad. Not the safest place for
the *Phillipa* to go, but northern Hilad was mostly unin-
habited, and Hephyra was confident she could get the
ship in and out without being seen.

They had crossed into Hiladi waters earlier this evening. How Captain Hephyra could tell one patch of
ocean from the next was beyond Danielle.

"Tala," said Jakob, standing up in his crib. "Tala!"

"Go to sleep, little prince." The sweaty spikes of his hair meant he must have slept for a time before awakening. Danielle hoped it hadn't been her peeking through the mirror that had awakened him.

"No. Tala now, now, now!"

The cabin door opened, and Talia peeked in side. "Captain Hephyra said you were looking for me?"

"Tala!" Excitement lit Jakob's eyes.

"Yes, thank you." Danielle passed the mirror to Talia. "He's been asking for you."

Talia's dark skin almost hid her blush. She squinted into the mirror. "It's late, Jakobena. You should sleep."

"Jakobena?" Danielle asked.

"It means 'Tiny Jakob.' " Talia started to return the mirror to Danielle, but Jakob yelled again.

"What does he want?"

"I think he wants me . . . to sing to him." Her glare all but dared Danielle to smile.

A year's worth of training in court manners helped Danielle keep her expression under control. "I don't think I've ever heard you sing." The unspoken question hung between them.

"I visit the nursery at night sometimes," Talia admitted. "There's room for me to work out undisturbed, and I'm quiet enough to avoid waking him."

Danielle wasn't buying it. "The armory is large enough to practice in. So is the great hall, or one of the guest rooms in the southern towers, or—"

Only Talia could turn a shrug into a threat. "Given how easily your stepsister attacked you in your room last year, I'd think you'd be happy to have someone guarding your son."

"Guarding him . . . by singing?" Danielle teased.

Another shrug. "Sometimes he has bad dreams."

"Tala, Tala, Tala!" Jakob's voice rose with each repetition. Soon he would be loud enough to bring Nicolette running.

"I'm here, Jakobena." Talia scowled at Danielle one

last time, then turned away. She brought the mirror close to her lips and began to sing. Her voice was low and clear, every note perfect.

> *"Silver moon crawls through the sky*
> *and asks if you might play.*
> *Peeking through the clouds, so shy,*
> *the lonely moon has slept all day.*
> *So close your eyes, O tiny child,*
> *and with the moon you'll fly away.*

> *"Silver moon and Jakobena*
> *dancing through the sky.*
> *Now close your eyes, my little one.*
> *Close your eyes and fly."*

Talia pressed her lips to the glass, then returned the bracelet to Danielle.

"That was beautiful." Danielle could see Jakob burrowing into his blankets. "Why don't you sing more often?"

"My voice is another of the fairies' gifts," Talia said. "It's not something I like to think about."

Danielle started to say more, then stopped herself. The tale of Sleeping Beauty was a popular one, but only a handful of people knew the truth of that tale. No princely kiss had awakened Talia from her cursed sleep. Instead, a prince had found Talia's body and used her to satisfy his own urges. The pains of labor roused Talia as her body expelled twin children from her womb. Children she had left behind when she fled her homeland.

"Thank you for watching over him," Danielle said, returning the bracelet to her wrist. The wires tightened, and Jakob's image disappeared.

"I'll watch him, sure. Just don't expect me to change any diapers."

Danielle covered a yawn. "Is Snow still with Morveren?"

"Where else would she be?" Talia raised one leg and

pivoted, slowly moving through a series of close kicks. "Lannadae was snoring in the boat when I passed, but Snow and Morveren are still chattering away about turning people into frogs, or whatever it is witches talk about when they get together."

"You're just mad because their plan doesn't include you pummeling Lirea," Danielle teased.

"If Snow thinks she and Morveren can control Lirea long enough to get that knife, I'm not going to stop them." Talia launched a particularly vicious sequence of punches.

Danielle knew that expression. "You're worried about her."

"She let Morveren transform her into a mermaid." Talia bent her leg, allowing her body to sink lower, then repeated her kicks. "You're the naive one who insists on trusting everyone you meet. Snow knows better."

"She's wanted to learn transformation magic ever since we came back from Fairytown," Danielle said. "The change was temporary, and Snow seems fine."

"I've never seen her so eager. So hungry. She's hardly spoken to me."

"You haven't exactly been bubbling over with warmth either," Danielle pointed out.

Talia turned away. "None of this would have happened if Morveren hadn't used magic to try to change her granddaughter."

"That was what Lirea asked for," said Danielle.

Talia struck the wall with the edge of her hand. "Lirea was little more than a child. She didn't know the risks. Morveren did."

Danielle ran her fingers over her bracelet, thinking about Jakob and how hard it was to refuse when he wanted something. "She made a mistake. Now she's trying to find a way to help Lirea."

"There's the naiveté I'm used to," said Talia.

"Morveren didn't turn her granddaughter into a murderer. Lirea is the one who killed her prince."

"After that prince used and discarded her." Talia relaxed, wiping her forehead on her sleeve. "Lirea's story has a lot in common with yours, actually. You both gave yourselves to men you hardly knew. In your case, Armand turned out to be a good man. Lirea wasn't as fortunate."

Danielle shook her head. Even if Armand betrayed her, she couldn't imagine killing him. Not even if her life depended on it, as Lirea's had. "Armand wouldn't have treated me like that."

"Why, because he danced so well? Because of his charming words and kind smile?" Talia began another series of kicks. "Armand asked you to marry him a lot quicker than Lirea proposed to Gustan."

"If Prince Gustan was so horrible, why would Lirea keep going back to him?" Danielle asked.

"Probably because Gustan knew how to be every bit as charming as your own husband, if not more so. Because Lirea was young and inexperienced, and a man like Gustan knows exactly how to con a girl into his bed. And because growing up, Lirea wasn't as lucky as you were."

A sputtered, "Lucky?" wasn't the most dignified or royal response, but it was the one that emerged from Danielle's lips.

Talia sat down on the opposite cot. "You weren't born into royalty. You were raised in the real world, and you learned very quickly how cruel that world can be. But you also had a mother who cared so much that she stuck around long after her death, just to look after you. You learned to take the blows fate strikes, and you learned what love really means. I assume that's how you've managed to cling to that idealism of yours for so long.

"Lirea was raised a princess, surrounded by guards and shielded from all of life's hurts. As Jakob grows up, you'll see how different his upbringing is. When you're royal you learn that most people will obey your every wish. You start to believe you're better than everyone around you. It's not arrogance, it . . . well, it is. But when you're young and you've never known anything else, that's simply the way the world works."

Talia dug through her small trunk at the foot of the bed, pulling out a small wooden pipe and tobacco pouch. She filled the ivory bowl while she talked. "Your parents teach you about politics and manipulation, but you always believe you're protected. That nothing truly bad can happen to someone like you, because you're royalty. You're special. When life finally shatters that illusion, you don't know how to cope."

Danielle watched Talia closely, but her expression never changed. "So I'm lucky because the way I suffered at the hands of my stepmother and stepsisters prepared me for the world's abuse?"

"The first time somebody strikes you, you're shocked. You lack the reflexes to block or dodge the blows or to roll with the ones you can't. The earlier you can learn those skills, the easier it is to deal with the next fight."

Talia crossed the cabin and lit a small taper from the flame in the lamp. "People learn to cope in different ways. You clean things when you're upset." She pointed, and Danielle realized she had been polishing her bracelet with the corner of her bedsheet. "Lirea slaughters people."

Danielle deliberately set the sheet down and folded her hands. "So how does Snow cope?"

"She sleeps with men and tampers with the nature of reality." Talia puffed on her pipe, then blew a ring of smoke toward the door. "One way or another, it's all about control."

Snow had spent much of the night transforming flower-worms into butterflies. When the butterflies flew away, she used magic to call them back. All except the one that fell victim to a bedraggled three-legged cat.

"Good," said Morveren as Snow completed another transformation. They sat together at the foremast, having left Lannadae to sleep in the cutter. "Your songs are already more precise. You're a natural spellcaster, child."

Snow grinned and modified her spell. The butterfly fluttered over to land on the tip of Morveren's nose.

The mermaid laughed. "I don't read your language very well, but are those your initials on its wings?"

Snow started to answer, but her attention was drawn to Captain Hephyra striding toward them.

"Undine?" Snow asked, once Hephyra had climbed onto the foredeck.

"I felt three of them passing beneath the hull, brushing my roots. It tickles." She patted the mast, her fingers sinking ever so slightly into the wood. "Two remain below. They've already poked us with their spears."

"Testing your strength," said Morveren. "If this were one of Lirea's raiding parties, there would be more warriors. These are guards, protecting the nesting sites. If you turn out to be a threat, they'll sing for help and sink you from below."

"Fortunately, we're going to stop them before they realize how big a threat we are," Snow said. Hephyra didn't look reassured.

Snow moved to the side of the deck. The water was so dark that she could barely see where the ocean ended and the sky began. The only exception was a broad stripe of white moonlight painted along the waves. A faint shadow along the horizon might have been land, or it might have been a trick of the eye.

"Will they be able to hear you down below?"

Snow jumped, then turned to Talia. "You know how much I hate it when you sneak up on me."

"So maybe you should pay more attention." Talia leaned out over the rail. "Hephyra knew I was here."

"That doesn't count," said Snow. "Hephyra *is* the ship. If you stepped on me, I'd know you were here too."

"I'll remember that next time."

"There," said Morveren, pointing to a lone undine. He bobbed in the water like a buoy. "If anything happens to him, one of his friends will sing a warning to the tribe while the other attacks from below."

Snow rubbed her hands together. Before the undine scout could speak, she leaned out to shout, "There you are! I was beginning to think Lirea had forgotten us."

The undine swam closer, coming into the light of the lanterns burning on the ship. His hair was like matted white wool, and his face was almost as wrinkled as Morveren's. He wouldn't have been Snow's first choice for a guard.

"Who are you?" he demanded.

"What do you mean, who am I?" Snow slapped her palms against the rail. "I am a friend of Lirea. She wished to speak to me alone, regarding her grandmother. Where is she?"

"Lirea is no friend of humans," said the merman.

"Captain Varisto told us otherwise." Snow stretched out her senses as Morveren had taught her. One hand moved toward her choker.

"Stop that," Morveren hissed, keeping her body low. "You don't need it."

Snow made a rude gesture, but she lowered her hand. Her eyelids fluttered. She could sense the one at the surface, but where were the other two? Lulling this one's suspicions would do nothing if the others realized what was happening.

"Varisto is a special case." The merman swam closer. "You speak the tongue of Lorindar, not Hilad."

Snow concentrated on the undine she could see. Using magic to fool a cat into attacking his own tail was one thing. Fooling a trained warrior was far more difficult. His suspicion was plain, so obvious she could almost touch it. She reached out to do just that, pushing back against his doubts.

"Bring Lirea to us." She sang softly, focusing her voice on him alone.

A second undine surfaced. This one was a girl, little more than a child. She whispered to the elder merman.

Behind Snow, Morveren began to hum, lending her strength. Morveren's time on the ship had obviously done her good, and Snow could feel the extra power flowing through her song. She smiled and tried again. "Go now, and tell Lirea we have news of her grandmother. News for her alone."

"She never said anything . . . she can't." The merman shook his head. "Lirea is needed. If she leaves now—"

"If she doesn't, she loses Morveren. Do you know what she will do to you if you cost her that chance?"

Snow could feel his fear. He knew how desperately Lirea wanted Morveren dead, but still he resisted. "A human wouldn't understand."

"Maybe if you ask nicely?" Talia muttered.

"No." The sound of Morveren's voice made Snow jump.

"I can do this," Snow said, concentrating on the merman. "Help me—"

"Can't you smell it? The tribe is spawning. They won't allow Lirea to leave. They can't." Morveren lifted her head, peeking out at the water. "I should have guessed. The stress of war would increase the pressure to breed. All those of mating age will have gathered around Lirea."

Snow studied the two undine. An old man and a child. No doubt the third was also of an age unlikely to reproduce this year.

"The tribe needs her," said Lannadae, pulling herself up the ladder to the foredeck. "Without the queen's scent in the water, the females won't be receptive to the men's seed."

Talia raised an eyebrow. "Aren't you a little young to know about—"

"When the mating scent fills the water, every undine feels it, from the eldest merman to the newborn mermaid. We can't all act on those feelings, but we all understand them." Lannadae smiled. "You humans conceal so much, hiding your bodies and your mating habits as if they were precious secrets."

"Some of us do, anyway," Talia said, glancing at Snow.

Snow adjusted her shirt. "Is there any way to lure Lirea away?"

"Ask them how long it's been since the spawning began," said Morveren, keeping her body low and out of sight.

Snow did so, and the merman responded, "Lirea returned less than a day ago."

"She won't leave," said Lannadae. "Not for four more days at least."

"We can't just anchor the *Phillipa* off the Hiladi coast while we wait for her to finish," Talia said.

"No." Morveren looked up at Snow. "You will have to bring her to us. The tribe will be distracted." She stretched out on the deck. "Such wonderful distractions. I miss those days."

"What about the tribe?" asked Lannadae. "If Lirea leaves in the middle of spawning—"

"I don't understand the urgency," Snow said. "Undine are long-lived. Even if there were no births this year, it would hardly affect the size of the tribe."

"You speak as a human," Morveren answered. "The undine can no more ignore the urge to breed than you could ignore the urge to breathe. To interrupt the tribe in midcycle will cause confusion, possibly even violence."

"Sounds like a good way to distract them from attacking our ships," said Talia.

"They'll likely turn that violence outward, becoming even more aggressive." Morveren reached over to stroke Lannadae's hair. "Lirea's scent will linger for another day, maybe longer. If we can save her in that time, she could return to control the tribe. This is our best chance."

Snow turned her attention back to the two undine in the water. "Forget what you found. Return to your tribe, and say nothing of us."

She could feel their resistance. They had grown more suspicious, and on some level, they knew they were being controlled. Their minds fought to throw off Snow's commands. Snow clenched her fists and pushed harder, expanding her spell to capture the third undine still hidden beneath the ship. "Forget!"

"Be careful," Morveren said. "Too much power in such a spell can damage their minds."

"Letting them tell Lirea we're here can damage us," said Talia.

Snow adjusted her spell, remembering the things Morveren had taught. Banishing a memory required a great deal of raw power, but walling that memory away for a day or two . . . She touched her choker, using the mirror's magic to seal her spell.

As one, the undine disappeared into the water. Snow staggered back, and only Talia's quick reflexes stopped her from falling.

"I don't know how long my spell will last." Snow sat down on the deck. "Go wake Danielle. Tell her we're going for a late night swim."

Danielle yawned as she waited for Captain Hephyra to finish stringing a makeshift curtain of old sailcloth across the poop deck.

"You and your modesty," Hephyra said. "You've little to be ashamed of, you know."

"Thanks," Danielle said dryly.

"This is a hell of a spot for a swim." Hephyra yanked the final knot tight, then tugged the curtain aside to allow Danielle to join the others. "Are you sure you wouldn't rather stay here while your friends go after the mermaid?"

"Captain Hephyra, are you worried about me?"

Hephyra shrugged. "You get yourself killed, your prince gets angry. If he blames me, well, let's just say I don't need that kind of hassle."

Danielle started to answer, but Talia was quicker. "Danielle has to come. She gets cranky when we try to leave her behind. She pouts for weeks."

"I do not!" Her heart wasn't in the protest. Talia's

smile, fleeting though it might be, was worth a little teasing.

"Lirea already tried to kill you once, Highness," said Hephyra. "What's to stop her from trying again?"

"They are." Danielle cocked a thumb at Talia and Snow.

"Remember, undine aren't like you," Lannadae said. "We don't seek privacy when we breed. The tribe might be distracted, but if you draw attention to yourselves, they'll notice."

"Don't worry, we'll be fine." Snow was already unbuttoning her shirt. Lannadae stared, obviously curious about human anatomy.

Danielle checked the curtain, then made sure nobody was watching from atop the masts before following suit. She stepped out of Lannadae's view before shrugging off her robe and unlacing her nightgown.

"The transformation is unpleasant at first, but you get used to it," Snow said. "It's actually a lot of fun, once you figure out the breathing."

"I don't like this," said Lannadae. "It's magic that drove my sister mad. Magic that hurt your queen. Isn't there another way?"

"Not unless you and Morveren want to swim in and fetch Lirea," said Snow.

Talia was the last to disrobe, moving to the edge of the deck and keeping her back turned to the others. She refastened her belt over her bare skin, making sure both knives were secure in their sheaths. Two shorter knives were strapped to her forearms. "I'm not thrilled with the plan either."

Danielle picked up her sword belt and pulled it tight around her bare waist. The buckle pinched her skin, and the leather dug into her hips.

"I'll be able to use my mirrors to deflect attention when we approach," Snow was saying. She frowned at the mermaid doll Morveren had given her. "How am I supposed to carry this thing?"

"You could put your shirt back on," Talia said without looking.

Morveren untied the harness she wore and passed it to Snow. "Your body is still too skinny, and your chest is too big, but this should work. You won't be comfortable, but you'll be able to carry the doll and anything else you might need."

Snow shrugged into the harness and used a length of twine to secure the doll to the strap beneath her left arm. Once the knots were pulled tight, she transferred her knife to the other side of the harness.

"It's not unusual for young undine to join other tribes this time of year," Morveren said. "If questioned, say you've come to join the line of Ilowkira. Use the magic we've practiced to draw Lirea out. Her anger and fear will work in your favor. Her body will be weary, so she'll be slower than usual. The rest of the tribe will be reluctant to leave. You can encourage that reluctance to make sure they don't follow. Once you lead her to the ship, we can work together to capture her."

"More magic," said Lannadae. "What if this only makes things worse?"

"More magic is the only hope your sister has," Morveren answered. "It's the only way to save her life."

"If she can take care of everything with her magic, what does she need these two for?" Hephyra jabbed a finger at Talia and Danielle.

Talia scowled. "If everything works the way Morveren describes, Snow will be fine. Personally, I don't have a lot of faith in her judgment."

"So send Lannadae," said Hephyra.

Lannadae's scales puffed out at that suggestion, and her fear was easy to read. She didn't speak; she simply turned to Morveren, eyes wide.

Morveren shook her head. "She's a royal. The moment her scent fills the water, they'll know she's there. If she were older, her scent might be strong enough to wrest control from her sister. But young as she is, I can't think of a faster way to get you all killed."

"We'll be fine." Danielle hugged herself against the wind. She felt exposed and a little embarrassed. Childbirth had left its lines on her, and she couldn't help comparing her body to Snow's unblemished form. But her discomfort was nothing compared to Talia's. Talia was as stiff and tense as Danielle had ever seen her. She refused to look at anyone. Words would only make her more uncomfortable, so Danielle simply asked, "Can we please hurry?"

"Snow can transform herself." Morveren crawled toward Talia. "I'll take care of these two. I've rested enough to do that much."

Talia's hand shot out, catching Morveren's wrist. "Touch me and I'll break your arm."

Morveren tugged free and backed away, scowling. Danielle moved between them. "Talia, she's not going to hurt you."

"I know that," Talia whispered. "I know it's the only way to reach Lirea, but I don't like people using magic to tamper with my body. I don't want her touching me."

Danielle did her best to swallow her own anxiety. "I'll go first." She sat down on the deck, gasping as her backside touched the cold, wet wood.

Her palms grew slick with nervous sweat as Morveren pulled a scale from her tail and prepared to cut her skin. Danielle forced a smile for Talia's sake. Morveren's hands were swift and steady, completing the cuts almost before the pain hit. Almost.

Soon Danielle's legs were crushing together. She clenched her jaw, biting back a shriek. Her nails dug into the deck as she waited for the shock to pass.

Morveren turned to Talia, the bloody scale still in her hand.

"You've got to be joking," said Talia.

"What if Snow casts the spell instead?" Danielle asked.

"No," said Morveren. "She should conserve her strength for Lirea. I can—"

"I'll do it." Snow lay on the deck, wearing nothing but her choker and Lirea's harness. Her red-scaled tail flapped against the sailcloth curtain.

Talia sat down and closed her eyes. "Make it quick."

Danielle studied her own undine body. Her torso was thicker, similar to the way it had looked in those first weeks after Jakob's birth. Her hair felt coarser, and there was more of it than before.

"I hate this," Talia whispered. She hadn't made a sound during her transformation, but her face was sweaty. Her tail was a deep blue, fading to green near the fins.

"You're beautiful," Lannadae said. "You all are."

"You shouldn't waste your power playing color games," Morveren said, frowning.

"But Talia looks so much better in blue," Snow insisted, climbing up onto the railing. Before Morveren could respond, she dropped backward into the water.

Danielle reached over to take Talia's hand. For once, Talia didn't pull away. "It won't last long," she said. "Snow will remove the spell as soon as she can."

Talia took a deep breath, then straightened. "I guess we'd better follow to make sure she doesn't get into trouble. Come on, Princess. The sooner we leave, the sooner we'll be able to shed these scales."

"I'll take the *Phillipa* west to make sure we're out of sight," said Captain Hephyra. "I'd come with you if I could. Spawning season sounds like fun."

"You're as bad as she is," Talia said, gesturing toward Snow. She shook her head and dove in after Snow.

"Remember your promise," said Morveren. "Please bring my granddaughter back to me."

"We will." Danielle studied the railing. There was no graceful way for a mermaid to climb over. Well, Talia had made it look graceful, but that didn't count. Danielle scooted forward and grabbed a belaying pin to pull herself up. The wood scraped painfully against her chest. She twisted around, balancing on her hips. Her weight shifted, and her body tilted toward the water.

She overbalanced and fell, and her back hit the water hard. Her body sliced into the water. She pushed away from the ship, kicking to the surface. Her muscles launched her higher than she intended. This body would take some practice.

"We'll be waiting for you," Captain Hephyra shouted.

"Thank you!" Danielle waved, then blushed when she realized the sailcloth curtain no longer shielded her from view. Her cheeks burned. She sank lower and swam over to Talia, who had kept close to the hull. Lowering her voice, she said, "Let's not tell Armand about this part."

"Personally, I plan on drinking until I've pushed the whole thing from my mind," Talia answered.

"Lirea's will is strong, but her thoughts are chaotic," Morveren called down. "Brute force won't help you. Use her confusion to trick her into following."

"I will!" Snow leaped from the water like a dolphin, then vanished beneath the waves.

"Be careful, Cinderella!" Lannadae shouted from the ship.

Talia snorted and disappeared after Snow. Shaking her head, Danielle followed them both.

To Danielle, the sea had always been an impressive thing, but ultimately dull. Water was water, fish were fish, and seaweed was seaweed.

She soon discovered how mistaken she had been. Swimming through the ocean was like flying through another world. Her body felt light as air. The currents were gentle winds, pushing her to the right. Those winds grew stronger and colder the deeper she swam.

Dark shapes passed beneath her. A school of fish, or creatures larger and more distant? There was no way to be certain.

For the most part, she stayed close to the surface, skimming just beneath the waves. She kept her arms at her sides, imitating Snow's movements. The water washed over her face, rinsing the sweat from her body.

Breathing water for the first time had been a shock, but after a few coughing fits, she had finally mastered the trick. She doubted she would ever get used to the water flowing through her gills, or the sensation of her neck opening and closing with each breath. Equally difficult was learning to clamp shut the muscles deep within her chest, sealing air in the bottom of her lungs to help her float.

Her stomach hadn't cramped this badly since she had Jakob. Her tail muscles seemed well adapted for swimming, but her stomach and back would ache for weeks. Either she still didn't have the movement quite right, or else she simply lacked the strength and endurance of a true undine.

Still, they were making better progress than any human could, having closed more than half the distance to shore. She looked back at the *Phillipa*. In the moonlight, the ship was a shadow the size of her fingertip.

"How far to Lirea?" asked Talia from up ahead.

Water fountained from Snow's lips, clearing her lungs. She grabbed the doll in one hand and closed her eyes. "She's directly ahead. We should be there before sunrise."

Danielle turned onto her back. Swimming this way used different muscles, bringing some relief, though it meant the air chilled her wet skin. At least now she understood why the undine went without clothes. Her sword belt tugged at her hips with every stroke of her tail. How much slower would she have been with clothes dragging against the water?

She dove deeper to escape the wind, doing her best to keep up with Talia and Snow, both of whom were in better physical condition. Something brushed her tail fin, and she streaked to the surface, yelping in alarm. She ducked her face back into the water to see a school of mackerel passing beneath her.

Snow laughed and splashed Danielle with her tail. "They're nothing to be scared of. You're a bigger fish than they are."

"Barely." Some of those fish looked almost as long as Danielle.

"Stay close to Talia," Snow said, still giggling. "She'll protect you if we have to face any killer tuna."

Danielle closed her eyes and whispered silently to the closest fish.

Moments later, Snow shrieked and leaped from the water. "They nibbled my tail fin!"

Danielle smiled and kept on swimming. As the water grew shallower, she began to notice the rocks below. Back home, the seabed would have been covered in white sand and stones from the cliff. Here, rocks jutted from the bottom like broken claws. Some were high enough to rip open any ship unlucky enough to pass this way.

"Where is this place?" she asked.

"The northern edge of Hilad," said Snow. "The land is the same black rock, completely uninhabitable. Some say dragons scorched the land. Others believe the earth itself opened up, belching fire over the entire town."

Danielle studied the shore. The sky ahead was lighter, illuminating a half-submerged wall rising from the water. Low arches as wide as a ship allowed the water to pass through the wall. Beyond, she could make out the ruins of a palace. Broken towers stood to either side of a larger structure with a teardrop-shaped roof.

"They say the bones of a former Hiladi emperor are entombed in the rock," Snow said.

"How do you know all this?" asked Talia.

Snow shook her head. "When we get back, I'm sealing you in the library until you've read at least five books."

Danielle pointed to a mottled, serpentine creature arcing through the water in front of the wall. "Does your library tell you what that thing is?"

"A kelpie," said Snow. "A big one. Imagine a cross between a giant horse and a sea serpent. The undine use them to haul their belongings when they migrate. They've been known to ride kelpies into battle, too."

Danielle glided through the water, trying to get a better view of the kelpie. *Kelpies,* she corrected, spotting a second. Each animal was probably half the length of the

Phillipa. A third kelpie raised its head farther down the wall. Silhouetted against the faint orange light of dawn, the head appeared vaguely equine. She could just make out the shape of several undine clinging to the kelpie's body beneath the head.

"Lirea is beyond the wall," said Snow, staring at her doll.

Talia was double-checking her knives. "Can your magic get us past the merfolk?"

"I'm offended you even have to ask." Snow tightened the knot holding Lirea's doll to her harness. "The kelpies might be trickier. But the merfolk shouldn't give us any trouble. If Morveren was right, they're not going to worry about a few strangers."

Danielle was beginning to feel a little distracted herself. The water tasted different here. Both sour and sweet, the faint tang made her mouth water and her heart beat faster. She found herself exquisitely aware of the waves caressing her bare skin.

Snow shivered. "Have any of you ever wondered how a merman and a mermaid—"

"No," snapped Talia.

"But don't you want to know where the mermen keep their—"

"Snow, please." Danielle raised a hand to stop her.

The taste of the water took Danielle back to those first nights with Armand. The feel of his hands exploring her body, the way her skin had tingled and tightened at his touch.

"It wouldn't have to take long." Snow swam up behind Talia. "Don't be such a prude. We could—"

Talia put both hands on Snow's head and dunked her beneath the water. Snow popped up a moment later, sputtering and wiping her face.

"I'm going to find Lirea," Talia said. "If you'd rather mount a merman than save Queen Bea's life, don't let me stop you."

Snow shook her head. "I was joking, Talia. What's the matter with you?"

"With me?" Talia shouted. "You're the one who's been acting like this is some sort of holiday. Giggling over your new magic, staying up all night with your mermaid friend, and now you want to run off to have a quick romp with a merman?"

"You know, I wondered why you only brought knives along this time," Snow said. "Usually you carry a lot more weapons. That was before I figured out you've got one of your fighting sticks wedged up your ass."

Danielle swam between them. She had seen Snow and Talia argue before, but not like this. "This isn't helping."

Talia turned away. "It's making me feel better."

"The water carries Lirea's scent, remember?" Danielle said. "The closer we get to the shore, the more we'll be . . ."

"Aroused?" Snow asked. "You know, if we could bottle this stuff, we could make a fortune."

Talia shook her head. "And you think something's wrong with *me*?"

Danielle took another gulp of air. "Keep your heads above water. Breathing air seems to dilute the effect."

Danielle swam past them both. The air helped, but she could still smell Lirea's scent. If the water was affecting the others the way it was her, this was going to get a lot worse before they reached Lirea.

She braced herself as she swam toward the shore. She wasn't sure what exactly to expect. An orgy of merfolk thrashing about in the water, or something more . . . *human*?

She gasped the first time one of the undine passed beneath her. This was an older merman, his matted hair streaming over his back like seaweed. He glanced up, frowned, and rose to the surface.

"Who are you?"

Snow's choker pulsed with blue light. The suspicion faded from his face. Smiling, Snow said, "Could you please tell Lirea we've come to join her tribe?"

He swam uncomfortably close, until his green tail fin

brushed theirs. "Welcome. You're wise to join us while you still can."

Danielle glanced at Snow, wondering what that meant. Snow gave a tiny shrug.

"Lirea lives apart from the tribe for her own protection," the merman continued. "I will bring you to Nilliar, the queen's spearbearer. She can—"

Snow frowned. "I'd really like to meet Lirea."

"Even if Lirea were willing to see newcomers, I'm afraid that would be impossible. Her home is inaccessible to undine." He took Snow's hand and pulled her close. "There's no hurry, if you and your friends would prefer—"

"No," said Talia.

Danielle winced, but the merman didn't take offense. "Does Lirea really mean to war against the humans? In our tribe, humans and undine were allies."

The merman paused. "Which tribe would that be?"

"Does it matter?" Snow asked. Her voice was playful, but a pulse of light from her choker hinted at the magic she was using to manipulate the merman.

"The Ilowkira were friends with the humans," he admitted. "But Lirea means to restore the undine to our former glory. To unite us all and give us back our rightful place as rulers of the sea. Those who refuse will face her wrath, human and undine alike." His eyes practically shone. Had he been human, Danielle would have thought he was in love with his queen. How much of that was due to the strange taste Lirea fed into the water?

"And the gold?" Danielle pressed. "What are we going to do with human treasure?"

"That is Lirea's concern, not ours. Come, let me bring you to Nilliar."

Snow frowned and rubbed her thumb over her choker. "No, thank you. I think we'll find our own way." Another flash of magic, and the merman was swimming away.

"He doesn't even question why they've turned against their friends," Danielle said.

Snow turned to face the ruins. "Humans obey poor

leaders all the time. It's even harder for an undine to question their royalty. There's a reason the blood of a royal mermaid can be used to make potions of mind control. Though he seemed more ... fanatical than I would have expected."

"Come on," said Talia. "Let's get Lirea before someone else comes along and tries to help."

"How close do you have to be to work your magic on Lirea?" Danielle asked.

Snow pursed her lips. "I'll have a better chance if I can see her. I should be able to make her trust us long enough to lure her back to the *Phillipa*. But there's a problem."

"Isn't there always?" Talia asked.

"He said she was inaccessible." Snow grabbed the doll and closed her eyes. "Lirea is inside that palace."

Which meant getting past the kelpies, through the wall, and sneaking into the palace. Danielle watched the kelpies patrolling the water. They stayed out from the wall, avoiding the shallows where the rocks might cut their bodies. This wouldn't be easy.

Another undine passed beneath her. Danielle blushed when she realized it wasn't one undine but two, their bodies pressed together so tightly she couldn't tell where the man's fins ended and the woman's began. They were singing a low harmony which grew faster with the undulation of their tails. Danielle didn't need to understand the melody to feel the urgency in their duet.

"They won't all be that preoccupied," Talia said.

"They will be when I'm finished." Snow adjusted her choker.

"You're going to enchant every merman and mermaid in the tribe?" Talia asked.

"Let me try to distract the kelpies instead," Danielle said, hoping they couldn't see her cheeks burning. "We can swim through in the confusion."

"How?" asked Snow.

Danielle turned toward the closest of the kelpies. Large as they were, kelpies were still animals. *Sharks are following us,* she said. *Many, in the deeper water. Please help!*

The closest kelpie surged through the water, earning a startled cry from one of his riders. His speed made the undine look like clumsy humans still learning to swim. Before Danielle could react, the kelpie was racing past her. The water buffeted her as the kelpie went off in search of sharks.

A second followed close behind. The third ... Danielle smiled. The third kelpie was swimming away as fast as he could. This one kept close to the surface. His riders shouted and pounded his scales, but he ignored their protests.

"You big coward," she said.

Some of the undine had already surfaced to see what was happening. Others crowded together for safety. Few paid any attention to three mermaids swimming along the bottom.

Most of the undine stayed close to shore. Some had retreated into oversized nests of stones and silt. Danielle slowed to get a better look at the undine's homes. Curtains of woven vines surrounded some of the nests. The vines clung to the rocks, making it easy to move the curtain. The nests were small, but Danielle saw three, four, even five undine crowded together in each one, sleeping or ... not sleeping.

A few undine approached, but the magic of Snow's mirrors turned them back until the three were through the center archway of the great wall.

Beneath them lay the remains of what might once have been a road. Here and there, broken paving stones poked through rippled black rock. Seaweed grew from the cracks. A black crab crawled along the rusted, half-buried remains of a gate.

Beyond the archway the water grew deeper again, as though a moat of some sort had once surrounded the palace. Talia pulled them to one side, where the wall would block them from view of the undine outside.

"Where is she?" Talia asked as she surfaced.

Four towers surrounded the central structure. Danielle could just make out the remains of secondary buildings around the former palace. Only the occasional broken pillar or crumbled wall marked a castle that in its day would have rivaled the one back home.

Snow pointed to the closest tower, which sat partially submerged at the edge of the moat. The tower would allow Lirea to hide away from the world, but her scent would still wash out to the rest of her tribe. The wind was stronger here, raising whitecapped waves along the moat and chilling Danielle's skin.

"Air spirits," Snow said.

"Can they see us?" asked Danielle.

"I'm not sure." Snow turned to look along the shore. "They're racing up and down the edge of the land. I can feel others farther back."

"The air spirits guard the land while the kelpies guard the sea," said Talia.

They crossed the moat to shallower water. Danielle guessed this to have been a garden of some sort. Green algae covered a submerged statue of a winged horse, giving it a monstrous appearance. Broken fountains formed the boundaries of a path.

Danielle studied the tower. Rock and rubble lay piled around the base, blocking any entrance. The only way in was through the windows. Lirea could take human form and climb the wall, but no other undine would be able to follow her. Nor could any human approach by land or sea without being spotted. "This is the one place she can feel safe."

Snow was still staring into the sky. "The spirits share an empathic bond with Lirea. They have no specific orders, but they share her fear. I should be able to ease that fear long enough for us to get inside."

Talia shook her head. "I've broken into a lot of places, but I'm not about to sneak into this thing naked."

Snow had already crawled onto the shallow rocks. She pulled her tail to her chest, eyes squeezed shut as her body began to change. Skin enveloped scales, and her fins pressed flat against her legs and feet. She doubled over, coughing water from her lungs.

Her voice hoarse, she said, "Make sure to exhale all of the water before I remove the spell." To Talia, she added, "If you'd prefer to wait behind while Danielle and I go after Lirea, that's fine."

She might as well have spat in Talia's face. Talia followed her onto the rocks. "Just cast the damn spell."

Danielle looked up at the tower, then down at her pale skin. This was not going to be fun.

CHAPTER 9

T ALIA MOVED AROUND THE BASE of the
tower ahead of the others on the pretense of scout-
ing the terrain. She hurried until she reached the ankle-
deep water in the back. Here, unseen by undine or her
fellow humans, she collapsed against the wall and fought
to regain control.

The pain wasn't a problem. Returning to human form
might feel like being skinned alive, but at least the pain
had helped to distract her from whatever potion Lirea
had spread through the water. And now that she was human, the scent and taste of the water no longer seemed
to affect her.

Her own mind was another problem. Every time she
closed her eyes, she saw Snow bobbing in the waves, her
hair slicked back, water dripping down her body ... Deliberately, Talia turned to study the mountains in the distance,
little more than a serrated shadow cutting across the sky.

It wasn't as though this was the first time she had seen
Snow naked. Several of their previous missions for the
queen had required them to switch disguises in a hurry,
but on those occasions Talia had been able to control
her body's reactions. Not this time, thanks to Lirea pushing her to the edge.

Her skin tingled when she heard Snow and Danielle
approaching. Snow was fully human now, wearing nothing but Morveren's harness, which accentuated—

"*In'a'een ya mavas*," she swore, digging her nails into her wrists.

"I should have brought shoes," Snow was saying. "The rocks are murder on my feet."

Talia tried not to look at either of them. "We can climb here. The undine shouldn't see us, and as long as Snow keeps the spirits busy, we should be able to sneak in."

Danielle stepped closer. "What's wrong, Talia?"

Talia didn't answer. Snow's poor powers of observation had always made it easy for Talia to keep her feelings hidden. Danielle, on the other hand, actually paid attention to such things. Damn her.

"Nothing's wrong," Talia whispered. "Aside from the two of you making enough noise to reach the *Phillipa*."

"Ignore her," Snow said. "She always gets uppity before a kidnapping."

Talia started to respond, but the words caught in her throat. What was *wrong* with her? Beatrice could be dying, and all she could think about was kissing Snow's lips, running her fingers through that sleek black hair.

A gentle touch to the middle of the back made her gasp. She twisted away from Danielle's hand.

"I'm fine." Talia's voice sounded hoarse even to her own ears.

Danielle looked past Talia to Snow, and compassion softened her face. "Snow, I've seen you cast illusions before. Would it be terribly difficult to use your magic to clothe us? I'm . . . I've always been self-conscious. This is too distracting."

Shame burned Talia's cheeks.

"You've got nothing to be self-conscious about," Snow said, grinning. "You'd never know that body spat out a prince."

"Please?" Danielle asked.

With a shrug, Snow touched her mirror. A low-cut blouse and trousers shimmered into existence, covering Danielle's body. Similar garments soon appeared on Snow and Talia.

Talia sighed. She recognized these clothes from Snow's

wardrobe, and they weren't too much better than being naked. Nor could they do anything to erase the images in Talia's mind. But it was better than nothing.

She started to thank Danielle, but that would mean acknowledging what Danielle had done. Instead, she turned to the tower wall. "Keep your body close to the tower, and try to put your hands and feet where I do. Move one limb at a time."

Illusory clothing did nothing to protect her body from the rough-hewn stone. The lowest window was three stories high, and she was soon bleeding from scrapes on her arms and legs. She peeked through arrow slits as she climbed, but the interior was too dark to see anything.

The marble sill of the window was wet and slick to the touch. She found a higher foothold and pushed herself up. She held her breath, listening for any sound inside: a footstep or a quick breath as someone prepared to decapitate her. The only sounds were the lapping of the water below and Snow's muttered complaints.

"Wait here." Talia pulled herself through the window, landing lightly on a stone floor inside. There, she waited for her vision to adjust. She could make out an orange glow rising from the center of the room. The light showed the outline of a pit where the center of the floor had crumbled away. She didn't trust the broken floor enough to investigate more closely.

A staircase wound along the outer wall. Overhead, she could see the fading stars through holes in the roof.

She returned to the window and reached down to help Danielle and Snow through. Danielle's sword clinked against the windowframe as she climbed inside. Talia froze, waiting for some sound from below, but if Lirea was down there, she didn't appear to have heard.

"Stay close to the wall." Talia led them to the steps. "Keep quiet."

This must have been a guard tower originally. The very top would have held cannons or ballista, as well as a signal bell. The weight of all that equipment was probably what had broken through the floors.

The stairs descended through a makeshift armory. Many of the old weapon racks were bare or broken, but Lirea had built up a fair collection of her own. Undine-style spears and knives carved from wood, stone, and bone stood in neat rows. Lirea kept enough weapons to fight a small army. Further along were more exotic weapons. Danielle picked up a grooved paddle that curved into a hook at one end.

"Spear thrower," Talia whispered, helping herself to a curved sword. The blade was tarnished but still sharp. It wasn't old enough to belong to the tower's original inhabitants. How many of these weapons had come from sunken ships? Her fingers tightened to fists when she spotted a knife with a polished white stone set in the cross guard. Such knives were common in the northern part of Lorindar, and the shine of the blade meant this was a new acquisition. "Come on."

They descended through another room, this one lined with broken, moldy bunks. Through the broken floor, Talia could see candle flames reflecting on the water below. Rusted hinges showed where a trapdoor had once locked the lowest part of the tower off from the rest. A dungeon of some sort? That might explain why it had been built below sea level. Locking prisoners in waist-deep water would be a good way to break their spirits. For humans, at any rate. For a mermaid, this was probably the perfect bedroom.

Talia kept her sword ready as she crept down the stairs, searching for Lirea. Dead, moldering flowers hung from the walls, filling the air with the sick-sweet smell of rot. Polished shells were mounted between the flowers, the kind of random decoration a child might have done.

On the far side of the tower, a sickly tree grew from the water. It resembled a willow, but with shriveled pink leaves. Many of the leaves had withered and fallen, floating on the water like tiny boats. The top of an ancient bell rose from the center of the water like a corroded island. Iron rings in the wall which might once have chained prisoners now served as candleholders.

"There." Snow pointed to the tree.

Within the curtain of leaves, a pale shape stood un-moving in the water. It was broader than the mermaid Talia had fought. She studied it more closely, until a flicker of candlelight showed not skin but white marble. She was looking at a statue.

A second form huddled at the base of the statue. Li-rea lay curled around the statue's feet. She whimpered, and Talia switched her sword to her left hand, drawing a knife with her right. But Lirea didn't move. She ap-peared to be asleep.

"I can kill her from here," Talia whispered. One throw and it would all be over.

"You can't." Danielle grabbed her arm. "We prom-ised Morveren."

"You heard that merman." Talia tugged free. "Lirea is the one leading them to war and glory. Without her, the attacks against Lorindar will end. You're princess of Lorindar, remember? You have a duty to protect your people."

"What about my duty to Beatrice?" Danielle asked. "You think Morveren will help us if we betray her and murder her granddaughter?"

Forget Lirea. Maybe she would just kill Danielle in-stead. She glanced at Lirea to make sure the mermaid hadn't heard their whispers. "We'll still have the knife. Snow can save Beatrice."

"Are you sure?"

They both turned to Snow. Her only response was silence.

"We take Lirea back," said Danielle. "Maybe Mor-veren will be able to help her. Either way, I don't intend to simply let her go free. We'll still protect Lorindar, and Beatrice will live."

"Lirea has killed too many people already." But Talia moved aside to make room for Snow. "Someone has to pay for those deaths."

Snow stepped down the stairs, squeezing past Talia. The illusion of clothing did nothing to mediate the sensation of skin against skin. Talia tightened her jaw and concentrated on Lirea, ready to kill her if she so much as twitched.

"The stairs are slimy." Snow held the doll in both hands as she hummed to herself. Her brow wrinkled, and she turned toward Talia. "I can hear her dreams. Her memories of her time with Gustan." Her eyebrows shot higher. "Mermaids are awfully flexible."

"Stop prying," Talia hissed. "Cast the damn spell."

"I'm trying. But her dreams are *intense*." Was Snow actually blushing? Talia wouldn't have thought it possible. "It probably has something to do with the spawning."

"Snow, please," said Danielle.

"Sorry." Snow swallowed and turned back to Lirea. "Her dreams are so happy, but her mind is an angry, frightened place."

Talia twirled her knife through her fingers as Snow resumed her spell. Talia started to ask how long this would take, then caught herself. Snow was too easily distracted as it was.

"She's fighting me, even in her dreams," Snow said. "She shouldn't be able to—"

The branches of the willow tree exploded outward, and Snow screamed. Talia threw her knife, but a sudden wind knocked it away to clatter against the wall.

Talia leaped from the stairs, her stolen sword clutched in both hands. Across the room, Lirea was sitting up, her eyes impossibly wide. She looked like a child roused from a nightmare.

The wind slammed into Talia from behind, knocking her into the water. The damned air spirits again. She tried to push herself up from the slime-covered rubble at the bottom, but the wind was too strong. She pulled her legs beneath her, pushing harder until she was able to raise her face from the water. The wind was so strong it created a bowl-shaped impression in the water.

She managed a single breath before another wind hit her from the side, tossing her off-balance and pressing her down again. Between the pressure in her ears and the roar of the wind, she barely heard Danielle's shouted warning.

Lirea dove from her shelter beneath the tree, swimming toward Talia. She carried a long spear, similar to the one she had used back on the *Glass Slipper*. Talia wrenched her sword around to knock the spear aside, but Lirea's body slammed into her, knocking them both underwater.

Talia tried to stab upward, but Lirea was pressing down on her. She dragged Talia over rocks and debris until they slammed into something harder. The fallen bell. Talia braced herself against the bell and dropped the sword, reaching instead for the shaft of Lirea's spear. She caught the end and pushed, using the spear as a lever to pry Lirea away. Her lungs were already burning from lack of air.

Lirea fought back, and Talia shifted tactics. She drove her knee into the mermaid's side. Lirea's grip loosened, and Talia kicked free. She gasped for breath, stepping back to give herself space to act. She dodged another thrust of Lirea's spear, and then the air spirits struck again, slamming her into the bell.

Lirea was too fast in the water. She moved about like a demon, diving one way then another before Talia could react.

Talia barely twisted out of the way of the next attack. Lirea's spear rang off of the bell, and then one of her tails swept beneath Talia's legs. The other tail flipped up and around her chest, pinning her arms. Lirea fell backward, dragging Talia back beneath the water and squeezing the air from her lungs.

Talia dug her fingers between Lirea's scales and pulled. The scales sliced her fingers, but she pulled until she felt Lirea's skin tear. Lirea refused to give in. Talia's vision began to sparkle, and her blood pounded in her skull. She heard shouts in the distance, and then Lirea was swimming away.

Talia pulled herself up and tried not to vomit. On one side of the room, Danielle staggered against the wind, her glass sword clutched in both hands. Lirea had recovered her spear, but it looked as though Danielle's enchanted blade had sheared off the point.

The wind-driven spray made it hard to follow Danielle's movements. She was backing away from Lirea. If Talia hadn't been able to beat the mermaid, Danielle wouldn't last long. "Where's that magic, Snow?"

Danielle jabbed her sword toward the stairs. Most of the candles had died, but Talia could just make out Snow's body crumpled on the steps, her legs submerged in the water. She wasn't moving.

Danielle was trying to get past Lirea to the stairs, but Lirea clubbed her in the arm with her spear. Danielle hit the spear again, cutting it in two, and then the wind tossed her into the water.

Lirea dropped her broken weapon and retreated up the stairs, her tails shifting into legs. She pulled her knife from her harness and grabbed Snow's hair, yanking her head up to expose the throat.

"Lirea!" Talia ducked behind the broken bell, taking shelter from the wind as she drew a knife from her belt and threw. The air spirits slapped it aside with ease, but it was enough to make Lirea jump.

Talia braced herself against the wind. She pulled both knives from her forearm sheaths and threw one left-handed. Like the first, this one flew wide. But even as that blade clattered against the wall, Talia was gauging its path and throwing the next. This time, she aimed to the right, a throw that would have gone wide ... if the wind hadn't altered its course.

It wasn't a perfect throw. Not even Talia was that good. But the blade sank into Lirea's shoulder.

Lirea screamed and dropped her own weapon. She ripped Talia's knife from her shoulder and flung it aside. "Stay out of my mind!"

Talia was already wading toward the stairs. All she could see was Snow lying on the steps. In that moment, she wanted nothing more than to tear Lirea apart with her bare hands.

Lirea disappeared up the stairs, her incoherent shouts echoing throughout the tower. Talia followed into the dark room above. She leaped off of the stairs, balanced to dodge another attack, but Lirea seemed intent on escape. Her footsteps slapped against the stairs above as she fled.

"Snow's hurt!" Danielle shouted. "We have to get her out of here."

It was probably the only thing that could have broken Talia's rage. She hesitated, then turned back.

"What happened?" Talia asked. Now that she had stopped running, her legs threatened to give out. "Snow started to cast her spell, and—" Her voice broke.

"The air spirits flung her against the wall." Danielle waded through the water, searching the filth on the bottom.

Talia knelt beside Snow. Her illusions had vanished when she lost consciousness, and Talia could see the rise and fall of Snow's chest with each slow breath. "You said you could do this. Lirea was *asleep!* You said you were strong enough, damn you!"

"Check to see if she has any other injuries," Danielle yelled.

Blood trickled along the step from the back of Snow's head. "Don't do this to me," Talia pleaded. "You're going to be fine. Just wake up!"

"Yelling at her isn't going to help." Danielle reached into the water, grabbing the knife Lirea had dropped. "We have to get her out of here."

"Her skull could be cracked," Talia said. "Her brain might be bleeding. Snow's the healer, not me. If we try to move her, she could die."

"If we stay here, she will. We all will." Danielle climbed the steps and slapped the knife into Talia's hand. "I've got no way to carry it."

Talia slid Lirea's knife into one of her sheaths without taking her eyes off of Snow. "I can't lose her, too." She was babbling, but she couldn't stop herself. "Not Snow. Danielle, I—"

Danielle punched her in the cheek. It wasn't a strong blow, but it was enough to get Talia's attention, as much from shock as from pain. Danielle swung a second time, and Talia automatically snapped her forearm up to block.

Danielle winced and rubbed her wrist where Talia had struck. "Help me carry her."

Talia wondered if she had learned that tone from the queen, or if it was just a mother thing. It was a voice that held no room for argument. Talia took Snow's arms while Danielle scooped her legs. Together they carried her up the stairs, moving carefully to keep from falling. The air spirits could have knocked them all down with ease, but the air had gone still when Lirea fled.

"She's probably alerted the other undine by now," Danielle said.

"We could retreat over land. They won't be able to follow."

Danielle shook her head. "Carry Snow across barren rock with no food or water? Where would we go? You'd mock me for weeks if I suggested something like that."

She was right. Talia might be able to reach the mountains on her own, but she wasn't sure about Danielle. Carrying Snow, they would all end up dead of exposure. "We can't fight our way past all the undine."

"Don't worry about fighting," Danielle said. "Just worry about carrying Snow up to the window. That's a command, Princess."

Talia felt like a marionette, dragged along by the strings of Danielle's voice. She continued up the steps, her breath hissing through clenched teeth at every bump or misstep. When they reached the third story, Danielle set Snow down and circled the room, inspecting the windows. Talia pulled Snow close, cradling her like a child. "If you'd let me kill Lirea when I had the chance—"

"You think her air spirits would have let your knife reach her?" Danielle interrupted. "If you want to be angry, fine. But we have to get out of here right now. I don't see Lirea anywhere."

"Snow's still bleeding."

The rising sun painted Danielle's face orange. "Talia, please. I know how you feel about her, but I need your help. Snow needs your help. Can you carry her and climb down at the same time?"

Talia scooped Snow into her arms and brought her to the window. Even if she had a way to secure Snow to herself, it would be a slow descent, leaving them vulnerable to the merfolk. She tightened her grip on Snow and steeled herself. "We have to jump."

"We have to *what*?"

"If we push off together, we should clear those rocks." Talia was already turning around, sitting on the sill with her back exposed to the morning air. She scooted to one side to make room. "Sit beside me."

Danielle looked past Talia, then nodded. "Will this hurt her?"

"Maybe." Talia bowed her head. "Probably. How much depends on how serious her injuries are."

"I'm sorry," Danielle whispered, squeezing onto the sill beside her.

Talia bent to kiss Snow's forehead. "So am I."

Each of them wrapped an arm around Snow's body, holding her close. With her other hand, Talia grabbed the back of Danielle's belt. Danielle did the same with Talia.

"We'll hit the water hard," Talia said, trying not to think about what they could be doing to Snow. "Keep her close so our bodies cushion her, especially the head. We go on the count of four."

Talia counted fast, leaving no time for fear, and then they were kicking out from the window. Snow started to slide free, but Talia dug her fingers into Snow's skin, holding her tight.

The impact slammed the air from her lungs. They sank through the water, hitting the rocks a moment later. Talia pushed Snow and Danielle up before following. As far as she could tell, the water had protected her from broken bones, but her back would be an interesting collage of cuts and bruises.

The merfolk were already closing in, swimming through the wall and spreading out to block the moat.

"Where's Lirea?" Danielle asked.

"Gone." Talia picked up a rock and hurled it at the approaching warriors. It glanced off the side of a merman's head, knocking him back. Another threw a spear, but the throw was clumsy, and the spear ricocheted off the wall behind her. Talia drew the knife they had taken from Lirea. "They're sluggish, as Morveren said. Distracted. Get Snow and the knife away from here. Stay near shore but far enough back to avoid their spears. If . . . when Snow wakes up, she should be able to summon the *Phillipa*."

Talia tossed Lirea's knife onto the rocks by Danielle, then reached into the water for another fist-sized stone. The merfolk slowed. They might be tired, but they weren't stupid. She counted at least twenty, with more likely hidden beneath the water. Even on land Talia would have been hard-pressed to fight so many, and Lirea had a literal army waiting beyond that wall. Talia threw, but this time her target twisted aside, and the rock splashed harmlessly into the water.

Three merfolk swam through the moat, weapons extended like lancers charging. Talia leaped back as the merfolk burst from the water. Talia twisted sideways, bending her legs in a sik h'adan fighting stance. She sprang between two of the merfolk, positioning herself close enough that they shouldn't be able to spear her.

They floated low in the water, most of their bodies beneath the surface. Talia struck one with her knee, but in the deeper water she lacked the power to do much damage. Still, the blow brought the mermaid's face up, allowing Talia to smash an elbow into her nose. She spun sideways and hit the merman behind her with the same elbow.

"Get ready," Danielle shouted.

"I thought you were supposed to be retreating!" Talia grabbed the mermaid's hair, twisting her around to keep her between herself and the uninjured merman.

Beyond the wall, one of the kelpies reared from the water and bellowed an enormous *Gronk!* Bowing its head, it lunged toward the large central archway of the wall.

Blocks tumbled from the arch as the kelpie burst into the moat. Waves surged ahead of its passage, tossing Talia and merfolk alike. Talia scrambled back, trying to escape from the kelpie's path. She could see a lone rider clinging to the kelpie, pounding its neck and shouting.

"Your doing?" Talia asked.

Danielle smiled. "Could you do something about that merman on our kelpie?"

Talia's next rock hit the rider square in the back. He yelled and dropped into the moat.

"Don't be afraid," Danielle shouted. She returned Lirea's knife to Talia, then waded into the water. "We're not going to hurt you!"

Two enormous flippers, each one longer than Talia herself, dug into the rocks as the kelpie reared back. The kelpie's underside was pale blue, darkening into bands of brown and muddy green. Huge nostrils flapped open, snorting sour air. Its head was vaguely equine, with an elongated snout and spines along the neck. Dark ropes nested behind each of the bony ridges circling his body. Each rope was knotted with large loops for riders to cling to.

"We're not going to hurt you, you coward!" Danielle shouted. "We need your help."

Talia searched for a weapon. "They've trained that animal to obey. If you can't control it—"

"I don't control them," Danielle said. "I ask for their help. But he knows we're not undine, and he can probably smell the blood in the water. I think he's scared."

The undine had fallen back to avoid the kelpie, but they appeared to be regrouping. The three Talia had fought were circling around, while others crept toward the shore behind the kelpie. "How scared?"

"Can't you see him shaking?"

"Good. Tell it Halaka'ar the three-headed sea dragon

is coming. Halaka'ar consumes light and breathes darkness, and he wears the skulls of his prey around his necks. His gaze petrifies all who look upon him, and his jaws devour body, mind, and soul. I know the prayers to divert Halaka'ar's wrath, but it has to help us."

Danielle stared. "Remind me not to let you tell Jakob any bedtime stories."

"Halaka'ar guarded the river of the dead," Talia explained. "My tutors taught me the old religions." She shook her head, remembering. "They also told me Halaka'ar would come for any child who snuck sweets during lessons."

Danielle closed her eyes, presumably relaying Talia's story. Moments later, the kelpie dropped flat. The merfolk hesitated, clearly distrustful of their beast's strange behavior. Talia grabbed Snow and waded toward the animal's harness. She hoisted Snow up, threading her arm through one of the loops on the harness. "Hurry up, Princess."

The kelpie's body was warm, trembling hard enough to send wavelets knocking past Talia's legs. She finished pushing Snow's other arm through the harness, then grabbed another rock. The rock knocked the closest merfolk back, giving her time to grab another of the kelpie's loops. She held the back of Snow's harness with one hand, keeping her tight against the scales.

"Hold on," Danielle warned, taking the next loop of rope beside Snow.

The kelpie reared up and twisted to face the wall behind. Merfolk fell back as the kelpie surged toward the arch and the open sea. Talia swore and pressed herself and Snow flat as they passed through the arch. The rock scraped skin from her shoulder blades and backside. Any tighter and she would have been torn free or crushed.

The kelpie began to sink as they reached deeper water. Talia shoved Snow higher on the kelpie's back. "Danielle?"

"We can't breathe water," Danielle shouted. "And my friends are injured. Their blood could attract sharks!"

The kelpie bobbed up like a cork. Its long tail undulated like a snake, shooting them through the water.

"They have other kelpies," Talia shouted. "They'll be after us as soon as they regroup."

Danielle nodded and closed her eyes, resting against the kelpie's body. Talia didn't know what she said, but the kelpie began to swim even faster, paddling with its large fins. The movement of its body reminded her of a horse's gallop.

Talia stretched her legs, bracing her feet against the bony ridge behind her to take some of the weight off of the loops around her arms. This would be more comfortable if she could get Snow to the top of the kelpie, where they could rest on a relatively flat surface. But she couldn't climb and hold onto Snow at the same time. Even with Snow's arms through the harness, her body draped down the kelpie's side, her toes trailing through the water.

Blood dripped slowly down Snow's neck and back. The bleeding didn't look too bad, especially for a head wound, but she still hadn't woken up.

"I shouldn't have made her cast the spell on me, back at the *Phillipa*," Talia said. "Morveren told me to let Snow conserve her strength."

"Snow thought she had enough power—" Danielle began.

"Snow's a powerful sorceress," Talia said. "Almost as strong as she thinks she is. But she's never been good at accepting limits."

"Unlike you?" Danielle teased. In a softer voice, she added, "This isn't your fault."

Talia twisted her head, looking back at the shrinking shoreline. Danielle was right. Even if Talia had tried to kill Lirea while she slept, the air spirits likely would have thwarted her attack. Knowing that didn't lessen the anger. "Can't this stupid thing go any faster?"

CHAPTER 10

L IREA CLUTCHED HER ARM where the human's knife had stabbed her. Voices taunted her as she fled, mocking her weakness and her fear, but she couldn't stop swimming.

She had been dreaming of Gustan, so real she could still feel his hands on her body, the tiny hairs on his legs that tickled her skin as he moved. She could smell the sweat that dampened the curls on his neck. He had never been gentle with her, but humans were known to be rough.

And then her dreams had shifted. Tears streamed from her eyes as she staggered up the beach, smiling through the pain of each tortured step. Naked and pathetic and human, she called out to him. She had been little more than a child, weak and desperate. She had begged for his love, and in doing so earned only contempt.

And now that weakness surfaces again. The voice sounded distant, though the words were no less sharp. How could Gustan ever love such a coward?

They came to my home, Lirea protested. *Cracked open my mind like a seabird digging the meat from a snail.*

So you flee like a child frightened by a passing cloud.

Another whisper, this one almost lyrical in tone. *Lannadae . . . Morveren . . . the humans . . . you've failed too many times, and soon you will be punished.*

More voices joined in, coming from all around her.
There is no escape.

No matter how far and how fast you swim.

You'll never be safe.

Lirea swam to the surface and screamed until the
sound threatened to scrape the skin from her throat.
Only when her lungs gave out did she look around to see
the undine gathered behind her. Nilliar was the closest,
watching her with worried eyes. Beyond them, Lirea's
palace was a shrunken smudge in the distance.

Lirea waited, but her screams appeared to have
drowned out the other voices for now. They would return soon enough. They always did.

"You're injured," Nilliar said. "What happened?"

"They stole my knife. They tried to steal my thoughts."
Lirea's scales flared, and she shivered at the memory.
The pain in her arm was nothing compared to the touch
of another's mind in her own. "How did they find me,
Nilliar? They came into my home and ripped open my
head and—"

"I don't know, but you're safe."

"No. None of us are." Why was she so afraid? Where
was her strength? Lirea squinted at the horizon, searching. "Which way did they flee?"

Nilliar pointed to the west.

"They must have a ship. Why didn't we see them approaching? Who was patrolling those waters?"

An older warrior named Toskoth swam forward. He
had served Lirea's mother and father for most of his
life.

"I spoke with three undine who said they wished to
join our tribe," he said. "I was there when the humans
escaped. They were the same. Somehow they were able
to take our shapes."

"Morveren." Her grandmother must have enchanted
the humans so they could come here to destroy her. Lirea beckoned, and Nilliar pressed a spear into her hand.
"You were my father's spearbearer, Toskoth. Did you
ever once allow murderers to attack *him*?"

"I'm sorry, my queen."

Lirea thrust her spear into his chest, pushing until the tip broke through the skin of his back. His gills flared, but he made no sound. Lirea shoved him away. Blood and bubbles rose from the wound as Toskoth sank through the water.

The other undine spread back. Even Nilliar appeared shocked, but none dared to speak. None but the whispers in Lirea's mind.

Toskoth played with you as a child and sang songs of times long past.

Lirea ducked beneath the water. This time her scream was sharper, a summons loud enough to be heard by every kelpie in the tribe. Once she heard their answering cry, she surfaced and said, "They mean to carve me apart until there's nothing left."

"You need rest," Nilliar said softly. "You're hurt, and you need time to recover. The tribe is in the midst of breeding. You can't—"

"They've torn me in two." Lirea swam closer and ripped the second spear from Nilliar's harness. "But a queen must be strong."

White crests approached from the shore, marking the arrival of the kelpies. Lirea gripped the spear in both hands and whispered, "I will be strong."

The harness straps dug deep into Danielle's arms. She would be horribly bruised . . . assuming they survived at all.

A faint call carried over the waves, and the kelpie slowed. He looked behind, his body quivering like a horse preparing to bolt. Danielle didn't know if the call was a summons or simply a cry of pain, but it was obvious the kelpie had been trained to respond.

"Please don't go," Danielle said. "You have to get us to our ship. It's the only way to stop Halaka'ar."

The kelpie turned back toward the *Phillipa*. The fins and spikes near his head flared out as he answered the call. The sound threatened to burst Danielle's ears.

"Please don't do that," she said.

In the distance, Danielle could hear other kelpies. She had no doubt they were following, along with the undine. The *Phillipa* was still barely more than a toy floating in the distance. They should reach it before their pursuers, but they wouldn't have much time to escape.

Beside her, Snow stirred and mumbled, "Too loud."

"Snow!" Danielle and Talia spoke as one.

Snow's face crinkled in protest. "I said too loud, and you shout at me?"

Talia shifted position, bracing herself with her legs and freeing one hand to touch Snow's face. "Open your eyes, Snow. Look at me."

Snow squinted in the light. "What happened?"

"You were hurt," Danielle said. "We're going to take care of you. We're almost back to the ship."

"I remember the tower . . ." Snow started to say more, and then her eyes widened. Before Danielle could react, Snow turned her head and threw up. She would have fallen from the kelpie if Talia hadn't grabbed her.

"Sorry." Snow closed her eyes and lay back.

"It's all right," Danielle said in the same soothing tone she used when Jakob was upset. "We'll be at the *Phillipa* soon."

"My head hurts." Snow tried to sit up again, but Talia held her in place.

"That's because Lirea's air spirits hit you with a tower," said Talia.

"Lirea." Snow closed her eyes. "She's awfully angry. She shouldn't have been able to feel my spell."

"Just rest," said Talia. "Try not to move."

Snow nodded and laid her head back against the kelpie. Her lips were pale, and her eyelids kept fluttering open. "Talia?"

"I'm right here."

Snow smiled. "My head hurts. What happened?"

Danielle's stomach tightened. She looked at Talia, whose face was taut. Danielle forced a smile. "You're going to be fine, sweetie."

"Oh." Snow appeared to consider this. "That's good."

"Talia, why can't she remember—"

"I don't know." Talia wouldn't look at her. "Sometimes when the head is hurt . . . she needs to rest."

Danielle turned back to the *Phillipa*. They were close enough now for Danielle to see the crew scrambling about, preparing for an attack. A heartbeat later, she realized the crew was getting ready to attack *them*.

"Wait!" Her voice barely carried over the noise of the water. She pulled one arm out of the harness and gripped the loop with her hand. "Hold Snow."

"I've got her," Talia said, slipping both arms around Snow's body.

Fear overpowered the cramps in Danielle's arms as she hauled herself higher on the kelpie's back, climbing the bony ridges and praying he didn't make any sudden turns. When she reached the base of his neck, she grabbed another of the harness' loops to brace herself and drew her sword. She waved the blade through the air, turning it so the glass caught the light of the rising sun. The crew thought they were undine, but no undine carried a glass sword. Nobody did, save the princess of Lorindar.

Below, Snow giggled. "You're naked."

"That's because somebody insisted on turning us into mermaids before we left." Danielle kept her body hidden behind the kelpie's neck the best she could, but continued to wave her sword until the crew stopped pointing weapons their way. She whispered silently to the kelpie, who slowed as he neared the ship. Danielle could see large fishing nets in the water, presumably lowered to fight the undine.

Captain Hephyra hopped onto the railing. Thrust through her belt was a thick, unfinished bludgeon of pale wood. "I hope you're not planning to keep that thing as a pet!"

"I know that kelpie!" said Lannadae, crawling up beside Hephyra. "I remember when he was just a hatchling!"

Danielle guided the kelpie between the nets. Hephyra tossed down a rope, which Danielle and Talia looped beneath Snow's arms. Talia grabbed the rope with one hand, using her other arm to keep Snow steady as Hephyra hauled them both on board.

"Be careful," Danielle shouted. "She's hurt."

Hephyra didn't appear to strain as she pulled Snow and Talia up. Lannadae was waiting with blankets, and soon it was Danielle's turn.

"Did you get what you needed?" Hephyra asked.

"We have Lirea's knife." Danielle climbed over the rail, and Lannadae threw a blanket over her shoulders. Most of the crew were too busy preparing the ship for battle to ogle the three women, though Danielle did see one gunner walk right into the capstan.

"What about Lirea?" Morveren crawled out of the cutter. "What happened to my granddaughter?"

"Snow couldn't control her," Danielle said. "The air spirits—"

The fins along Morveren's legs slapped the deck. "I warned her! Finesse, not power. The stronger the spell, the easier it is to detect. She pushed too hard!" She peered into Snow's eyes, and her fins rippled again.

Snow groaned and pulled away. "Will someone please make the ship stop spinning?"

Danielle tried to smile, but inside she was feeling more useless with every passing moment. "The air spirits threw her against the tower wall." She could still see the surprise on Snow's face as she flew back, just as she could still hear the horrible thump of Snow's head striking stone. "She didn't wake up until we were almost back to the ship."

"She will get better, won't she?" Lannadae looked from Morveren to Danielle, her eyes wet with tears. "She's Snow White. She has to get better."

"Maybe." Morveren adjusted her tails, tucking them both to the side. "Depends on how hard she was hit. She needs rest."

Outside, the kelpie bellowed again. The answering calls were louder than before.

"Your pet is leading his friends right to us," Talia said.

Danielle shook her head. "They know which way we went. They would have found us anyway." She could see the kelpies in the distance, but right now Snow was more important. "We should get her inside the cabin."

"I don't want to go in the cabin," Snow protested as Talia picked her up.

"Can you go with them?" Danielle asked Lannadae. "Snow's hurt, and she'll need someone to watch over her."

"You should go too, Princess," said Hephyra. "We're going to have enough trouble without you getting in our way."

Danielle shook her head, trying to focus. "Do you have anyone else on board who can tell those kelpies to return home?"

Hephyra looked out at the kelpies. "Do what you can. Try not to get killed." Drawing her weapon, she turned around to shout, "I want every gun loaded and ready to fire. Hold her steady. Any man who looses so much as a single crossbow bolt before my order gets fed to the sea monster."

Danielle moved to the edge of the ship, holding her blanket closed with one hand. "Thank you for saving us!" The kelpie should be able to hear her without words, but between the noise of the crew and the honking of the other kelpies, it couldn't hurt to shout. "Now go, quickly, before Halaka'ar finds you. Tell your friends to follow. You should be safe back at shore."

The kelpie's answering warble sounded confused. He bobbed his head, splashing hard enough to spray Danielle.

"Go!"

Waves rocked the ship as the kelpie disappeared into the water. Danielle watched his shadow retreat through the water, heading directly toward the approaching undine.

"Here." Talia tossed Danielle a long, dark green tunic. Talia had donned a similar one, along with a pair of knee-length trousers. She'd rolled her sleeves up, exposing the knives on her forearms. She must have rearmed herself while Danielle was talking to the kelpie.

Talia reached out to hold the blanket while Danielle changed. "I thought you might want your dignity back."

"Thanks." Danielle yanked the tunic over her head. She was just buckling her sword belt over the tunic when a cheer broke out among the crew. Another kelpie had turned to follow the one Danielle had sent away. She could see the riders shouting and slapping the kelpie with their spears, but it made no difference. Soon a third kelpie began to retreat.

"Well, squeeze my taproot," Hephyra said. "We might survive this thing after all."

Their triumph was short-lived. Another kelpie reared up from the water and called out. This one was a deep yellow color, spotted with green. Danielle could feel the vibration of the call through the ship's hull. The rest fell back into formation.

This new kelpie carried only a single two-tailed rider. Lirea guided her mount closer to the *Phillipa*. Undine warriors dropped from their kelpies, spreading out through the water. They kept their distance for now, no doubt waiting for the order to attack.

Danielle turned to Morveren. "Can *you* try to control Lirea?"

"I've tried before, remember?" Morveren pointed to the stubs of her tails. "She knows me, and her hate is too strong. I had hoped an unfamiliar mind would have better luck."

Danielle tried again to send the kelpies away. A few shifted in the water, but none moved.

"Can the guns hit them from here?" Talia asked.

Hephyra shook her head. "It would be like shooting a fly with a longbow at fifty paces."

"No guns!" Morveren said, crawling toward them. "You promised to help me save my granddaughter."

"We tried." Talia didn't bother turning to look at Morveren. "She stabbed Beatrice. She nearly killed Snow. I'm not giving her another chance to hurt anyone."

This time, Danielle was in complete agreement. "If you want to protect her, help us find a way to stop her."

Lirea raised her spear in one hand and began to sing. It was a harsh, grating sound, barely recognizable as song. The rest of the undine soon joined her, their voices rising like a hundred flutes trilling in unison.

"A war song," Morveren said. "She orders the tribe to fight until death. Ours or their own."

"Target the leader," Hephyra shouted.

Morveren moaned, but she said nothing. She simply crawled away, back toward the shelter of the cutter.

The undine disappeared into the water. The kelpies appeared to leap forward, sinking deeper as they charged the ship. Lirea held back, still singing.

Hephyra pointed her weapon. "Somebody shut that bitch up."

Four guns fired in quick succession. One lucky shot hit Lirea's kelpie in the neck. It was a glancing blow, but the animal reared back, squealing in pain.

"Ready the nets," Hephyra yelled, running toward the back of the ship. "Your crossbow bolts will lose their speed in the water, so don't bother shooting unless your target's near the surface. Don't forget to watch the port side!"

The gun crews were already reloading. Danielle had seen the process before on the *Glass Slipper,* but never with such grim-faced urgency. Young boys ran fresh powder cartridges up from below while others hastily swabbed the inside of the cannons, cleaning out any embers that might prematurely ignite the next charge.

As the undine approached the ship, Danielle heard another sound. Morveren had begun to sing. The sound was like a blanket that grew heavier with every passing moment, pressing Danielle down. She tried to step back, but her legs wouldn't obey.

The first wave of undine leaped from the water to hurl their spears. The crew made no effort to dodge. Danielle saw four men fall, dead or dying.

A crossbow clattered to the deck. Another followed. One man tumbled out of the yards, cracking his arm and shoulder when he landed. Even Captain Hephyra stumbled against the mast, clinging to the wood as though she would fall without its support.

Though Morveren's song wasn't identical to the one she had sung against the Hiladi, it was similar enough for Danielle to recognize the magic. This song was more emotional than the last, driven by fear and anger and desperation. This one also sounded stronger to Danielle's ear.

"Grandmother, no!" Lannadae crawled out of the cabin. She paused to shake a fallen crewman, but with no effect. "No more magic! Lirea will kill us all!"

"I won't let that happen." Morveren worked the words into her song, never missing a note. "I'll find a way to protect you both."

"Lannadae, stop her!" Danielle's voice was nothing against the power of Morveren's, but Lannadae turned toward her. "Please!"

The *Phillipa* trembled as one of the kelpies rammed her hull. Fainter thuds followed, probably caused by the undine trying to splinter the ship from below.

"I can save her," Morveren said. "I can save us all. Get off the deck and go somewhere safe!"

"These people tried to help us!" Lannadae grabbed Moveren's arm.

Without breaking her song, Morveren struck Lannadae on the side of the neck. Lannadae's gills flared out, and she fell back, weeping. She lay there for a moment, gasping for breath.

"I'm sorry," Morveren sang. "Now go!"

Even Danielle could feel the power in that command. Lanndae crawled away, still crying.

Help us, Danielle pleaded, concentrating on the kelpies. She could still see Lirea's kelpie circling the ship at a distance. Blood dripped from his neck, but the wound obviously wasn't a crippling one. Neither he nor the other kelpies acknowledged Danielle's plea. She closed her eyes to try again, this time directing her request somewhere closer.

The scrape of claws on wood marked Stub's arrival. He scrambled up from below, then raced across the deck in a streak of dark fur. For days he had reluctantly obeyed Danielle's request to not stalk these strange half-fish visitors. Now, with Danielle's blessing, he pounced, sinking teeth and claws into the exposed skin at the stump of Morveren's left tail.

Morveren shrieked and twisted about. Stub scrambled up Morveren's side, claws raking her skin and tangling in her hair.

Danielle pushed herself up, trying to reach her sword. She had to get to Morveren before the mermaid recovered, but her body felt like water.

Morveren caught Stub's tail. He turned and bit her hand between the thumb and forefinger. She yelled as she ripped him from her skin. Stub continued to claw her arm as she drew back and threw the cat toward the mast.

Danielle pushed herself up, but there was no way she would get there in time.

Captain Hephyra stepped around the mast to snatch the cat from the air. Bringing Stub to her chest, she said, "I don't appreciate guests attacking my crew."

Danielle finally freed her sword and raised it overhead, stumbling toward Morveren. She saw the mermaid flinch back, arms raised to protect her head.

Danielle hesitated. With Snow hurt, killing Morveren would likely mean letting Beatrice die as well. In that moment of doubt, Morveren opened her mouth to sing.

Talia was faster. She fell on Morveren, driving her shoulder into the mermaid's chest. Morveren pushed her back, and Talia snapped an elbow to her jaw. She grabbed Morveren's thumb and twisted, eliciting a shriek of pain as she drove Morveren face first into the deck.

Danielle heard bone snap as Morveren fought to break free of Talia's hold. She swung one of her tails into Talia's side, knocking her down. But even as Morveren tried to crawl away, Talia rolled over and kicked her in the stomach. A second kick caught her in the bridge of the nose. Morveren's head snapped back, and she slumped to the deck.

"Did you kill her?" Danielle asked.

"Not yet."

"We still need her." Danielle used her sword to cut a strip from her discarded blanket. "Gag and bind her, but don't kill her."

"What about kicking her a couple more times?" Talia yanked Morveren onto her stomach, then shoved the gag into her mouth. "We should make sure the other one doesn't get any ideas either."

"I don't think Lannadae would—" Danielle bit her lip. She hadn't thought Morveren would turn on them either. For all of Lannadae's fear, she cared about her sister and her grandmother both. Danielle wanted to trust her, but mistakes could get people killed. "Go ahead."

Talia ran toward the cabin, pausing only to snatch a thrown spear from the air and hurl it back toward its owner. She grabbed the cabin door and tugged. When the door wouldn't budge, she stepped back and kicked it.

"Do you mind?" Hephyra demanded, still holding Stub. "She's not getting out of that door unless I want her to. I've swollen it shut, and the wood's thick enough to muffle her if she tries to sing."

"What about Snow?" Talia asked. "She's in there too."

"Your mermaid friend isn't about to hurt Snow. She's huddled against the door, bawling like a jilted lover. Nothing happens on this ship without me knowing. Now get out of my way and let me defend my ship."

Cannons and crossbows began to fire again as the crew shook off Morveren's song. Their weapons had little effect on the undine, most of whom were too close to the ship. The cannons couldn't be pointed straight down, and the water slowed the crossbow bolts.

"Work the nets!" Hephyra was already hauling one of the lines strung through the yardarm, pulling a net up along the starboard bow. Three undine flopped within the net. Two managed to flip free, though the second took a crossbow bolt to the arm. Three more men fired, killing the last undine before he could escape. "Get to the bow and drag the nets beneath the keel. Otherwise they'll crack the ship like a nut and drown us all."

Danielle watched over the rail as a wounded undine retreated. Another cannon fired, and the water erupted directly in front of the undine. He floated to the surface, stunned.

"There are too many," said Talia. "We can't stop them from up here, even with the nets."

Talia was right. The crew knew it too. Danielle spotted James standing in the forecastle, crossbow cocked as he searched for a target. There was no longer any fear in his expression, only grim determination.

The ship shook as another kelpie rammed the side. Two more cannons fired, and the kelpie's cry of pain made Danielle cringe.

"Talia, grab Captain Hephyra and come with me." Danielle ran toward the ladder to the lower decks. She blinked as she passed into the darkness. Down here, the cannons sounded like thunder, and the motion of the ship was even more disorienting. Fighting a wave of queasiness, Danielle made her way deeper, toward the magazine where the powder was stored. There were no lanterns here, not with the damage a single open flame could cause.

"What are we doing?" Talia asked.

Danielle nearly collided with a boy running fresh cartridges to the guns. She stepped around and pushed through a damp curtain into the magazine.

The room was almost pitch black, save for a few cracks of weak light that pierced the walls. A shadow of a man rose as Danielle entered. "You can't be down here."

"She can if I say so," said Captain Hephyra, entering behind Talia. "That's one of the perks of being captain."

"We need a powder barrel." Danielle was already searching the room the best she could. She bumped one barrel sitting against the wall. The top of the barrel came to her midthigh. A single push told her it was far too heavy to lift. Too heavy for a human, at least. "You saw the cannons firing at the undine. They missed, but the impact stunned one of the undine."

"So we need a bigger impact." She could hear Talia's grin.

"Stand aside." Hephyra grunted as she dragged the barrel onto its side and rolled it out of the magazine toward the ladder. When she reached it, she wrapped her arms around the barrel and hoisted it into the air. "We'll teach those bottom-feeders to hack at my ship."

The ladder creaked from the strain. With each step, Danielle held her breath, certain Hephyra would overbalance or drop the barrel. But Hephyra climbed as though rooted to the ladder.

Danielle ran after her. Hephyra was already rolling the barrel toward the side of the ship.

"We'll need a way to set it off," Talia said.

Danielle grabbed the linstock from the nearest gun crew. The gunner yanked it back, raising a fist before he realized who stood before him. He blanched, but didn't release the linstock. "Princess, we're almost ready to—"

Hephyra cleared her throat, and the man let go as though the slow match at the end of the linstock had burned him. Danielle handed it to Talia, who hefted the iron rod in one hand.

"Think you can hit a barrel with that thing?" Danielle asked. The slow match was a short distance back from the tip of the rod. Talia would have to throw hard enough to pierce the barrel and drive the ember into the powder.

Talia raised an eyebrow. "You're joking, right?"

Hephyra raised the barrel above her head and tossed it over the rail. It splashed into the water, nearly landing on one of the undine. "If it blows so close to the ship, the explosion might crack the hull."

"Imagine what it will do to the undine." Danielle backed away. "Everyone clear the starboard rail!"

"You break my ship, I'll use you for compost." Hephyra turned around and shouted, "Get back and brace yourselves!"

Talia leaned over the rail, raised the linstock, and threw. As soon as the linstock left her hand, she leaped back from the rail. Danielle heard a thunk as iron hit wood. For an instant, she thought her plan had failed.

The sea exploded. The *Phillipa* pitched sideways, and even Talia stumbled. Over the ringing in her ears, Danielle could hear shouts and curses from the crew. She moved toward the rail, grimacing at the plume of black smoke rising from the water.

Several undine already bobbed on the surface. Most appeared to be breathing, though the explosion had killed at least two. Others followed, floating to the surface and drawing cheers from the ship. The kelpies were already retreating, their head fins flared in fear. A cannon fired on the fleeing kelpies, driving them beneath the water.

"Not bad." Hephyra grinned and ran back to the ladder, though she didn't bother to use it. She simply jumped, hair flying as she vanished into the darkness.

Talia pulled Danielle down as a fresh wave of spears flew toward the ship. Some of the undine had obviously escaped the explosion. The crew returned fire, sending three crossbow bolts into the water for every spear the undine threw.

Soon the floating bodies began to disappear, no doubt dragged to safety by the still conscious undine.

Even from this distance, Lirea's scream of rage was enough to make Danielle stumble. Lirea guided her kelpie around, pointing her spear and urging her people to attack. Most of the undine were underwater, making it hard to follow their movements. Their bodies were little more than pale streaks doubling back toward the *Phillipa*.

At the back of a ship, the helmsman screamed as the wheel spun out of his grip. Even from here Danielle could see that his arm was broken. The undine must have cut the line to the rudder.

"Talia, are you ready?" Hephyra climbed onto the deck, another barrel in her arms.

This explosion was even closer to the ship. Once again undine floated to the surface, but still they obeyed Lirea's commands.

Danielle concentrated on the kelpies. *I warned you. That horrible sound is the call of Halaka'ar. He comes to devour all in his path.*

Two of the kelpies fled. Even Lirea's mount reared higher, head twisting about to search the water. A blue-tailed mermaid was climbing up the side of Lirea's kelpie. They appeared to be arguing.

"Fifty crowns to the gunner who takes that bitch down," Hephyra said.

The men raced to reload and fire, but Lirea was too far from the ship. Their shots splashed harmlessly in the water. Lirea's kelpie sank from view. Peering down, Danielle saw the last of the undine swimming away.

"We should go after them," Talia said. "Chase them back to land and take out Lirea for good. I counted at least four more barrels in the magazine. That's more than enough to—"

"The *Phillipa*'s taking on water." Hephyra leaned against the rail. She appeared weary. "The undine know their work. Another explosion like that will sink us."

Danielle stared out at the water. Patches of rust-colored foam littered the sea. Blood, she realized, bubbling up from the undine's wounds. "Get us home," she said, fighting a bout of nausea that had nothing to do with the movement of the ship. So many dead, human and undine alike. "The faster we get that knife to Beatrice, the better our chances of saving her."

Talia looked back at the main deck. Morveren was groaning and clutching her stomach. Blood and tears marked her face. "What about her?" Talia asked. "I suppose you're going to tell me she was only protecting her granddaughter. That we should forgive her and pretend she *didn't* almost kill everyone on board."

Behind Talia, the crew was gathering the dead and wounded. Undine spears had killed at least eight men.

Danielle's throat tightened when she spotted James. He lay unmoving, a spear pinning him to the deck. He still clutched his crossbow in his hands.

"No," Danielle whispered, staring at James. "I mean, yes, she was trying to protect Lirea. I don't believe she'll try to hurt us again. But I won't risk being wrong, either."

Hephyra laughed as she limped toward them. "You talk like it's your choice, Princess. Royal or not, this is my ship, and if you ordered that mermaid left free, I'd have tossed the whole lot of you overboard." She shoved her hair back from her face and shouted, "Lock that witch in the hold, and make sure she stays gagged. Anyone not on the sheets or tending wounded had best get down to the pumps."

"How bad is it?" Danielle asked. "Will we make it back to Lorindar?"

Hephyra's grin was more than a little wild. "Ask me in a day or so."

Chapter 11

L IREA SANG A COMMAND, drawing her kelpie
to a halt. She relaxed her grip on the harness, allowing herself to fall into the water. Her surviving warriors
spread into a circle around her.

You've failed yet again.

She screamed to drown out the whispers in her head,
then returned to the surface. "How many did they
kill?"

Nilliar swam toward her. "At least twenty, with twice
that number wounded."

*You underestimated them. You should have taken ev-
ery last undine and swarmed that ship until nothing was
left but splinters and blood.*

"They can be replaced," Lirea said. "Have our scouts
found the nesting grounds of the other tribes?"

"Two more tribes have been found," Nilliar said.
"We've collected enough gold to destroy one of them.
Once the humans have poisoned their waters and
killed their queen, any survivors will be free to join the
Ilowkira."

*Murderer! Conspiring with humans against your own
kind!* Lirea held her breath, trying to shut out the con-
demnation. It was the only way to unite the tribes and
restore her empire. The other queens would never willingly surrender to Lirea. She had to kill them.

She would be sure to kill the human alchemists as

well. If they could poison one tribe, they could poison the Ilowkira.

"Forgive me," said Nilliar. "I doubted you when you told us of Morveren's return."

"Lannadae led the humans to Morveren, and Morveren brought them to me." Tears streamed down Lirea's face. She felt so tired, and her arm throbbed. The wound had started bleeding again, and the pain flowed all the way to her hand with each beat of her heart. "They'll never stop coming until I'm dead."

"Morveren's song stopped their attack," Nilliar said. "Perhaps she—"

"She lured us close, making us believe the humans were helpless." Lirea could still hear the explosions. "They want me dead. They want to punish me for killing Gustan."

Lirea raked her nails down her chest, remembering Gustan's death and how the voices had urged her to drive the blade into her own body. Blood welled over her ribs. Thin and weak, neither human nor undine. Morveren's spell had turned her into a broken, twisted, pitiful creature. No wonder Morveren sought to erase that failure, to replace Lirea with her sister. With a "pure" undine.

Another whisper. *There's still time to make amends. Still time to finish what you began in Gustan's bed. Take your spear, bury the point in your heart and end the pain. A single thrust, and you will finally know peace.*

"Has there been any word from Captain Varisto?" she asked.

Nilliar shook her head.

The human ship had showed signs of recent fighting. Most likely he too was dead. The thought brought new tears.

"I will stop Morveren for you, my queen," Nilliar said. "Let me lead another attack against the humans. Their rudder is disabled. We can attack in small groups, so their explosions harm only a few at a time."

"I should lead the attack," Lirea said. "I can't—"

"The tribe needs you. We can't risk your safety again."

Nilliar gently pushed Lirea away, a liberty no other undine would dare. But Nilliar was her spearbearer, and she had been Lirea's friend for many years. "Go, my queen. Return to the spawning grounds and rest. Allow your spearbearer to fight in your stead, and I promise to put an end to Morveren's threat."

Slowly, Lirea nodded. She watched as Nilliar picked fifteen warriors to accompany her. The remaining warriors passed over weapons, rearming Nilliar's force. They swam away singing a song of victory.

Long after that song faded, Lirea could still hear Morveren's laughter in the waves.

A stabbing pain jolted Snow awake. She sat up slowly, touching the back of her scalp with one hand. Dried blood crusted her hair, coming away in dark specks on her fingertips. A bloody bandage had slipped from the wound, tangling in her hair. She pulled it free.

"How do you feel?" asked Talia.

"Like I drank too much pixie beer." She looked around. Where . . . oh, yes, the cabin on the *Phillipa*. The movement made her queasy, and a second Talia sprang into being behind the first. Snow squinted, trying to force the phantom Talia back into the original.

Danielle was here as well. Two Danielles, rather. Sitting on blurry cots and watching Snow like a mother ready to reach out and catch her baby.

"What's wrong?" Danielle asked.

"Nothing." Snow's vision still split the world in two, but the effect wasn't as bad if she kept her eyes half-closed.

"Do you remember what happened?" Talia's voice was deceptively calm.

Snow started to shake her head, but that only made things worse. She remembered climbing the wall to Lirea's tower. After that, there was nothing but darkness.

Her hands were scratched and sore. Someone had dressed her in a rather plain shirt and trousers, and her hair smelled of salt water.

She must have hit her head. Loss of memory was normal for such a blow, as were problems with vision. Snow knew as much, but it was one thing to read about the symptoms. It was quite another to experience them. She frowned and sniffed her hair again. "Did I throw up?"

"Twice," said Danielle. "Once on the way back to the ship, then again in the cabin when Morveren started singing."

"Morveren—" That was right. Snow remembered Morveren's song, the magic falling over the ship, pressing her down. She had tried to fight the spell, but the effort had been too much. She looked down at her sheets.

"I changed them for you," said Danielle.

"Thank you." She started to say more, but a faint buzzing sensation drew her attention to the knife on Talia's belt. Lirea's knife. "You got it."

Talia nodded. "Lirea escaped, but we have the knife."

"May I?" Snow held out a hand.

Talia hesitated but passed her the knife. As soon as Snow touched the hilt, she could feel the tension within the spells. The hairs wrapped around the hilt were taut, like the lines of the sails when the winds gusted.

Snapping those spells should be simple enough. Cut the hairs and the whole thing would unravel. Unfortunately, there was no way to know what that would do to the souls trapped inside. When lines stretched so taut finally snapped, they often did so with enough force to kill.

She brushed her finger over the blade. The abalone felt warm and wet to the touch, as though the blood it had tasted had never truly dried. She wiped her hand on her shirt.

"You should rest," said Danielle. "Can we get you anything? If you're still nauseated, I could prepare some of that tea you brought for me."

"I need to talk to Morveren," said Snow. "I need her help to—"

"Morveren tried to kill us." Talia kept looking at Snow, then glancing away.

"I don't understand." Snow stared at Talia, then at Danielle, who nodded. "She *helped* us. She was teaching me—"

"Her lessons and advice nearly got you killed." Talia turned away. When she spoke again, her voice was calmer. "She's locked in the hold. When we reach Lorindar, you can work with Father Isaac—"

"No. It's at least a day's journey to Lorindar," Snow said, trying not to think about Morveren. "Can Beatrice afford to lose another day? I assume you've already spoken to Armand?"

"While you slept," Danielle admitted. "Beatrice is . . . she's alive, but she's not doing well."

Snow touched the front of her choker, feeling the warmth of the mirrors. She squinted, trying to force the twin knives to blur together. Beatrice was inside that knife, somewhere. "Mirror, mirror in my—no, that doesn't rhyme."

"What are you doing?" Danielle asked.

The throbbing in Snow's head grew deeper as she concentrated. "Mirrors with your silver sheen, help me speak with my trapped queen."

Not her best rhyme, but the words helped. Morveren would have been disappointed, but right now Snow needed the extra power of her mirrors. Without that power, she didn't know if she could cast even the simplest charm.

Both Talia and Danielle leaned closer, as if they too hoped to hear Queen Bea's voice.

Snow did her best to shut out the sounds of the ship and the crew. There was something . . . a buzzing sound, like an argument in a distant room. She couldn't concentrate enough to make out the words.

"I need privacy." Snow stood, and the room shifted around her. She reached for one of the ceiling beams to steady herself, but her vision had doubled again, and she missed. Talia caught her by the elbows before she could fall.

"You need rest," Danielle said.

Keeping one hand on Snow's arm, Talia reached over to pluck the knife away. "How about I take that? You won't do us much good if you fall and impale yourself."

"Actually, that might work," Snow mumbled. "The knife was designed to hold a single soul. Stabbing more people might snap the spells completely. That might still destroy the souls, though. Hm . . ."

She pulled out of Talia's grip and placed one hand against the ceiling for balance. Pain pulsed through her skull, blurring her vision with every beat. "I'll need a new bandage, too."

Talia moved to block the door. "Do I have to tie you to the bed to make you sleep?"

She would, too. She was awfully stubborn that way. Snow sat back down. "Actually, Danielle, some tea might help settle my stomach."

"Of course." Danielle squeezed Snow's hand, then slipped away.

Talia dug through Snow's things, pulling out clean rags to use as bandages. Talia was more skilled at inflicting wounds than patching them up, but Snow knew she had also gotten plenty of practice with the latter.

"Thank you." Snow leaned back in the bed and closed her eyes. She could hear Talia sitting down on the trunk. "You're staying?"

"You think I'm going to let you sleep with that kind of wound and not keep an eye on you?"

"I'll be fine." Snow took a deep breath and began to hum to herself. "I'll sleep better alone."

"Since when?"

Snow grinned despite herself. Gathering her magic as lightly as she could, she nudged Talia's mind. "Go. Captain Hephyra could probably use you in the crow's nest, watching for undine. You wouldn't want them catching us off guard again, would you?"

"That's true enough," Talia said slowly.

"You should probably leave the knife here." Snow pushed harder. "We're better off keeping it out of sight."

The pressure in her skull squeezed tears from her eyes, and the pounding grew worse. Snow maintained her concentration until she heard Talia rise. The trunk's oiled hinges made hardly a sound as Talia stowed the knife.

Talia started to leave, then hesitated. Snow held her breath, uncertain how much more she could push without Talia realizing what was happening. She opened her eyes, squinting at the sight of two Talia's bending over her. Talia's lips brushed Snow's forehead, and then she was gone.

Snow had an easier time keeping Danielle away. She didn't even need to use magic, which was fortunate. After Talia, she felt as though any magical effort at all would cause her head to burst like an overripe grape. She accepted the cup of tea from Danielle, took a few sips, then lay back with a fatigue she didn't need to fake. "I'll be fine. You should go check in on your son."

"How?" asked Danielle. "He wouldn't be in the nursery right now."

Snow smiled. "Do you have any idea how many mirrors I've hidden throughout the palace? Your bracelet will find him."

Danielle pushed back her sleeve and raised the glass to her lips.

"I'm sorry, but would you mind going elsewhere?" Snow said. "The magic . . . it makes my head ache."

That much was true. Snow felt as though she had the world's worst hangover and hadn't even had the chance to enjoy herself first. She rested a while after Danielle left, until the pain began to ease. Before, she had felt as though six ogres were trying to dig their way out of her skull. Now there were only five.

She gently tugged one of the mirrors from her choker

and studied herself in the tiny reflection. Wraps of white cloth circled her brow, and her hair was an utter disaster. How could her friends have left her in such a state?

She picked up a pearl-handled comb and went to work, carefully tugging through the worst of the blood and vomit. She surveyed the results with a grimace, then crawled out of bed to retrieve her hat. Ever so lightly, she lowered the hat over the bandage, concealing the worst of the cloth.

Much better, at least from what she could see in her mirror. Strange that her sight through the mirrors was so clear when the rest of the world remained blurred and doubled. More evidence that the mirrors worked through senses beyond mere sight. She would have to study them more closely when she got home.

For now, it was time to stop stalling. Snow locked the cabin door, then struggled to cast a small charm to prevent Talia from picking the lock. She leaned against the door until the pain receded, then moved to the trunk, digging through Talia's things until she found the sheathed knife.

From her own trunk, she retrieved a small bundle wrapped with white leather. She returned to her cot, cradling the knife in both hands. There she waited, sweat dripping down her face, until the worst of the pain receded.

When she could move again without nausea, she unrolled the bundle on the mattress. A set of slender silver tools lay within. Knives and needles, mostly—all too small to serve as weapons. She picked a long needle, strong and sharp enough to pierce double-folded leather.

"I know you're in there, Bea." Carefully, she pressed the needle's tip into the hair wrapped around the knife's hilt, separating the hairs to reveal a crack of dark purple. More digging showed the edge of a scale. These were Lirea's scales, similar in size to those from the doll Snow had lost at the tower.

The scales made sense, given the knife's purpose.

Morveren's spell was meant to bind Gustan's soul to Lirea.

And they had taken that knife away. What would happen to Lirea now? How far could Lirea be from Gustan's soul before Morveren's original spell claimed her life?

"You shouldn't have made the transformation permanent," Snow muttered. "Every kid thinks she's in love with her first. Give her some time as a human and see how it goes. Don't marry her off to a man she's barely spoken to, save for a few clumsy nights together."

She picked up a short-bladed knife, suitable for dissecting seeds and tiny creatures. She pressed the razor-sharp tip to her thumb, wincing as it nicked the flesh.

Fear and excitement quickened her breath as she dabbed the blood over the abalone blade. Nothing happened at first. She squeezed her thumb, spreading more blood onto the hilt.

If she hadn't been waiting for it, Snow might not have noticed the knife's magic reaching out to her. Morveren's magic was both strong and subtle. Snow's thumb grew cold, tingling as though asleep. She drew her hand back and sucked on the wound as she studied the knife. The magic felt like a cobweb sticking her thumb to the hilt. Right now, she could sever that bond with ease. With more blood, it would soon become unbreakable.

"Queen Bea?" Beatrice didn't respond, so Snow fed the knife another drop of blood. She was rewarded with a soft buzzing in the back of her mind. Voices, too distant to make out. "Bea, it's me. Please hear me."

Magic tugged her hand, like a fish nibbling a line. Snow pulled back. "Stop that."

The bindings on the knife reminded her of the spells she had touched on Morveren's soul jars. She still hadn't found time to take out the jar she had ... borrowed ... and investigate it more closely. She wondered if the core of the knife's hilt, like those jars, would turn out to be hollow.

Snow picked up her needle and pressed it beneath the edge of a scale, prying it back. The voices grew louder, their tone more urgent, but Snow couldn't understand what they were saying. They could be telling Snow she was on the right trail to unwind Morveren's magic, or they could be screaming in terror and pain.

More blood helped somewhat. The voices didn't seem to come from the knife itself. Rather, Snow heard them inside her head, through the bond she had established with her blood.

"Beatrice?" Snow could almost hear her. Not a single voice, but a chorus, all singing different tunes. Pain and confusion and fear and hope and fatigue, as though Beatrice had fragmented into a hundred voices. Then, without warning, *recognition*.

Snow blinked back tears as she spread more blood onto the hilt. "I'm here, Bea. I've got you."

For a heartbeat, the chorus spoke as one. *Snow?*

Other voices clamored to be heard. No, not voices, but a single voice crying out as many. Stronger than Beatrice, drowning her in his rage and his terror.

"Prince Gustan?" There was no response. Either he couldn't hear her, or else he no longer recognized his own name. Neither Gustan nor Beatrice was aware enough to help her from within the knife.

"I'm going to get you out of there," she promised. The cacophony of voices grew louder. She blinked, trying to clear her vision. Her head was pounding so hard she could barely see. When she tried again to reach Beatrice, Gustan's anger drowned everything else.

Snow couldn't blame him. She'd be mad too if her lover drove a knife into her chest and trapped her soul. She tried to push past Gustan's thoughts—

Her mind touched Gustan's. What was left of it, rather. Little more than disjointed memories and emotions. She saw him with Lirea, his fingers digging into her arms as they rocked together.

This was familiar . . . Snow tensed. She had seen pieces of this vision in Lirea's dreams, before the touch of Snow's magic had roused Lirea from her sleep. Before Lirea's air spirits had almost killed her.

She forced herself to stay with Gustan. They were on a docked ship, the cot rolling with the movement of the waves. Lirea's body wasn't yet human. Gustan's hands clutched her tails, pushing them apart farther than any human could have endured. Lirea clung to her prince, inexperienced but eager.

The images fragmented, and then Gustan was greeting his brother Varisto at the docks. Gustan laughed and joked as he helped the men unload the ship, while Varisto stood with his arms folded in disapproval.

Who was Varisto to question him? Varisto would be lucky to inherit some minor title, deep in the arse end of Hilad. He was as bad as Father, a whimpering child too afraid to take what was rightfully his. The empire needed strength to survive.

A third memory. Lirea limping up the beach, begging for forgiveness. Gustan laughing as he told her how he had taken a new girl. Lirea wept, telling him she would die without him. Slowly, Gustan wavered.

Was there still power in Lirea's voice, some trace of undine magic to help sway Gustan's mind? Snow couldn't tell. He had already rebuffed her request for marriage, but the sight of Lirea's body overcame his distaste. Gustan pushed her down on the damp sand. She kissed his neck, and then he fell back as something within him was tugged away, pulled toward Lirea. He rolled off of her. Lirea followed, her confusion plain. Gustan grabbed her by the throat and flung her to the side, cursing.

Lirea climbed back onto him, pressing her body to his and renewing the ripping sensation within his body. Snow recognized Morveren's magic, a barely heard melody reaching deep into Gustan. With a snarl, he struck her face, knocking her aside. He drew back to hit her again, and Lirea drove a knife into his chest.

Snow gasped, feeling the impact as vividly as if it were she on that beach with Lirea. She opened her eyes, but the memories didn't fade. She could still feel the blade grating against her ribs, and she could still see the shock on Lirea's face. Shock and the slow realization of what she had done. Rather, what had been done *through* her.

Snow tried to separate herself from the memories, but the knife's grip had grown stronger. She pried back her fingers and dropped the knife, but its power clung. How much blood had she given it? Or was it that she had gone willingly, reaching into the enchantments to try to find Beatrice? She could feel the knife's magic fighting to pull her in.

Her mouth was dry, and her lips stuck to her teeth as she whispered.

"Gray stones, gray stones,
hear my call.
Gray stones build a
great big wall."

Slowly, she raised a shield between herself and the knife, weakening the bond between them.

Snow?

She had never heard fear from Queen Bea before. But Snow wasn't strong enough to help. If she stayed any longer, she would lose herself. With a shudder, she wrenched free. "I'm sorry, Bea. I'll be back soon, I promise."

Snow leaned over to retrieve the knife. Best to return it to Talia's trunk before she returned. She bent down, and the blood rushed to her head. The room went dark. The world felt like it was tumbling around her. The last thing she heard was a distant voice, singing from Gustan's shattered memories.

"Oh, pixie farts," she said, and passed out.

Danielle sat on the cot, studying the broken door. The edge was splintered at the latch, as was the frame. Captain Hephyra had already expressed her displeasure about the damage, but Hephyra hadn't been able to overcome whatever magic Snow had used to seal it. Talia, on the other hand, had always been good with locks.

Most she could pick as easily as if she had the keys. As
for the rest . . .

"Did you injure yourself?" Danielle asked.

"Just bruised. Hephyra has a tough tree." Talia
stopped massaging her foot and glanced over at Snow.
They had moved her from the floor onto the other cot.
"What I can't decide is whether to kill her the moment
she wakes up, or if I should give her a chance to explain
what in the six hells she thought she was doing. And
then kill her."

"After Lirea attacked Beatrice, you were ready to
dive in after her." Danielle kept her voice gentle, trying
to ease Talia's anger. "If we're killing people for foolish
choices, should I be going after you, too?"

"You're welcome to try." Talia jumped to her feet and
began to pace. "I'm used to Snow taking stupid risks.
That's why I never would have left her alone with that
knife. But I did. The next thing I knew I was climbing in
the rigging watching for undine. Snow used her magic
on me. She had to. How could she do that to me?"

"She's scared." Danielle studied Snow's face. She appeared to be frowning, her eyebrows pushed low by the
bandages around her head. The room was dim, but Danielle could still see the shadows beneath Snow's eyes.
Her breathing was slow but steady.

"She played games with my thoughts." Talia stopped
in front of the single lamp, her shadow falling across
Snow's form. "With those of the crew, too. Amusing herself by tugging their strings, making them obey whatever
silly whim struck her fancy."

"She needed to learn that magic to try to control Lirea. She wasn't hurting anything."

Talia's face darkened at the mention of Lirea's name.
"Not yet."

"Snow will be all right," Danielle said. Snow was
dreaming, judging by the way she twitched and mumbled to herself.

"You don't know that." Talia twisted on the balls
of her feet. Lirea's knife hung at her hip, with several

lengths of twine securing the weapon in place. "You can't know that."

Snow rolled onto her side. "I'm sorry my cat ate your spider, Mother." Her muffled words dissolved into a sleepy giggle.

Danielle blinked and turned to Talia, confused.

"Snow had a pet cat for a while. But it snuck into her mother's things. Made a horrible mess. Her mother made her watch as she killed it." Talia's shoulders slumped. She opened her trunk, retrieving a dented flask, then collapsed back onto the cot beside Danielle. "Maybe it's better if . . . if she doesn't try to save Beatrice. This time the effort knocked her out. Who knows what it will do next time? Father Isaac and Ambassador Trittibar could talk to Morveren, try to understand how to—"

"You know Snow will insist on helping," Danielle said.

Talia brought her legs to her chest. "Snow's the one who found me when I first came to Lorindar. She and Beatrice. I had stowed away on a cargo ship. The *Verdant Ogre,* I think. I pried the lid from a crate of cloud silk and curled up inside during the day, listening to every voice, every footstep. The hold was dark as death, and most of my time was spent alone with only the scurrying of the rats for company. Each night I snuck out to steal food and to check the stars, making sure we hadn't turned back."

Danielle tried to imagine how frightened Talia must have been. Awakening after a hundred years, her friends and family long dead. Her home overgrown and crumbling, her land ruled by another. She was no princess, only a magical oddity from another age, and the one who helped awaken her had also used her horribly.

"I wanted to sleep again, even if it meant I would never wake up."

Danielle bit her lip. Talia wouldn't appreciate sympathy. Had the room not been so poorly lit, she doubted Talia would have spoken of those times at all.

"Beatrice and Snow came to the docks. Bea *knew* I

was there. She's always been able to sense when someone needed her help. Like with Lannadae." Talia took a quick swallow from her flask. "Her guards boarded first, searching the hold until they found me. They pried open the crate and dragged me out. I was too stiff and sore to resist, but I tried. I knocked one down and dislocated the thumb of another, but I could barely walk, let alone run."

"How did you learn to fight so well?" Danielle asked.

"I didn't leave Arathea right away. I was ... angry. I wanted to fight back. Against the family who had taken my land, against the fairies who had done this to me, against everyone. I found people who could help me. I stayed with them for more than a year, until the prince's family learned of my whereabouts."

Talia took another drink. "I escaped again, but not before I saw the prince's men kill four of my protectors. By the time I arrived in Lorindar, I think a part of me was hoping the guards would kill me and put an end to it all. And then Beatrice came down into the hold, with Snow behind her."

Danielle could hear a faint smile in Talia's voice.

"Beatrice doesn't get angry like other people do. She neither shouts nor threatens. All she did was walk across the hold, squeezing past barrels and crates and one moaning guard, but the way she looked at those men ... if Bea had been a witch, every last one of those guards would have died on the spot. When she reached me, she turned to the guards and said, 'I told you this woman was our guest.'

"One of the guards stammered an apology and loosened his grip on me. I kicked the other one in the groin and ran right past Beatrice and Snow, thinking if I could only reach the docks, I might be able to disappear."

Danielle closed her eyes, following Talia's flight in her mind.

"Instead, Beatrice turned and said, '*El-sak fasiv byattu ayib*?' Is this the behavior of a guest? Her accent was atrocious, but her tone reminded me of my own mother. I was so stunned to hear my own language, I stopped running."

"What happened next?" Danielle asked.

Talia snorted. "Snow stepped out from behind the queen and smiled at me. I had never seen anyone like her ... so beautiful I wasn't sure if she was human or fey. I started to say something, and then she poleaxed me with a spell from her mirrors. It felt as if she had smashed the whole ship over my head. By the time I woke up, we were in the palace.

"I had been bathed, dressed in decent clothes, and there was an entire tray of food sitting beside my bed. Fish fillets with that orange jelly you people like so much, fresh grapes, almond biscuits with butter melting down the sides. Do you know how good a real meal tastes when you've spent two weeks living on stolen scraps? I was mopping up the last of the jelly when it finally occurred to me that they might have put something in the food."

"Beatrice wouldn't—"

"I know that now," said Talia. "But back then ... I assumed they were planning to turn me over to the royals back home. The only reason to hold me prisoner was so they could negotiate a better price for my return. They hadn't left anything to use as a weapon, so I broke the tray and took the longest, sharpest piece I could find.

"They had put me in the northeast tower, in the room with the sunrise tapestry on the wall. The one with the window facing out over the cliffs."

"Jakob loves that tapestry," Danielle said, smiling.

"I was more interested in the window. I thought about trying to climb down, but I didn't know if I was strong enough to reach the sea. I swore I'd throw myself onto the rocks before I let them send me back. And then Snow unlocked the door."

Talia tipped back the flask, swallowing loudly. "Her first words to me were, 'You're Sleeping Beauty? I always imagined you as a blonde.' I still had my makeshift wooden knife, so I pointed it at her and asked who and what she was. She flashed that perky smile and said, 'I'm Snow White.'"

Talia shook her head. "I thought she was mocking me, so I punched her in the face and ran. Beatrice was waiting for me in front of the stairs. I raised my weapon and told her to get out of my way.

"She didn't answer right away. She stood there frowning, until I started to squirm. Then she said, 'I expected better manners from a princess. Still, given what they did to you, you have every right to your anger.'

"Beatrice pulled out a knife of her own. I didn't want to fight her, but I wasn't going to be anyone's prisoner. She wasn't trying to fight me, though. She held the knife out and said, 'If you stay, I can protect you. I can give you shelter and perhaps someday a home. But if you choose to leave, you'll need something better than a broken dinner tray.'"

Talia returned to her trunk, pulling out a knife and handing it to Danielle. The hilt was smooth ivory, and in the faint light she could just make out the blue jewels inlaid in a flower pattern at the hilt. The blade was mottled steel, curved back at the tip. "It's beautiful."

"It's Arathean. Beatrice set it on the ground between us, then stepped aside, saying, 'If you do choose to stay, I hope you'll do me the honor of teaching me to use that. I've never been strong with the knife.'

"She knew who and what I was," said Talia. "What I had done and what had been done to me. And there she was, inviting me into her home. I started to answer, but then Snow came out of the room, holding a bloody cloth to her nose. I expected her to be angry, but she just said, 'If she stays, we have to make a rule against punching me in the face.'"

Danielle returned the knife. A part of her envied Talia her years with Snow and Beatrice. They had all welcomed Danielle into their fold, but sometimes she could still sense the deeper bonds between them, the time they had spent together before Danielle arrived.

She pushed such uncharitable thoughts aside. "Both of them will be all right, Talia. We have Lirea's knife, and we'll be back in Lorindar tomorrow."

Talia stared at Snow. "I don't know what I'd do without them."

"You won't have to find out," Danielle promised.

Talia shook her head. "Sorry, Princess. Just because your story had a happy ending doesn't mean everyone else's will."

CHAPTER 12

THE *PHILLIPA* MADE GOOD TIME despite the damage inflicted by the undine. Hephyra had ordered barrels lowered into the water on either side of the ship. By manipulating the ropes to the barrels, they could be tilted up or down. Tilting the barrels on one side of the ship so the water rushed into their open mouths would turn the *Phillipa* in that direction. It was clumsy and slow, but it worked.

The sun rose above the horizon, turning the waves to flame just as the cliffs of Lorindar came into view. Danielle yawned and rubbed her face as she watched the palace grow.

Snow appeared to be sleeping normally, and neither Talia nor Danielle was willing to wake her. Rest would help her to heal more than anything else they could do.

Danielle glanced around to make sure nobody was watching, then kissed the mirror on her bracelet. Armand soon appeared in the glass.

"Danielle! Where are you?"

The urgency in his tone burned away her fatigue. "What's wrong? Is Beatrice—"

"She's still alive." The image jogged about, presumably while Armand found a more private place to talk. "I've tried to reach you, but your friend neglected to tell me how to make this mirror work. Prince Varisto of Hilad arrived in Lorindar last night. He says you invaded his land? Are you all right?"

"We're fine," Danielle said. "We should be home in less than an hour."

Armand lowered his voice. "Danielle, he's threatening to declare war against Lorindar."

"He attacked us! He would have sunk the *Phillipa* if Morveren hadn't helped us."

"He's saying Morveren is an enemy of the Hiladi Empire."

From behind Danielle, a tired voice said, "He's right."

Snow grimaced and adjusted her hat to block the worst of the sun. She kept one arm around Talia's shoulders for support. Shadows swelled the skin beneath her eyes, and she hugged a heavy cloak around herself for warmth.

"Varisto is demanding we surrender Morveren to him," Armand said.

Danielle shook her head. "She helped us find Lirea. We need Morveren's help if we're going to save Beatrice."

"Where is Morveren?" Snow asked.

"Down below." Talia's words were as stiff as her posture, and she wouldn't even look at Snow. "Captain Hephyra wanted her locked away for the rest of the journey."

"I'll meet you at the docks," Armand said. "I don't believe Varisto will try anything here, but I'll have guards ready just in case."

"Thank you." She kissed the mirror again, then turned to Snow. "How do you feel?"

"Foolish." Snow gasped in pain as she rested her forearms on the rail. "Also a little sore."

Danielle started to reach for her. "Did you hurt yourself?"

"You know how your whole body aches when you get sick?" Snow asked. "It's kind of like that, with the added pleasure of blurred vision, a cracked skull, and memories that aren't actually mine."

"The knife?" Danielle guessed.

Snow started to nod, then winced. "I heard her, Danielle. I heard Bea's voice. She's in there. She's scared, but she's still . . . still *her*."

Danielle smiled, and even Talia relaxed slightly.

"I heard . . . I *felt* Gustan, too. What's left of him. He's in bad shape. Fragmented." Snow closed her eyes. "I watched Lirea kill him. I saw the expression on her face when she realized what she had done."

"What do you mean?" asked Danielle.

"Morveren created the knife to complete her spell and save Lirea's life. But Lirea refused to use it. She had chosen death rather than kill the man she loved."

"Stupid," Talia said.

"Young," Snow corrected. "He was her one true love. Without him life wasn't worth living, and woe was her. Weren't you ever young and foolish?"

Talia scowled but said nothing.

"I saw her face." Snow bowed her head. "When she stabbed Gustan, she didn't know what she was doing. Any more than Talia did when I made her leave the knife behind last night. I could hear Morveren's song in Gustan's memories."

"You're saying Morveren used magic to force Lirea to kill Prince Gustan." Talia's voice was taut as the lines running to the mainmast.

"That's what destroyed Lirea," said Snow. "Morveren warned me that struggling to control a mind could damage or even destroy that mind. This was no gentle nudge. Morveren used magic to rape Lirea's mind. When Lirea regained control and saw Gustan dying in front of her, you could see the horror in her face. She covered her ears and fled, screaming."

"Morveren wouldn't allow her granddaughter to die," Danielle whispered. "All along, she's wanted to save Lirea. It's the only thing she seems to care about."

"That's why I couldn't control Lirea." Snow turned to Talia. "She might not be trained, but some part of her recognizes the touch of that magic and remembers what happened the last time."

Danielle nodded. "Morveren said Lirea was gifted."

"She said the same of me." Snow's voice was so quiet Danielle barely heard. "Talia . . . I'm sorry."

"It's not the same thing," Talia said, shifting uncomfortably. "You didn't force me to kill anyone."

"Not to kill, no. But I did force you. Because I could." She laughed, though there was little humor in the sound. "You'd think I would have learned better than to trust witches by now."

"Morveren helped us find Lirea and that knife," Danielle said. "We still need her."

"No." Snow took a slow breath. "I want no more of her help. Leave her locked in the hold, or give her to Varisto. I can help Beatrice on my own."

Talia snorted. "You can barely walk on your own."

Snow pulled away from Talia and turned back toward the cabin. "We're docking soon, and I'm still wearing the clothes I slept in. I have to change."

Talia followed, catching Snow's arm. Talia's anger was obvious, but she handled Snow as though she were porcelain.

Danielle turned away, watching as Lorindar slowly grew in the distance. She stared at the docks until she spotted the fleck of red that marked Varisto's ship.

Talia had wanted to kill the crew of that ship. Danielle was the one who ordered them left alive, and now Varisto was threatening war against Lorindar.

"I'm surprised they made it, given the damage we did," Talia said, walking up behind her a short time later.

"Do you think they've fixed their guns yet?" Danielle asked.

"Don't worry. He wouldn't dare attack us again, not with a good twenty ships of Lorindar to either side."

Danielle looked down, watching the waves break against the *Phillipa*'s hull. "If Morveren forced Lirea to kill her prince, that would explain why Lirea attacked

Morveren so brutally and why she wouldn't trust Lannadae, but . . ."

"What is it?"

"Lirea ambushed the *Glass Slipper.* She's begun an
offensive that could cripple the naval power of every nation around. At the same time, she's brought new undine
into her tribe, expanding her numbers beyond anything
we've ever seen. Do those sound like the actions of a
woman with a broken mind?"

"Princess Whiteshore, is that *suspicion* I hear in your
voice?" Talia shook her head. "I've fought Lirea twice.
She's strong, but she has no strategy, no tactics beyond
rage and pain."

Danielle turned toward the cabin. "It makes me
wonder exactly how closely Gustan's soul is bound to
Lirea."

Like the *Phillipa,* the Hiladi vessel still bore the scars
of battle. Bright planks had been nailed into place and
tarred to cover the worst of the damage. Armed men
worked on the deck, replacing lines and mending sails.
They had lowered one of their boats into the water at
the back of the ship, where two men had been inspecting
the rudder. Now they stood watching the *Phillipa* glide
closer. Even from this distance Danielle could feel their
anger.

"I think they remember us," Talia said, coming up beside her.

The docks were packed more tightly than Danielle
had ever seen. High tide was normally a busy time, but
not one of these ships appeared ready to leave. Nor had
the *Phillipa* passed any traffic on their way in, save for a
pair of three-masted naval ships patrolling beyond the
harbor. The storms had departed Lorindar with the *Phillipa.* Only fear of the undine kept these ships docked
now.

Captain Hephyra stood balanced on the bowsprit,
one hand raised in an obscene gesture toward the Hi-

ladi. Glancing over her shoulder, she shouted, "Lower anchors!"

The deck vibrated beneath Danielle's feet as the anchor chains played out. The *Phillipa* jerked once before dragging to a halt.

By the time the crew had readied the cutter, Snow had emerged from the cabin wearing a green jacket trimmed with gold cord over a low-cut white shirt. A polished leather belt gleamed at her waist, matching her knee-high boots. She had kept the tricorn hat, though it didn't really match the rest of her finery.

"Are you up for climbing?" Talia asked.

"I'll be fine." Snow waved them away and climbed down the rope ladder into the boat. She moved slowly but reached the cutter without incident. Danielle wondered if anyone else noticed the sheen of sweat on Snow's face.

"We have a welcoming party," Snow said as Danielle and Talia joined her.

Prince Armand waited at the dock, surrounded by a handful of guardsmen. His hair was a rumpled mess, and he seemed a little short of breath. Had he run all the way from the palace rather than waiting for a carriage? No, looking back along the boardwalk, Danielle could see several horses tied near the barracks.

Her stomach tightened as she spotted Captain Varisto standing with her husband. He wore the same red sash as before but had changed into a bright yellow sleeveless tunic which left his muscular arms bare. Gold bracelets shone at his wrists.

The men rowed harder, pulling alongside the dock. They braced the boat as Armand reached down and helped Danielle onto solid footing. She had barely caught her balance when he wrapped his arms around her and squeezed. "I've missed you."

"I missed you, too." Danielle kissed him hard enough to earn an appreciative whistle from Snow. She pulled back, studying Armand more closely. His eyes were red and shadowed, and she could feel the tension in his neck and shoulders.

Captain Varisto coughed. "Princess Whiteshore."

"Prince Varisto." Danielle drew herself up the way Beatrice had taught her and did her best to match Varisto's formal tone. "Welcome to Lorindar. Thank you for not firing on us this time."

He merely bowed his head. "Your husband tells me Queen Beatrice is in dire health. My sympathies."

"Thank you," said Danielle. "When Lirea attacked—"

Varisto held up his hand. "Please consider your words carefully, Highness. I have no quarrel with you personally, but if you insult my sister, I'll be forced to take offense."

"Your sister?" Snow stood on her toes and studied his neck. "I don't see any gills."

"When my brother married Lirea, she became my sister by Hiladi law." He turned back to Armand. "Much to the dismay of my parents, I'm afraid. For months I kept his secret, but after his murder, I had no choice. Only my mother's intervention stopped Father from striking Gustan's name from the imperial histories."

Snow folded her arms. "He never—"

"We were told Lirea and Gustan never wed," Danielle interrupted. "That your brother merely used Lirea."

His face darkened, and he started toward Danielle. "My brother was a good man."

Talia moved between them and folded her arms, almost as if she wanted him to attack. Armand cleared his throat, and the guards stepped closer.

Varisto visibly composed himself, then turned to stare at the *Phillipa*. "I was there when Lirea saved my brother's life. She swam through the night, holding him against her. The journey would have exhausted even the strongest undine, but Lirea was determined. I remember the infatuation on her face, the way her gaze lingered on him as he stumbled onto shore. She was such an innocent girl, full of joy. I . . . worried that Gustan might take advantage of such love. My brother had his share of conquests, the more exotic the better. But you've seen how the wind obeys Lirea's wishes?"

"The air spirits, yes." Danielle looked upward. The sky was clouded, but the malevolence of Lirea's winds was gone. "We're familiar with them."

"Those spirits have served my family for generations. My family and no other. No mermaid could command them unless she was joined to that family." He was still watching the ship. "For the past year I've tried to find a way to reach Morveren. I couldn't protect my brother, but I vowed to see his murderer punished."

"You know Morveren was responsible for Gustan's death?" Danielle asked.

"I know Lirea's sisters were no more pleased with her love for a human than my family would have been. I know they conspired with Morveren to end that relationship, and that it was Morveren who used her magic to force Lirea to kill my brother." He sighed and turned back to face Danielle, stepping just close enough to make her aware of his greater size and strength. "Lirea would see her sisters dead for that betrayal, but I won't ask for Lannadae. Just give me Morveren."

Armand spoke up for the first time, his voice hard. "That sounds suspiciously like a demand, Your Highness."

Varisto bowed slightly. "No offense was intended, Prince Armand. But I must point out that it was your wife who invaded Hiladi waters and attempted to murder my sister. Were my father to learn of this, he would be far more ... demanding ... than I."

Now it was Snow's turn to stare at Varisto. "The northern coast of Hilad is a wasteland. How would you know about any invasion?"

Varisto's lips pressed into a tight smile.

Danielle put a hand on Snow's shoulder. "Our queen is dying, Prince Varisto. Morveren's knowledge might save her life. I will not sacrifice Beatrice so that you can have your revenge. Now please step aside."

"Yet you delayed your return in order to invade my country and attack my sister?" His bracelets rang together as he hammered a fist into his palm. "If you continue to conspire with this murderer, you will—"

"You attacked the *Phillipa* without warning." Danielle's voice broke, thinking of the bodies they had lowered into the sea. Between the Hiladi and the undine, almost thirty people had died since they left Lorindar. James had been one of the last. Hephyra had given them all a burial at sea. Danielle could still see his pale form sinking into the water, rejoining the rest of his crew.

She moved closer to Armand, drawing strength from his presence. "I expect you to answer for the deaths you caused. But not today. Queen Beatrice is dying, and you are preventing us from bringing her the help that could save her life. So you will either stand aside of your own will, or you will be thrown aside."

Armand winced, but said nothing. The guards were holding their breath, watching Varisto. Danielle could see Talia shifting her weight, lowering her body as she prepared to make good on Danielle's threat.

Varisto laced his fingers together, bringing his hands to his mouth as he glared fire at Danielle. He took several deep breaths before saying, "I *will* have the mermaid who took my brother from me. If you try to protect her—"

"That's enough," said Armand. "I understand your grief, Highness. There will be time to talk later. You and your crew are welcome to stay as guests—"

"Forgive me if I mistrust the hospitality of liars and murderers. I will stay with my ship." With that, Varisto backed away, never taking his gaze from Danielle. "I have spent a year of my life hunting that mermaid. Do not test my patience."

Danielle watched him leave. "He might try to sneak his men onto the *Phillipa* to take Morveren. We should—"

"I wouldn't worry," said Talia. "Captain Hephyra will be watching them, and I'm sure she's just waiting for an excuse to play with the people who hurt her ship."

Armand took Danielle's hand in his as they walked toward the horses. "Remind me to have Ambassador Trittibar talk to you about diplomacy. Did you really invade Hilad?"

"Only the very edge," said Snow. "And it was only the three of us. There was no looting or pillaging or anything like that."

Talia coughed and looked away. "I might have pillaged a few things."

"Perhaps it would be best if you don't tell me," said Armand.

Danielle quickened her step. After so many days at sea, it was strange to feel solid ground beneath her feet. She had finally grown accustomed to the rocking motion of the *Phillipa*. "We'll need a carriage for Snow. She's hurt, and riding wouldn't be good for her injuries."

"A horse is fine," Snow protested. "I've been riding since I was five."

Danielle pointed to the barracks. "If you can tell me how many horses are tied there, you can ride whichever you please."

Snow adjusted her hat and squinted, her lips moving silently. She closed one eye, then switched to the other. "I think . . . it looks like there are . . . oh, go fondle a dragon."

Armand ordered one of the guards to prepare a carriage. To Snow, he said, "I'll have Tymalous look to you as soon as we reach the palace. Will your injuries keep you from being able to help my mother?"

Danielle glanced back at the ship. "We should arrange to have Morveren and Lannadae brought—"

"No," said Snow. "Varisto is right not to trust Morveren. I can help Bea without her help."

From the way Talia's brow wrinkled, she didn't like that answer any more than Danielle. They had both heard Snow express such determination before. She would do whatever she had to in order to save Beatrice . . . no matter the cost to herself.

*　　*　　*

When they reached the chapel, they found Father Isaac trying to spoon broth into the queen's mouth.

The queen had never been a large woman, but this was the first time Danielle had ever thought of her as fragile. Her face was taut, the cheekbones protruding beneath sunken eyes, but it was her hands that chilled Danielle's heart. Beatrice's hands were clasped over her stomach. Her fingers were like interwoven sticks. The skin was dry, sagging from the bones beneath. She wore no jewelry save her wedding band, which was so loose it could have fallen off.

A pair of silver incense burners hung on the walls to either side of the altar. The smoke was heavily perfumed, making Danielle's eyes water.

"Tymalous and I have been able to protect the wound, keeping it from turning gangrenous," Father Isaac said without looking up. "In the beginning, she appeared to be healing, albeit slowly. But being unable to swallow means her body has lost the strength to repair itself."

"She's starving," Danielle whispered.

Snow had retrieved Lirea's knife from Talia. She carried it in both hands as she approached the altar. Her movements were stiff from pain, but she said nothing.

Isaac stared at the knife, his expression a mix of curiosity and revulsion. "She's trapped in that thing, along with another. Can you free them?"

Snow glanced back at Danielle. "Beatrice is so weak . . . I don't know what will happen when both souls are released. There's a chance Gustan might try to take her body. I had hoped Beatrice would be strong enough to help fight him off. I could try to enter the knife myself, to restrain Gustan until Beatrice is able to—"

"No!" Danielle wasn't sure who spoke first—herself, Talia, or Father Isaac. She hurried to Snow's side. "Talia, will you stay with Snow to make sure she doesn't try any more experiments?"

Snow rolled her eyes and gave a melodramatic sigh. "Fine. I'll find another way. Father Isaac, could you come with me to help—"

He shook his head. "I can't leave the church. Nor is it safe to tinker with such spells so close to the queen."

Snow started to argue, then turned around, studying the church walls. She sniffed the air. "The incense?"

"As well as certain enchantments worked into the stained glass," said Isaac.

Danielle looked at the windows. "I don't understand."

"He's protecting her." Snow pointed to the incense burners. "He's mixed a potion into the incense. No, two potions." She sniffed again. "One to ward off certain demons, and another to . . ." She turned to Father Isaac. "Is that a sleeping potion?"

"Not exactly," said Isaac. "I think of it as a potion of peace. Try to strike me."

Snow shrugged and raised a hand. Midway through the movement, she turned away, yawning.

"The greater the anger or hostility, the stronger the magic," said Isaac.

Both Snow and Danielle turned to look at Talia, who scowled. Either her anger had eased, or else her curse protected her from the effects of Isaac's potion.

"The windows are warded as well," said Snow. "They block out external magic and suppress spells cast within the church. Even if I could work here, our spells would interfere with each other."

"It's necessary," said Isaac. He tipped his spoon, allowing several drops of broth to fall past the queen's lips. Perhaps he hoped such a small amount might make its way down Beatrice's throat, even if she couldn't swallow to help it along. "Man was not meant to stand on the border of life and death. In this state, your mother is highly vulnerable. I must remain here to protect her."

"So summon Trittibar," Armand snapped. "Call every witch and conjurer from the city and put them to work on this knife."

"Trittibar is a fairy," said Snow. "His magic comes to him through the hill in Fairytown. His spells are too different from Morveren's." She bent down to kiss Beatrice's forehead, then stepped back from the altar. "As for witches, you've heard the expression about too many cooks?"

Armand nodded.

"Too many spellcasters is worse." Snow's smile held no humor. "Worse as in smoking craters and charred corpses."

"If you cannot free the queen, please bring the knife back to me," said Father Isaac.

Snow stopped moving. "What can you do?"

"I can destroy it." Isaac met and held Armand's stare. "I can release the queen and the knife's other captive. I can give them both peace."

"I can give her life." Snow left without another word. Talia started to follow, turning back when Danielle called her name.

"Take care of her," said Danielle. "Don't let her—"

"I will," Talia promised.

Though she never would have admitted it to Talia, Snow knew she was in no condition to climb down the ladder hidden in Danielle's room. Fortunately, there were other ways to reach the secret chambers beneath the palace. Ways that would have been far more convenient without the two servant girls making up the bed in the king and queen's bedchamber.

Snow cleared her throat as she entered the room. She tried to remember the servants' names, then gave up. "The prince sent us to find you. He wants—" She glanced around the room, searching for a plausible excuse.

This room was similar in shape and size to the one Danielle shared with Armand. Both rooms were tiled in black and white, with soft carpet covering most of the floor. Tapestries covered the outer walls. One showed the Lorindar navy at sunrise, while another depicted a young girl in a field, surrounded by six white swans.

The first tapestry had been made here in Lorindar. Snow could tell from the gold and burgundy border, as well as the knots used on the white tassels. But she had never been able to identify the second. The violet star-shaped flowers in the field were like none she had ever seen, nor did she recognize the stylized flames that bordered the piece.

Talia cleared her throat. Snow turned to see both of the servants staring at her, making no effort to hide their amusement or disdain. Right . . . Snow's mind was wandering. The throbbing in her head made it difficult to concentrate on anything.

"The prince is hungry," she said. "Run to the kitchen and fetch him something to eat. You'll find him in the chapel."

"Just 'cause you're the queen's favorite doesn't make you head of this household," muttered one. Miriam, that was her name.

Snow smiled. "That's all right. I'll tell the prince you were too busy to answer his summons." She turned to go.

Miriam beat her to the door. "I never said I wouldn't do it, you old—"

"The prince asked for wine as well," Talia said, turning to the second girl. "Could you please find him something from the cellar?" Once they were gone, Talia shook her head. "You're as bad as Danielle. She still thinks she's a serving girl, and you still think you're a princess."

Snow stuck out her tongue. "I tried being nice back when I first arrived. They all hated me anyway." She had quickly learned not to bother trying to befriend the servants. The girls were jealous of her beauty, and the boys . . . well, they were boys. Add to that Snow's closeness to the queen, and she was shunned by most of the staff. Not that she minded, much. Snow had spent most of her life alone and preferred it that way.

Snow knew they had given Talia a hard time in the beginning as well, but that hadn't lasted long. Two weeks after her arrival, Talia had found herself alone in a hallway with a blacksmith's assistant named Brendan who had been known to harass the girls. Nobody knew exactly what Brendan had said or done, but Talia had broken both of his arms, blackened his eye, and might have killed him if the queen hadn't come running. Nobody bothered Talia after that.

Once both servants were gone, Snow shut the door and walked to the fireplace. She picked up an iron poker, then crouched down, flinching at the heat. The fire had died down, but the embers still glowed in the ashes. She wrinkled her nose and held her breath. Given the pain in her head, a single sneeze would probably knock her unconscious.

"There you are," she whispered, jabbing the poker into a cracked brick at the back of the fireplace.

The wall beside the fireplace slid open, revealing steps spiraling downward. The staircase was so narrow Snow had to walk sideways, but it was much easier and safer than the ladder in Danielle's room. She whispered a spell, casting candlelight from the mirrors of her choker.

The stairs circled around, following the contours of the tower wall until they reached another hidden doorway. The door was as narrow as the passage, opening through the side of the archway connecting the armory and the library. Talia slipped past her, checking the darkness as she always did.

"Have you mentioned these stairs to Danielle?" Snow asked.

"Not yet. She needs the exercise."

Snow called sunlight from her mirrors and followed, only to find Talia waiting with folded arms.

"You know, those servants *might* just notice an open door beside the fireplace," Talia said.

Snow blushed and hurried back to close the door.

By the time they reached the bottom of the stairs, Snow's vision was flashing with each drumbeat in her skull. She did her best to ignore the pain as she lit the lamps and made her way into her study.

Snow brushed her hands over the platinum frame of her mirror, whispering words Trittibar had taught her. Slowly, the vines cast into the metal twisted and peeled away from the glass, reaching down to the floor. Snow stepped back, smiling as the vines lifted the mirror from the wall, tilting it until the mirror stood flat like a table.

She pulled a stool up to the mirror. "Trittibar showed me that trick. What do you think?"

"Can you teach it to fetch and roll over, too?" asked Talia.

"I tried, but there's too much power in the mirror. It ran off and tried to mount the queen's leg. She made me stop experimenting after that." She smiled and set the knife on the glass, then went to the bookshelves. Running her finger along the spines, she selected four tomes.

"What are you doing?" Talia asked.

"The mirror helps me to see the weave of Morveren's magic." She set the books on one end of the mirror, then waved a hand over the glass. The light in the room brightened. "Mirror, mirror, on the floor. Show me now the mermaid's lore."

"You really need to talk to a bard about those rhymes," said Talia. "Someone to tutor you in matters of word choice and rhythm."

Snow made a gesture she had picked up from Captain Hephyra. Then she reached out and moved the knife to one side.

The reflection of the knife remained behind. Snow bent over the mirror and willed the image to expand. The colors in the mirror brightened as the reflection grew, from the rainbow shimmer of the abalone blade to the cracks of purple where Lirea's scales peeked between layers of hair.

Snow massaged her forehead as she studied the knife.

"Are you sure you don't want me to get Trittibar?" Talia asked.

Snow glanced up, then groaned. Squinting, she addressed the Talia on the left. That one appeared slightly more solid than the other. "His magic and mine don't obey the same rules." She rapped her knuckles on the metal vines beneath the table. "I spent three weeks translating his spells to make this trick work for me. Even if Beatrice had that kind of time, Trittibar doesn't know anything about binding or releasing spirits. I asked him about it last year after we returned from Fairytown."

Snow turned her attention back to the knife. Working with the mirror was a tremendous relief. Like her smaller mirrors, its magic didn't seem affected by her blurred and doubled vision. She brushed her fingers over the reflection, wiping away the likeness of the knife and leaving only the image of Morveren's magic.

The binding spell was clearest: loops of green light where the hilt had been. Inside those loops, two shadows moved about like bottled smoke.

Snow rested her cheek on the glass, trying to see into the end of the loops. She expected a cap of some sort, a symbolic net to keep the souls from escaping. Instead, spokes of light crossed through the entire length of the hilt.

Talia's reflection appeared beside the knife. "What is it?"

"Morveren's spell." Snow rubbed her eyes, but the images didn't change. She grabbed the soul jar she had stolen from Morveren and set that on the mirror. When she moved the jar away to study the magic, the differences were obvious. The jar's spells formed a hollow prison, as she had expected. She looked back at the knife, with its tendrils of magic that pierced both souls.

"The knife doesn't just trap souls." Snow blinked back tears and pressed a finger to the glass, trying to reach through to Beatrice. She could hear Talia moving closer. "It's feeding on them."

Talia whispered an Arathean curse. Snow was already grabbing the top book from her pile, a treatise on ghosts written sixty years ago by a dwarven priest. She flipped pages, searching for the chapter that talked about binding spirits, but the words blurred and swam together. She had hoped her vision would have improved by now, but instead it seemed to be getting worse. The dwarf's handwriting didn't help matters either. Gritting her teeth, she squinted and tried to force the words into focus.

This was going to be a long night.

Chapter 13

TALIA HOOKED ANOTHER LOOP of green yarn, pulling the row tight. She tugged more wool from the skein and studied her progress before starting the next row. A flat snake of green and black squares, barely as wide as her hand, sat in her lap. "Maybe I should just make the kid a scarf instead of a blanket."

She rested her shoulders against the wall, shifting ever so slightly to loosen the muscles of her back. The light from Snow's mirror really wasn't bright enough for knitting, but Talia had learned these patterns as a child. She could stitch a rayid-style two-color row blindfolded, thanks in no small part to the "gifts" of her fairy patrons.

"I'm sorry," Snow mumbled. "I'll try to be gentler."

Talia tensed. "What was that?"

Snow looked up and squinted. "Didn't you ... sorry. I thought you said ..." She yawned and rubbed her eyes. "Wait, are you knitting?"

"I didn't want to disturb you." Talia gathered her would-be blanket and yarn.

"But you're *knitting*." Snow smothered a giggle.

Talia held up one of the needles, a bronze spike as long as her hand. "A woman with proper training can kill a man with this needle and never spill more than a single drop of blood."

"I suppose you're knitting a garrote?"

Though Snow's voice was playful, her eyes were bloodshot, and her lips had lost much of their color. She kept rubbing her thumb, smearing a thin layer of blood over the skin, though she seemed unaware of it. "When was the last time you took a break?"

"Beatrice can't wait." Snow wiped sweat on her sleeve. "Stop being such a hen." She turned back to the knife and her books.

Talia's needles clicked a staccato rhythm as she watched. It wasn't long before Snow was mumbling to herself again. She sounded like she was speaking Allesandrian. Talia didn't recognize the exact words, but the tone was unmistakable.

Soft footsteps announced Danielle's arrival. "Has she made any progress?"

"How should I know?" Talia rolled up her knitting and jabbed the needles into the skein. "Is there news from upstairs?"

"Nothing good." Danielle sat down next to Talia and watched as Snow flipped through another book, turning pages roughly enough to tear the paper. "King Theodore asked me to join him in the throne room. They've brought out the crystal, and he's been meeting with other rulers to discuss what we've learned."

Talia nodded. The crystal was a polished sphere the size of a human skull, enchanted to allow the king to communicate with the lords of other nations, as well as his own nobles. "What did they say?"

"It was hard to hear over all of the shouting," she said ruefully. "They weren't happy to hear about Hilad's involvement with Lirea. Lyskar is ready to declare war."

That made sense. Lyskar hadn't suffered as personally as Lorindar, but they had still lost ships to the undine.

"Lyskar paid Lirea's tribe for free passage three days ago," Danielle said. "Now they're demanding repayment from Hilad, both for the ransom and the damage to their fleet."

Talia snorted. "The Hiladi must have loved that."

"They'd probably be sending warships after one another if Theodore hadn't calmed them down." Danielle absently rubbed at a stain in the carpet with her thumbnail. "Lord Montgomery is rallying some of our nobles, trying to pressure the king into joining Lyskar against Hilad."

"Ask if he'll be the one to lead the attack," Talia said. "That should shut him up."

"It's not just the nobles, Talia. The merchants have been raising their prices. The cost of food has doubled in the past week. If shipping doesn't resume soon, the people could riot."

"The undine are all busy breeding." Talia pulled out one of the needles and twirled it in her fingers. "What are they so afraid of?"

"Most of them are breeding," Danielle said. "They've still hit three more of our ships, including one down in Emrildale that was still docked. We've heard similar reports from Morova and Najarin. Mostly the elder undine and the very young, but once the undine finish spawning—"

"It's going to get worse," Talia finished. Theodore had to know what was coming if Lirea wasn't stopped. Fighting between Hilad and Lyskar would only make it easier for Lirea to destroy them all.

"I know," Danielle whispered.

Talia didn't envy Danielle her time upstairs. Talia wouldn't have lasted a single hour in a room full of angry, frightened nobles before breaking someone's nose. "What does he intend to do?"

The answer confirmed her expectations. "Nobody wants war, but we have a better chance against Hilad than we do against the undine. Theodore will be taking the crystal to his chambers. He means to talk to the Hiladi emperor alone about an attack against Lirea's tribe. We know where she is, and Hilad isn't the power it once was. If Hilad finds itself at war against both Lorindar and Lyskar . . ."

"What about holding Varisto hostage?" Talia suggested.

Danielle looked shocked. "And do what? Cut his throat if the empire refuses to help us?"

Talia sighed. Danielle was so naive. "The threat might be enough to ensure their cooperation."

Danielle looked over at Snow. "The only other choice is to stop Lirea now. There are some who feel we should destroy the knife, even if it means letting Bea die."

"I'm impressed someone had the courage to suggest—"

"Montgomery didn't get the chance to finish his suggestion." Danielle shrugged. "I'm afraid my response wasn't very princesslike. I excused myself shortly after."

"Snow will figure this out," Talia said. "Once she has, we can destroy the knife. That should take care of Lirea, right? Snow might need a few more days, but—"

"Every day is another chance for Lirea to move her tribe elsewhere." Danielle lowered her voice. "We should bring Morveren to the palace."

"No!" Snow rubbed her eyes as she turned away from the mirror.

"Morveren might still be willing to help you," Danielle said.

"She might also be willing to cut my throat and steal the knife for herself," Snow said, grabbing another book.

Talia shook her head. "Not with me here she won't."

"You don't understand. What Morveren did to Lirea . . . it would have been kinder to let her die. And her magic, the way the knife feeds off of souls. I think it's more than just the knife."

"What do you mean?" Danielle asked.

Snow picked up a green jar. "Morveren was too weak to escape her island. She needed my help to fight her own defenses. But afterward, she was stronger. Because she had a chance to feed."

Even from here, Talia could see the guilt in Snow's eyes. Snow had gone down to Morveren's home, but hadn't realized what the mermaid was really doing there.

Danielle stood and walked to Snow, looking down at

the knife and the books. "How long will it take you to free Beatrice?"

"I can do this," Snow insisted. She spun back to her mirror, knocking one of her books to the floor. The jar would have fallen if Danielle hadn't grabbed it. "If people would just shut up and let me work."

"All right." Danielle backed away and glanced at Talia before leaving. Talia stood to follow.

Danielle waited for her inside the armory. "Snow's exhausted. If she keeps working like this, she's more likely to hurt herself than to save Bea."

Talia couldn't argue. "If we bring Morveren here, we don't know what she'll do."

"We need her." Danielle glanced away, her gaze distant.

"You couldn't have known Morveren would turn against us," Talia said, guessing at Danielle's thoughts. "What happened to James and the others isn't your fault."

"But it is my responsibility," Danielle said. "That's what it means to be a princess, right?"

Talia didn't answer.

"Can you keep Morveren under control?"

That earned a smile. "I'll fetch a scaling knife on the way down."

"Don't hurt her if you don't have to." Danielle peeked through the archway. "I don't suppose I could just command Snow to take a break."

"Allow me." Talia walked silently to the mirror. Once there, she reached out and began to comb Snow's hair back with her fingers, being careful not to disturb the bandage. Snow's hair smelled like chrysanthemums, one of the scents Snow mixed herself. This one was sweeter than usual, with the faint scent of honey blended into the floral smell.

Talia moved her hands to Snow's shoulders, kneading the knotted muscles. Her thumbs moved up the base of Snow's neck.

Snow gasped as Talia pressed down on a particularly

stubborn knot. "The spells in the knife weren't meant to last this long," Snow mumbled. "The knife was a stopgap to keep her alive."

"What does that mean?" Talia asked, moving her hands down to work the muscles between Snow's shoulder blades. Snow groaned and lay her head down on the mirror. The bandage was still white, which meant Snow's bleeding had stopped. That was a good sign.

"Don't know," Snow said. "Gustan was just a component in her spell. But Lirea fought back. Morveren didn't expect that."

"Like she fought back when we stole the knife."

"She's strong. Morveren must have been mad when Lirea wasn't interested in learning magic." Snow yawned. "Morveren's a good teacher. How can such a bad person be a good teacher?"

"When I tried to teach you swordfighting, you said I was an awful teacher."

Snow giggled. "You are. You're too impatient, and you're always showing off."

Talia's face grew warm. She rarely showed off her fairy gifts, but with Snow . . . "Well, you're not much of a student sometimes. Do you remember when you refused to pick up a sword for a full week because the practice jacket was 'too unflattering'?"

The only answer was a low snore. "Believe me," Talia whispered. "That jacket was plenty flattering."

Danielle crossed the room to retrieve the knife from Snow's mirror. "I'll deliver this to Father Isaac for now."

Talia grabbed quill and paper and scrawled a quick note. "And where will you be?"

Danielle groaned and looked upward. "Upstairs, trying to help Theodore avoid a war."

Talia was stopped only once on her way out of the palace. She sighed, feigning annoyance as she explained that the princess had forgotten something on the ship, and of course she needed it fetched *right now*. Soon she was riding a horse and wagon down the road toward the docks.

The ride seemed to take forever, though the moon had barely moved by the time Talia arrived. The same excuse got her past the harbormaster's man, who was understandably curious why a lone rider needed to reach the queen's ship at this time of night.

Talia hailed the *Phillipa,* and was unsurprised when Captain Hephyra answered. As far as Talia could tell, Hephyra slept almost as infrequently as Talia herself.

"Nice to see you again," Hephyra called. "Shall I send a boat?"

"No need." Talia kicked off her sandals and dove from the end of the dock. By the time she reached the ship, Hephyra had already lowered a line into the water. She hauled Talia up as though she weighed nothing at all.

"Come to take me up on my offer?" Hephyra asked.

"Not today." Talia squeezed water from her hair. "I need to borrow one of your guests."

"Take them both," said Hephyra, her annoyance obvious. "The crew will be happy to see them gone. They're down in the hold. Before she left, your friend Snow rigged a circle to keep Morveren from using her magic. Nearly killed herself from the effort, but it seems to have worked."

"Thank you." Talia clenched her jaw and crossed the deck toward the ladders.

"Want an escort?" Hephyra asked.

Talia dipped into the pouch at her waist and pulled out a ball of beeswax. She squeezed off two small pieces, pressing them into her ears. "No thanks."

The air grew cool as Talia descended to the bottom of the ship. The boards creaked beneath her feet. Below this deck, rocks and soil provided ballast for the *Phillipa.* The air smelled like a farmer's field after a heavy spring rain.

Talia wrinkled her nose. A heavily fertilized field.

Her bare feet splashed through puddles. Crates and barrels were secured to either side, creating a dark,

cramped hallway of sorts. A single lantern burned farther along, hung from the central beam.

Talia ducked her head and made her way past extra
rope, provisions for the crew, and several barrels that
smelled of tar. Morveren sat at the rear, where the miz-
zenmast was secured through the decks all the way
down to the keel. Chains bound Morveren to the mast.
Through the puddles, Talia could see faint scratches in
the floor where Snow had cast her spell.

Lannadae lay in the circle beside her grandmother,
both tails curled against Morveren's. Lannadae was
asleep, but Morveren's eyes watched Talia as she
approached.

"I need you to help free Beatrice from that knife,"
Talia said.

One of Morveren's tails slapped the deck. "I
should save your queen when you couldn't save my
granddaughter?"

"Lirea didn't seem interested in being saved." Talia
sat down on a crate. "But that didn't stop you, did it?"

"I gave her what she wanted."

Talia drew the curved knife Beatrice had given her all
those years ago. "You used magic to force your granddaughter to kill Gustan. That makes you a murderer. If
you prefer not to help us, I'd be happy to turn you over
to Captain Varisto. He's wanted to get his hands on you
for quite some time." Talia turned the knife, testing the
point. "I imagine he'd be even more upset if he learned
what you'd done to his brother's soul."

"Is that true?" Lannadae was awake now, her eyes
wide. "You forced Lirea to kill Gustan?"

"Would you rather I let her die?" Morveren snapped.
"Gustan was a cruel man, and he deserved far worse."

"But Lirea loved him," Lannadae protested.

"Lirea will die if you don't help us," Talia said. "If
Snow can't free Beatrice, they mean to destroy the
knife."

"You can't!" Morveren pulled against the chains.
"She's queen of the undine. Through Lirea, we will re-

store what we once were and take our rightful place in your world."

Talia leaned against a barrel, trying to read Morveren's expression. Her gills were open, exposing the red lines along her neck. The fins on the side of her tails kept opening and snapping flat again. "You *wanted* Lirea to lead the undine to war."

Morveren didn't answer.

"Why would you do that?" Lannadae backed away. "I don't understand."

Morveren closed her eyes. "I see no reason to explain myself to a child and a human servant."

Talia stabbed the knife into the barrel. "I am Princess Talia Malak-el-Dahshat." Merely stating her true name brought back memories of her childhood. Her chin rose, and her hands came together in preparation for the ritual bow. She could almost hear her mother chastising her for venturing out with her hair unbraided, like a common harlot. "You will explain, and you will help my friend, or I will finish what Lirea began with your tails."

"You're a princess too?" breathed Lannadae. "Really?"

"Princess or no, you have no authority over me," said Morveren.

Talia pulled her knife free and flicked it at Morveren. It thudded through one of her fins, pinning it to the deck.

Morveren squealed. The sound made Talia flinch, but if there was any magic to the sound, Snow's circle and the plugs in Talia's ears blocked it. Talia had aimed for one of the smaller fins near the end of her left tail. There didn't seem to be any blood, but the wound obviously hurt. Morveren grabbed the knife with both hands, trying to work it free.

"I have more knives," Talia said. "Explain yourself, mermaid. Lirea asked to be human. You twisted her into something else."

"She *can't* be human." Morveren gave up on the knife and sagged backward. "None of us can."

"Why not?"

"To be human requires a soul."

Lannadae grabbed Morveren's arm. "Grandmother, you can't believe those horrible tales."

Morveren slapped Lannadae's hand. "They're more than tales, you silly child. We were created incomplete. More animal than human. I've studied souls for two centuries. You could stab Lirea's abalone blade into my chest, and it would kill me as dead as anyone else, but I would not join Gustan and your queen. Nothing of our people survives beyond our death. We are monstrosities, formed of seafoam and magic, but we *can* be more. Through Lirea."

There was an intensity to her words that made Talia take a step back. If not for Snow's circle, she would have believed Morveren's words carried magic. "So you wanted to give Lirea a soul. Gustan's soul."

"Not only Lirea," Morveren said, lunging forward until her chains and the knife in her fin stopped her. "Her children. And her children's children. A new line of undine, one with the ability to live on land or sea. She will unite the tribes and save our race."

"And her war against humans?" Talia asked.

"That was unplanned," Morveren admitted. "Gustan was both aggressive and ambitious. Traits Lirea needed. That's one of the reasons I pushed them together. I suspect it's his influence turning her against the humans."

Trying to reclaim the glory of the Hiladi Empire, Talia guessed. If not for Beatrice, she would have killed Morveren right then.

Lannadae was shaking. "No wonder Lirea hates me. She thinks I helped you to murder Gustan."

"You didn't know." Talia crouched in front of Morveren. "Tell me about the storm that drove Gustan's ship against the rocks."

"I was stronger back then. I managed to influence his pet spirits long enough to arrange matters." Morveren lay back. "I don't care about your people. Give me the knife. Let me complete my work and save my granddaughter. I'll make sure she leaves Lorindar in peace."

"That's why Snow said the magic in the knife was incomplete." Talia reached down to tug the knife loose. "Killing Gustan trapped his soul and sustained Lirea, but you weren't finished. You need to force that soul into her body."

"I can save your queen and my granddaughter both."

"I have a better idea. You'll help Snow to save Beatrice, and then I'll let Danielle decide whether or not to let you live."

Morveren spat. "Why should I agree to that?"

Without looking, Talia sent the knife into the meat of Morveren's tail, near the stump. Morveren's scream hurt her ears even through the beeswax. Raising her voice, Talia said, "Because Danielle has an overblown streak of mercy, whereas I take a very dark view of people using magic to 'improve' their children."

"My people will remember you as a devil," Morveren said, clutching her tail. "One who damned us all."

Talia's smile was cold enough to make both mermaids flinch. "I've been called worse. And anything has to be better than that silly Sleeping Beauty tale."

Tiny feet dug into Danielle's ribs. She groaned and rolled over, trying to make room for a child who, despite his size, had somehow managed to claim well over half the bed for himself. She rubbed her eyes and sat up, balancing on the edge of the mattress. Armand lay on the opposite side, his position equally precarious. Danielle dimly remembered carrying Jakob into the room late last night, but she couldn't recall when Armand had finally come to bed.

Sleep was a losing battle, but she tried again. Moments later, she heard the privy door creaking open. "She stole it!"

The indignation in Snow's voice brought Danielle

fully awake. Stifling a yawn, she climbed out of bed and crossed to the doorway. "What?"

"The knife. Talia took it." Snow waved a crumpled piece of paper in Danielle's face. Her clothes were rumpled. She hadn't even taken the time to change before coming to see Danielle. Her eyes were shadowed, and she still tended to squint.

Danielle pried the note from Snow's hand and held it to the light of Snow's choker. "She says to meet her in the chapel when you wake up."

"That's another thing! She put me to sleep!"

Danielle glanced back, but neither Jakob nor Armand had stirred. Taking Snow by the hand, she dragged her out into the hallway and shut the door. "She should have made you sleep longer. You're grumpy."

Snow drew herself up. "I am not! I'm trying to save Beatrice's life."

"So am I." Danielle waited a heartbeat, watching Snow's eyes narrow with suspicion. "Talia took the knife because I told her to."

"I told you I could—"

"You were exhausted," Danielle said. "You're still hurt. I'm amazed you made it up that ladder."

"I stopped to rest a lot," Snow admitted. She snatched the note back and crumpled it into a pouch on her belt. "Where did she go?"

"To get Morveren." Danielle peeked back into the room while Snow fumed. Armand and Jakob were both still asleep. "Wait here."

She stepped inside and dressed as hastily as she could, while Snow fumed.

"I'll get her for this," Snow was muttering when Danielle returned. "The next time she smokes that pipe of hers, I'm changing it into a newt."

"Aren't you the one who used magic on Talia to get that knife in the first place?" Danielle asked.

"That's right, tease the cranky sorceress. Don't think I'm letting you off the hook either. It's going to be newts for everyone."

Danielle fastened the clasp of her cloak as they walked outside. Dew covered the grass of the courtyard. She waved to the gardener, who was already up and pulling slugs from the young shoots.

"Slugs might work, too," Snow said thoughtfully.

"Tell me the truth. Could you even read those books you had out, or were you too exhausted?"

Snow stuck out her tongue.

Incense made Danielle's eyes water as she stepped into the chapel. She spotted Talia at the front of the church. Beside her, Morveren rested on the steps which led up to the altar. Lannadae was here as well, curled up next to her grandmother.

"She shouldn't be here with Queen Bea," said Snow.

"Father Isaac agreed it was safe." Talia pointed to one of the incense burners. "The potion should work on undine as well as humans, so she can't use her magic against us. This place is as safe as her prison on the *Phillipa*. Safer, really. Even if she tried to escape, where is she going to go?"

Danielle frowned. There was a fresh bandage on one of Morveren's tails. "What did it take to persuade her?"

"Talia and I have already spoken of her 'persuasion,' " said Father Isaac, emerging from the vestibule at the back of the chapel. He carried Lirea's knife in both hands. "While I can understand her urgency, I fear her passion will lead her down dark paths."

"You have no idea," said Talia.

Snow stomped through the church and snatched the knife before whirling on Talia. "How did you trick me into falling asleep, anyway? I don't remember drinking anything."

"Magic." Talia waved her fingers. "Now sit down. If you're going to break Morveren's spells, you need to know the truth about what she tried to do."

Danielle walked slowly through the palace, Armand at her side. She was still trying to process everything Talia had shared. How many people had died because of

Morveren's quest to "improve" her race? "Do you believe her? That the undine have no souls?"

Armand shrugged. "There are some who say the same of the fairy folk. I'm told there was a time women were thought to be soulless as well, and children weren't named or accepted as human until their fourth birthday."

"But Morveren's magic lets her manipulate souls. Wouldn't she know the truth?"

"Perhaps," he admitted. "Or perhaps the undine are simply different."

They had just reached the kitchen when a page came running. "Princess Whiteshore," he gasped. "Captain Varisto demands you meet with him."

"Thank you, Fenton." Danielle stared longingly through the kitchen door, inhaling the smell of fresh-baked bread and cinnamon. "I suppose I should be grateful he waited this long."

"I'll grab something for you," Armand promised. "You go get ready."

"What do you mean?"

Armand's eyebrow quirked. "You're going to be meeting with a prince of Hilad. You might want to run a brush through that hair, and maybe even grab that crown you love so much."

Danielle groaned and turned back toward her room.

Two handmaidens were already waiting when she arrived. Before she could protest, they began stuffing her into a formal forest green gown, cinching the waist tightly enough to interfere with her breathing.

"What have you done to yourself?" asked the older girl, Aimee. She grabbed a hank of Danielle's hair and tugged a comb through the ends. "Did you spend your entire time at sea standing in the wind, just to make our jobs more difficult?"

Danielle grimaced, but didn't struggle. She had learned a long time ago that fighting only made it worse. "If I'd had to endure this to attend the ball, I think I would have left Armand to my stepsisters."

The other girl, Sandra, pressed a hand to her mouth to cover a giggle. She turned away to pull out a drawer at the base of the wardrobe, retrieving a pair of glass slippers.

Danielle shook her head hard enough to yank the comb from Aimee's hands. "I haven't been able to fit into those since before I had Jakob."

Armand returned a while later, bearing a cinnamon-topped pastry in one hand. He pressed it into Danielle's hand, then retrieved her sword from beside the bed where she had left it the night before.

"Bless you," Danielle said, taking an enormous bite of the pastry. Armand stepped around behind her, strapping the sword belt to her waist despite Aimee's protests.

"She's meeting a Hiladi prince," Armand said. "If she goes unarmed, he'll believe her weak. Given that they've already faced one another in battle, he'll likely take it as an insult." He stepped back and gave Danielle an appraising look. "You shouldn't need to use it, as long as you refrain from any further insults. But carrying a weapon means you respect him as a threat."

Aimee stood on her toes to set Danielle's crown onto her brow. The braided circlet of silver and gold was heavier than it looked. The metal felt cold against her forehead. She closed her eyes as Sandra dabbed an eye-watering scent onto her neck.

"How did he find out about our . . . visit to Hilad?" she asked.

Armand shook his head. "I don't see how the undine could have reached him so quickly, and I can't imagine he sailed close enough to spy on you. Not without Hephyra noticing. That woman has eyes like a hawk."

"I've never seen eyes so green," Danielle said.

Armand snorted. "You should see her in the fall. They change with the seasons, turning the most amazing shade of hazel."

Danielle stood as her handmaidens adjusted her hair, her gown, and even tugged her sword belt around so the hilt rested at a more attractive, if less practical angle. "The gem in the pommel doesn't really match the gown," Aimee said. "Sandra, get the ocean-blue gown with the gold—"

"Don't make me use this," Danielle said, laying a hand on her sword.

Armand smiled and offered an arm. "Are you ready?"

Danielle's throat went dry as it sank in. She was about to meet with a foreign prince. A prince who had the might of the Hiladi Empire behind him. A single misspoken word and history would remember Cinderella not as a filthy girl who won a prince but as a foolish princess who helped plunge Lorindar into war. "Is it all right if I throw up first?"

He lowered his voice. "The first time my father presented me at court, I was so nervous I forgot to relieve myself beforehand. By the time I was introduced to the last baron, it was a miracle I wasn't standing in a puddle."

"Are you sure you or the king wouldn't be better off—"

"My father has enough to worry about."

"Of course," Danielle said, guilt rushing through her. "I'm sorry."

"I'd talk to Varisto if I could." Armand shook his head. "His grievance is with you. I'll be there, but you have to face him." He led her toward the door. "He's waiting in the courtyard, by the fountain."

Danielle spent the entire walk trying to plan her responses to Varisto's accusations. He was the one who had attacked the *Phillipa* without warning. Her words on the docks might have been impetuous, but she refused to apologize for worrying about Beatrice.

As they walked through the halls, Armand cleared his throat and whispered, "If you're not going to eat that . . ." He reached toward Danielle.

Danielle looked down at the forgotten pastry in her hand. She took another bite, then held it protectively to her chest, out of her husband's reach. His playful grab missed, but it was enough to make her smile. She was still licking crumbs from her hand when they reached the courtyard.

Captain Varisto was easy to spot, thanks to his red sash. He stood with Ambassador Trittibar at the fountain in the courtyard, a large circular basin resting on a square pedestal. In the center of the basin, water trickled from four figures carved from a single pillar of white stone. On one side, water dribbled from a wizard's pipe. On another, a slender dragon breathed water from his nostrils. As Danielle approached, she could hear Trittibar explaining the fountain's history in painful detail.

"The figure who stands atop the pedestal is Malindar himself, who forced my people into a treaty with the humans," Trittibar said. "This was carved nearly a hundred years ago by a gnome named Rigglesnip. It was a gift to the humans, though you can tell Rigglesnip wasn't happy about the assignment. He made Malindar's nose too big, and concealed extra pipes within his statue. This wasn't discovered for several years. After a heavy enough rain, that water will spray from Malindar's nostrils as well. Now over here we have the dragon Nolobraun, who—"

"Prince Armand!" Varisto's relief was plain as he hurried away from Trittibar.

"I apologize for the interruption." Neither Armand's expression nor his tone betrayed his amusement. "We can come back at another time if you wish to continue your conversation."

"No!" Varisto stiffened and turned his attention to Danielle. "No, I have waited long enough." His eyes took in the sword at Danielle's side. He too was armed, carrying a spiked ax through his belt. "You captured Morveren, a feat I have failed to do. I know your darkskinned friend smuggled her here last night. I will overlook your attack on Lirea in exchange for Morveren. This is my final offer, Highness."

Without thinking, Danielle said, "I'm sorry for your loss, Prince Varisto."

Varisto started to respond, then cocked his head. "What?"

"I had no brothers or sisters." This wasn't what she had planned. She hesitated, feeling exposed. But how much more exposed must Varisto feel, alone in the palace and surrounded by strangers? "My stepsisters were ... not the kind of family I had hoped for. I know you cared for your brother. To lose him must have been painful, and I offer my condolences."

This obviously wasn't what Varisto had expected. He stared at her. "Thank you for your words, Your Highness. If you would also offer his killer, I would be indebted to you."

"When your brother lay dying, if there was one who could have saved him, would you have sent that one away?" Danielle folded her arms. "Beatrice is more than my queen. She's my friend and my family. Should I let her die so you can have your vengeance?"

Varisto started to speak, then shook his head. His shoulders sank, and his voice softened. "No. But after, then. When Morveren has worked her magic. You will give her to me then."

Danielle looked at Trittibar, standing behind Varisto. Trittibar's face was sympathetic. Ever so slightly, he shook his head no.

"I captured Morveren, as you said." Danielle swallowed and hoped this was the right response. "I promise she will be punished for what she's done, both to Lirea and to your brother. That's the most I can offer you."

Varisto's hand moved toward his ax, and his face clouded. "You expect me to accept a woman's idea of justice?"

"I expect you to remember you are a guest of Lorindar," Danielle said, fighting to keep her voice steady. This was more than simply standing up to her stepsisters. She spoke for an entire nation. "Remember also that men died when you joined Lirea's war and attacked our ship. Do their souls deserve justice as well, Prince Varisto?"

He bowed slightly. "I loved my brother, Princess. I would give my own life if I could bring him back."

"Some of those men had brothers, too."

"I . . . I know." For a moment, his facade slipped and Danielle saw not a Hiladi prince but a young man struggling against his own doubts. "But I took a vow to protect Gustan's wife."

Across the courtyard, Danielle spotted Talia leaving the chapel. Danielle tensed, but Talia was moving with her normal purposeful stride. If something was wrong, she would be running. She turned back to Varisto. The man's arrogance annoyed her, and she couldn't forgive the deaths of her people, but the pain on his face was genuine. Her instincts told her he deserved the truth. Praying she wasn't making a mistake, she said, "Varisto . . . your brother never married Lirea."

Trittibar stepped forward. "Perhaps this isn't the time for such matters, Princess."

"I've seen his air spirits come to Lirea's aid," said Varisto.

Danielle shook her head. "Gustan was a prince of Hilad. Do you believe he would have risked his future to wed a mermaid? Would your people ever have accepted her as their queen?"

"I wouldn't have believed, but I was wrong." Varisto gripped his ax. Both Armand and Trittibar tensed, but Varisto didn't try to draw the weapon. "I thought he was only—I misjudged him."

Danielle watched his face, the way he stared at the earth as he spoke. This was guilt as much as grief. "You thought he was using her. You know how he treated her, don't you?" Danielle thought back to what Lannadae had told them. "That's why you argued with him about Lirea."

"He liked to fight, to prove himself stronger than all others. There were times in our youth when he would beat me for some unintentional slight," Varisto said, his gaze distant. "Lirea was a pleasant child, but she didn't know our ways. Her words were often impertinent or disrespectful. I told him—" He stiffened, and then he was a prince once more, calm and formal. "These matters are none of your concern, Princess."

"The air spirits don't obey Lirea." Danielle could see Trittibar's apprehension. Even Armand appeared tense. Varisto was young, angry, and unpredictable. But he was also Gustan's brother. It was wrong to keep this from him. "They obey Gustan."

Varisto whirled to face Armand. "What is she saying?"

"Morveren created that knife to trap your brother's soul," Danielle said. "To bind him to Lirea. It's through that bond that the spirits follow her will. That same knife now holds our queen as well. We entered Hilad in order to retrieve that knife and save Queen Beatrice."

"You lie." He drew his ax.

Danielle started to grab her own weapon, but that would only guarantee a fight. Instead, she folded her arms and said, "I trust you have more honor than to attack a defenseless opponent, Prince Varisto."

"Think, boy," said Trittibar, circling Varisto. "You stand alone in Whiteshore Palace."

"He's my brother." Varisto's voice shook.

Talia stepped past Danielle, her stance low as she moved inside Varisto's reach. Danielle hadn't even realized she was there.

Talia drove her fingers into Varisto's wrist and the ax dropped to the ground. He grabbed for her, but Talia moved too quickly. Danielle saw her fingers jab the soft flesh beneath Varisto's chin, and then she was spinning, one leg sweeping the prince's legs. Varisto slammed to the ground.

"And she's my princess," Talia said, kicking his ax away. "I'll thank you to leave her in one piece."

"Talia, please." Danielle beckoned Talia back.

"You tell me Morveren stole my brother's soul, yet you protect her." Varisto sat up, twisting his sash in his hands. "I know the knife you speak of. I've seen it many

Chapter 14

THE WORST PART ABOUT BEING FORCED to work with Morveren was that deep down, a part of Snow was enjoying it.

They sat on the floor near the front of the chapel, while Talia watched from the altar like an angry, well-armed hawk. Even with Father Isaac's protections, Talia looked like she would cut Morveren's throat at the slightest threatening sound. But Morveren had barely spoken, save to instruct Snow as they crafted a new soul trap.

Snow still hadn't forgiven Talia. They hadn't spoken more than a handful of words to one another, but Talia's cockeyed smirk said it all. *Now we're even.*

Maybe so. There would still be newts and slugs aplenty when this was over. But Snow's anger soon gave way to fascination as she watched Morveren work.

Morveren's skill surpassed even that of Snow's mother, though her power was less. Morveren reminded her of a scrimshaw artist who had once carved a portrait of her mother in whalebone. His knife had moved in small, careful strokes, each one following the next with no hesitation. Morveren displayed that same care as she set one hair after another over the mouth of a golden chalice, fixing each one in place with a bead of white wax.

"What happens to them?" Snow asked.

"Who?"

"The souls you consume for their power."

Morveren spliced another hair through the web. "I don't know. I use them until their strength fades. Eventually they slip away. I like to believe they find their way to whatever world awaits them." She picked up the cup and moved it toward Snow. "Be careful. Too much power will destroy the trap. I could come with you to—"

"You're staying here." Snow calmed herself as she took the cup. Her vision had improved slightly with sleep, but her eyes still watered if she tried to focus on fine details like the individual hairs.

Each of those hairs had been carefully trimmed from Beatrice's locks. Morveren had used them to weave a white web, one which should allow Beatrice to pass freely while trapping Gustan. A hole at the center would allow the hilt of the knife to rest in the cup.

Snow held her breath, afraid to disturb the web as she carried the chalice toward the door. Stepping through that door was like throwing off a stifling blanket. It wasn't that she couldn't use magic inside the church. She had tested a spell or two, and with the help of her mirrors, Snow suspected she could overpower Father Isaac's wards if she had to. Probably. But even her aborted efforts had left her drained, her head pounding.

The pain in her skull returned as she wove power into the web on the chalice. She could feel the hairs vibrating like lute strings.

"Your eyes are watering." Talia stood looking down at her. Snow hadn't heard her approach. "You need rest."

"Are you offering to take over?" Snow ran a finger over the hairs. Physically, she could have snapped them with ease, but to the trapped souls, the bonds would be strong as steel. To Gustan, at least.

Assuming Snow hadn't poured too much magic into the trap. Or too little. And that Beatrice was still strong enough to escape. "It's ready. I think."

"That's all?" asked Talia.

"Magic doesn't always involve smoke and lights and explosions."

"You wouldn't know it from some of your experiments."

Snow stuck out her tongue and carried the cup back into the church. The cup felt heavier, and she could feel the wards pressing in on her spells, but the enchantment was already in place. Trying to ignore the pain in her head, she carried the cup toward the altar.

"Well done," said Morveren. "You see? A delicate touch is all a true witch requires. You can—"

"Are you sure Gustan won't be able to escape?" Snow said. "If he finds Beatrice's body, he could try to take it for himself."

"Even if he does find a flaw in the soul cup, he won't be able to take your queen. If bonding soul to flesh were so simple, I would have claimed one for myself years ago. More likely, his struggles would kill her and destroy what's left of his spirit." Morveren sagged against the altar. "Snow, I know you don't agree with what I've done, but you can't let Lirea die. This isn't her fault."

"No. It's yours," said Talia.

Morveren ignored her. "Separating Lirea from the knife will have weakened her. Together we can use her connection to the knife to control her, to stop her from attacking your people. Please keep her alive until I can find a way to complete her bond with Gustan." She cried as she spoke. Magic and urgency filled her words, though the wards of the church protected Snow from the power of her voice.

"I'm sorry," Snow said.

"Lirea is innocent." Morveren turned to Lannadae. "Help me, child. This is your last chance to save your sister."

Lannadae had spent the past hours with Father Isaac, talking in low voices so as not to disturb Snow or Morveren. She drew herself higher, balancing on her tails. Tears wet her cheeks. "Your magic destroyed my sister."

"You can't—" Morveren crawled toward Lannadae, only to stumble. Snow could feel her struggling to throw off the effects of Father Isaac's incense. Morveren raised her head. "It's not too late, child."

Snow brought the cup to the front of the church and set it on the corner of the altar, out of Morveren's reach. "I'm ready."

"I'll fetch Danielle and the others." Talia hesitated, then turned to Father Isaac. "Will they be—"

"Morveren can do no harm while the incense fills the church," said Isaac.

Snow pressed her thumb carefully through the gap in the center of the web. When she pulled back, she could feel the web tugging, similar to what she had felt when she experimented with the knife.

Snow would have tried to use raw power to trap Gustan while Beatrice returned to her body. She might have beaten him, but what damage would she have done to Bea in the process? Without Morveren's help, Snow might have destroyed them both. "Talia was right to stop me."

"She cares for you," said Morveren as she tried to find a comfortable position. Too much time out of water had left her hunched, much as she had been when Snow first saw her. Morveren groaned with every movement, but until this moment she had fought to carry herself with some dignity. Now she sagged against the frontmost bench, broken and defeated. Wincing, she rubbed her wounded tail with her hands.

"Most of the time," Snow agreed. "Though there are days I'm sure she wants to toss me off the palace walls."

Morveren frowned. "You mean you don't know how she feels about you?"

Snow's next quip died on her lips. "What do you mean?"

"Talia loves you. I noticed before, on the ship. When she came to bring me here, her feelings were unmistakable. Even out of water, I can smell her feelings. I assumed you knew."

"That's not—She's my friend." Snow set the cup down to keep from dropping it. She thought about Talia's discomfort when they were swimming together to Lirea's palace. Or how annoyed she always got when Snow flirted with men.

Not annoyed, but jealous.

Snow bit her lip, remembering how strangely Talia acted when Snow first recovered from Lirea's attack. Talia had looked almost frightened, a childlike vulnerability Snow had never seen from her.

"You don't care for her?" Morveren asked.

"It's not that simple," said Snow. "She's not ... I don't—"

"Humans." Morveren snorted and rested her head against the bench. "I forget how you complicate these matters."

Morveren was right. Snow would have seen it long ago had it been anyone but Talia. One hand went to her shoulder, remembering the way Talia had massaged her to sleep. How long had she felt this way? As far as Snow could recall, Talia had never shown romantic interest in anyone, male or female. Given her history, Snow could understand Talia's reluctance, but—

The chapel doors swung open. Father Isaac escorted King Theodore inside, followed closely by Armand, Danielle ... and Talia. Talia was watching Snow, though she quickly looked away. Too quickly.

Prince Varisto was the last to enter, along with Tymalous, who took a seat at the back of the church. Varisto had left his ax behind. He moved like one lost as he followed the others to the front of the church.

"How is she?" asked Theodore.

Father Isaac stepped past Snow and Morveren, climbing the steps to the altar. "Unchanged."

Snow shook her head to clear her thoughts, which turned out to be a mistake. Her vision swam, and the back of her head began to throb. She groaned and clutched her skull with one hand.

"Are you all right?" asked Talia.

"I'm fine." Snow swallowed, hoping that hadn't come out as sharply as it sounded. Without looking up, she untied Lirea's knife from her belt and gripped it in both hands.

"Please," Morveren said. "Don't let her die."

Snow could feel the power in her words, fighting through even Father Isaac's protections to press against Snow's thoughts. How long had Morveren gathered her strength for this one final attempt?

It wasn't enough. As Morveren's power faded, she curled her tails around herself and began to weep.

"This is the witch?" Prince Varisto stood staring at Morveren, his hands clasped.

Talia stayed beside him, presumably to make sure he didn't kill Morveren right then. Talia had never been one to rely on magical protections. "This is Morveren."

Varisto turned to Snow. "And that knife. My brother . . ." He reached out, then hesitated. "Does he still live?"

"The mind I touched was splintered," Snow said. "Little remains of your brother's spirit."

Varisto touched the hilt. He closed his eyes. "I feel nothing. I . . . I had hoped—" His fingers tightened into a fist, and he jerked back. "Please finish this. Give him the dignity of death."

Father Isaac moved to the end of the altar. Clasping his crucifix in both hands, he bent his head and began to pray. Snow could feel his power spreading through the church, waves of warmth and protection.

Snow moved the knife toward the queen's arm. She saw the king start to rise, but Prince Armand caught his hand.

"Blood renews the bond between body and soul," said Morveren. "You have to do this, to help her to find her way back."

"I'm sorry, Bea," Snow whispered, then jabbed the tip of the knife into Beatrice's forearm. She blinked back tears as blood welled from the cut. Reversing her grip on the knife, she spread the queen's blood onto the hilt.

Morveren pulled herself higher, her bent tails supporting her like two thick serpents. "From this point forward, you must be swift. Both souls sense the presence of her body. Already they will be fighting to escape. If your queen is strong enough, she will—"

"Shut up." Snow set Lirea's knife through the web in the cup so that the pommel rested on the bottom of the cup. The hairs held the knife in place, with the blade pointed to the ceiling. "She's strong. She can do this."

Gritting her teeth, she touched her choker. Her head exploded with pain as Father Isaac's protections fought to suppress her magic, but the true power of Snow's spell was far from here, safely hidden beneath the palace.

She called enough power to set the whole chapel alight, but only a single beam of magical light pierced the wards. Being careful not to touch the strands of the web, she directed that light into the cup, to the hair wrapped around the hilt of Lirea's knife. The first few strands were slow to break, but with each passing moment, more of the hair snapped and curled away. She could almost feel the trapped souls adding their strength from within, fighting to break free of their prison.

Magic flared through the web on the cup as both souls escaped the knife. Snow's legs gave out, and she would have fallen if Father Isaac hadn't caught her.

"Thank you," she whispered, pushing herself upright. She concentrated on the soul cup. Each hair glowed golden, a glowing web over the mouth of the chalice. Voices cried out from within. Snow felt Beatrice's presence as she started to pass through the web, only to fall back into the cup. "Gustan is fighting her."

"She must fight back," Morveren snapped. "Fight back, or both will be lost forever."

Danielle approached the altar. "Beatrice, it's us."

"The soul can't hear you," said Morveren.

Snow tore a mirror from her choker and dropped it through the web. The glass rang against gold.

"What are you doing?" Morveren asked, trying to pull herself higher.

The mirror held the reflection of the glowing web. Snow concentrated, spreading that reflection beyond the boundaries of the glass, creating an illusory web within the cup. Like a bird to a window, Gustan broke away from Beatrice and lunged toward the mirror, seeing it as a second portal to freedom.

"It's done," Snow whispered, pain and tears blinding her. "She's free."

Father Isaac rested a hand on Beatrice's forehead. "Her body and spirit are one."

Everyone gathered around the altar. The king took Beatrice's hand in his and asked, "How long until she awakens?"

"Not long." Morveren backed away from the altar.

"What of my brother?" Varisto asked.

Snow wiped her face on her sleeve, blinking to try to clear her vision. She reached to take the cup and knife. The cup tilted onto its side and rolled toward the edge of the altar. Talia jumped to catch it . . . and missed. The cup bounced once on the floor, and then a gust of wind blew it into Morveren's waiting hands. "I'm sorry, child. I can't let you murder my granddaughter."

"Lirea's air spirits," Snow whispered. "They're here. All of them."

The doors exploded outward. Wind spun through the church, knocking Snow back before she could ready her own magic. She could feel the power of the incense burning the spirits, but with every moment the wind blew more of the incense from the chapel. Candles toppled to the ground, their flames extinguished. Hangings on the wall tore free and whirled around the air. Talia sprang toward Morveren, one foot sweeping up in a kick, but Morveren dove aside, crawling beneath the bench.

"How did they get in?" Danielle shouted.

"They were already here." Snow turned to the knife. "We carried them into the church ourselves."

Father Isaac spread his hands and approached Morveren, his robes fluttering. "Allow Gustan to move on."

The wind had knocked Danielle down. Other spirits

held King Theodore and Prince Armand pinned against the benches. But so far nobody had actually been hurt. Snow held the altar with both hands, using her body to shelter Beatrice from the wind.

Morveren clutched the cup to her chest. Her humming grew louder. Snow's ears popped as the wind gained in strength, and then all was still. She could feel Isaac fighting to suppress the spirits' anger. His own magic seemed untouched by the chapel's protections.

"Go in peace." Isaac reached for the cup.

One of the windows shattered in a storm of colored glass. A second followed, broken by the spirits.

"Grandmother, stop!" Lannadae tried to reach Morveren, but the wind tossed her aside like a doll.

Varisto clapped his hands. The ringing of his bracelets echoed throughout the church. Snow could hear the sound reaching beyond the walls, a summons of some sort. Breaking the window had weakened the wards. Moments later, Varisto's ax spun through the open door, slapping into his hand. He leaped to strike, but the wind knocked him back.

Snow squinted at Morveren, trying to understand. There was another spell worked into the chalice. Several of the hairs seemed to extend beyond the lip of the cup, reaching toward Morveren.

"You wove your hairs with hers." And Snow had missed it. She fought to maintain her balance. Her head pounded as she tried to erect a magical wall around Morveren. If she could sever Morveren's connections to her spirits, they should dissipate.

"A small thing, but enough to connect me to our trapped prince," said Morveren. "Skill, rather than power. Now please move aside. I have no desire to hurt you."

"No." The wind howled louder. Snow's hair whipped about her face, blinding her. She grabbed her own knife, flipping the catch to reveal the mirror in the cross guard. She thrust the blade up, willing the strike to cut past mere air to the spirit's heart. Her arm shook from the effort, but the wind diminished as the spirit fell back, wounded but not dead.

"You're a strong one," Morveren said. "But you lack experience."

Even as Snow struggled to hold off one spirit, the rest attacked in unison. They smashed through her defenses, lifting her into the air.

"Snow!" Talia jumped to catch Snow, arms wrapping around her waist. The wind threw them both to the side, but somehow Talia managed to twist her body, taking the brunt of the impact.

Through doubled vision, Snow saw Morveren rise, held aloft by her spirit slaves. She flew out of the church, vanishing before anyone else could react. The doors slammed shut behind her.

Talia was already up and running. She lowered her shoulder and crashed into the doors, but they refused to budge. "They're held from the outside."

Snow pulled herself up, keeping one hand on the wall as dizziness washed over her. Nothing felt broken, but she would have a number of new bruises. She had always bruised so easily. She touched her hair, and her fingers came back bloody where the fall had reopened her injuries.

Snow stumbled toward the door, her knife still clutched in one hand. She had cut herself when she fell, a long gash along her side. Any deeper, and she could have killed herself.

Her neck warmed as she pulled power from her choker. Sparks danced from the mirror in her knife. Talia started to speak, then swore and jumped aside as the doors creaked.

Snow could feel the air spirits outside. Morveren had left two to bar the doors. With every step, Snow pushed harder. The pressure in her head increased as well, but she kept going. Slowly, the doors bowed outward.

She threw her knife.

The blade wedged into the gap between the doors and quivered in place. Moments later, the doors exploded.

Boards and splinters burst inward, but the same magic Snow had used to push open the doors also deflected the debris. The air spirits vanished.

Talia jumped through the doorway, knives drawn. "She's gone."

Snow could hear shouts from outside. Cries of confusion and fear, but Morveren had already escaped.

"Snow!" Danielle and the others had gathered around the altar. "Beatrice is moving."

Snow turned away from the door. There was nothing she could do to catch Morveren now. If the air spirits were strong enough to carry her, she could go anywhere.

Beatrice lay shivering. Her lips were cracked and bleeding, but she was smiling. Her smile grew when she saw Snow. "I heard you. Even within that dark place, I could hear you calling me."

The words triggered a coughing fit. King Theodore helped her to sit up, holding her until she recovered. Beatrice leaned her head against his chest. "Is everyone all right?"

"Our son tried to smash through a bench with his leg," Theodore said. "He might have broken the bone."

"Where's Isaac?" Snow turned around until she spotted him slumped against the wall beneath the cross. He had been the first target of Morveren's attack. Tymalous was already running toward him, moving with surprising speed for a man of his age.

"He's alive," said Tymalous. "God willing, I might even be able to keep him that way."

In the far corner, Snow spotted Lannadae huddled and crying. "I'm sorry," Lannadae said. "I didn't know."

Snow glanced at the ruined doorway. A crowd had begun to gather outside the church. "Morveren means to finish her spell, to make Lirea the first of a new breed of undine."

"Lirea is still queen," Danielle said. "The entire tribe will attack Morveren the instant they see her."

"Not all of them," Lannadae whispered.

Snow crouched beside her. "What do you mean?"

"There have always been those who believe as Morveren does, that we are soulless. Some among the tribe want what Lirea has. To move about on land as well as the sea. They envied her that ability, even as they feared and pitied her madness." Lannadae shuddered, finally looking up to make eye contact. Salt-streaked tears crusted her cheeks. "Morveren has followers among the tribe. Undine who will obey her in return for that gift. She . . . she offered to do the same to me if I helped her to escape."

The church had fallen silent. All those at the altar were listening to Lannadae's confession.

"When was this?" asked Danielle.

"Last night. Normally the queen's control is absolute, and Lirea's scent is stronger than any I've known. But Morveren is royal as well. She told me she had protected some of her followers from Lirea's control." Lannadae tugged on her scales. "I told her I wouldn't let her do to me what she had done to Lirea. I'm sorry I didn't tell you."

"She probably made sure you wouldn't tell," Snow guessed. When she squinted, she could see faint traces of Morveren's spell lingering like cobwebs over Lannadae. Lannadae was timid by nature. It wouldn't have taken much to ensure her silence.

"She intends to unite the undine," whispered Lannadae. "All those who refuse to follow Lirea will be killed."

"How?" asked Danielle.

"The gold Lirea collects." Lannadae bowed her head. "She means to hire human alchemists to poison their waters."

Snow rose. "I know where she's going." Morveren's escape would have weakened her. How much power waited for Morveren back in her wrecked ship? All of those soul jars, still safe after so many years. "We'll need to take the *Phillipa* back out to sea."

"That's dangerous," said Armand. His face shone with

sweat as Danielle helped him toward the altar. "The undine have already increased their attacks. They struck Lyskar again last night."

"Lirea will kill Morveren if she can," Lannadae said.

"She can't," Snow said. "Lirea might have fought Morveren's control before, but now that Morveren has Gustan—"

"Because of you." Varisto held his ax with both hands, seemingly lost as he stared into the engravings on the head. "Because your people allowed her to live. Because you brought her here and placed my brother's soul within her reach. And because once again I failed to save him."

"Prince Varisto?" Beatrice's voice was stronger, though she still held Theodore for support.

"Your Majesty." Varisto bowed his head. "Forgive me, but your people should have destroyed that cursed knife."

"And let me die?" Bea closed her eyes. "Perhaps."

"Damn your stubbornness. Gustan's as well." Varisto stomped away. As he left the church, Snow heard him say, "Had he listened to me, he might still be alive."

"We know where Morveren's going," Snow said. "If we sail straight for Hilad, we can intercept her before she reaches Lirea. The *Phillipa*—"

"You saw how fast she flew," said Talia. "Even the *Phillipa* isn't fast enough to catch her air spirits."

"She is," Beatrice said, pressing closer to Theodore. "For me, she will move like the wind itself."

Lirea rested her head against the legs of Gustan's statue, listening with all of her being. The voices had gone quiet, and she didn't know whether to laugh or scream. Every movement ached, as though her body were that of an old woman. Yet this was the closest she had come to peace since before Gustan. She had almost forgotten what it was like to be alone with her own thoughts.

Her solitude had been short-lived. Already she could feel Morveren trying to pry into her mind, like a turtle burrowing in the sand to lay her eggs. In the past, Morveren's touch would have roused the voices to such fury her head felt as though it would burst from their screams. Now Lirea simply slid into the water, savoring each moment until she lost herself once again.

The songs of her tribe drifted through the windows of the tower. Their numbers were greater than anyone could remember. One tribe had already been poisoned. The survivors had come seeking revenge, only to fall under Lirea's sway.

Morveren had done something to her scent. From the moment Lirea murdered Gustan, she had grown in power, twisting the loyalty of her tribe from her father to herself. She could unite all undine into a single tribe. Gold coins glittered in the water, tribute from the first nation to give in to her demands. Soon the entire ocean would be hers.

There was no exhilaration. Lirea wanted only to rest, to sleep.

But with sleep came dreams. The screech of her knife as the blade scraped bone. The hot blood splashing her hands. The shock on his face. Shock that twisted into hatred.

She sank lower, allowing the water to wash away the tears. One by one they abandoned her. Nilliar hadn't returned. Lannadae and Morveren still conspired against her.

She dragged a hand through coins and sand, stirring tiny vortexes of dirt in the water. Her father had been the first to turn against her. To punish her for giving herself to one of *them*. He had shouted and struck her, threatening to strip away her title and banish her forever. She could still hear his words, telling her she had shamed her family yet again. Her mother had sat by and said nothing. She wouldn't dare contradict the emperor.

Wait . . . Lirea's mother had died long before she met Gustan. These were Gustan's memories, not hers. His father, beating him and shouting at him for rutting with mermaids. With *animals*.

Lirea's song was little more than a moan as she pressed herself to the floor and tried to separate her thoughts from the rest. Gustan had never loved her. He had used her, and like a fool, Lirea had let him.

He still used her. Gustan and Morveren both, their desires twining with hers, twisting her mind, propelling her actions. Her moans grew louder as she clung to that sense of self, even as the whispers filled her mind, pulling her down . . .

Outside, a merman called for her, his song urgent enough to jolt Lirea from her thoughts. The water swallowed her screams as fins flattened into flesh. A shock of cold ran through her body. She pulled herself onto the stairs, the hard edges digging into her body.

The transformation took longer than usual, leaving her exhausted. She gasped with pain as she strained to draw the last scales into her skin. When she finally pushed herself to her hands and knees, she felt as though she crawled upon knives. Eventually, she made her way to the upper window, where she could look out at her people.

Undine filled the moat. The first rush of spawning had passed, and most of her people were ready to go forth. Pride filled her chest at the sight of her army.

A merman warrior sang from the front of the crowd, quieting the others as he requested his queen's permission to speak. Lirea didn't recognize him. The entire tribe was alien to her. They had grown too much, and she no longer knew her people by sight or by smell.

"What have you found?" she asked.

"Captain Varisto's ship," the merman said. "He docks at Lorindar. With Morveren and Lannadae."

Not Varisto too. She gripped the window with one hand as anger flooded her body. How could he turn against her? The miserable traitor. All that time he had pretended to aid her, hunting for a way to break Morveren's power when in truth he wanted only to help Morveren destroy her.

The air was strangely still. Lirea rested her head

CHAPTER 15

T HE ONLY SOUND WAS THE RATTLING of the
carriage wheels over the paving stones. The tension
made Danielle want to leap out the window.

Armand was furious about his injury, hardly saying a
word since they left the palace. Tymalous had splinted
his leg after tending to Father Isaac, but there was no
way he would be able to get about on a ship. Even on
land, Armand had to use a crutch to hobble about. He
sat on the far side of the carriage, his leg propped up on
the opposite bench.

Rarely was Armand's resemblance to the king more
pronounced than when they were both upset. King
Theodore hadn't spoken either. He sat with Beatrice,
their hands twined together. He hadn't tried to argue
Beatrice out of her decision, but it was clear to everyone how badly he wanted to. He fumed in silence, and
Danielle found herself leaning to the side to try to avoid
his scowl.

Even Snow was uncharacteristically somber. At first,
Danielle thought it was guilt. Snow blamed herself for
Morveren's escape and for Father Isaac's injuries. But
she kept staring at Talia, then turning away. If Danielle didn't know better, she would have thought Snow
looked embarrassed.

The queen alone appeared relaxed, resting with her
hand twined with Theodore's. She had taken both tea

and wine but said she had no appetite for solid food yet. Danielle hadn't been able to talk to her since she awoke in the church. Selfish as it was, she desperately wanted time alone with the queen, time to tell Beatrice what she had done, to ask if she had made the right choice about Morveren.

Armand finally broke the silence. "You're not well, Mother. You shouldn't even be out of bed, let alone—"

"I'm still your mother, not to mention your queen," Beatrice interrupted with a trace of her old spark. "That means I outrank you twice."

"That's right," muttered Talia. "If she chooses to head into battle half-starved, the stitches in her chest still seeping blood, who are we to question her wisdom?"

Bea's smile was pale but loving. "Precisely."

Talia stared heavenward. She was the first out of the carriage when they arrived, practically leaping through the door to escape. Danielle followed with only slightly less speed. The familiar salty mist of the sea sprinkled her skin, and the gulls cried out in greeting.

Prince Varisto stood waiting at the end of the dock. He met her with a slight bow, which Danielle returned.

"I didn't expect to find you still here," Danielle said.

Varisto shrugged. "I'm aware of your plans, Princess. As prince of Hilad, I thought you might want to ask my permission before invading my nation a second time."

"You've been in touch with your father?" Danielle watched him closely, but his face was stone. "The emperor still refuses to grant permission for any ship to encroach on Hiladi waters."

Varisto watched as Snow stepped lightly from the carriage. "My father's priorities ... do not match my own. Were you to sail with an escort, one captained by a Hiladi noble, he could hardly object. Lirea knows me and my ship. My presence will assure your safety."

Talia helped the queen down, while the king assisted from within the carriage. Once Bea was down, the king passed her a polished black cane. Beatrice held both the cane and Talia's arm for support. "Your ship would never keep up, I'm afraid."

Varisto stared at the *Phillipa*. "So instead you will take a single ship against Morveren and her air spirits? A ship that has already endured at least two attacks, to my knowledge? I'm amazed she still floats."

"My ship heals quickly, Prince Varisto." Beatrice waved to Captain Hephyra.

"Then let me join you on your ship," Varisto said again.

King Theodore stepped out and studied Varisto. "I've spent much of the night trying to negotiate with your father. You would defy his wishes?"

"It's my duty, both as a prince and as a brother, and—" He blushed and turned away.

"What is it?" Danielle asked.

Varisto shook his head. "Gustan was always the better warrior. Not once was I allowed to forget that fact. All my life I dreamed that one day I would be the one to come to his rescue."

Theodore's mouth remained set, but Danielle thought she saw his eyes wrinkle with what could have been amusement. He glanced at the queen, who nodded. To Varisto, he said, "As you say, it would be improper for Lorindar to invade your nation again without permission."

"Thank you." Varisto's lips tightened into a smile. "And when I see my brother again in the next life, I plan to make sure he knows exactly how his little brother had to save him."

Danielle found Captain Hephyra waiting at the top of the ladder when she boarded the *Phillipa*. The dryad held a thick cudgel in one hand, and her eyes were a darker green than Danielle remembered.

"I remember that one," Hephyra said, jabbing her weapon at Varisto. "That's the bastard who attacked my ship, may lightning split his mainmast. What in the name of the king's right ball is he—"

"He's here as my guest," Beatrice said. She climbed

slowly, using both hands to pull herself up each rung. Talia and Snow climbed behind, ready to catch her should she fall, but Beatrice made it without help. She took her cane from Talia, then stepped toward Hephyra. "I trust you'll treat him with the same care and respect you would me."

"But he—"

Beatrice rapped her cane against the deck. "Is my ship ready?"

"He attacked my—"

"We're in a hurry, Captain," Bea said.

Hephyra threw up her hands. "The rudder's repaired. She's not stocked for a long voyage, but we've managed to load some basic supplies, including four barrels of guts for the princess' shark friends. As long as you don't plan to stay at sea for more than a few days, we can cast off any time you're ready."

Varisto ran a hand along the rail, then grimaced. He used his teeth to pull a splinter from his palm. Hephyra lowered her head, smiling slightly before turning away.

Danielle tossed a line down to Lannadae, who was swimming beside the ship. "It's time!"

"Let me swim for a while," the mermaid shouted. "I can keep up with any human ship."

"Not *this* one." Frail as she was, Beatrice's smile had lost none of its mischief. She leaned heavily on her cane as she made her way to the back of the ship. Once there, she took the wheel with both hands. Some of her pain seemed to slip away. She straightened, and her breathing eased. "Captain?"

"Anchors are raised, Your Majesty," said Hephyra. If she resented Beatrice's mastery of her ship, she did a good job of hiding it. "She awaits your command."

At the front of the ship, the swan carved into the bowsprit spread its wings and let out a deafening cry, a trumpeting sound that echoed from the cliffs. Silver sails unfurled with no human help, and the *Phillipa* leaped away from Lorindar. Danielle stumbled, catching the rail to keep from falling. She wasn't the only one. Prince

Varisto fell to the deck. He had been digging at another splinter but now sat staring in amazement as the docks shrank behind them.

Alongside the ship, Lannadae clung to the rope Danielle had thrown. Danielle and Talia worked with several of the crew to haul the mermaid on board.

Lannadae's gills were spread wide, and she panted for breath. "I've grown so weak. There was a time . . . I would have swum circles . . . around this ship."

Beatrice looked down and smiled. "Oh, good. Now let me show you what the *Phillipa* can really do."

The swan trumpeted again, and the masts creaked as the sails snapped taut. The wind wasn't terribly strong, but the ship sailed forward as though propelled by a gale.

"Can you help Lannadae settle in?" Danielle asked.

Talia nodded. "Where are you going?"

She clutched her stomach and hurried toward the rail. "To lose whatever's left of my lunch."

Snow smiled at the sailor. Jeffreys, she thought his name was. He was talking about his time on the *Phillipa,* though his words were growing more and more jumbled. That happened a lot when she gave a man her undivided attention.

The sea spray misting her shirt probably didn't help matters either.

"I was one of the first to crew the queen's ship," Jeffreys said. "Back when the queen gave it to the queen. The fairy queen, I mean. Gave it to our queen. Queen Beatrice."

"She's a fast ship." Snow tilted her head, allowing the wind to catch her hair.

"Yes, ma'am. Very fast."

Snow gave him one of her best sidelong glances. "Some of us prefer to take things slowly."

Jeffreys turned a delightful shade of red.

A cough made them both jump. "Don't you have duties to attend to?" asked the queen.

"Yes, ma'am." He turned back to Snow, stammered, then fled.

Beatrice sighed and leaned on her cane. "I'd appreciate it if you didn't distract my crew when we're sailing into a battle."

Snow shrugged. "Maybe you should get an uglier crew."

"Isn't he a little old for you, anyway?"

Snow watched Jeffreys busy himself by the mainsail, checking the lines to make sure they were holding up to the strain of the ship's speed. The man couldn't have been more than thirty. Thanks to the price Snow had paid for certain spells, she appeared several years his elder. She tucked her hair back behind her ears, pretending not to notice the strands of white. "I'll be twenty in a few months, you know."

Bea stared out at the sea. The sun was nearly set, gilding the waves with fire. "How is your injury?"

"I'm fine," Snow said automatically. Her headaches had grown worse after the fight in the chapel, and the rolling of the ship did nothing to help her vision, but she would recover.

"You're a poor liar," Bea's smile took the sting from her words. "Your flirting always gets more desperate when you're upset."

Snow pulled her hat lower. "What do you mean, desperate?"

"Talia tells me you and Morveren spent a great deal of time together."

"Talia talks too much."

That earned a laugh from Beatrice. "Oh, yes. *Talia* is the loquacious one."

Snow hated being embarrassed. Her pale skin made the slightest blush evident to anyone within view. "Morveren was teaching me magic. I've never had a teacher before, not like her. I should have realized what she was. She nearly killed us all to stop us from hurting Lirea, but even then a part of me wished—" She broke off. "Morveren used her magic on the cup in the chapel, and I missed it."

"As I understand things, Morveren has had more than two hundred years of practice," Beatrice said. "It's not your fault."

Snow was blushing again, remembering precisely what Morveren had said to distract her. How long had Morveren known about Talia's feelings? Snow looked around for Talia, eventually finding her at the front of the ship with Danielle, watching the waves.

Bea followed her gaze. Thankfully, she misunderstood the intent. "Talia distrusted Morveren from the start, I assume?" When Snow nodded, Beatrice only laughed. "Talia distrusts everyone in the beginning. Even yourself, if memory serves."

"I've never been good at reading people," Snow said. "Everyone else knew my mother was evil, too. Everyone but me. When I was young, I'd hear the servants whispering. They made me so angry. I thought they were ungrateful and spiteful, filthy little commoners who didn't understand how great and powerful she really was." She rubbed her eyes.

"Talia expects to see the darkness in people, and thus she's more likely to find it," said Beatrice

"I wonder sometimes if the reason I couldn't see who Morveren really was is because—"

"You are not like her." Bea brushed Snow's hair back from her face. "Nor are you your mother. I trust you."

Snow closed her eyes, thinking of how she had reached into Talia's mind, manipulating her thoughts. "I don't."

"I know." Bea kissed her cheek. "Now go. Your friends need you. Particularly Danielle, judging by her shade of green."

Most of the night passed without incident, once Danielle had imbibed an entire pot of Snow's ginger tea. Snow used magic to chill the glass, and the tea tasted surprisingly good at that temperature. Of course, that much tea

had a price, and Danielle awoke several times that night
to visit the head.

Once she stopped to check on Beatrice, who remained
on deck. When the queen wasn't at the helm, she slept
in a hastily rigged hammock, staying close to the wheel
and Captain Hephyra. Talia remained with her through
the night, bringing her food and drink, though she took
little of either. Beatrice smiled at Danielle's concerns
and shooed her back to bed.

It was still dark when Danielle woke again. Men
were shouting, and she could hear footsteps thudding
across the ship. The door creaked open and Talia peeked
inside.

"Good, you're awake. Get out here."

Danielle glanced at Snow, who had kicked her blankets to the floor and lay sprawled with one arm hanging
off the cot. "What's going on?"

"The watch spotted debris up ahead. Looks like a
wrecked ship."

Danielle grabbed a cloak and hurried out after Talia.
"Where are we?"

"We crossed into Hiladi waters a short time ago.
Looking at the charts, we should be in position to intercept Morveren by midmorning."

The crew had lit oil lamps along the sides of the
ship. Danielle hurried to the rail, peering at the water.
Wooden planks, barrels, and other wreckage bobbed on
the surface. "What can I do?"

Talia jabbed a finger at the water. "Those sharks you
summoned are still with us, and there could be survivors
out there. You might want to tell the sharks not to eat
them."

Danielle leaned out. *There are people in the water.
They're my friends. Show us where they are, but please
don't hurt them.*

A scream made her jump. Two sharks circled a man
who clung desperately to a broken door. More cries followed as the sharks sought out other survivors.

"Have someone feed them," Danielle said. "The sharks, I mean. I don't know how hungry they might be."

"That ship was Hiladi." Talia pointed to a broken yardarm. "You can tell by the knots in the lines. They rig their sails more tightly than we do."

"We should wake Varisto." As the cold air swept the last of the fatigue from Danielle's mind, she realized those men who weren't helping to rescue the wrecked sailors were gathering weapons. "Lirea's tribe did this, didn't they? They've turned against Hilad."

"They'll do worse when they find us," said Talia.

A breeze caught Danielle's cloak. She spun, heart pounding. After her encounters with the air spirits, the gentlest wind was enough to make her jumpy. Talia didn't seem to notice. Her jacket appeared untouched by the wind. Danielle frowned, studying her more closely. "How many weapons do you have weighing that thing down?"

"That depends on how you define 'weapon.' "

Before Danielle could think up a response to that, a man near the bow shouted, "Captain Hephyra! Kelpies sighted to the port side."

Moments later, six kelpies leaped from the water. Undine clung to their harnesses, dozens on each mount.

"I didn't think they'd find us so soon." Talia tugged Danielle back from the railing. "They must have seen us approaching. You'll want to talk to those sharks again."

The crew doubled their efforts to pull survivors from the water. Captain Hephyra crossed the deck carrying a small powder barrel in her arms. She winked at Danielle as she hoisted the barrel overhead. "We don't have much, but we should be able to put up a decent fight."

"Talia, get Varisto. The undine might still listen to him." Danielle looked to see Beatrice still at the helm. "Then get to Beatrice and keep her safe."

Captain Varisto was already staggering up from below. He was barefoot, his shirt unbuttoned, but he had taken the time to don both his war hammer and a thick-bladed knife as long as Danielle's forearm. He stumbled and swore, stopping to rip a splinter from his foot.

"Hephyra, stop tormenting him," Danielle snapped. "We need his help."

Varisto cursed when he saw the survivors being brought on board. "That was one of our ships!"

"We're going to join them if you can't turn the undine away," Danielle said.

He cupped his hands to his mouth and bellowed, "I am Varisto, friend of Queen Lirea."

Undine dropped from the kelpies like rain, diving into the sea. Danielle silently summoned the sharks closer. She could see nothing beneath the surface, and only the occasional dorsal fin hinted at the sharks' presence.

A single undine surfaced, spear in hand. "Lirea named you traitor, human."

Varisto swore and twisted aside as the undine threw his spear. It slammed into the cutter behind them.

"How much longer do you mean to talk?" asked Hephyra. "This barrel isn't as light as it looks, you know."

"There are so many," said Lannadae.

Danielle spun. Lannadae sat behind her, staring through the railing. "I don't recognize them all. How did Lirea bring so many undine into our tribe?"

"You shouldn't be here." The words came from Varisto, to Danielle's surprise. He moved to stand in front of Lannadae, shielding her with his body. "They'll rip the ship apart to get to you if they learn you're with us. Get to shelter and stay there."

The *Phillipa* shuddered as one of the kelpies rammed her hull. That kelpie reared from the water moments later, and Danielle saw two sharks tearing at its flesh. Waves marked the passage of another kelpie who veered away from the ship.

"Give me to them in exchange for passage," Lannadae said.

"No!" Varisto and Danielle spoke as one. Danielle knelt beside her. "I will not turn you over to be killed."

"Beatrice almost died trying to protect me. I'm the

one who told you to free Morveren from her exile. You've risked so much, and I've done nothing but hide behind you." Lannadae crawled toward the rail.

Shouts and splashing from below showed where the undine had begun their attack. The sharks fought back, but they were outnumbered. Captain Hephyra hurled her barrel into the water, and the undine scattered. Word of this tactic had obviously spread. Hephyra held out a hand and shouted, "Spear!"

One of the crew slapped a fishing spear into her hand. The point had been covered in pitch. Hephyra leaned over the rail and thrust the spear into one of the lamps, breaking the glass. The pitch burst into flames.

"You're a royal," Danielle said. "Does that give you any power over the undine?"

"Not much." Lannadae bowed her head. "I'm still young. My scent is weak. Lirea is ... her scent is stronger than any mermaid I've ever known. Her power blossomed after Morveren transformed her. Even away from her, they'll still obey her commands."

"Good." Danielle ran toward Hephyra. "Captain, wait!"

Varisto followed. "Perhaps I don't know your language as well as I thought. How exactly is this 'good'?"

"Because it means the tribe will attack Morveren, too. All we have to do is lead them to her." To Hephyra, she said, "We outpaced Lannadae when we left Lorindar. Can this ship outrun kelpies?"

"I doubt it."

Danielle searched the water, but if any others had survived the shipwreck, the undine had dragged them down. "Then you'll want to bring up the rest of the powder. Beatrice, show them how fast this ship can fly!"

The *Phillipa* surged ahead. The kelpies started to follow, but Hephyra threw her spear. It disappeared into the water without even a splash.

"Rotting hell!" Hephyra grabbed another spear, lit it, and tried again. This time, the spear slammed into the barrel. The resulting explosion scattered kelpies and undine alike, not to mention most of Danielle's sharks.

We have more barrels, Danielle warned the kelpies. *Approach too closely, and we'll use them.*

The crew cheered as the kelpies fell back. Some of the undine still clung to the side of the ship, bracing themselves with their knives and spears. A few crossbow shots soon rid the ship of those hangers-on.

"Did I hear thunder?" Snow yawned as she approached Danielle. She looked around, staring first at the three Hiladi sailors who sat dripping by the mast, then at Captain Varisto. She studied him for a longer time, taking in the muscled lines of his chest and arms, until Danielle cleared her throat.

"What? I'm allowed to look." Snow yawned again, then reached into her shirt and pulled out a slender green bottle. "Besides, I thought I should let you know. My dead friend here says Morveren's on her way to Hilad."

CHAPTER 16

DANIELLE HELD HER CLOAK TIGHT against the night air as the *Phillipa* raced to intercept Morveren. Though hours had passed with no sign of the mermaid, Snow assured them it wouldn't be much longer.

"Looks like they're trying again," Hephyra shouted. She picked up a barrel and hurled it at the nearest kelpie. Their pursuers scattered in all directions. Talia raised a spear, but Hephyra shook her head. "No need. That was an empty."

So it had gone throughout the night. Time after time the kelpies would draw close, only to flinch back as Captain Hephyra hurled another barrel into their midst. At these speeds, even Talia had trouble hitting the barrels with her spears. More exploded than not, and the kelpies learned quickly. They fled from the barrels whether they exploded or not, so Hephyra had begun tossing empty barrels as well in order to preserve their supply of black powder.

All too soon, the kelpies resumed their attack. The skies had begun to lighten, making it easier to see the kelpies as they swam parallel to the ship, drawing ahead and closing ranks to form a living blockade.

"Hold on to something," Beatrice said, pulling the wheel left.

The *Phillipa* threaded its way between two kelpies, close enough to strike the one on the starboard side. The ship shuddered, and the kelpie honked in protest, and then they were through. Guns thundered as the crew fired a quick broadside. Given how little powder remained, Hephyra had ordered only half the guns loaded. It was enough. The crew cheered as one of the kelpies fell back, bleeding from the chest.

Such exchanges had their cost. Four men had fallen to undine spears, and nine others had been wounded. The foreyard was cracked from the last time they had rammed through the kelpies.

Beatrice sagged back into her seat. The ship's carpenter had secured a tall chair in front of the wheel, nailing the legs to the deck. The queen appeared ready to pass out, but still she steered the *Phillipa* through the waves.

"How much longer can they keep this up?" Danielle asked. "The poor kelpies must be ready to collapse."

"Some of them have," said Snow. "A second group joined them a while back."

Danielle rubbed her eyes. She hadn't even noticed. Living with Jakob had helped to prepare her for sleepless nights, but between the explosions and the honking cries of the kelpies, she felt tense enough to shatter at the slightest blow. "What about Morveren?"

"She's getting closer. She's moving almost as fast as we are." Snow clutched the green bottle in both hands. "Faster than I expected. I wonder if she found kelpies of her own."

"Is that one of Morveren's trapped souls?" Danielle asked.

"I borrowed it. I'm close to being able to re-create the jars." Snow held the bottle to the light of the rising sun. "I can't actually communicate with the soul, but I can feel Morveren through it. The wax she used to seal the cork is mixed with a bit of her spit and blood. She's commanding all of her souls, using their strength to power her magic."

"To do what?"

Snow shrugged. "I'm sure we'll know soon."

Danielle stretched, grimacing as her armor dug into her shoulders. She longed to remove it, but Talia had insisted. The hardened blue leather was molded for a taller woman, one who hadn't recently given birth. She reached beneath her cloak, trying to loosen the straps and buckles.

"Let me." Snow handed the soul jar to Danielle, then moved around to fix her armor. She pulled Danielle's cloak aside and began yanking various straps.

Snow wore similar armor, though hers was white and better fitted to her body. Flowering vines were molded into the breastplate, accentuating the curves of her chest. Heavy pads covered the shoulders, and a series of leather strips hung down to shield the thighs. Danielle still didn't understand how all of the straps and buckles fit together, but if it helped protect her from undine spears, she wasn't going to complain.

"Captain!" From the crow's nest, the watch cupped his hands to his mouth and shouted, "We've got another ship coming up behind us to the port side."

"Stay ahead of it," Hephyra shouted.

"Morveren," Snow whispered, reclaiming the soul jar.

Captain Hephyra tossed one more barrel, which Talia quickly speared. As the ringing of the explosion faded, Danielle saw Hephyra running toward the port guns, ordering the men to ready the cannons. The gunners worked quickly, packing powder and shot, then hauling the cannons into position at the edge of the deck.

Danielle reached for the queen. "We should get you out of sight. Let me help you—"

"No. The ship needs me here." Beatrice's voice was strained, and she clung to the wheel as though she would collapse without its support.

Danielle glanced at Snow, who was concentrating on her stolen soul jar. Snow sucked her lower lip as she watched the distant ship. "This isn't going to be fun."

The wind picked up, splashing water over the deck. "Secure your lifelines," Hephyra yelled.

Talia was half-running, half-sliding toward them. "What kind of ship is that?"

"A dead one," Snow said, her eyes half-shut. "That ship sank over a hundred years ago. Morveren's using the spirits of the crew to sail her. It's their memories keeping the ship afloat."

A low, mournful song swept over the ship. Danielle tensed. "Can you block Morveren's song?"

"That's not Morveren," Snow said.

Danielle turned toward the cutter. Lannadae sat on the middle bench, hands gripping the ropes as she sang. Her voice was weaker than Morveren's and uncertain, like a child still learning to sing. But Danielle could still feel the fear and the desperation in her voice.

"I'm trying to warn the tribe about Morveren!" she said.

Danielle moved to the edge of the ship, leaning out to see if the undine would answer. The kelpies had raised their heads from the water, but they still pursued the *Phillipa*.

We have an undine on this ship, a royal, Danielle said, adding her voice to Lannadae's. *The people on that ship behind us mean to kill her, and then they'll destroy your queen.* If the kelpies heard, they gave no sign.

The wind grew stronger. One of the topsails ripped free of the yard and flapped like a flag.

"Furl the thrice-damned sheets before the masts snap," Hephyra shouted.

Lannadae stopped singing.

"What's wrong?" Danielle made her way toward the cutter.

"My voice isn't strong enough. Not in this wind." Lannadae watched the other ship approach, her eyes inhumanly wide.

By now, Morveren's ship was close enough for Danielle to make out the broken masts and a large gash in her hull. Barnacles and seaweed covered most of the wood. Gray ropes trailed through the water behind the ship. Morveren lay at the bow, resting against the splintered stump of the foremast.

"She's not alone," Danielle said, spying another form

beside Morveren. She soon counted more. Close to twenty figures moved about the ship.

"That looks like Nilliar," Lannadae said. "The one with the crossed spears on her back. She was Lirea's spearbearer."

Danielle shook her head. "She looks human. She can't . . ." Her voice trailed off. The shapes were still dim, but she could see the glint of scales protecting Nilliar's body. "Morveren changed them, like she did Lirea."

"They abandoned their queen to follow Morveren," Lannadae whispered, staring at the other ship.

A gust of wind knocked Danielle against the cutter, which creaked from the strain. "We have to get you out of there." She reached up to take Lannadae's arms, helping her over the side of the boat.

Another wave crashed over the side, knocking them both down. Lannadae twisted away from Danielle and crawled toward the edge of the ship.

"What are you doing?" Danielle shouted.

"The tribe can't hear me from here. They don't know what's happening." Lannadae grabbed the rail and pulled herself up. "I need to get out of the wind."

"Lannadae, you can't—"

"They're my people." Lannadae's tails wrapped around the railing for balance. "They've seen Morveren's ship, so they know something's wrong. They might listen to me now."

"Or they might kill you."

"They'll have to catch me first." She disappeared into the next wave before Danielle could stop her.

"She's right." Varisto reached down to help Danielle to her feet. "We can't fight that ghost ship and the undine at the same time."

"Where have you been?" Danielle asked.

"In my cabin, trying not to throw up." Varisto grimaced. "Have I mentioned how much I despise the sea?"

The cannons thundered, and several of the figures on Morveren's ship cried out as the *Phillipa*'s guns raked her deck. Morveren's ship was too old to have guns of its own, but the winds' fury increased in response. Water sprayed down so hard it felt like hail.

Danielle and Varisto made their way back toward the helm, where Snow's magic appeared to be deflecting the worst of the air spirits. Captain Hephyra had retreated to the wheel as well, adding her strength to Beatrice's.

"We need to board her," Talia shouted. "Before she passes us and escapes."

"How?" Varisto pointed to the ship. "Even if the wind doesn't divert your grapples, they'll likely just rip right through that wreck."

Beatrice and Hephyra yanked the wheel, bringing the bow into line with Morveren's ship. Beatrice gave them a tight-lipped smile. "You might want to hold on to something."

Danielle held the ladder up to the poop deck and watched as Morveren's ship grew closer. She could make out the individual undine standing about the deck, but where had Morveren herself gone? The rigging had long since rotted away, but swaths of seaweed and the broken remains of masts and the upper deck provided plenty of cover.

One crewman fired his crossbow, but the air spirits swept the bolt away. Talia covered her head and started toward the port rail, her body bent into the wind. Morveren's ship didn't even bother to turn away. Either Morveren couldn't see what was about to happen, or else she didn't care. Danielle tightened her grip on the ladder.

The *Phillipa* rammed Morveren's ship at an angle, striking the middle of her starboard side. The impact flung Snow to the deck. Danielle dropped to her hands and knees and crawled toward her.

The ship shook a second time as the *Phillipa* turned to starboard, aligning with the other ship. The impact had cracked much of Morveren's hull, but she showed no sign of sinking or taking on water.

Danielle made her way toward Snow, who was clutching her head.

"I'm all right," Snow said, shoving Danielle away. "Go, but be careful. All of those souls, trapped and angry and lost . . . I don't know what it will do to her."

"Aside from making her stronger?" Danielle asked.

"Well, yes." Snow pushed her hair back from her face. She had lost her hat during the collision. "I'll do what I can to help from here."

Varisto stomped past, running toward the rail. Both ships were pressed together, but the rounded shape of the hulls left a significant gap between the two decks. Now the other ship tried to pull away, but Hephyra and Beatrice kept the *Phillipa* tight beside her.

Danielle unfastened her cloak and hurried after Varisto. Talia had already crossed onto the other ship. Danielle could see her fighting two of Morveren's undine.

"I hate sailing," Varisto muttered. He placed one foot on the rail and leaped, crashing to the deck and drawing his weapon. Bellowing, he launched himself at the nearest undine.

Another crewman followed, only to be knocked back by a sudden gust of wind. His screams were cut off as he dropped between the ships.

Danielle looked down at the gap. Already Morveren was pulling away, and it looked as though fewer than ten people had made the jump.

"Here!" Talia kicked her second opponent in the knee and tossed her aside, then used a knife to cut a length of seaweed from the wreck. She grabbed one end and tossed it toward Danielle.

Though wet and slippery, the plant felt strong enough. Danielle coiled it around her wrist twice, prayed, and jumped.

Talia pulled, yanking Danielle forward as she flew. The wind slammed her down. Even with Talia's help, she wasn't going to make it. She braced herself as her body struck the side of the ship hard enough to crack the old wood. At least, she hoped that sound had come from the wood.

Talia reached down to grab her wrist, hauling Dani-

elle on board. "If you have to fight, remember these undine aren't used to legs. Sudden movements will throw
them off-balance, and they don't know to protect their
knees."

A quick search showed no sign of Morveren. She
must have retreated below. Talia had cleared this part
of the ship, so Danielle made her way over the broken
deck, peering through jagged holes into the darkness
below. Seeing nothing, she grabbed a crossbeam and
swung down.

Talia followed, grimacing as she landed in the ankle-
deep sludge. "Morveren could be anywhere."

Danielle drew her sword. This section looked to be in
slightly better shape than the upper deck. Slime and silt
covered the floor. The wind was quieter here, whistling
through the gaps in the hull. She slashed her way past
more seaweed until she reached a round pit.

"This is probably where the capstan sat," Talia said.

"Snow said Morveren was using the crew's memory
to keep this wreck afloat." Danielle turned toward the
back of the ship. "She'd want to keep those soul jars below, where they would be safe."

Talia nodded and climbed down through the hole.
"I don't suppose Snow lent you an extra choker for
light?"

Danielle pushed back her sleeve and studied the
bracelet with Snow's mirror. Snow had said she could
use it to talk to Jakob or Armand. Would it also reach
Snow herself? She closed her eyes and imagined Snow,
concentrating until she had a clear image in her mind.
Bringing the mirror to her lips, she planted a quick kiss
on the glass, as though she were kissing her friend's
cheek.

"I'm a little busy right now!" Snow's voice was
strained. "Air spirits, remember?"

"We need light!"

"And I need a massage and a bottle of gnomish ale,"
Snow shot back. But a warm light began to shine from
the mirror.

The light was dimmer than Snow usually produced, but it was better than nothing. Danielle climbed down after Talia.

The sludge was thicker here, covering the wall to the left as well as much of the floor. Danielle could see tiny crabs and other creatures scurrying in the muck. Water dripped from the ceiling, and Danielle tried not to think about what else might be falling into her hair and clothes.

"Do you think she'd give us Gustan if you offered to clean the place?" Talia asked.

Danielle shook her head. "Even I have limits."

The ship rocked to the side, groaning as though it would shatter. The sound of the two hulls grinding together raised bumps along Danielle's skin.

"Over here." Talia waded through filthy knee-deep water toward a rope curtain.

Danielle splashed after Talia. She couldn't see anything in the darkness beyond the makeshift curtain. A gentle swing of her sword severed the ropes, allowing the light of Snow's mirror to penetrate into a smaller storage chamber.

Two undine sprang from the water, lunging with short forked spears. Talia pushed Danielle to the side, moving both of them away from those spears.

Remembering Talia's advice, Danielle parried one of the spears with her sword and jumped forward. The merman arched backward as though he were trying to swim away. Instead, he overbalanced and fell.

The merman tried to stab her from the ground, but the angle was bad, and his spear slid off Danielle's armor. Danielle pressed her advantage, knocking his spear away.

A crooning wail made her stumble. Morveren bobbed in the back of the room, only her head visible above the water that lapped the broken edges of the floor. Danielle's body grew heavy, as it had back when they first encountered Varisto's ship.

The light from Snow's mirror flickered. "Brace yourselves," Snow said through the glass. Moments later, the room seemed to explode.

Danielle clutched her head, fighting to remain standing. This must be what a cannonball heard as it shot from the cannon. The undine fell back, and even Morveren appeared stunned. Morveren tried to sing again, but her voice was distant.

Talia threw the spear she had taken from her opponent, but the wind knocked it aside. "I'm getting tired of those things!"

Danielle barely heard. She grabbed the edge of the doorframe, pulling herself closer. The wind wasn't as strong as she expected. Perhaps Morveren had kept only one or two spirits to defend her, sending the rest to speed her ship along. Danielle took another step, and then her chest cramped as though a giant were squeezing her ribs.

"I meant it when I said I have no quarrel with you, Princess. I didn't want to use this." Morveren held up a scale. "This is the scale I used to transform you into one of us. The scale knows your blood. It knows you."

Danielle's legs gave out. She felt herself falling, and then Talia's arms caught her and pulled her back through the water. Talia grabbed Danielle's wrist and shouted into the mirror. "Snow, we need some magic in here!"

"Snow can't fight me from your ship." Morveren's voice was strained. "Nor will killing me end my spell on Danielle," she added quickly, stopping Talia in midstep.

Danielle held her breath, but that only increased the pressure. Yet every time she exhaled, she had a harder time filling her lungs. Bit by bit, Morveren's spell squeezed the air from her body.

"What did you do?" Talia demanded.

"Human lungs are such fragile things, so easily shrunken." Morveren rose higher, sitting on the broken floor so the water washed against her stomach. "You can kill me if you'd like. Fight your way past my spirits and cut my throat. But how much time will you waste—"

"Just kill her," Danielle croaked.

Talia sheathed her knife and grabbed Danielle's collar, hauling her back. Danielle's vision was starting to sparkle. She dimly saw a merman lunge toward them, only to scream and fall back as Talia rammed Danielle's sword into his belly. Even as she suffocated, Danielle was relieved Talia had remembered her sword.

"Hold on." Talia's voice sounded hollow. "Snow, if you can hear me, get ready to fix our princess!"

Danielle gasped, trying to force more air into her chest. Talia tossed the sword up through the pit, then lifted Danielle onto her shoulder, shoving her onto the next deck.

Talia would never be able to drag her all the way to the upper deck. Danielle tried to speak, but her chest felt like it was crumpling inward.

Instead of carrying Danielle higher, Talia turned and hauled her toward the side of the ship. Through a haze of sparks, Danielle saw Talia step back from the hull, spin, and smash her heel through the wall. A flurry of kicks widened the hole, breaking away the rotted wood. Talia switched legs and continued to kick, splitting the outer boards of the hull.

Danielle felt herself being lifted. Her feet dragged over broken planks, and then she was falling. She doubled over as the cramps in her chest worsened. Her heart was beating so loudly she could barely hear. She plunged into the water, the shock of impact driving any remaining air from her lungs.

Another set of hands took her, and then she was racing across the water.

She heard Lannadae's voice say, "I've got her." Snow was shouting something, but Danielle couldn't make out the words.

Moments later, the bonds squeezing Danielle's chest eased. Her head pounded, and she gasped for breath. Slowly, her vision cleared. Lannadae and Talia held her as she coughed. They floated in the water, surrounded by humans and undine both. "Lannadae?"

"Quiet," said Snow. She sat behind Danielle, balanced on a floating isle of ice. "Don't try to talk yet."

Danielle turned her head until she spotted the ship. The *Phillipa* lay on her side. Her masts rose at a low angle from the water, and debris littered the waves. Most of the crew clung to the rigging or bobbed along on bits of flotsam. Fighting another bout of coughing, she asked, "What happened?"

"The merbitch sent her rot-eaten air spirits against us." Captain Hephyra stood on the starboard side of the ship, balanced on the hull. "They struck hard, pushing us off-kilter. We held steady, but once the cargo shifted, there was no saving her." Hephyra was more somber than Danielle had ever seen her.

"How long?" asked Danielle.

"More water rushes into the hull with each swell," Talia said, pointing. "The *Phillipa* is more watertight than most, but I suspect she'll sink before the sun lifts above the horizon."

"Snow, can you—"

"I'm not the one with a hundred trapped souls to serve me," Snow said. "I tried to freeze the water as it rushed inward, but there was too much." She lowered her voice. "Hephyra will survive for a while. Weeks, maybe even months before her tree finally dies. But she'll be trapped here."

"Do me a favor, Talia," Hephyra shouted. "The next time you see the fairy queen, punch that uptight bitch in the mouth for me."

Danielle looked around. Her chest still hurt with each breath. "Where's Beatrice?"

"Safe." Snow used her hands as paddles, turning her frozen island about to point toward the front of the ship. "Hephyra ripped the cutter free with her bare hands and helped Beatrice into the boat. We should get you in there as well."

"What then?" Danielle asked. Morveren's ship had already shrunk in the distance, appearing no larger than a toy. The undine had formed a loose ring around the

Phillipa and her surviving crew. If they chose, they could drag every last human down with hardly any effort. From the wary looks on the men's faces, they knew it too. She rubbed her bracelet. "I should call Armand. I need to warn him."

Warn him that she had failed. That Morveren had escaped and would soon control Lirea and the undine. How many more ships would they sink because of that failure? How many undine would die for refusing to join them?

"I never should have rescued her from that island," Danielle whispered.

"Don't be stupid." Snow splashed ice water in Danielle's face. "If we're about to die, I do not want to spend my last moments listening to you wallow in guilt."

Lannadae bobbed to the surface between them. "You're not about to die. Not right now, at least."

Danielle grabbed one of Lannadae's hands. "Thank you for saving me. I'm glad you're safe."

Lannadae beamed. "I sang the true story of Morveren, how her magic allowed a human to corrupt our queen, and how the princesses Cinderella, Snow White, and Sleeping Beauty fought to save Lirea from Morveren's power."

Talia's fingers tightened on Danielle's arm. "You told them *that*, did you?"

"Would you like me to sing it to you?" Lannadae asked.

"Does that mean they'll help us?" Danielle interrupted before Talia could answer.

"Not exactly." Lannadae gave a well-practiced shrug that looked almost natural. "They agreed to not kill you. And they believe I should have the chance to tell my story to the queen."

"That's a start," said Snow.

It wasn't enough. Lannadae's influence had kept them alive for now, but Lirea would order them killed the moment she saw them. Danielle squeezed Lannadae's hand. "You did wonderfully. I'm proud of you."

"I'll have that mermaid's head on a pike," Varisto yelled, paddling toward them. He and the other Hiladi survivors of the Hiladi shipwreck clung to an open trunk. Clothes floated on the waves nearby. Snow's clothes, now that Danielle looked more closely. To a passing glance, the shirts looked uncomfortably like bodies.

Varisto was bleeding from a cut to his arm but otherwise appeared unharmed. He looked around, and his bravado faded. "What do we do now?"

Was he asking *her*? Danielle clutched her bracelet. Even if Armand sent every ship in the fleet, they would never arrive in time to stop Morveren. Most of the crew would likely drown before help arrived.

"Come on." Talia and Lannadae took Danielle's arms and pulled her toward the cutter.

"You should have killed her, Talia." Danielle gripped their arms. "You would have stopped Morveren and Lirea both."

"You're saying you'd rather be dead?" Talia scowled and shoved Danielle into the boat.

Beatrice pushed herself to one side to make room. The benches had been removed, and the queen lay at the front of the boat, her back sloped upward with the curve of the bottom. Stub the cat was curled in her lap, drenched but purring.

Danielle looked back at Talia. "You know what I'm saying."

"You're right, I should have." Talia grunted and grabbed the side of the cutter, helping Danielle climb on. "That's what I get for spending so much time with overly sentimental princesses."

From here, Danielle could see the exposed underside of the *Phillipa*. A network of long, pale tendrils lay limp against the hull. Roots, she realized.

"I can't drown out here," Varisto said. He sounded like he was talking to himself as much as anyone else. "Gustan's shade would never let me rest if I died trying to save him. I'm *not* spending the next life listening to him gloat."

Danielle grimaced as she pulled herself upright. Her chest and stomach burned from the effort. "Lannadae! Tell your people we need them to take us to Hilad. The kelpies might be fast enough—"

"I can't command them," Lannadae said, swimming up beside her. "Lirea named me traitor. To follow my orders is to commit treason. I'm too young, and my scent isn't strong enough to break Lirea's hold."

"You said they listened to you," Danielle protested.

"Because we were helping to fight Morveren, another traitor. You're asking them to escort us into the heart of the tribe."

Danielle looked around at the undine floating on the surface. "You saw Morveren's ship!" she shouted, fighting tears. "You have to know Morveren will destroy your queen. Is this what you want? Will you obey Lirea's orders even if it enslaves you to a witch who devours the souls of her enemies?"

"They *can't* disobey," Snow said softly. "Do you remember what happened when we swam through their waters last time?"

"Yes," Danielle said, her face hot. "What does that—"

"The scent Lannadae and Morveren talk about is a kind of love potion. Given time, I might be able to counter it, but . . ."

"But some of the undine did leave Lirea," Danielle protested. "They joined Morveren."

"Who probably used magic to help them resist Lirea. You remember the song she sang on the *Phillipa*, back when Lirea attacked?"

"When she almost killed us?" asked Talia.

"Morveren is skilled enough to sing two spells at once, and nobody would have known." Snow rubbed her hands together, blowing on them for warmth. "I think she was calling to her followers, severing Lirea's hold on them. I'll keep trying to do the same, but you and Talia might want to start coming up with another plan."

Danielle realized Snow was close to passing out. Her face was bloodless, her movements stiff with pain. She had already fought Morveren's air spirits and broken the spell that nearly killed Danielle.

"Stop," Danielle whispered. "You need to rest before you kill yourself."

Snow started to shake her head, but the movement made her gasp.

Danielle looked at Beatrice. "What do I do?"

"You have to stop Morveren," Bea said gently. "You know that."

Danielle searched for Morveren's ship, but it had already disappeared from view. She turned to watch the kelpies circling. Raising her voice, she called out, "I surrender myself to Lirea. I helped to shelter Lannadae. Bring me to your queen to face justice."

Talia yanked the side of the boat, nearly dumping Danielle into the water. "What are you doing?"

"Can you think of another way to reach Morveren in time?" Danielle asked. Talia's jaw tightened, and she shoved away from the boat.

"Me too!" Snow's eyes were closed, but her voice was firm. "I'm the one who prepared Lannadae's cave for the winter. I even read her stories."

"I sheltered her too," Talia said grudgingly. In a lower voice, she added, "Brilliant plan, Highness."

"Do you have a better one?" Danielle asked.

"As prince of the Hiladi Empire, I demand you capture me as well!" Varisto bellowed.

Danielle still had a hard time reading undine expressions, but their confusion was clear. They swam together to confer, gesturing and pointing at the humans.

Danielle didn't wait. Taking advantage of the confusion, she whispered to the kelpies, who swam closer in response to the urgency of her summons. Moments later their heads disappeared into the water.

Beatrice grabbed the sides as the cutter rocked with the waves. "What are you doing?"

"Watch." Danielle pointed toward the *Phillipa*. "Hold tight, Captain!"

"To what?" Hephyra shouted. The ship shuddered as

the first kelpie pressed his head against the hull. Hephyra staggered backward. Two more kelpies joined the first, straining to right the ship.

At first, they simply pushed the *Phillipa* sideways through the water. Danielle ordered two of the kelpies around to the opposite side to brace the bottom as the rest lifted. Whatever else happened, she would at least save this crew.

Slowly, the ship began to right herself.

"Harder!" Hephyra crowed. "Put your fins into it!"

Water poured from the deck and the portholes. Hephyra danced along the hull, whooping as the *Phillipa* rose higher.

"Overbalance her to starboard," Hephyra yelled. "We need to shift the weight back to center. Easy, now. Not too far."

Waves shoved the crew back as the kelpies rocked the ship to and fro. Their fins and tails sent small vortices dancing over the water. Danielle did her best to coordinate the kelpies' efforts, tilting the ship as Hephyra raced about the deck.

"That's good enough for now." Hephyra began tossing ropes down from the deck. The ship sat much lower in the water than before, but she appeared stable for the moment. "What are you lot waiting for? Get up here and man the pumps! The rest of you get below and secure that mess. If I sink, I swear to the gods I'll take every last one of you with me!"

"She still won't be seaworthy for days," Beatrice said. "Even with all of Hephyra's magic."

"That doesn't matter." Lannadae bobbed in the water, her pride obvious even to Danielle. "They've agreed to capture us. We're going to Hilad."

Chapter 17

THE KELPIES RACED THROUGH THE WATER
toward the black wall ahead. Some of the undine
had fallen behind, unable to match the kelpies' speed.
If Danielle's silent urgings had increased that speed, so
much the better.

"This is fun!" Snow still appeared wan and weak,
but she was smiling. She lay with her feet through
one of the loops of the kelpie's harness, clinging to
another loop. "Danielle, can we get a kelpie for the
palace?"

"If we do, I'm not feeding it," Talia said.

Danielle's stomach clenched as they neared the coast.
Even from this distance, Morveren's song was strong
enough to make her shudder. Danielle knew little of
magic, but even she could hear the power in that voice.
Morveren sang a chorus of anger and despair. Danielle
could almost hear the individual souls Morveren was using to feed her power.

"Anyone have any wormwax?" Snow asked. When
nobody spoke, she closed her eyes and said, "I could
have used a longer rest, but I guess we'll have to do this
the hard way." She began to hum a quiet harmony to
Morveren's own song.

"By the emperor's blood, the mermaid sails as poorly
as my brother!" Varisto stared at the wreckage of Morveren's ship. She had crashed the ship directly into the

archway in the wall, all but blocking the way. The water around the shore teemed with undine.

One of the undine broke away, hurling a spear. It bounced off of the kelpie's thick hide, but others quickly followed. Another spear tore through a merman's leg, and he dropped from the harness with a scream.

"Morveren," Snow said.

"She's controlling them?" Danielle guessed.

"Nothing so crude." Snow spoke in a broken rhythm, humming between pauses. "She's heightening their fear and hostility. Nudging them into attacking of their own will. I can protect this small group, but I don't have the lungs to fully counter her song."

"She's turned them against us." The mermaid who spoke wore a necklace with two oysters, a symbol that appeared to denote some kind of rank. She sang a shrill command, drawing the kelpies to a halt.

"She'll do worse than that, Nevidhal," said Lanna-dae. "She enslaved my sister to a human soul. You saw how she's changed. Morveren intends to rule this tribe through Lirea, and to do the same to all of us. You have a duty to protect your queen."

"I know my duty." Nevidhal glanced toward the shore. "How do you mean to stop her?"

"Do you think you can fight your way through that many?" Danielle asked, glancing down at Talia.

Talia made a show of counting the endless swarm of undine. "Depends. Can you lend me a few more knives?"

"I will deal with the undine." Captain Varisto pulled himself higher on the kelpie's body.

"What are you doing?" Danielle asked.

Varisto's eyes were wide. "You think my brother was the only one given spirits to guard him? We were each bound to the empire as children. Gustan was given the spirits of the air."

"And you?" Snow asked.

Varisto stripped off his shirt, revealing a jagged brown tattoo on the left side of his chest. "I was bound to the rock of the earth." A geyser of steam shot into the sky from beyond the wall. Varisto bared his teeth. "And in this part of the country, if you crack the rock, you'll find fire."

The archway began to collapse, enormous blocks of ebony stone plunging into the water and crushing Morveren's ship. More steam rose from the water, and Danielle glimpsed orange fire flowing *beneath* the waves, pouring forth like syrup. The undine fled, seeking the safety of deeper water. Even Morveren's magic couldn't hold them here to be boiled alive.

"That's what happened here all those years ago, isn't it?" Snow stared at Varisto. "One of you unleashed fire over the land."

"There was a rebellion, back when the empire first began to crumble." Varisto never took his eyes from the shore. "From what I've read, it was a very short-lived rebellion."

Smoke rose from the wreckage of Morveren's ship. The land shook again, and flames raced to engulf the ship. Varisto's gaze appeared to reflect the fire as he watched it burn.

"You remember we can't swim through fire either, right?" Talia asked.

"Take us around to the edge of the wall." Danielle pointed to the right of the palace. "Just be thankful we have clothes this time."

"What was that?" Varisto spun around so fast he nearly fell from his kelpie. "My spirits told me of your intrusion, but they seem to have omitted certain details."

Lannadae sang a command. The kelpies veered to the right, swimming through fleeing undine toward the blackened shore.

"We can't follow Morveren onto land," Nevidhal said. She brought her kelpie around until she faced Danielle. "Even if we could, her song is too strong."

"Get Lannadae away from here and keep her safe." Danielle jumped down from her kelpie. The water was shallow enough her toes touched bottom. She pushed to the surface and grabbed the kelpie's rear fin for support.

Nevidhal hadn't moved. "What of our queen?"

"We'll protect Lirea," Danielle said. "I promise."

The air rippled from the heat. The smell of sulfur was stronger here, and the steam left droplets of water on her skin and hair. The water was warm as well, though not unpleasantly so. But anyone swimming toward Varisto's fire would be boiled alive.

"Danielle!" Lannadae clung to her kelpie. "I want to help!"

"Help by taking your people away from here," Danielle shouted. "Sing as loud as you can to help them block Morveren's song."

Lannadae started to protest, but Nevidhal said, "Lirea and Morveren have taken their battle beyond our reach. We must get you away from here."

Danielle kept her smile hidden. Already Nevidhal and the other undine began to treat Lannadae as a royal instead of a banished criminal. She and Talia helped Snow down, and together they swam toward shore, giving the pillars of steam a wide berth.

Several undine tried to attack, but most were more concerned with escaping the liquid fire crawling through the sea. Those who approached were easily knocked aside by Talia. Varisto bellowed at another, raising his ax to frighten the merman away. Morveren's magic worked against her now, inspiring the undine to greater panic.

The rock scraped Danielle's hands as she climbed onto land. Was it her imagination, or was the earth warmer than before?

Talia appeared to be having similar thoughts. "The rest of this place isn't going to crack open and spit fire, is it?"

"Not unless I so command," said Varisto.

"How reassuring." Talia began to jog toward the palace. "Where exactly are they, Snow?"

"Morveren is by the tower. The same one as before. I think Lirea is inside."

"Wait." Danielle stared at the distant tower. She knew what she had to say. She had known since she spoke with Beatrice, back at the boat. She bowed her head. "Talia, try to get into the tower. If Morveren is too strong—" She swallowed. "If we can't stop her, you'll have to kill Lirea."

Talia turned around. "You promised the undine—"

"I know." Danielle drew her sword, trying not to hate herself. All Lirea had wanted was to be with the man she loved. Instead, she found herself discarded by her prince and enslaved to her grandmother's magic. "This is only the beginning of Morveren's plan, and too many people have already died. You saw her crew. Other undine transformed like Lirea. She said Lirea's children would be the start of a new race, but do you think she'll stop there? How long before she creates more of those knives? How long before the undine who follow her begin hunting human souls? Without Lirea, Morveren's scheme falls apart."

Talia nodded. "It's a good plan, Highness."

"No, it's not." Danielle started toward the tower. "But it's the only one we have."

Approaching on land, her vision blurred by clouds of steam, Danielle could imagine the palace as it had once been. The wall that separated the moat from the open sea angled back, forming a five-sided barrier around the palace. Observation towers stood at each corner, surrounding the larger structures in the center. There must have been other buildings, now completely wiped away by fire and magic. All that remained was rippled black rock, leading to the crumbled ruins of the wall. In some places the wall still rose high enough to block her view, but most was little more than broken blocks of stone.

Even here the steam scalded her skin. Danielle wondered how many undine had been caught by Varisto's fires, not to mention the fish and other sea creatures. She could see crabs scrambling over the rock, but many more would have perished the moment the fire poured from the rock.

Once they crossed through the broken wall, Danielle spotted Morveren hovering outside of Lirea's tower. Her air spirits kicked up swirls of dirt and rock as they held her aloft. On the ground, Morveren's transformed undine surrounded the tower with weapons ready.

A spear flew from the tower window, but the air spirits knocked it aside.

"You don't understand," Morveren shouted. She clutched the cup with Gustan's spirit in her hands. "You're dying, Lirea! Let me save you!"

"I can reach the tower." Talia hadn't taken her eyes from the undine standing guard. "Once I start climbing, can you stop them from putting one of those spears up my—"

"It will be our pleasure," said Varisto.

Danielle joined him, following a curved path that would hopefully draw the undine away from Talia. "Snow, we can keep the undine busy, but you'll have to deal with Morveren."

Snow was still pale, but she smiled as she plucked the largest mirror from her choker. "Mirror, mirror, in my hand. Drag that mermaid back to land."

Morveren squawked as she fell. Her air spirits raced to catch her, slowing her drop, but she still hit hard enough to knock the breath from her chest.

"You realize we're badly outnumbered," Varisto commented, readying his ax. He took up position in front of Danielle as Morveren's undine ran toward them.

Talia had already split away from the others, running along the edge of the moat toward the tower. A few of the undine turned to follow, while the rest continued toward what they perceived as the greater threat.

A silver blur buzzed past Danielle, catching one of the undine in the shoulder. He fell, tripping another. Snow grinned and threw a second of her steel snowflakes. This one took a mermaid in the arm. It also came awfully close to taking out Danielle's earlobe.

"Do you mind?" Danielle asked.

"Sorry," Snow said. "My vision still isn't quite right."

She turned to Morveren, who had risen from the ground and begun to sing. Snow countered the melody, but this close even the dissonance of their songs was physically painful, like a knife scraping along Danielle's bones.

"She used most of her power to get here," Snow said. "But she's still stronger than I remember."

"Strong enough to beat you?" Danielle asked.

Snow rolled her eyes. "Oh, please."

Varisto settled into a low stance, ax ready. "Stay behind me, Princess. I'll protect you and your friend for as long as I can."

Danielle raised an eyebrow. A silent request brought the crabs skittering toward the approaching undine. Morveren had spread scales over the bodies of her warriors for protection, but those scales ended at the ankles. The first undine yelled as he fell, a large crab clinging to his toes. Another followed, and more crabs swarmed onto the bodies. Soon more than half of Morveren's undine were busy stomping and stabbing Danielle's reinforcements.

"Thank you for the kind offer of protection, Your Highness." Danielle stepped forward and raised her sword. Varisto merely grunted.

The first of the undine threw her spear as she ran. Danielle ducked, barely recovering fast enough to parry a downward slash by a second mermaid. Danielle grabbed her sword near the tip, using both hands to brace the weapon as the mermaid pressed down. The enchanted glass wouldn't cut Danielle, but even so she was no match for the mermaid's greater strength. Varisto stepped sideways and struck the mermaid's shoulder with the butt of his ax before turning away to intercept another attack.

"How much time do you need?" Danielle asked, cutting the mermaid's spear in half.

"A week would be nice," Snow said, her voice tight.

Danielle stomped her foot, feinting at a merman. They were strong, but as Talia always said, footwork was key to fighting. The undine had possessed feet for less than a day. She swung hard, trying to keep them back and off-balance.

Varisto let out a tremendous shout as he smashed a spear, then kicked a merman in the stomach. "If need be, I can destroy this place. My spirits can crack the land, destroy the tower, send us all into the hot sea."

"All of us?" Danielle asked, parrying another spear.

"If they go, we all go. All but the flying fish-woman over there. My spirits are strong, but I'm afraid they're much less discerning than my brother's."

"Then let's hope Snow succeeds."

Talia drew two knives from her forearms without breaking stride. She threw one with each hand as she ran, and two of the undine fell. Another tripped over the body of his companion, leaving only two between Talia and the tower.

She started to run between them, watching as they both drew back to swing. Talia bent backward, sliding to the ground as their attacks passed over her. They managed to avoid striking one another, though. Talia's luck was never that good.

Talia kicked out the knee of the mermaid to her right, then rolled away to avoid another spear thrust. She grabbed the spear and allowed him to pull her to her feet. Stepping in close, she slammed a knee into his crotch.

Mermen might keep their equipment hidden within their scales, but there was only so much those scales could do. He dropped, groaning. Talia snapped a kick to his cheek, then turned to plant her heel in the nose of the other merman.

That left only the one who had tripped over his friend. He charged, spear outstretched.

Talia slipped her toes beneath a dropped spear. She waited until he was almost upon her, then kicked the fallen spear up into her hand and dropped low.

The merman's spear passed over Talia's shoulder. Talia's sank into his stomach.

Soon Talia was scaling the tower wall, circling around to the ocean side in order to keep the tower between herself and Morveren. All it would take was one of those damned air spirits to rip her from the wall and dash her onto the rocks.

When she reached the window, she pulled herself up to peek into the tower. Lirea sat on the far side, her legs pulled to her chest and her head buried in her knees. Another of Morveren's transformed mermaids was with her, her body between Lirea and the window.

"Sorry, Danielle," Talia whispered. "I don't intend to wait." She pulled out her last knife, the one Beatrice had given her. Moments later she was through the window, balanced on the balls of her feet. Raising her voice, she said, "Excuse me, but you're in my way."

The other mermaid spun. As Talia had hoped, the movement exposed Lirea. Talia was already throwing her knife. The blade spun across the tower, only to veer right, sucked out the window by one of Morveren's spirits.

"I am tired of those damned things." Talia ran, but a gust of air knocked her into the wall. Her shoulder scraped stone. The other mermaid was coming at her with a sword.

"You see?" the mermaid said as she attacked. "The humans will never stop trying to kill you. Morveren is the only one who can save us."

"What if I no longer want to be saved, Nilliar?"

Talia ducked and tried to step back, only to be shoved into the wall again by the wind.

"She can give you back your prince." Nilliar swung again, cutting Talia's arm. "It won't be like before. You have to let Morveren complete her spell. Gustan still loves you, Lirea."

"No, he doesn't," said Talia, scooting backward. The wind was weaker here at the wall. So long as she kept her body pressed to the stone, the air spirit couldn't do much more than push her from side to side. Of course, that severely limited her options. If she kept backing up, the wind would either push her out the window or toss her down the steps. "He never did. You know that, deep down."

"He said I was most dear to him," Lirea said, hugging herself. Tears shone on her cheeks. "He was kind to me in the beginning."

Talia dropped onto her back, kicking at Nilliar's legs. She missed the knee, but caught Nilliar's shin. It wasn't enough. Nilliar's sword rang against the stone where Talia had been a moment before. Talia tried to rise, only to be tossed away from the wall, toward the broken edge of the floor and a long drop to the bottom of the tower. She pressed herself flat, clinging to the floor.

"People lie." Talia waited for Nilliar's next attack. This time, she rolled toward the mermaid and rose up on one knee, wrapping an arm around Nilliar's waist for balance. Her other hand slid along Nilliar's arm, reaching not for the sword but for the fingers that gripped it. She found the thumb and tugged. The sword clattered to the ground.

The air spirit attacked them both, driving them past Lirea and toward a window. It meant to throw them both down to the rocks.

Talia didn't fight it. Instead, she added her strength to the wind, pushing Nilliar back. With her left hand, she tugged her zaraq whip from her belt. A snap of the wrist launched the weighted line at Lirea, twirling it around her neck.

Talia twisted, shoving Nilliar through the window. Nilliar tried to grab the edge, but between the wind and Talia's own weight, her grip wasn't strong enough.

"If it's any consolation, I've never had much luck with romance either." With that, Talia yanked the whip with both hands. Lirea staggered across the floor, and then Talia was tumbling back through the window, dragging the mermaid after her.

Snow's vision swam. There was too much magic, too many spells to counter. Three Morverens appeared to float outside of the tower, and she couldn't begin to count the number of undine fighting Danielle and Varisto. She closed her eyes, calling forth another burst of sunlight from her choker. It was enough to distract the undine, giving her friends a momentary advantage. But there was only so much she could do.

She could feel Morveren reaching out to the tower, trying to work her way into Lirea's mind. Morveren was far more skilled than Snow, her touch light as air. One strand at a time, she wove her web around Lirea's will.

Snow concentrated on the cup, trying to erect a magical wall to sever Morveren's connection to Gustan. Without that connection, there should be a very satisfying crunch as Morveren dropped onto the rocks below. But Morveren punched through the wall with ease, widening the cracks between Snow's imaginary bricks.

"Power is subservient to skill," Morveren shouted. She waved a hand, and one of her air spirits broke away. Rocks and sand rained against undine and humans both. The humans took the worst of it, since they couldn't turn away to protect their faces without exposing themselves to attack.

"Maybe." Snow pulled out the green soul jar she had taken from Morveren's ship. Another few days and she would have figured it out. She was sure of it.

Snow bit the stopper in her teeth spat it aside. She peered through her lashes at the faint web of Morveren's magic laced through the inside of the jar. Closing her eyes, she reached into the bottle with one finger, ripping a hole in the bonds that had trapped this soul for over a hundred years. The freed spirit rushed past, feeling like hot velvet over her skin. There was power in that soul, but Snow allowed it to escape.

Varisto yelled as a rock struck him in the knee. Another glanced off Snow's forehead, redoubling the pain in her skull and driving her to one knee. Blood trickled down the side of her nose. With a gentle push, she nudged the strands of the jar's magic, sending them outward like a fisherman casting his line. As soon as those strands touched the air spirit, Snow allowed the spell to collapse back into the bottle, dragging the spirit along.

The rocks and sand died down. Snow pressed a thumb over the mouth, a crude seal, but effective for the moment.

Snow could hear Morveren redoubling her efforts to reach Lirea's mind. Shouts rose from inside the tower. Talia stumbled into the window, fighting a blue-scaled mermaid. Talia twisted, pushing the mermaid through. She fell to the ground with a scream. The drop wasn't necessarily a fatal one, but the mermaid fell head first. Snow could hear the crack of bones breaking.

Talia tumbled out the window, clinging to her whip. The other end of the whip was looped around Lirea's throat. For a moment, it looked as though she would drag Lirea down, but Lirea caught herself. She clutched the windowframe with both hands.

"Snow!" Danielle slammed her sword down, snapping a merman's spear and cutting deep into his shoulder. "Help her!"

Talia braced her feet against the wall and pulled, but Lirea was too strong. Morveren swooped down, drawing a knife. Snow recognized the abalone blade from here, as well as the remnants of broken spells that still clung to the knife like leeches. Talia pushed herself to one side, barely avoiding the attack.

Snow still held a mirror in her left hand. She removed her thumb from the jar, placing the mirror over the mouth. The air spirit fought to escape, but she pushed him back. Using her magic to reach into the heart of the mirror, Snow struck the glass from within.

The mirror crumbled to powder, glittering as it fell into the bottle. "Mirror, mirror, crushed so fine, lend strength to this spell of mine."

The remains of her mirror melted into the bottle. Soon both the inside and outside gleamed like quicksilver. Snow waited, but the mirror's power held the spirit trapped. She stumbled toward Morveren, head throbbing with every step. Another of the air spirits attacked, only to be drawn into the jar.

Morveren floated higher, this time bringing her knife toward the whip. Talia tried to stop her, but the winds knocked her against the wall, and then she was falling. She spun in the air, but the spirits slammed her to the ground too quickly. She rolled with the impact and tried to stand, only to stumble as her left ankle gave out.

Morveren renewed her assault against Lirea. She floated closer, reaching into the tower. "Let me save you, child."

"Morveren!" Snow smiled. "Sometimes raw power has its place too."

She threw the soul jar. It spun through the air, and as it passed beneath Morveren, the spells within the jar reached out to entangle the remaining air spirits. The jar clinked against the tower wall and dropped to the ground, the mirror's power protecting it from the impact.

Morveren screamed as she fell, but she caught the windowsill with one hand. She pushed the cup into the tower, then pulled herself up and through the window.

"No fair!" Snow muttered. To Talia, she asked, "Are you all right?"

"I'm fine," Talia snapped. "Get her."

Snow closed her eyes, trying to listen the way Morveren had taught her. Morveren's magic was easy to detect. All her power was concentrated on Lirea now, digging into her thoughts and emotions.

"You asked for this, remember?" Morveren asked. "You begged me for it. All I've ever done is try to give you what you wanted."

"No."

Slowly, Snow reached into Lirea's mind. She was gentler than the last time, but Lirea still sensed her touch. Unlike before, Lirea lacked either the strength or the will to fight one more intrusion.

Snow pressed deeper, until she began to see through the mermaid's eyes. Morveren still held the knife in one hand. With the other, she picked up the cup and thrust it at her granddaughter. Lirea tried to push it away, but Morveren was too strong. Lirea's hands reached out to take the cup from Morveren's hand.

Snow could hear Gustan raging within the cup, the sounds more animal than human. She had no doubt Lirea could hear him as well. Little remained of the Hiladi prince but anger and confusion.

Snow tried to unravel the threads of Morveren's control, but there were too many. Lirea twitched, her muscles rigid.

"Drink, child," Morveren whispered. "Drink, and be great. Be complete."

"I don't want to go back," Lirea said, but she was too weak to fight. She stared at the cup. "I didn't want any of this."

So be it. Snow couldn't break Morveren's hold on Lirea, so she would have to try something more direct. No subtle threads of magic were these; Snow seized Lirea's mind like a rag doll, yanking her hands back. The cup clattered to the floor and rolled toward the edge of the broken floor.

"No!" Morveren grabbed the cup before it could fall. "You'll destroy her mind!" She brought the cup back to Lirea, forcing it to her lips.

Lirea wrenched away, looking toward the window. Toward Snow. "Please don't let them take me."

"I won't," Snow whispered. She could feel Morveren tightening her grip on Lirea, expending her own strength to prevent Snow from wresting control away. Lirea whimpered as something within her tore. Slowly, Lirea's hands moved back toward the cup.

"Please," Lirea whispered.

Morveren was too strong and too skilled for Snow to fight directly. Instead, Snow simply nudged Lirea's right arm so she reached not for the cup, but for the knife in Morveren's other hand.

Before Morveren could react, Lirea wrapped her hand around Morveren's and shoved the abalone blade into her grandmother's chest.

"Sometimes brute power beats skill," Snow whispered.

The cup fell. Tears filled Morveren's eyes. "I tried to save you."

Lirea didn't appear to hear. Or if she did, there wasn't enough of her left to understand. Now completely under Snow's control, Lirea crawled to the window and ordered the remaining undine to break off their attack against Danielle and Varisto.

As the pounding in Snow's skull darkened her vision, she swallowed and sent one last command. Inside the tower, Lirea picked up the cup with Gustan's soul. Though Lirea's mind was in tatters, a part of her still reveled in taking the knife and slashing through the web of hair, freeing Gustan before flinging both cup and knife out the window to clatter against the rocks below.

Chapter 18

SNOW SPENT MUCH OF THE NEXT TWO WEEKS
in bed, under orders from Tymalous. Several times
when she tried to sneak away, she found Talia waiting at
her door. There were no words. One look at Talia's face
was enough to send Snow hobbling back to bed.

Much of what happened had the blurred, fantastical
feel of a dream. She remembered fighting Morveren and
then later, while they waited for a ship, working to try to
undo the spells Morveren had cast on Lirea. And then
there was the part where she was flying naked over the
ocean, surrounded by very handsome, very large pix-
ies . . . but she was fairly certain that really had been a
dream.

The back of her head was still tender, but Tymalous
had pronounced her well enough to join the others for
one more voyage on the newly repaired *Phillipa*, under
the condition that she do no magic for at least another
month.

"Magic excites you," he had said. "Your heart pounds
harder, your blood rushes through your body, and your
injury worsens. You may have already done yourself
permanent damage. You will, if you don't allow yourself
time to recover."

Beatrice had been quick to broaden that prohibition
to . . . other forms of excitement, and Snow had grudgingly agreed. With the exception of one spell.

It was that spell that brought Snow to the queen's cabin on the *Phillipa*. Snow had tried three times to talk to Beatrice, and each time her courage had failed her.

Snow knocked lightly on the door. There was no answer, so she cracked open the door and peered inside. Beatrice lay in her bed, her eyes closed. She had spent much of the first day's journey resting. Snow stood frozen until she heard the slightly strained sound of the queen's breathing.

Squeezing through the door, Snow set a cup of tea on the floor beside the bed and turned to go.

"Thank you." The queen still hadn't opened her eyes. "That smells wonderful. Dare I ask what you put into it?"

"You probably shouldn't," Snow admitted. "It will ease the pain."

Bea sat up and reached for the mug. Snow was faster, placing it into her hands. Bea took a sip, then wrinkled her nose. "In the future, let it be known that the queen's medicines should be mixed with elven wine." She took another drink, then set the mug back down. "So how long do you intend to wait before you tell me?"

"Your Majesty?"

"Call me that again and I'll have Hephyra lock you in the hold." Bea reached out to take Snow's hand. "When do you mean to tell me that I'm dying?"

Snow couldn't look at her. "How did you know?"

"I've lived in this body for fifty-eight years. I know when it's given up the fight." Almost absentmindedly she touched her chest, where fresh bandages covered the old stitches beneath her shirt. "How long?"

"I used the mirror at the palace." It had taken days to work up the courage to speak the rhyme, once she began to suspect. *Mirror with your truth so cold. Show me what her future holds.*

"How long, Ermellina?"

Snow made a face. "A year. Maybe two. Morveren's knife damaged your spirit, and your body was near death. There are other medicines I can try, spells I can—"

"I'm sure Tymalous has done what he can. We've already risked more than we should have to save me." Beatrice's gaze was distant, staring out the window at the sea. "I'd consider it a favor if you didn't tell anyone else until I've had a chance to talk to Theodore."

"Of course," Snow said. "But once Father Isaac recovers from his injuries, he and I could work together to—"

"I've lived an amazing life, Snow. I've spent more than half of my years married to the man I love, and I've seen my son grow up to become a father. I always regretted that I couldn't have another child, but I couldn't be more proud of you and Talia if you were my own daughters."

Snow stood and hoped the queen couldn't see her blushing. "I should let you rest."

Beatrice merely chuckled. "So beautiful, and you still haven't learned to accept a genuine compliment from someone who loves you."

"You're teasing me. You know there are worse things I can put in your tea."

The queen raised her hands in surrender. "Before you go, will you tell me what else is bothering you? I assume it's something to do with Lirea."

With a sigh, Snow sat back down on the carpet. "I keep remembering what I did to her. I thrust a knife into her mind and twisted until there was nothing left. I *felt* her thoughts fragmenting, ripping apart like rags."

"Is that why you worked so hard to reverse the spells Morveren had worked upon her, back in Hilad?" Beatrice asked. "Danielle told me you kept passing out, but each time you awakened you insisted on trying again."

"I managed to bind Lirea to one form," Snow said. "The transformation from human to undine and back was a tremendous strain. I can't completely restore her body to what it was . . . she no longer produces a scent, and her voice will never heal. But now that she's free of Morveren and Gustan, unable to change, she might survive for years. A part of me wonders if it would have been kinder to kill her."

"You did what you had to in order to free her."

Snow snorted. "Free her to what?"

"To a life with a sister who still loves her. And perhaps, as time passes, a life of peace." Bea climbed out of bed and held out her hand to Snow. "Help me find Danielle and Talia. There are few things more beautiful than sunset at sea, and I'll be damned if I'll let them miss it."

Snow bit her lip at the mention of Talia's name. The undine had kept her too busy to think about Morveren's revelation, but now that the crisis had passed . . . She still didn't feel ready to face that truth. "I think I'd rather be alone, if you don't mind."

"I do mind. Since I'm queen, that means you're coming with me." Beatrice put her hands on Snow's shoulders. "None of us live happily forever after. But we can choose to be happy today. I'm choosing for both of us. Argue, and I'll make you wake up tomorrow morning to watch the sunrise as well."

Slowly, Snow smiled. "Yes, Your Majesty."

The next morning Danielle stood on the forecastle with Beatrice, watching the waves. The queen tried not to let her pain show, but Danielle could see the tightness in her expression and the way she rested after exertion. Though she did appear stronger here on the *Phillipa*.

Beatrice glanced at Danielle. "You seem to have gained your sea legs at last."

Danielle smiled and shook her head. "Without Snow's tea, I'd be huddled away in my cabin with a bucket."

Perhaps it was the magic of the ship, or simply being out in the sea air, but Beatrice's face had more color this morning than in the past two weeks. She still used a cane for support, and she couldn't stand too long without rest, but she was alive. Alive and healing.

The ship wasn't fully recovered either. Hephyra said it would likely be several months before the foremast finished regrowing. But she was seaworthy, and Beatrice refused to set out in any other vessel.

"King Theodore was right," said Danielle. "You shouldn't be here. You need rest."

"If I spend one more day in bed, I'll go mad. They treat me as though I were a crystal doll who'll shatter at the slightest touch."

"How foolish," Danielle agreed. "It's not as though you were stabbed, had your soul ripped from your body, fell from a sinking ship, ripped your stitches, and nearly bled to death on the journey back to Lorindar."

Beatrice snorted. "You sound like Talia. I think I liked it better back when you were afraid of offending me."

From high in the mainmast, the watch shouted, "Hiladi ships sighted to port."

"That would be the *Prince's Triumph* and their escort," said Beatrice. "I'll have to ask Snow, but I don't believe a Hiladi vessel has ever attended an undine ceremony before."

Danielle pulled down her hat to block the sun as she searched for Varisto's ship.

"You should get Snow and Talia. We'll be there soon, and Lannadae will be disappointed if they aren't present."

Danielle turned around. "They're already coming." Snow and Talia were making their way from the cabin. Snow was trying to shove a sheathed shortsword into Talia's hands.

"He'll be offended if you don't wear it," Snow said, laughing. "If you didn't want the sword, you shouldn't have accepted it."

"Why not?" Talia sprang onto the ladder, pulling herself onto the forecastle. "It's a beautiful weapon. Light, well-balanced, and matched with one of those magical bracelets. Do you remember how Varisto summoned his ax back in the chapel? I could use a weapon that came when called. I thought this was his way of thanking me."

"You didn't see the coiled snakes on the pommel?"

Snow asked as she followed. "Or the garnet chips worked into the scabbard?"

"What's wrong?" Danielle asked.

"The snakes and jewels mark this as a hakris sword," Snow explained. "Varisto gave it to Talia before he left Lorindar last week. She must have impressed him. The hakris weapon is a token of a suitor's intentions. It's not an engagement, but the next best thing."

Talia snatched the sword from Snow's hands. "You were there. You knew!"

"If you'd spend more time reading and less time learning new ways to kill a man with your bootlace, you'd have known too!"

Danielle reached out to take the sword, squeezing between them before Talia tossed Snow overboard. She was used to their teasing, but over the past few days, there had been an edge to Snow's joking. Whatever had happened between them, Danielle hoped it would pass soon. "I'll explain to Varisto that Talia is oath-bound to serve Beatrice and thus unable to accept other commitments."

"Are you sure, Talia?" Snow pressed. "You don't have to marry him, but the wooing could be fun. He's strong, attractive . . . you both seem to like pummeling people. I thought maybe you might—"

"I count six warships," Talia interrupted, squinting at the approaching Hiladi vessels. "You'd almost think they didn't trust the undine anymore."

Danielle glanced at their own escort. Four ships sailed alongside the *Phillipa*, each one carrying large nets, extra guns, and twice as much powder as necessary. Danielle just prayed fear and hatred didn't lead one of the humans to fire on the undine. The undine attacks had stopped soon after Morveren's death, but Danielle suspected it would take years for humans to once again feel safe at sea.

Danielle shivered when she spotted the undine approaching, their bodies cutting through the waves. How long would it be before *she* felt safe again?

"There they are," said King Theodore, climbing up to stand beside his wife. His skin appeared faintly green, but it was an improvement over the previous day. Snow's tea had helped the king as much as it had Danielle.

Theodore's advisers had warned him against coming, citing dangers ranging from vengeful undine to the angry ghosts of Morveren's victims. The king's response had been succinct and had left at least three nobles red-faced and coughing.

Danielle had no doubt Armand would have been here as well, if not for his leg. She looked forward to returning home to him and Jakob soon.

There were no displays of undine strength or skill this time as Lannadae's tribe approached the gathered ships. Nor would there be any gifts. Only a formal end to hostilities.

The undine swam in a series of inverted Vs, with Lannadae in the lead. Her escort was armed, weapons pointed not so subtly at the human ships, but Lannadae herself hardly appeared to notice. Her chest heaved, and she appeared to be breathing harder than her companions. She was still out of shape from her long hibernation and exile. But her skin had lost its blue tinge, and she was smiling. She wore the oyster necklace Danielle remembered seeing on Lirea.

There were fewer undine than Danielle remembered. Lannadae was too young, her scent still weak, and many of the undine had left her tribe.

The Hiladi ships dropped anchor a short distance behind and to the right of the undine. Some of Lannadae's warriors shifted, clearly uncomfortable at the number of humans and cannons. Lannadae merely swam closer to the *Phillipa*.

"Greetings, Queen Beatrice!" Lannadae waved. "And to Princess Danielle and her two companions."

Danielle had asked Lannadae not to share the truth about Snow and Talia. From the delighted smile on Lannadae's face, she took great joy in keeping that secret.

"Hello, Lannadae," said Bea. "I'm glad to see you again."

"Is that your mate?" Lannadae asked.

The king laughed. "I am. My name is Theodore of Lorindar. I'm honored to meet you at last, and I am pleased to see you doing so well."

"Thank you, friends. For everything." With that, Lannadae disappeared into the water and swam toward the Hiladi.

Danielle blinked. "That's it?"

"She named us friends," said Bea. "The undine aren't big on ceremony."

"We've waited two weeks for her to name us friend?" Danielle demanded. "She could have done that the moment she accepted leadership of the tribe!"

Bea smiled and patted Danielle's arm. "It wasn't the undine who delayed us. Theodore and I haven't had an easy time convincing our people to let go of their hostility. There were many who wished to punish the undine."

Theodore scowled. "With the return of trade, I've ordered all merchants to return their prices to what they were before the crisis. A handful of gougers have been arrested, but the rest are falling into line. That should go a long way toward making the people happy. Though Montgomery still presses to punish Hilad for their role in this mess."

"Name Montgomery ambassador to Hilad," Beatrice suggested. "Send him to live among them for a year."

The king laughed and squeezed her hand. "Who would I be punishing, Montgomery or the Hiladi?"

Lannadae returned a short time later. She sang to her people, her voice louder than Danielle had ever heard. In response, one of the kelpies surged forward, head held high. On the kelpie's back, four undine carried a large chest.

"Most of the gold my sister collected will be returned, but I wanted to give you this," Lannadae said. "I hope it will help to repair some of the damage Lirea caused."

"Thank you," said Bea. "How is your sister?"

Lannadae's expression fell. "She refuses to leave her tower. We've dug a tunnel through the wall, but when I visit, she only hides. She hasn't spoken since Morveren's death. I don't know how much she remembers. She's like an infant, with no voice and no understanding of the world around her. But she seems to enjoy it when I sing to her. Yesterday she even came out into the open to listen."

Lannadae swam closer, smiling through tears. "Thank you. All of you."

"How are you adapting to your role as queen?" Danielle asked. "I know how overwhelming such a change can be."

Lannadae beamed. "Oh, I'm not the queen. Lirea holds that title until her death. But when the queen is too old or injured to rule, her consort is allowed to act in her name."

Danielle turned to Beatrice, certain she had misheard. For once, Bea looked as surprised as Danielle felt. "Her consort?"

Lannadae laughed. "You look like gulper eels."

"But she's your sister," said Danielle.

"Yes, of course." Lannadae's laughter grew, until she could barely stay afloat. "Oh, Danielle. Next you'll be expecting me to wear clothes, too."

Theodore raised a hand, disguising his own laughter with a cough.

"As consort, it falls to me to care for Lirea and our tribe." Lannadae's tails swayed gently beneath the waves, keeping her close to the ship. "I'll still have suitors, of course. I might even take a mate of my own. Mermen from this tribe and others." She flushed, the expression making her look almost human. "After so long in exile, I'm looking forward to that part."

"What of Morveren's followers?" Talia asked.

Lannadae's smile faded. "Morveren's magic wore off within a day. Their transformation was temporary, unlike my sister's. Those who fought for Morveren have been banished. If there are others who believed as she did, they've decided to keep those beliefs to themselves."

She swam back to the gathered undine. Taking a spear from another mermaid, Lannadae raised her weapon in salute. "Farewell, my friends!" She turned to the Hiladi, saluting them as well.

"Will we see you in the fall for the migration?" Beatrice asked.

Lannadae lowered her spear. "I look forward to the strawberries." And then she was gone. Moments later, no trace of undine remained.

"We could learn from them," Beatrice commented, smothering a yawn. "I know nobles who would have stretched this ceremony out for three days."

"*Now* will you rest, Your Majesty?" Danielle asked.

"I've already spent too much time in that stuffy cabin." Beatrice shook her head. "Give me the wind and the rolling of the deck beneath my feet."

Danielle groaned. "I'll take the bed, I think."

"I wanted to thank you, Danielle." Beatrice's voice was somber.

"Snow was the one who freed you from the knife. And Talia—"

"That's not what I meant. Don't misunderstand, I'm grateful to be free." She looked back at Snow and Talia, who were still bickering. "Neither of those women trust easily, but they trust you. For several years, I've worried what would become of them after I'm gone. You've eased that fear. For *that*, I thank you."

Theodore chuckled and added, "That and helping us avoid all-out war, of course." He kissed Beatrice on the cheek.

Danielle turned to stare at the water. "So is this what the queen does? Rescue princesses and prevent wars?"

"You didn't think the job was all balls and banquets, did you?" Beatrice's eyes twinkled.

Danielle watched the waves breaking against the *Phillipa*. "Lannadae is so young. Snow said her scent wasn't yet strong enough to control the tribe, and she's been through so much. Will she be—"

"Lannadae is stronger than she knows. She has a kind heart, and she cares for her people. For now, they will stay with her because they choose to. Because they know she came back to protect them." Beatrice squeezed Danielle's hand. "She may feel uncertain, even scared, but she will be a good queen."

Danielle flushed. "I ... imagine she must feel overwhelmed. There's so much to learn."

"There always is," Beatrice said, smiling. "But thanks in part to you and your companions, she already knows those things that are most important."

Before Danielle could answer, Beatrice took her hand and tugged her from the rail. "Now come, I want you to try your hand at the wheel."

"I don't know how—"

Beatrice's eyes sparkled. "Princess Danielle, do you remember what I told you when you said you didn't know how to swim?"

Danielle swallowed. "Yes, Your Majesty."

"That's more like it." Beatrice took Theodore's hand, allowing him to help her down from the forecastle. "The voyage home is far too short, and there's much I intend to teach you."

Once upon a time...

Cinderella—real name Danielle Whiteshore—did marry Prince Armand. And their wedding was a dream come true.

But not long after the "happily ever after," Danielle is attacked by her stepsister Charlotte, who suddenly has all sorts of magic to call upon. And though Talia the martial arts master—otherwise known as Sleeping Beauty—comes to the rescue, Charlotte gets away.

That's when Danielle discovers a number of disturbing facts: Armand has been kidnapped; Daniellie is pregnant; and the Queen has her own Secret Service that consists of Talia and Snow (White, of course). Snow is an expert at mirror magic and heavy-duty flirting. Can the princesses track down Armand and rescue him from the clutches of some of Fantasyland's most nefarious villains?

The Stepsister Scheme
by Jim C. Hines

"Do we *look* like we need to be rescued?"

DAW 130

Jim Hines

The **Jig the Goblin** series

"Clever satire… Reminiscent of Terry Pratchett
and Robert Asprin at their best."
—*Romantic Times*

"If you've always kinda rooted for the little guy,
even maybe had a bit of a place in your heart for
Gollum, rather than the Boromirs and Gandalfs
of the world, pick up *Goblin Quest.*"
—*The SF Site*

"This exciting adult fairy tale is filled with
adventure and action, but the keys to the fantasy
are Jig and the belief that the mythological creatures are real in the realm of Jim C. Hines."
—*Midwest Book Review*

"A rollicking ride, enjoyable from beginning to
end… Jim Hines has just become one of my
must-read authors." -—Julie E. Czerneda

GOBLIN QUEST   978-07564-0400-0
GOBLIN HERO   978-07564-0442-0
GOBLIN WAR   978-07564-0493-2

To Order Call: 1-800-788-6262
www.dawbooks.com

DAW 100

John Zakour

The Novels of
Zachary Nixon Johnson
The Last Freelance P. I.

"If you like your humor slapstick and inventive,
you need look no further for a good fix."
—*Chronicle*

Dangerous Dames*   978-07564-0496-3
(The Plutonium Blonde & The Doomsday Brunette)
Ballistic Babes   978-0-7564-0545-8
(The Radioactive Redhead* & The Frost-Haired Vixen)
The Blue-Haired Bombshell   978-07564-0455-0
The Flaxen Femme Fatale   978-07564-0519-9
    *co-written with Lawrence Ganem

"No one who gets two paragraphs into this
dark, droll, downright irresistable hard-boiled-
dick novel could ever bear to put it down until
the last heart-pounding moment..." —*SFSite*

To Order Call: 1-800-788-6262
www.dawbooks.com